BY THE SAME AUTHOR
Telling Stories

*Valerie Windsor*

# SAINT AND WARRIOR

VIKING

To Sue Mayo
With love and gratitude

VIKING

Published by the Penguin Group
Penguin Books Ltd, 27 Wrights Lane, London w8 5tz, England
Penguin Books USA Inc., 375 Hudson Street, New York, New York 10014, USA
Penguin Books Australia Ltd, Ringwood, Victoria, Australia
Penguin Books Canada Ltd, 10 Alcorn Avenue, Toronto, Ontario, Canada m4v 3b2
Penguin Books (NZ) Ltd, 182–190 Wairau Road, Auckland 10, New Zealand

Penguin Books Ltd, Registered Offices: Harmondsworth, Middlesex, England

First published 1996
1 3 5 7 9 10 8 6 4 2
First edition

Copyright © Valerie Windsor, 1996
The moral right of the author has been asserted

All rights reserved.
Without limiting the rights under copyright
reserved above, no part of this publication may be
reproduced, stored in or introduced into a retrieval system,
or transmitted, in any form or by any means (electronic, mechanical,
photocopying, recording or otherwise), without the prior
written permission of both the copyright owner
and the above publisher of this book

Typeset in 11/13.25pt Adobe Sabon
Typeset by Datix International Limited, Bungay, Suffolk
Printed in Great Britain by Clays Ltd, St Ives plc

A CIP catalogue record for this book is available from the British Library

ISBN 0–670–86875–2

The self is exempt from evil, untouched by age or death or sorrow, untouched by hunger or thirst: its desire is the real, its idea is the real.

>From the Chandogya Upanishad

Morality does not help me ... I am one of those who are made for exceptions, not for laws. But while I see there is nothing wrong in what one does, I see there is something wrong in what one becomes. It is well to have learned that.

The supreme vice is shallowness.

Oscar Wilde, *De Profundis*

# ONE

This is just a room, like any other.

I recognized it at once. The bed. The thin, blue-striped coverlet. The bookshelf. The window over there with the blank wall beyond. I've lived in this room time and time again. I know the bones of it, as the saying goes where I come from.

'Oh, yes,' I said to the woman who showed me in. 'This is perfect.' I thanked her. I smiled. She looked at me as if I were mad.

It's odd the way I keep coming back, again and again, to this room. This is what reincarnation must feel like.

Let's get one thing straight right from the start. I'm not looking for sympathy. I don't want anyone thinking this is some touching moral tale of Innocence Betrayed and Virtue Ruined. Don't fool yourselves that once upon a time, before I went astray, I was nice girl. I was never a nice girl. I was born with the worm of original sin crawling across my skull. By the time I was old enough to chew a rusk it had burrowed its way under the skin and deposited its eggs in the blood-rich tissues of my vital organs.

So where do I start?

At the beginning.

The man they took me to see today, the one with the beard who is clearly some kind of mind doctor, is keen on beginnings. In the beginning is the root of all neuroses, he says. Or some such rubbish. He says he would like to use hypnosis on me. It's possible, he says, to take a person back to the moment of birth. This seems a particularly pointless exercise to me.

'Why can't I just *tell* you what I remember,' I say. 'I have a very clear memory.'

'Ah,' he says, 'no, because you'll edit it with the benefit of hindsight. People always do.'

'How do you know that I won't edit it under hypnosis?' I ask.

He chews the end of his pencil. His eyes twinkle in an offensively friendly way. 'Well, we shall just have to take that risk, shan't we?' he says.

He uses the word 'we' as if we are already in collusion. I shall have to watch this man.

'I don't think so, no,' I say.

He leans forward and looks at me so greedily, with such hungry relish, that I'm surprised he doesn't rip off one of my arms and start chewing on it.

Excuse that diversion. It's difficult to concentrate in here for long. There's so much noise, so much coming and going, so many meals.

The beginning, then.

I was born at a time in history when nothing much was happening; or if it was, people were too tired to notice.

I was the eldest of three, and by far the most beautiful, which I can say without boasting because it's got nothing to do with me: it's genetic. From my father I inherited my build. He came from old sea-going stock, but his roots were still in the African bush. His bones were long and slender, the bones of a man built to run long distances across sunburnt plains bearing a message in a forked stick. His skin was chocolatey smooth. He had a dashing, villainous kink in his hair and bloodshot eyes bulging with melancholy.

My mother was Irish. Her skin was so pale it was transparent. You could trace a whole continent of rivers across the map of her body. Her hair was the colour of the sun setting over the East Lancs. road on a winter's afternoon. She was short-legged and broad-hipped, with an arse on her the size of a battleship.

I was lucky. I got the best of both parents. From my Dad I inherited my height, my long powerful bones and my permanent tan. From my Mum I inherited sparky copper lights in my hair, a luminous complexion and chips of gold in my eyes.

I was born on a Sunday.

'The child who is born on the Sabbath Day is bonny and blithe and good and gay,' the midwife recited as I slithered into her hands. I blinked at her and made my first conquest. I was, she swore, the most beautiful baby she had ever delivered.

'Look at the eyes on her,' she marvelled. 'And that skin. And those fingers.'

They were so lost in their rapt admiration of me, the midwife and my mother, that they forgot all about the afterbirth, and only remembered it when my Mum suddenly started haemorrhaging. Nor did either of them notice the almost invisible worm lying hidden like a dark shadow along the course of one of my cranial veins, its head already piercing the skin.

'Ah, will you look at the little angel,' the midwife cooed, mistaking beauty, as most people do, for goodness.

From then on, faces dangled into my pram like pale planets eternally circling the sun. 'Little angel,' the faces murmured. 'Oh, what a blessed little darling,' they marvelled, warming themselves in my reflected light. I smiled at them, a smile which, though toothless, was, I am told, so heart-piercingly sweet that the circling planets fell into further ecstasies of reverence, all of which, of course, was quite natural and no more than my due. Even as I sat in my pram graciously accepting the world's homage, I was aware that I had been born for some special and significant purpose.

And what are you going to do when you grow up,

Sandra, people asked when I was old enough to answer them. The consensus was that with looks like mine I could go on the films, like Elizabeth Taylor.

I gave them my most perfect and most calculated smile. No, I announced, when I grow up I'm going to be a saint, and was offended when they laughed. How dare they laugh? It should have been as obvious to them as it was to me that I was going to be something far more extraordinary than any of *them* was capable of imagining. Besides, by this time I'd begun to believe my own publicity: I too equated beauty with goodness. I had only to look in the mirror to see that I was inevitably marked out for spiritual perfection. I shone. 'Jesus bids us shine with a pure, clear light,' my Mum sang to me sometimes at bedtime. God knows where a lapsed Catholic picked that one up from. By 'us', of course, she meant me. Nothing about my Mum shone any more, except her hair when she'd just washed it. I was the one who shone, with a light so pure, so clear, so fierce, it could blind people.

It was a pity, really, that I wasn't born in Lisieux or Assisi. There was nothing particularly numinous about Belmont Road, except perhaps the local cemetery which we overlooked.

It was huge, Andwall Cemetery. It was so big I thought the streets on the other side were part of a foreign country which was only attainable after a long and hazardous journey. It was contained by a blackened sandstone wall. On each of its four sides, iron gates of formidable Victorian splendour opened into an avenue of cypresses. Where the four avenues met was the chapel of rest and the crematorium. Gravel paths ran between rows of headstones and soot-bitten angels. Dogs chased each other across the grass. Lovers fucked in the darkness on dry beds of pine droppings. Kids played kick the can, and made dens and hung out at dusk smoking in the earthy hidden places between the rhododendrons.

This vast necropolis was my playground and my nursery. From infancy the mysteries and rituals of death were played out regularly for my consideration. I was as deeply rooted in the place as the dead themselves.

(Do you note how grandly I use these resonant, classical, uncomfortable words like 'numinous' and 'necropolis'? You probably think I've been scanning the N section of the dictionary, but I haven't. I don't have one. They're not my words: I just borrow them sometimes.)

Because of the cemetery – the trees, the lawns, the Victorian statuary – Belmont Road was considered a posh place, a serious place, a place of worth. You were somebody if you lived there. Despite the exotic colour of my Dad's skin, and the hordes of visiting Irish relatives, both of which ought to have counted against us, the Bagnalls were class. My Dad was a steel erector, but he earned big money so *how* he earned it was politely overlooked. He was paid in fistfuls of tenners. He came home with his pockets bulging with double-time and danger money and bonuses. My Mum was a ward sister on the chest unit at the Children's Hospital. Money *and* professional status – it was an unbeatable combination in the class stakes.

Number 22 was a three-bedroomed Tudor semi. It had all the right qualifications for deepest suburbia: a flowering cherry at the front, a prefabricated garage at the side, a cracked concrete drive. I slept in the coffin-shaped boxroom above the porch. From my window I could see straight over the road and into the cemetery, which at night was full of nervy, flitting shadows. The light from the street lamp spilled over the wall and turned the paths a turgid orange, so that after dark it looked as if the furnaces of hell were burning dangerously close to the surface.

Once, one of my visiting Irish cousins told me the story of a dead woman whose skeletal fingers had clawed through the surface of a turnip field. She had grabbed a farm worker's ankle and with an icy grip dragged him down to her peat-bog grave.

'He was never seen alive again,' my cousin Padraic whispered. 'It's true. It was in the papers.'

Padraic was staying with us while his mother had her gallstones removed. They were all pale and red-haired, my cousins. I didn't like any of them, except Padraic. He had an interestingly morbid turn of mind. He was very thin with bony wrists and feet, and he smelled of some vile oil he dropped into his ears to counteract a chronic ear infection.

'How many dead people are there altogether in the world?' I asked him.

'Zillions,' he said. 'Everybody who's ever lived so far. Zillions and zillions.'

'Where do they all go?' I was very worried about this. I knew their souls went either to heaven or to hell, but what about their bodies? I imagined subterranean coffins like streets of terraced houses, a simulacrum of the world above, where the soulless dead walked up and down, nodding their fleshless skulls, and dragging scraps of mildewed grave-cloths behind them.

'They decay,' my cousin said. He was older than I was. He was at senior school and knew things. 'They turn into dust. Dust and ashes.'

This was a very unsettling piece of information. It changed the way I looked at people (and also, necessarily, the way I looked at dust), but once the initial shock had subsided I accepted it without too much trouble. It didn't, after all, apply to me. I was already marked out for some kind of unimaginable and painless transubstantiation, although I was nearly eight at this time and had learned not to say such things out loud.

'Will you for God's sake stop putting such disgusting ideas into the child's head?' my Mum said, slapping Padraic sharply across his head.

After tea on summer evenings, the kids along Belmont Road and Chapel Street East climbed over the wall into a bed of dusty rhododendrons and played kick the can. I ran about shrieking with all the others but secretly I was playing a far more exciting game. I chose my route straight over the graves, racing across the bodies of the dead, kicking at their headstones and knocking over their vases of wilting flowers. 'You're all dead,' I jeered at them, challenging them to push their bony fingers through the earth and try catching *me* by the ankle. 'I dare you,' I taunted, because I knew I was safe. I was alive, I was here and now. The blood roared in my ears and my lungs grasped great mouthfuls of air. They couldn't touch me, the dead. They were impotent. They were firmly locked up in their walnut coffins. Although, to be honest, at dusk I lost a little of my certainty about this, and ran so fast I think I was flying. My feet skimmed the marble chippings, and the rush of displaced air scattered daffodils and chunks of Oasis and jamjars in my wake. I was, I *was* flying, and my heart was hammering against the bones of my chest and never, never was I more dangerously or more powerfully alive.

So there we were, a normal, ordinary family in the middle of the twentieth century. History happened elsewhere in those days. We'd had enough of it. We left it to foreigners. And for a decade or so we jogged quietly along, hardly aware of what was happening elsewhere. Suez caused a flutter I believe, but I was still safely floating in the womb then, and as vague about what was happening beyond my immediate environment as most people in Andwall were. The Berlin Wall got built, the troubles in Indo-China escalated, the Cuban missile crisis was averted, and in Belmont Road our neighbours tutted as they watched newsreaders on the telly telling them of wars and disasters in posh, serious voices, but it was all too far away to be more than an intriguing fiction devised to keep them entertained. Only in Andwall did real things happen, vital things, major, life-changing events like deaths and marriages and pregnancies and accidents and illnesses and separations and rumours of separations. And births.

*

Births occurred in our house at eighteen-month intervals. There was me, then there was Beverley, and then Joanne, after which my Mum put her foot down. Catholic teaching or no Catholic teaching, she said, three kids were enough for any woman. If God had seriously meant women to have babies every time men got horny, she said, then why had he given them brains? Who said God had given them brains, my Dad muttered, he'd not noticed it. My Mum clipped him across the ear and said: Well, Pope or no Pope, she was bloody well going to use *her* brains: she was going to get herself measured for a cap.

In those days my Mum went to Mass twice a year, just to keep her hand in. It was more of an insurance policy, a dark fear, than a true belief. She'd had a bellyful of religion when she was a girl, an overdose. Her bloodstream, she claimed, was probably permanently contaminated, but she thought the rest of her vital organs were more or less clear of the poison now. In County Mayo, she said, the priest knew if you turned over in bed at night: he knew if you burped. The very air you breathed, she said, was thick with controlling influences. It almost choked her. As soon as she'd saved up the fare from her Saturday job, she ran away to England to train as a nurse. And when that no longer felt adequately rebellious, she caused an uproar in Mayo by marrying a heathen, a savage, a man with the pure black genes of Africa only one generation away and no religion at all. Unless you count football as a religion.

Whenever visiting sisters or cousins expressed surprise that there was still no sign of a fourth baby, my mother hinted delicately at a gynaecological problem. 'Tubes,' she murmured. And when on subsequent visits they inquired whether her little trouble had been sorted out yet, she shook her head and implied that medical science was baffled by her case. In fact, her 'little trouble' lived in a shell-shaped plastic box on the bathroom window-sill, and disappeared miraculously every time the Irish relations came to stay.

*

It was fortunate that despite the gappy teeth phase, I continued to be so extraordinarily beautiful, or, as time passed, my aspirations towards sainthood might have taken a bit of a nosedive. My looks naturally excused me from the rules and restrictions that governed ordinary mortals, so I could indulge in minor sins – lying, nicking sweets, torturing my pug-faced sister Beverley – with guaranteed immunity. I slid out of trouble as smoothly as a snake pouring itself out of a crack in a wall. No one believed I was capable of even the mildest sin – a fundamental mistake: I was capable of anything.

Poor squat, short-arsed Beverley usually got the blame. I never bothered to put people straight on that score, mainly because it felt to me like some sort of natural justice. Beverley deserved to be punished on at least two counts: firstly because she was an insufferable cow, and secondly because she was so ugly. By a cruel accident of genetic chemistry she had inherited the worst of both parents: my mother's build and my father's bulging eyes. But in my book thick thighs, pan-scourer hair and a muddy skin are not, even in combination, sufficient reason for turning into a smug and sanctimonious bitch.

If you're beginning to feel sorry for Beverley, don't bother. She doesn't deserve it. She was born bloated with self-righteousness. Anyway, it was impossible to be nice to her. I did try. On and off. Occasionally I felt twinges of guilt that things had been so unfairly distributed between us. But you can't be kind to someone like Beverley for long. It's against nature.

Once, after she'd been punished for some crime of mine – a reasonable enough distribution of responsibility, I thought, and certainly nothing to make a fuss about – she accused me of being evil.

'*They* all think you're so perfect,' she hissed in her spitty, fat-snouted way. 'But I know what you really are. You're evil!'

I was winded by the injustice of her accusation: how could a putative saint be evil?

'There, you see,' she sneered, 'you don't know what to say now, because you know it's true' – and she slammed my bedroom door.

'Who's slamming doors up there?' yelled my Dad from the lounge.

'It's Beverley,' I shouted back. 'Will you tell her, Dad? I'm trying to sleep.'

'Stop disturbing your sister, Bev.'

She opened my door again. 'I hate you,' she hissed through the crack. 'I'll hate you till the day I die.'

I slammed the door hard on her in the hope that I might crush her prying, stubby fingers in it. I was twitching with outrage. How dare she criticize *me*. How dare she say she hated me. No one hated me. It was impossible. Everyone loved me. I seethed with self-justifications. But for the first time in my short life it occurred to me – briefly – that perhaps goodness and beauty were *not* the same thing. Perhaps I was supposed to make some kind of effort towards the fulfilment of my destiny.

As the searing indignation cooled, I imagined various good and noble things I could do. The best one I imagined was this: I was dressed in a long blue robe and I was standing at my castle gate receiving the sick, the halt and the lame, and miraculously curing them of their diseases. So overcome were they by the translucent beauty of my soul that they fell in attitudes of adoration at my feet and wept and kissed my skirts. It was such a pleasant scenario I replayed the best bits in my head several times, and completely forgot about questions of morality, which, I regret to say, has been a lifelong tendency of mine.

In 1968, the year of revolutions, the year I was eleven, something terrible happened.

I killed my sister.

You think I mean Beverley, don't you? Wrong. It was my youngest sister Joanne I killed.

It was August. Mum was working days. She left us sandwiches for dinner. I had the key because I was the eldest and in charge. I wanted to go down to the railway embankment on Bexton Lane and play on the rope swing, but Beverley said she hated the rope swing, it was dangerous, and anyway she was going next door to play one of her nauseous dolly games with her friend.

'Well, I'm going,' I said.

I had to take Joanne with me. She was too young to leave. She was eight. She was small-boned, and had a long neck and the darkest skin of all of us. I sat her on the go-kart and pulled her down to the end of Bexton Lane where the railway line ran through a tunnel and out into a steep-sided cutting. She sat sharply upright, like a small Egyptian princess floating down the Nile in her ceremonial barge.

At the end of Bexton Lane I shoved her through a gap in the railings on to the embankment. The lads from St Joseph's had tied a rope to an overhanging branch. I was scared of the big lads. They wore leather jackets and hunted in packs. If they'd been around I'd have scuttled off as fast as a beetle. If, if, if. All those ifs. The world hangs on them.

I made Joanne sit at the top of the cutting in a patch of peppery dog daisies where she could watch me. The rope was thick and grey. It had a knot near the bottom to stand on. Wispy bits came away in your hands and made your skin rough and hot and musty. I pulled the rope back to the farthest point, right up against the fence which ran along the rear of the gardens, and then kicked off into open space. Above me branches squeaked. Leaves flounced and loosened. Twigs broke away. Loose shale skittered down between the nettles and rosebay willow-herb to the track miles below.

'Look at me, Joanne,' I shouted. 'I'm flying.'

I loved flying. The noise of the rope sawing against the branch was the beating of my wings as they gathered power. The panicky fluttering of leaves was the wind streaming through my oiled feathers.

'Watch me,' I shrieked as I swung higher than the branch. The air lifted my skirt and rushed against my face. The rope burned the palms of my hands.

She sat watching me for a while. Then she began to get bored.

'I want to go home now,' she whined.

'In a minute.'

She started snivelling.

'In a *minute*,' I said.

Her small, self-possessed, Egyptian face crumpled. To stop her crying, I offered her a turn. I lifted her up so her feet were on the knot. I felt her small body tremble as she looked down. 'Ready?' I asked. I had her perfectly positioned at the top of a swooping arc.

Suddenly she panicked. 'No!' she screamed. 'Don't push! I want to get off!'

To reassure her, I held her very tight. This is what I tell myself. The reason, I say, that I held her so tight was to reassure her. I am lying, of course. I know that. Like all skilled liars, I have a needle-sharp eye for the truth.

'If you didn't want a turn then what did you make all that fuss for?' I said.

Her face screwed up in terror. 'Let me get off, Sand,' she begged.

'I'm going to count to three,' I told her. Oh, I was merciless. Torturing her was such a delicious pleasure. She was so little: her fear was so exquisite. 'And if you haven't got off by then, I'm going to push you.'

Tears squeezed from between her eyelids.

'One, two, three,' I gabbled. 'Push!'

She corkscrewed over the purple spikes of willowherb. Her tiny body gripped the rope with prehensile terror. As she swung back into my grasp, I heard her give a strange, hopeless little sigh. It was horribly exciting. Driven by an itch of pure evil as ravishing and as urgently in need of satisfaction as lust, I pushed her again, this time so violently that I overbalanced.

Above me, as I tumbled and slithered down the precipice of loose chippings, Joanne flew upwards.

The sawing noise of rope against wood segued into silence. The tree shuddered and then stilled. I watched my sister continue in her upward arc clutching the broken rope. She looked like the bulge in the stomach of a snake. She was flying. My sister Joanne was truly flying. I lay on the shale smarting with jealousy. I wanted to fly like that. I wanted to soar.

She rolled over in the air. I saw her mouth open and a long scream pour out of it. I saw her hands reach out to grasp at nothing. The broken rope collapsed and fell away beneath her. She plummeted like a shot bird. Her body dropped through the air and landed on the sleepers. There was a crack as her head hit the rail.

'It's OK,' I was shouting as I skidded to the bottom of the cutting. 'You're all right. Don't cry.'

But she wasn't crying. Her eyes were wide open. Black blood trickled from a cut on her forehead. I knelt down. 'Joanne,' I shouted in her ear.

It was her open eyes that unnerved me. 'Stop staring,' I told her. 'Stop it.' I prodded at her to try and make her move.

There was an odd noise in my ears. I thought at first it was the noise of fear, that icy pain which grips the bones of your head, but it wasn't. It wasn't coming from me. It was coming from the rails – like the clean crystal ringing note you get when you rub a wet finger round the rim of a glass. I covered my head with my arms. And then there was a noise like the beating of wings, as if the Angel of Death was swooping down from heaven to smite me. I was beginning to feel sick. My teeth rattled against each other. My muscles had gone into spasms. The noise from the rails grew louder and stranger. I realized suddenly and too late what it was. I forgot about Joanne. In my instinctive rush for self-preservation, I abandoned her. The train exploded out of the tunnel just as I managed to pull myself clear and grab on to a handful of ragwort.

It was the eleven thirty-four to Preston, and it sliced Joanne's small head clean away from her body.

No one blamed me. It never occurred to anyone that I was the instrument of my sister's death.

I remember being sick over a woman's feet. I don't know who she was: somebody who lived in one of the houses whose gardens backed on to the embankment, I suppose. And I went on vomiting until there was nothing left and my insides were raw.

An ambulance arrived and took me to hospital where I was treated for shock. A second ambulance took Joanne to the mortuary.

My Mum and Dad came and sat by my bed. Mum held my hand tightly in hers. I kept falling asleep. 'It's all right, love,' she said whenever I woke up. 'It's all right.'

It was assumed from the beginning that the lads from St Joseph's or one of the other local gangs had been involved. The police told my parents that whoever it was must have run away after the accident leaving me to pick up the pieces. When I say 'pieces', I am speaking literally. I was found kneeling by the side of the rails with Joanne's severed head cradled in my lap. I don't remember lifting it up. It must have weighed a lot. Perhaps I was trying to fix it back on to her body.

A policewoman came to talk to me while I was still in the hospital. 'So how many boys were playing on the swing, Sandra?' she asked.

I saw at once how they were thinking. I shook my head.

'Could you identify any of them?'

'No,' I said, and started to cry again. When I cried, people became uncomfortable and stopped asking questions.

Nobody ever asked me why I'd taken Joanne to the embankment. My mother blamed herself. It was her fault, she should never have left us, she should have made proper arrangements. She gripped my hand tightly and mumbled 'Oh, merciful God' over and over again, which seemed to me a contradiction since manifestly he wasn't merciful. Perhaps she was grateful to him for decapitating only one daughter.

My Dad kept shaking his head. Grief had completely baffled him. He couldn't speak.

I lay in bed for several days. People brought me bars of chocolate and comics. I ate continuously as if a sticky sludge of half-digested Mars Bars at the pit of my stomach might smother the sharpness of the pleasure I'd felt when Joanne's rigid body went hurtling out into space, or might sweeten the sour bile of fear. I went over and over the moment of choice, the moment when I'd had the power to lift her down but chose to torture her instead. It made my aspirations towards sainthood look uncomfortably hollow. Now the best I could hope for was to be like everybody else. But even that seemed to be beyond my reach. I had no idea at all how to be ordinary.

I was completely adrift. I wept a lot and hardly spoke. People were immensely kind to me.

Today I've been to see this mind-doctor person again. I asked him what his qualifications were. Well, I am not having my mind raked over by someone who bases his conclusions about me on the personal hang-ups of some nineteenth-century Austrian Jew. He shows me several framed degree diplomas on the wall from places like Edinburgh and Boston. He says he's a psychiatrist. Or did he say psychologist? Psychiatrist, psychologist – one or the other. It makes no difference to me.

He calls himself Rick. He pronounces his name in a manly sort of way. He thrusts out his hand. 'Rick,' he says. 'Rick Thomas.' Two masculine manly names. He has a lusty brown beard. He smells of hair and sweat and testosterone.

'Well, Sandra,' he says in his irritatingly understanding voice.

'Well, Rick,' I say. I smile at him and open my eyes wide. I watch him blench slightly and recover.

One thing: I will never tell this man about Joanne. I am not sure yet if I shall tell him anything.

The day before the funeral, the undertakers brought the coffin back to our house and manoeuvred it through the front door and into the dining-room. The house was full of relatives.

'You don't have to see her if you don't want to,' my Mum said, crossing herself. She had taken to crossing herself so often it was becoming an unconscious habit. A small gold crucifix hung round her neck. 'Would you prefer not to?' she said.

I shook my head. I was more afraid of *not* seeing Joanne than I was of seeing her.

The coffin was laid on the dining-room table between pale candles and wreaths of waxy, heavily perfumed flowers. Joanne lay on a satin pillow. They had dressed her in the bridesmaid's dress she'd worn for my Aunty Mo's wedding, and they'd tastefully arranged a chiffon scarf to cover what no one even dared think about. My Mum kept her arm tight round my shoulders as if she were afraid my head might roll off as well.

There was no air to breathe. The room was thick with the smell of death and flowers and too much furniture and shoe polish. 'She looks so pretty, doesn't she?' my Mum whispered.

I didn't think so. I thought that her face looked suspiciously plastic, as if she was wearing make-up.

'Do you want to kiss her?' my Mum asked.

I shook my head. I was nervous about the arrangements under the chiffon scarf. I wasn't sure how secure they were. Besides, kissing her seemed like a betrayal. Murderers do not kiss their victims. They have more pride.

My Mum, my Dad and some of the Irish relatives kept an all-night vigil by the coffin. I lay in bed listening to the murmur of their voices downstairs, the long gaping silences, the sudden fierce whispers, the cadences of an adult ritual from which I was excluded. I listened to the floors creak as they moved about.

The brief darkness of a summer night dragged on. The house was a separate place: it had nothing to do with Belmont Road any more. It was isolated by death. It floated in a grey silence above the petrol fumes and the misty lawns and the scents of suburban roses, its focus concentrated on two candle flames and the impenetrable mystery they symbolized. I yawned so much my jaw started to crack. I couldn't sleep. I tried praying.

'Dear God,' I recited politely, but that was about it. I didn't really have anything more to say to him. Praying for Joanne's soul felt as hypocritical as kissing her. Praying for *my* soul was probably pointless. So I tried asking him to make everything go back to normal again. I asked him to stop my Mum crying all the time and wearing a crucifix and crossing herself, and to stop my Dad looking so bewildered and defeated. Let there be an end to everyone behaving strangely, I prayed, and let things go back to how they were before.

The words curled upwards, thinner than smoke, and disappeared into the void. It was a meaningless prayer. You can never get back to 'before'. That's what 'before' means: a time you can never get back to, a time when there are still alternatives, a time immediately prior to the fraction of a second after which 'before' is irretrievably lost. I knew that it was pointless mourning for 'before'.

My mind drifted into silence. The sky beyond the curtains had turned a thick, dull white. Downstairs the vigil continued.

'I am the resurrection and the life,' the priest recited.

It was interesting to be part of a ritual I'd observed so often from my bedroom window. I was now the silent child in the back seat of one of those shiny black cars that slid along the avenue of cedars to the chapel of rest. I was the child in her best clothes watching the grown-ups hug each other and press tissues to their eyes.

'The tragic death of an innocent ...' the priest was saying. My Mum sat chewing her lips. Her knuckles were white. I knew she was digging her nails into the palms of her hands to give herself something else to concentrate on.

We followed the coffin from the chapel out into the cemetery. It was a sticky day. I stood on the edge of the hole into which they lowered the coffin, and watched the sweat gather like drops of oil on my Dad's forehead.

'Returning,' the priest intoned, 'from whence we came.'

How much more terrible it would have been, I thought, if *I* had been the child who had died, instead of Joanne. Certainly more terrible for me, and probably, I deduced, for the rest of the world as well. Joanne's life was manifestly expendable, but mine wasn't. I had important things to do, I had a destiny to fulfil; so it was a good thing I was indestructible. An earthquake could hit Belmont Road, a tidal wave could sweep over it, fire and pestilence could destroy what little was left, but I, Sandra Elizabeth Bagnall, I would survive. Nothing could kill me. I could hear my blood slapping against my artery walls. I could feel my nerve ends frizzle like burnt hair. I was so alive I couldn't keep still. My Dad held my arms down by my sides to steady me. 'Stop jigging about, girl,' he whispered. 'Behave.'

'How long does it take for a coffin to rot?' I asked Padraic when we were back at the house for the funeral tea. But Padraic was sixteen now and drinking beer with the men. He had passed into the adult world, where questions like that were in bad taste.

I was very anxious about this question of the coffin and its inevitable decay. I imagined the first damp swelling of the wood, the orange beads of rot, the widening split. I imagined dark trickles of earth sifting into Joanne's mouth, and glutinous grey worms nesting in her hair. 'How many years?' I persisted. Padraic looked embarrassed and pretended he hadn't heard. I didn't know who else to ask. I knew no one else with a sufficiently morbid cast of mind.

I started to dream about it. I saw Joanne lying in darkness with pale slugs stuck to her skin like seed pearls. I saw rusty millipedes squeezing out of her empty eye sockets. I was so afraid of these dreams I lay in bed rigidly resisting the first loose blurrings of sleep until I grew pale and red-eyed and started getting stomach pains. My Mum had to take me to the doctor.

Two weeks after the funeral I started at my new school – the Sacred Heart Grammar School for Girls. We wore blue blazers with SH♡GS embroidered on the pocket in red and gold. We were known as the 'Shags'. 'Here come the Shagbags,' the lads from St Joseph's yelled down at us from the top deck of the bus.

On the first day we were weighed and measured by a nun with rabbity teeth and glasses, which seem to be the basic qualifications for becoming a nun. Or maybe it's the other way round. Maybe a religious vocation is the natural consequence of advanced myopia and buck teeth.

I was the tallest in our class by a head. I was treated by everyone at the grammar school with hushed awe. People fell silent when I passed. I was the girl who'd knelt by the railway line and held her sister's blood-soaked head in her lap. Nothing so exotic had ever been seen at the Sacred Heart before. I could dream whole lessons away, hand homework in late or not at all, forget to bring in my games kit week after week, and no one said a word. Endless allowances were made. What I had seen was so terrible, so far beyond their experience, the teachers were afraid to look me in the eye in case the unspeakable vision of blood and gristle was imprinted on my retina. For several terms I walked along the school corridors on a different plane from my contemporaries, unchallenged and unaware of the petty rules that governed the other girls.

My sister Bev, who started at the Sacred Heart in the

following September, complained to our Mum about my behaviour. 'It's dead unfair,' she whined. 'You should see our Sand. She gets away with murder.'

During my first spring term at the Sacred Heart, I was confirmed.

It was Mum's idea. She had started going to Mass every Sunday now. She hung a print of 'The Light of the World' over the mantelpiece in the dining-room. It seemed illogical to me, this sudden reversion to religion. It was like a dog cravenly licking the hand of the master who'd beaten him. Why look to God for comfort, I reasoned, when he was the one who'd caused the pain in the first place?

The more I thought about it, and I thought about it a lot, the more I realized that he was as much to blame for Joanne's death as I was. I may have pushed her too hard, but he let the rope break. He let her bang her head on the rail instead of falling safely on to the embankment. He made the train come out of the tunnel before I could move her. He needn't have let any of those things happen.

I decided to make a bargain with him. The nuns said you couldn't do that, but I didn't see why not. They implied God might take offence, that he would fall into a fit of divine sulks, but I thought that was only likely if you were trying to make some kind of childish and trivial bargain with him, like promising never to tell another lie in return for a new bike. My bargain was a deadly serious one: if he was willing to forgive me not only for killing Joanne, but for what I'd *felt* just before I killed her, then I was willing to overlook both his part in her death, and the fact that it was he who had given me those feelings in the first place.

'Dear God,' I prayed, assuming that he was a rational God and would understand the logic of my argument, 'if you agree to these terms, then please give me a sign during my confirmation.'

I was pleased by that final touch. It seemed fair to give him time to think the deal through. I also thought my confirmation would be a particularly fitting occasion for us to establish a mutual understanding.

The dreams got worse. I dreamed of wings beating as thunderously as the pumping of my heart. I dreamed of a vast black open mouth. I dreamed that a steel head flew out of it, the bodiless head of a blind steel angel with nests of coiling worms for hair. And as it sped out of the void towards me, it spewed a stream of poisonous hissing vomit.

On the morning of my confirmation, I felt like St Theresa of Lisieux, fragile and burning with holiness.

My mother put her hand on my forehead. She thought I was sickening for something. She said to my Aunty Mo, who was sponsoring me, that she hoped it wasn't tonsillitis.

I could feel myself shining. I walked up the aisle transfigured with light. The other girls shuffled towards the altar rail, smirking sideways at their families, but I was so certain that I was going to receive a sign that already I felt myself touched by the hand of God, and walked with my head erect and my eyes fixed on the high altar.

I knelt at the rail, bathed in confidence. In their youth, some of the most famous saints had been the greatest sinners: St Augustine, for example, or Mary Magdalene, or Francis of Assisi. Killing my sister was not necessarily, I decided, a bar to sainthood. In fact, it might even be a necessary qualification, like buck teeth and glasses were for nuns. Perhaps God had deliberately made me do it, so that I was now bad enough to grow into an exceptionally gifted saint. It was a theory that made entire sense. I was convinced that in a moment God would reveal to me that I was right. I closed my eyes. The choir sang. The rich, sickly smell of incense burned in my nostrils.

The bishop had started at the far end of the altar rail. I waited. I was in a state of almost complete bliss. As he approached I bowed my head. My Aunty Mo put her hand on my shoulder. I had a distractingly good view of the bishop's shiny shoes.

Oh God, I prayed. Now. Give me the sign now. Do it now, God. Now.

The bishop rested his hands on my head.

I had expected a jolt of electricity to fling me prostrate and unconscious at his feet, or maybe just a warm, trickling sensation like water, or possibly an external sign like a dove flying into the church and hovering pointedly above me, or even something like a butterfly caught in a beam of sunlight. If the worst came to the worst, just the beam of sunlight would have been enough – anything really, anything would have done, anything that might remotely have been interpreted as a sign.

There was nothing.

I couldn't believe it. I stayed kneeling when I was supposed to stand up.

'Are you all right, Sand?' my Aunty Mo hissed in my ear as she yanked my elbow.

No, I was not all right. No, I was not. *Now*, God, I prayed so fiercely that I tripped over my own feet. *Now!*

Nothing.

If you want a sign badly enough, then almost anything will do: a sneeze, a police siren, anything. But there was such a marked, such a pointed lack of anything at all, such an implacable nothing, that I was forced to take the nothingness itself as a sign. God had taken umbrage. The nuns were right. He was not, after all, to be bargained with. He had pointedly refused either to forgive or to be forgiven. Unequivocally he had turned his back on me.

All right, then, I said to him. All right, if that's how you want it.

I took his absolute rejection of me as a declaration of war.

For five years I studied the enemy in minute detail.

What better place to learn his habits and his weaknesses than the Sacred Heart Grammar School for Girls? The nuns were innocent but eager accomplices in my campaign. They took their responsibilities towards their pupils' spiritual education very seriously.

Academically my years at SH♡GS were undistinguished. I managed to avoid learning anything that might have helped me to pass an exam. This was not because the teaching was second-rate, it wasn't. It was just that to acquire an academic education you had to make some kind of effort, whereas to acquire a religious one you simply had to breathe.

Oddly enough, the enemy was rarely spoken of. He was too mysterious and too important for us. We could only approach him tangentially through the priest, the Virgin, or a variety of saints. The more I learned about the saints, the more I wondered why I'd ever imagined I wanted to be one. They did absurd things like sitting on the top of poles and cutting their breasts off. It seemed to me that they were all mad and lacked any sense of perspective.

I said so to Sister Ambrose, who taught religious education to the first years. She was an elderly, anxious nun who might have been distantly related to a sheep.

She took my remark with such a sweet seriousness I ought to have been shamed into stopping, but I never was.

'Well, yes, Sandra dear,' she nodded. 'You may well be right. I think there's an element of madness in any great love, don't you? And I assume that someone who falls "madly" in love – that's the phrase people use, isn't it? – I assume that indeed they *do* lose their perspective on things. Which I suppose is what happened to the saints – they fell "madly" in love with Christ. Now why is that funny, Sandra? Why are you girls sniggering? I don't think there's anything funny in loving Christ. Stop giggling, dear. The next girl who giggles will get fifty lines.'

Depictions of Christ hung on every wall. Every corner you turned there was some representation either of him or his mother. Sometimes his hands were spread in blessing and he had a thin-bearded, soulful look as if he were high on dope. Sometimes his eyes had rolled right up into their sockets in some sort of epileptic fit. In the passage near the gym, where he hung from a crucifix, drops of scarlet blood fell from the wound in his side on to his loincloth. In the chapel, you could actually see into his chest cavity. A translucent sheet of skin made out of glass allowed a view of his deep red heart. If you stared at it long enough you could convince yourself it was pulsing.

'Why do we eat Christ's flesh?' I asked Sister Ambrose on a boring Thursday afternoon when we had RE after double physics. 'Isn't that cannibalism?' It was a predictable enough question. She must have been asked it a hundred times. I didn't expect it to upset her so much.

I was sent to Sister Perpetua, the headmistress. Sister Perpetua said if that was the worst I could come up with to upset Sister Ambrose, then standards of silliness were not what they were. She said that upsetting someone as vulnerable as Sister Ambrose was morally despicable and that if I wished to argue theology, then would I please find a more serious argument and come and discuss it with her.

I tried to be kind to Sister Ambrose. Sometimes I managed it for nearly a week, but I found her distress difficult to resist. I questioned the validity of the miracles, I questioned the meaning and the rationality of the parables, I questioned the logic of the resurrection. I could not stop taunting her. It was as if poor, woolly Sister Ambrose represented the furthest, most ill-armed and poorly trained outpost of God's army here on earth, and was therefore ideal material on which to practise the first feeble thrusts of my campaign.

At the end of my first year, Sister Perpetua wrote on my report: 'If Sandra could learn to channel her undoubted intelligence more profitably she should do well. She might also be a happier girl.'

My Mum was surprised. 'Are you not happy at school, Sand?'

I was, in fact, very happy there. I dreamed through the boring bits, and read magazines under the desk, and one way or another learned a great deal.

In the third year we stopped having Sister Ambrose for religious education. We were taken by Sister Carmel. I gave up arguing. Sister Carmel had a soft fat face. She wore thick glasses and moved sluggishly, but underneath this deceptively flabby surface was a mind like a Stanley knife. She could disembowel you with sarcasm alone. I still can't understand what a woman like Sister Carmel was doing devoting her intellect to a Church which she must have known had a humiliating and distorted perception of her sex.

Sister Carmel also taught maths, which was the one subject to which I occasionally paid attention. It was the idea of maths that intrigued me rather than its practice. I seldom did any. I just liked the words. Vectors. Logarithms. Antilogs. To the power of. That's what maths was to me – a powerful army, ordinates to the power of a hundred, to the power of a thousand, marching under the leadership of clean-limbed, muscular young vectors, left right, left right; well-armed quadratic equations cutting a clean swathe with sword and divisors through muddled thinking and superstition.

Maths was logic. It was the only subject that made any sense to me. It provided logical rules. For example, a rainbow is always 22½ degrees to the earth. This isn't something you can argue about: it isn't a received opinion or superstition dressed up as immutable law. It *is* immutable law. 'Maths Rules, OK?' I wrote on the front page of my algebra textbook. (I never got much beyond the front page.)

I was sent to Sister Perpetua for defacing school property.

By the time I reached the fourth year and my celebrity had faded a little, the rules that governed the other girls at Sacred Heart began to filter down to me.

In comparison with the dazzling perfection of the rules that governed maths, they made very little sense. One must not eat sweets in the street. One must not chew gum.

One must always wear one's school hat on the way to and from school. One must wear white gloves in chapel on certain particularly holy days. One must draw margins of precisely one inch on the left-hand side of the page. One must always walk on the right-hand side of corridors, not simply when the corridors were busy, but always, under any circumstances, because the right-hand side, through use and tradition, had become the correct side of a corridor on which to walk. It had long ceased to be an expediency, and had acquired the force of a moral absolute. My sister Bev still walks along the right-hand side of corridors. To walk deliberately on the left would, in her eyes, be roughly on a par with committing adultery. Such were the curious results of our education.

One Friday afternoon, at the end of a week when I had:
1. Failed to give in work.
2. Drawn margins narrower than the stipulated one inch. And crooked.
3. Been caught eating chips at the bus stop.
4. Been seen running down Manville Road without a hat.
5. Talked repeatedly in chapel.
6. Worn outdoor shoes on the polished floor of the hall –
Sister Ambrose turned the corner of the corridor leading to the cloakrooms and found me walking towards her on the left-hand side. She finally lost her sheep-like patience.

'Sandra Bagnall,' she said, 'you're doing that on purpose.'

She was wrong: I was not doing it on purpose. I had no desire whatever to break their rules. I just kept forgetting that they applied to me.

'Well, would it be all right,' I asked reasonably, 'if I stayed on the left but walked backwards?' (Although then, of course, I'd land up where I'd just come from so it wasn't an entirely satisfactory solution.)

Her woolly face wobbled with distress.

'No, it would not,' she said. 'Stop trying to be silly, Sandra Bagnall.'

'But, Sister,' I argued, 'I don't understand what's wicked about walking on the left-hand side of the corridor. Especially if there's no one else around.'

'What is wicked, Sandra, is your total disrespect for rules. It is not the rule itself that matters, but a respect for rules in general. You must learn, dear, to bend your will to the general good. None of us can exist without rules. And even you, Sandra Bagnall, cannot place yourself above them, because they come directly from God.'

I questioned the use of the word 'directly'. 'Where exactly does it say that God doesn't want us to walk on the left side of the corridor?' I asked.

Like most people in positions of authority, she had learned to answer the question she wanted to answer rather than the question she'd been asked. 'There will be an accident,' she said. 'Girls will get hurt.'

'Not if there's no one else in the corridor, they won't,' I said. 'Not unless they walk slap bang into a wall, or the ceiling falls down on them.'

'A rule is a rule, Sandra,' she bleated. 'If you only obey rules on the rare occasions that you concede that there might be a reason for them – well, good heavens, if everybody did that, where should we be? We should be in chaos.'

'But, Sister Ambrose, I have just walked down the left-hand side of the corridor,' – I couldn't resist it – 'and I am not aware of any chaos. Are you aware of any chaos?'

Her face blushed prawn pink. Her chin trembled. Her mouth dissolved into furry shapelessness.

'Follow me, Sandra Bagnall,' she said.

I followed her along the corridor – walking on the right – past the dining-room, past the kitchens, past the passage leading to the chapel and through the green baize swing doors which separated the school from the convent. I had never been in this part of the building before.

'Where are we going, Sister?' I asked, but the exertion of the argument had left her breathless and she didn't answer.

She crossed an empty room. The walls were the colour of weak custard. The wooden floors glittered with polish. It was a no man's land between one state of consciousness and another. To enter it was like dying. Ahead of us, on the far side of the room, across the satin floor, was a pair of carved double doors. She pushed them open. I had a moment's panic. I thought that if I followed her over this threshold I might never return.

She paused and looked back.

'I shall not keep you a moment,' she said. 'Follow me.'

So I followed her plump blackness into an inner hall. I suppose it was a hall. A glass-panelled door opened into the nun's private garden. The floor was tiled in black and white and at the bottom of the stairs was a huge statue of Christ carved in pale wood. I ran my hands along the banister rail. It shone so richly it begged to be stroked.

'Don't do that, dear. You will make sticky finger marks,' Sister Ambrose said. 'You are young and strong. You can surely climb stairs without support.'

At the top of the stairs everything changed again. We were in a functional corridor. There was a different smell – bitter, like the thin, burning yellow stink in your nostrils before you faint. On the left was a long row of doors. Sister Ambrose opened one. Each had a small glass peephole in it above which hung a metal cross.

'You may come in,' she said.

I was very interested to see inside a nun's cell. It was exactly how I'd imagined it: a single iron bed with a striped blue bedspread, a window, a desk, a chair, a single bookshelf on the wall.

Sister Ambrose looked along the shelf of books and took one down.

'I should like you to have this,' she said. It was a paperback copy of *L'Histoire d'une âme*. 'God has seen fit to let an appalling tragedy mark your life,' she said. 'But you must never for a moment doubt that he had a supreme purpose in mind when he allowed your sister to die. I am convinced, Sandra, utterly convinced that one day you will be required to use your terrible experience to his greater glory. Pray that you will be ready for the challenge.'

'Yes, Sister.'

'Which is why, Sandra, it pains me so much to see you constantly challenge his will. I should be sad to see you grow up into a ungovernable young woman.'

Her eyes were painfully bright. She took my hands in her plump, obscenely soft ones, and folded them round the book.

'Read it,' she said. 'Find comfort from it. Watch and pray.'

'Yes, Sister,' I said. 'I will.'

I didn't, of course. Either read it, or watch and pray. I took it home, flipped through it, and then lost it somewhere.

The day before the day before yesterday, or was it the day before that? – already I am losing track – I found a copy of *L'Histoire d'une âme* in the library here. Most of its pages are missing so I still don't know how it was that an ordinary schoolgirl from Lisieux made the journey towards sainthood. Perhaps I shall write 'L'Histoire de *mon* âme.' From Sandra Bagnall, putative saint, to Sandra Stevens, murderess. The trouble is I'm not sure if I've got a soul. I think it is an overrated and possibly mythical thing, like the G spot.

All the same, I seem to have been moved by a strong urge to write something. To explain myself.

I asked them yesterday for some paper. They were very accommodating. They brought me a thick pad of the stuff. I shall never use it all.

Today Mr Rick Thomas had a pile of newspapers on his desk.

'The tabloids are still after your blood,' he said.

There is a four-page spread about me in the *Sun* – photographs, comments from past acquaintances. I am a she-devil, a dangerous psychopath, a sad comment on our times – the list goes on and on. In the *Express* I occupy the centre pages. On one side is a picture of me aged about six. I don't know where they got that from. I am smiling. I look luminously angelic. On the opposite page is a picture of me with a blanket over my head, a faceless woman, a blinkered animal being led into the court. The headline says 'FROM ANGEL TO DEVIL'.

'That's a bugger,' he says.

He is doing it as a word game, from ANGEL to DEVIL changing one letter each time. It's the sort of thing Dysart could do without even bothering to write it down. Mr Rick Thomas gets very stuck. He writes:

>ANGEL
>ANGER
>AUGER
>LUGER
>LAGER
>LAVER
>LEVER
>LEVEL

and he still only has three letters in place. Besides which, I don't think there's any such a word as LAVER. And I am doubtful about AUGER. It looks wrong.

'Bloody impossible,' he says. 'Can't be done.' He pushes the piece of paper over to me. 'You have a try.'

I play with it for a moment but I can't do it either.

Anyway, I take issue with the premise.

They have a time here called recreation. The other prisoners sit around in a room full of institutional armchairs and watch telly or play card games. I am not allowed to join them yet. I'm not sure whether this veto is designed for my protection or theirs. When Mr Thomas has established what nature of creature I am, whether or not I will foam at the mouth, chew off a table leg and batter my fellow prisoners to death with it, then presumably an official decision will be made. In the meantime I am in a special wing.

It's an interesting word, recreation. I never thought about it before, but it precisely describes what I have been doing these last couple of days. I have 're-created' myself from the moment of birth to the age of sixteen. It was surprisingly easy. The words bounced out of my head and on to the page. I seem to have skimmed over sixteen years with insouciant ease. The trouble is, I am not sure if I sound serious enough. I think I sound more trivial than I meant to.

What I want to do is this: I want to make a sort of map. I want to trace the exact route I took from there to here. The first part is easy. I know it backwards. But from here on it gets harder.

Room service has just brought me some cocoa. It's lukewarm but quite pleasant. Already I am beginning to look forward to the time of day when cocoa comes.

Did I ever describe this room? I forget. I have it entirely to myself. The window looks out at a brick wall. I am used to this. I once lived for over a year in a similar room with an almost identical view, so I have grown fond of brick walls. This, by the way, is a particularly fine specimen. The colours of ageing brick are infinite in their variety. There are blues and ochres and greys, greens and pinks and rusty oranges. Perhaps I will give up map-making, and paint the view from the window instead. I could make it into a lifelong occupation. Like Pissarro, I could paint it in every kind of light and at every season. I could struggle daily against inevitable failure to catch the essence of this wall. I like Pissarro. 'Oh, not boring old Pissartist again,' I murmured silently for my own amusement as I trailed round some metropolitan gallery in Dysart's wake. But actually I had learned to love Pissarro's watery light, his obsessive bridges, his dense, liquid streets.

I left the Sacred Heart Grammar School without a single qualification. It didn't matter to me. I was sixteen, I was five foot ten and beautiful, I was going to be a model. You didn't need qualifications to do that. Not academic ones, anyway.

My Mum was bewildered. 'I can't understand it,' she said. 'It's not as if she's stupid, our Sand.'

I explained to her that it was pointless fussing: if I'd needed qualifications then I would have got some. I saw no point, I said, in wasting effort on things I didn't need.

What I did need was a portfolio. I asked my Dad for the money.

He pulled a wallet full of tenners out of his trouser pocket. He'd give you anything, my Dad.

I once asked him why he was so quiet. He said maybe it was because he wasn't very clever. 'Your Mum's the clever one,' he said. What he meant was that my Mum was the one who did all the talking. I think his quietness was probably something to do with working so close to the sky all day. It gave him a clearer perspective on things.

He gave me fifty pounds. My plan was to take my portfolio round the model agencies in London. I was very confident. Sometimes I flipped through *Vogue* in the newsagent's and thought coldly that none of the models had anything approaching my extraordinary incandescence. Some were pretty, and some were stylish, but they were all very much the same. None of them had dark gold skin like me, none of them had hair like copper sparks. None of them burned out of the page.

'You can't go working down there by yourself,' my Mum said. 'You're not old enough.'

Bev said I had too much bosom to be a model. Proper models have no breasts at all, she said, but this was just jealousy because she was all bum.

My Mum thought I'd be better off trying for a job at Boots.

There was no point in arguing with ignorance, so I said nothing. Instead, I went into town to get my pictures done. The photographer I chose was in Wellington Street. The photos in his window had style. They weren't all fat babies and smug over-coloured brides smirking out of gilt frames.

The photographer was a small, round man who wore a spotted bow-tie and a waistcoat. I told him I wanted a portfolio. I liked saying the word out loud, it made me feel professional.

The photographer said that he did a lot of work for people in the acting profession so he knew what I wanted. I made an appointment for the end of the week. As he bent his head to write it down in his book, a flurry of dandruff fell on to the page. Absent-mindedly he brushed it on to the floor.

His name was Alisdair Duff.

He introduced himself when I arrived for the session. He also introduced me to his assistant, Billy Fox, who had long permed hair with orange streaks and black roots.

No, wait, I have gone wrong. I have taken a short cut. I need to go back a little. I need to start the story of Billy Fox in a different way because it is all connected with my war with God.

The declaration of hostilities after my confirmation had been followed by a long, deep, offended silence on his side, and by those few feeble practice thrusts and parries on mine. Occasionally, when I was seduced by the ritual, the easy certainties, the sweetness of nuns' voices soaring into the vaulted ceiling, the smell of lilac on the altar, I felt my skin shrivel with fear and thought how dangerous it was, what a dangerous and unthinkable thing I had done. The full vengeance of God's terrible wrath might at any moment be visited upon my head. But the moment I got out into the fresh air again, away from the sensual diversions of plainsong and incense I thought, no, wait a minute, what about the full vengeance of *my* terrible wrath? Because I had ten times more cause for anger than he had.

Sometimes I thought God was way above petty

skirmishes and had forgiven me long ago. But I had forgotten about the difference between human and divine time-scales. God was biding his time. Just when I was beginning to think I was safe, just when I was finally off guard, he fired the opening salvo in our long-postponed engagement.

Billy Fox was his chosen ammunition.

Billy Fox was nineteen. A gold ring dangled from his left ear. A green and purple tattooed snake curled up his arm. He wore shirts covered in roses and tight black leathers and he played drums in a band called Dead Meat.

Mr Duff, the photographer, made me stand against a rolled white sheet of paper while he arranged lights and adjusted things. He kept sending Billy Fox off to find a reflector or move some cables. I got bored waiting and watched Billy out of the corner of my eye. He was wearing jeans that day. There was a faded bulge where the zip was.

'This is what you'll have to get used to, Miss Bagnall, if you're going to be a model,' Alisdair Duff said.

I was annoyed because I wanted Billy Fox to think I was already a model.

'All right, Miss Bagnall,' Alisdair Duff said an hour later. 'Shall we get started?'

I posed all afternoon, not for the camera but for Billy Fox. I flashed my wide and heart-stopping smile for him. I sucked in my cheeks to show him the carved perfection of my cheek-bones, I stared with provocative aggression at the camera. I imagined I was a tiger, I snarled, I sulked haughtily, I melted with languorous sweetness, I pouted kittenishly.

'A little less,' Alisdair Duff kept saying. He ran round me snapping like an overweight dachshund. 'Give me a little less. Hide yourself from the camera. Make it search you out. Make it seduce you.'

I was offended to hear a middle-aged midget with thinning hair and a bow-tie use the word 'seduce' to me. Who did he think he was? Did he think I was doing all this for *his* benefit? I closed up. I gave him nothing, which seemed to be exactly what he wanted.

'Superdoops,' he kept saying. 'Lovely. And again. Superb.'

When the session was over, he sidled after me into the shop. 'Do you by any chance enjoy the theatre, Miss Bagnall?' he asked in his velvet voice. 'Or perhaps dinner? Would you care to have dinner with me one night?'

'I'll think about it,' I said.

I was outraged by his presumption. How dare he? The backs of his hands crawled with hairs, like a mass of black spiders' legs. How dare a plump photographer with dandruff and hairy hands aspire even to *look* at me, let alone ask me out.

The truth was I knew nothing about men. Like death and school rules, sex was another of those things that didn't seem to apply to me. The other girls hung about in bus shelters waiting to see sixth-formers from Cardinal Latimer, and drooled over unattainable singers, but none of this touched me. Besides, I was far too alarming to be attractive to any of the lads I was likely to meet in Andwall. They liked petite blondes with sweet faces and blue eyes, or doe-eyed brunettes with pony-tails. They liked girls who giggled and bounced and whispered in corners and had a smart line in backchat and didn't in any fundamental way frighten them.

I frightened them a lot. I trailed after me a dead and headless sister. I made them very uncomfortable. So while my best mates, Janice Ainsworth and Melanie Bessman, swapped intimate details about Phil Derby, with whom at various times they were both going out, I listened and was mildly interested but nothing more. I was waiting for something much better than Phil Derby, who had a false front tooth and was doing a City and Guilds' in welding at the tech. I wasn't impressed by such callow underachievement. Besides he only came up to my ear lobe. I was waiting for someone with glamour and money and the power to make things happen to come along.

So it was a singularly clever opening shot on God's part to put Billy Fox in my way. Billy was so over-endowed with glamour that I failed to notice how lacking he was in either of my other two requirements. And when, finally, I did notice, I deceived myself into thinking that it didn't matter, his excess of glamour was enough. He had a way of moving his hips that muddled my usual clarity of thought.

He was behind the counter when I went in a week later to collect the contact prints.

'You want to come down Quags Saturday night, then?' he said.

'What's Quags?' I asked.

He didn't bother to answer. He took it for granted that I'd be there. He was above chat-up techniques. He seldom bothered even with the polite deference of a question mark. That was the larger part of his glamour, his contempt for personal charm. I was too intrigued by him to be properly offended, so I accepted his invitation. Next time, I told myself, next time he'd *beg* me to go out with him and I'd refuse, and only weaken when he crawled. But this time, just this once, out of curiosity, nothing else (and also because if I didn't he might never ask me again), I said, yes, all right.

Quags was one of those clubs that start up in a cellar and then extend at roughly the same pace as its reputation into adjoining cellars. It featured Heavy Metal bands. For a short time, in the seventies, it was the place to go. On Saturday nights it was a nun's vision of hell.

I stood at the edge of the floor near the exit trying to accustom my eyes to the sulphurous lights flicking across the dance floor like electric whips. The relentless pounding of the music smashed into my brain. The heat made me dizzy. Sweat trickled down my shoulder-blades. Heads – hundreds of them, black, unidentifiable heads like scorched skulls – surged and rocked. Black skeletal arms punched the smoky air.

I didn't know until I saw him in action up on a sort of stage, that Billy Fox was in a band. He played the drums. He was bathed in blue light. His arms flailed so wildly they were a blur, they were a hundred and twenty-four arms at any one moment. His body was crouched in obsessive concentration. He was somewhere else, on another planet. Pearls of sweat flew from his skin. Sometimes he leapt up as if convulsed by a sudden charge of power, as if lightning had struck the roots of his hair.

Suddenly a scream ripped through the smoke and Billy Fox went into a kind of fit. In a spastic frenzy he attacked the cymbals; he leapt in the air; he threw away his sticks; he ripped the guitar from the lead singer, lifted it high above his head and flung it down on to the stage. The scorched skulls went wild. They shrieked, they howled, they surged.

And that apparently was it. That was the end of the set. Billy Fox pulled off his T-shirt and wiped himself down with it. He swigged at a can of beer, and mopped his armpits where the hair was black and sticky. He had a fierce, brief argument with the lead guitarist, crushed his beer can in his fist, and then vaulted down on to the floor.

I watched him push his way through the crowd. He stood at the bar, drinking and talking to an older guy whose grey hair was scraped back into a pony-tail. I thought: If the man with the pony-tail goes away, then I will go and stand next to Billy Fox and see what happens.

Two heavily built men in jeans and vests appeared on the stage and started clearing up the mess. They pushed the discothèque forward. Lights started flashing again. The man with the pony-tail abandoned the bar and threaded his way across the floor towards the stage. I realized he must be the DJ. A swarm of girls moved in to fill the vacuum he'd left, but Billy Fox ignored them. He turned his back on the bar and stared up into the lights.

I thought, if I don't do something then the whole evening will be wasted. I wanted to stake a claim on him.

I walked up to him. I was as tall as he was. I stood dead in front of him, eyeball to eyeball, so that he'd have to look at me.

'Hiya,' I said.

He went on staring up at the lights. He seemed neither surprised nor pleased to see me. He had no observable feelings about anything.

'What do you want, then?' he said. 'A beer?'

I stood beside him, in silence, sipping the lager he bought me. He went on staring up into the lights. 'Fucking crap, this stuff,' he said. 'Fucking does your head in.'

'The lager?' I said stupidly.

He didn't answer. I realized that he must be talking about the canned music.

The lead guitarist wandered over to the bar.

'So who's this then?' he said and winked at me. 'Hi, gorgeous.'

Billy Fox flung his tattooed arm across my shoulder. I could smell the spicy heat of his armpit. 'Hands off,' he warned. 'Her name's Sandra. She's a model.'

His wrist dangled over my breast. He wore a silver identity chain. We stood there like that for hours, Billy Fox and his new consort, Billy Fox, king and superstar, holding court, Billy Fox showing off his new bird. Girls stared at me, their eyes cold, their mouths thin with bitchiness. Their boyfriends hovered round us in respectful swarms trying to get Billy to talk about obscure American Heavy Metal bands. He answered them in monosyllables. When he got bored, he sucked in his cheeks and stared up at the lights again. This was a sign. They backed humbly away.

'This is Sandra, right?' Billy Fox said whenever one of his entourage approached to find out who I was. 'So keep your fucking thieving hands off.'

I was weak with pleasure.

He drove me home in his van, which was used for ferrying the instruments around. I sat in the front passenger seat. There was a hole in the floor where my feet should have been. I watched the road streaking away beneath me. We drove in silence. He wasn't the sort of person who bothered much with language.

'See you Tuesday,' he said when I climbed out.

I faintly remembered an earlier resolution to make him beg. 'Where shall I meet you?' I asked.

'Outside the shop. Half six.'

He drove off without saying goodbye.

'So what time do you call this?'

My Dad was so angry he was spitting rivets. I'd never seen him like that before. My Mum was crying and crossing herself. 'We were just going to ring the police,' she said. 'Where've you been?'

'Out.'

'Who with?'

'No one you know.'

'Your Mum asked you a question, Sandra.'

'Oh, all right then,' I said, with exaggerated bad grace. 'All right. I was out with a lad called Billy Fox. He works at the place I got my photos done. He's a drummer. And I'm going out with him again on Tuesday.'

'And when are *we* going to meet this Billy Fox?' Dad said.

I shrugged. I couldn't imagine any circumstances in which I would even consider bringing Billy Fox back to Belmont Road.

What a sordid and tedious story this is. And it gets worse. I would skip it if it didn't, as one thing always does, lead on to another. Every boring cliché of a young girl's life, everything I assumed that as Sandra Elizabeth Bagnall, ex-saint-in-embryo and fearless warrior, I would automatically avoid, I fell into head first with both eyes open. Listen to what happened next. Actually, it's so depressingly ordinary, so embarrassing, I can hardly bring myself to write it.

On the following Tuesday, in the back of Dead Meat's

rusty Transit van, I lost my sixteen-year-preserved virginity.

I was so innocent I didn't even realize it was going to happen. I lay in Billy Fox's arms at the back of this van on some mildewed offcuts of carpet, and thought that I was in paradise. I loved the smell of his jacket and the creak of leather as his arms moved to push up my jumper. I loved the wet, grainy warmth of his tongue pushing into my mouth. What I loved most was his urgency. I didn't realize that anyone would have done: I thought it was *my* mouth he wanted, *my* tongue, *my* arms. I thought he wanted *me* as opposed to any other girl on earth. That's how innocent I was.

When I was beginning to wonder where all this kissing and pushing up of jumpers was leading, Billy Fox got up on to his knees, and unzipped his flies. He slid his jeans and a greyish pair of underpants down to his knees. He grasped my hand and clamped it round a dangling bag of skin with the texture of a boiled savoy cabbage leaf. He shuddered. I was very intrigued by this. I took my hand away and then put it back again. He closed his eyes and whimpered. It was fascinating; it was like pressing the stomach of a squeaking toy: it happened every time. I tried running my fingers over his buttocks. This time his response was even more extraordinary. He pushed me back on to the Axminster offcuts, stuck his hand up my skirt and started pulling down my knickers.

I let him do all this. Don't imagine he raped me. I was a willing if detached collaborator. I observed what was happening with objective interest.

'You a virgin?' he asked.

'No, of course not,' I lied.

I felt him nudging blindly against my pelvic floor. 'Where the hell is it?' he said, pausing to poke about ineptly with his fingers.

In the end there was very little resistance, and hardly any blood. Nothing seemed to tear. Nothing hurt. On the other hand there was no pleasure either. All I could feel was his weight above me and his tediously rhythmical pumping.

So this is it, is it, I thought, in the disappointed manner of countless other virgins before me. While Billy Fox pumped away like a piston engine, and I lay inertly beneath him, I occupied myself by wondering how it was that a moment so deeply insignificant, an act so dull and trivial, had been made to bear such a huge weight of cultural and moral significance. Resonances boomed in its wake: words like sin, defilement, shame. I was listing them in my head, when Billy Fox's rhythm changed. He began to pump faster. His thin body trembled. He moaned, he shook. I held him tighter because he seemed suddenly so vulnerable, and so frighteningly affected by what to me was nothing more than sore thigh muscles and a crick in the neck.

'Oh God,' he mumbled, his mouth hot and damp in my ear. 'Oh God. Oh Christ. Oh Mother of God,' and he went into a juddering spasm and collapsed on top of me like a dead jellyfish.

I was deeply impressed. I must be terribly good at this thing, I thought. I must have a natural talent for it. I felt huge and very powerful. I had reduced Billy Fox, king and superstar, to a limp splodge of jelly. And I could do this without even trying, just by lying on my back and thinking about something else. It was awesome. He sprawled across me snuffling like a small, sated pig, my nipple dribbling out of his snout.

When he woke up ten minutes later, he was Billy Fox again. In his sleep he had reassembled himself. His power was restored. He pulled his jeans back on and lit a cigarette.

'Pull your skirt down,' he said.

What a tactician God was. How simply and with what economy he managed to lay me low. You'd have thought, wouldn't you, that I'd have had my defences up, that I'd have parried so obvious a thrust. But simply because it *was* so obvious, I completely failed to recognize it for what it was: the opening move in his larger offensive. How he must have laughed. How well he understood the bottomless pit of my vanity.

I practised my new talent at the back of Dead Meat's Transit van several times a week. We parked in the cemetery car park and did it there. On hot evenings we sometimes did it in a clearing in the rhododendrons behind the crematorium. I learned new ways of pleasing Billy Fox. I learned how to make him sob, how to make him weak and soft, how to drain away his bones and blood, and then how to give them back to him again when I was ready, not before, when *I* decided it was time to let the small, pale worm that lay exposed and exhausted on the vast plains of my belly turn back again into a man. I was like the sorceresses in mythology: I could do this deep and terrible magic. I swaggered through the summer. I forgot about my plans to go to London and take the modelling world by storm. I got a job in an office instead. Me – Sandra Bagnall. I made tea and filed letters, and all because I wanted to go on seeing Billy Fox. I wanted to stand beside him on Saturday nights in Quags, bathed in the glory of being the drummer's girl. I was willing to hang around at home all evening for the sake of the half-hour he could fit me in after band practice.

It was the power that excited me, not the sex. The sex was irrelevant: it meant nothing. But the power was a drug. For weeks nothing else mattered. For weeks I was Circe and Medusa rolled into one.

I was so used to my sister Bev getting the blame for all my misdemeanours, this seemed so much the natural state of affairs, that I'd completely failed to grasp the fundamental law of nature which states that every action has its equal and inevitable reaction. If you hold a burning poker against your arm, the flesh will sizzle away. If you continue to have sex night after night in the back of a van, you will get pregnant. And yet even now, even as I write this, I can feel the tears stab the back of my eyes and I am moved to pity for my younger self and the first frightening realization that I was ruled by the same biological laws that governed everyone else, the truly immutable rules from which even I was not exempt. For the first time I grasped that I was controlled not as I thought by my own will, but by my chemistry. Already, and without my consent, my stomach was full of alien cells multiplying and dividing. Implacable, mathematical things were happening inside me, autonomous, invasive things. I was nothing at all in this equation except a vessel for some larger imperative. The pinkish moons round my nipples grew huge and spotty. Great veins like the ones that had ruined my mother's body ran like purple snakes under the skin of my breasts. I was revolted and very afraid. I railed against God. I accused him of perfidy and injustice. I accused him of ruining my life out of small-minded spite. I sat waiting for the doctor to give me a pregnancy test, and squirmed from one end of the bench to the other in a hopeless attempt to slough off this treacherous body.

Three days later I rang for the results. I made Billy Fox come into the phone box with me. 'Positive,' the receptionist said in a voice which dripped with nosy sympathy.

'Oh good,' I said, 'that's good, that's brilliant,' because I couldn't stand to have some self-satisfied, middle-aged receptionist feeling sorry for me.

Billy misinterpreted my response. He slumped against the door of the phone box in relief. 'So it's OK then, is it?' he said. It was the first real question mark I'd ever heard from him. 'It's negative?'

'No,' I said. 'It's positive. I'm pregnant.'

'Shit,' he said.

Never believe that the laws of nature do not apply to you. You can easily exempt yourself from the laws of priests, from the laws of men, maybe, but from the laws of nature – never. Nature will always get you in the end.

*

'Oh, Sand,' my Mum said. 'Oh Sand,' and burst into tears. She fished her crucifix out from the neck of her jumper and hung on to it so fiercely her knuckles were bursting through her skin.

My quiet, bewildered Dad turned paler than it was physiologically possible for him to turn. He was so angry that for nearly ten minutes he couldn't speak at all. He chewed his lips and sweated and trembled like a racehorse. I was terrified by their reaction. I'd assumed – as I've always tended to assume – that somehow I'd get away with it. Once the first sticky ten minutes or so were over, I calculated that they'd feel sorry for me, and relieve me of the problem. All I wanted was my own body back again.

'You little slut,' my Dad said. His eyes bulged with contempt.

My Mum sat weeping on the sofa. 'Have you been to confession yet, Sand?' she asked.

My Dad exploded. 'Never mind bloody confession. Confession's not going to help. It's decisions we need.'

'Well, there's no option is there?' my Mum said. 'She'll have to get married.'

'I want an abortion,' I said. I had reached that overexcited state when things are falling apart around you so fast, there's no point in trying to hang on to anything any more.

'Oh, Sand, love, no. You don't put one sin right by committing another,' my Mum said.

'But I don't *want* to be pregnant. I don't like it. I don't *want* a baby.'

My Dad said, 'You should've bloody thought of that before, then, shouldn't you? Before you started putting yourself about. You girls, you're all the same, you want the pleasure, but you don't want the consequences, do you?'

What pleasure? I was irritated by his assumption that there had ever been any pleasure involved. All I'd ever had out of it was the heady buzz of power, and even that had turned out to be a cruel deception. I was more powerless now than I'd ever been. Vanity and stupidity combined had reduced me to abject impotence.

'Well, anyway,' I said, 'I don't care what you think. I want an abortion.'

I cried so much that week that my eyes were puffy slits.

Dear God, I prayed in the early hours of one dark, hopeless morning. 'Dear Lord and Father, please find it in your heart to forgive me, and please can we start again. Let me have an abortion quickly, and I swear to you that I will never sleep with Billy Fox again. Or with anyone else. Ever.'

It was, of course, a totally wasted prayer. It floated upwards into implacable silence. Far too late to start waving the white flag at God now. He'd got the bit firmly between his teeth. He was enjoying himself. His strategy had the simple inevitability of a good chess game.

'I'm having an abortion,' I said to Billy Fox. 'I'm going to need money.'

I had expected him to back me to the hilt. I thought he'd be so eager to get rid of this inconvenience that he'd lend me all his savings, but I'd underestimated the strength of his patriarchal instinct. 'You're not getting shot of my kid,' he said. 'That's my son you got in there.'

So God set about assembling his allies. He did well. Billy Fox, his Mum, his Dad, my Mum and Dad – he recruited them all into his camp. They were all lined up against me. Naturally I lost.

Mr and Mrs Fox came to our house one evening and sat on the edge of the settee drinking tea. Billy came with them. He had a sheepish, stupid expression on his face. I hardly recognized him. I noticed for the first time that he had acne on the back of his neck. It was a very thin neck. I hadn't noticed that before either. Nor the way his Adam's apple slid up and down whenever he swallowed. He sat in an armchair trying to look cool.

My Dad, his lips dry and powdery, his eyes bloodshot, managed to shake hands with the Foxes, but refused to shake Billy's. For a quarter of an hour things were very strained. Mrs Fox clutched her handbag tightly on her knee and coughed into a delicate fist. My mother fidgeted with her crucifix. But eventually they started talking and once they'd got going, they couldn't stop. They made plans. They decided the future. They drank more tea and my Mum made egg and cress sandwiches. No one said anything to me. I tried to put my case, but they weren't interested in logic. They were powered by naked emotion, so it was an unfair contest.

'You can't kill a baby, Sand,' my Mum said.

I thought I could probably do anything. But she seemed so certain I couldn't that in the end I went upstairs and left them to it.

I sat on my bed and looked out over the cemetery. The wind bent the trees against the darkness. Distant lights were trapped in their roaring branches. I thought about Joanne. In my head she was now reduced to a pile of white bones lying on a bed of rotten wood. I envied her. Nothing could ever happen to her again. She was complete and diminishing, whereas I was multiplying. It must, I thought, be nice to embark on the clean, mathematical process of subtraction.

When I went down again, both sets of parents were still talking. They hadn't even noticed I'd gone. They had got the photograph albums out.

'She's such a lovely girl, your Sand,' Mrs Fox was saying. 'So striking.'

All of which was perfectly true and all the more reason why none of this horror should be happening to me.

They were discussing the details of the wedding now. I looked at Billy in his jeans and his leather jacket and tried to forget about the acne and the thin neck and the Adam's apple, and to remember that this was Billy Fox, Dead Meat's drummer, and that it might after all be quite exciting to get married to someone who was heading for stardom. We could go down to London after the wedding, and he'd become a famous drummer with a band and make hit records and go to glamorous parties, and as soon as the baby was born I'd start modelling and make loads of money, and we'd have a flat and an au pair girl and all our friends would be in the music business or in films. On the whole, I decided, things could be worse.

By this time my Dad had got the whisky out and found half a bottle of sweet sherry at the back of the cupboard, so everyone was feeling more optimistic.

And so it was that in February I married Billy Fox at St Joseph's. I wore an off-white dress with a lace veil. Billy Fox wore a sharp blue suit with a kipper tie and a white carnation in his buttonhole.

A sudden gale blew up during the ceremony. It buffeted us back into the porch when we tried to come out. We staggered against it to pose for photographs, clutching our hats and pushing down ballooning skirts. The wind whipped my veil off my head and blew it high over the trees and out on to the road where a passing lorry ran it over. It's all caught on celluloid, courtesy of Alisdair Duff. There we are, our clothes flapping against our legs, our hair streaking past our faces, our smiles frozen across our teeth like rictuses – and there is the veil flattened damply over my face like a grave-cloth. Running diagonally across it is the imprint of a muddy tyre mark.

Afterwards, I realized what the gale was: it was God's laughter gusting uncontrollably across Andwall. He must have laughed until he cried at this bleak ceremony of self-inflicted human misery.

So after a reception at the Three Feathers, followed by a piss-up at which the Irish relations sang 'The Wearing of the Green' and other rebel songs in the cheerfully maudlin way that drunk Irish relatives always do at weddings, we went back to the Foxes' house. This was where it had been decided that we should start our married life because they had the extra room. I said why couldn't we go to London, but the Foxes said there was Billy's job to consider and where would we live? My Mum and Dad said have the baby first before you make any decisions, and what if Billy couldn't find a job down in London, what would we live on then? That's right, said the Foxes, there's the baby to consider now.

Ted and Marilyn Fox lived in a bleak pebble-dash council semi between Garsditch and Spokely. They gave up their bedroom for us, the big front room with the bay window. It was decorated in apricot pink. I despised it. It smelled of bleach. It smelled as if someone had been very sick in there and cleaned it up with a bucketful of neat Domestos.

Outside the bay window, the dual carriageway roared into town. It was bifurcated – I think that's the right word, I must ask them if I can have a dictionary – by an island of thin, sickly grass where plastic bags and crisp packets fluttered frantically up and down like wounded birds. The air stank of exhaust fumes, of noxious gases from the chemical works across the river, of the damp, mousy stench of small, grey, poisoned lives.

My life grew smaller and greyer by the hour. In exchange for a dubious power over Billy Fox I had sold my soul. Even as I stood at the altar rail saying 'I do', I knew what a pitifully poor bargain I'd made.

The first few days of what was technically my honeymoon I spent in spasmodic bouts of tears. I lay on the apricot pink nylon bedspread choking on a cocktail of despair, traffic fumes and bleach. The window frames rattled as lorries thundered past outside. On the landing Ted and Marilyn whispered nervously to each other.

'What's the matter with her?' Ted hissed. 'What's she crying for now?'

'She's homesick, poor pet,' said Marilyn. 'She's only a baby herself. Tell Billy to come upstairs and sit with her.'

It wasn't *home*sickness. It was *self*-sickness. It was my self I was pining for. I wanted it back, my real self, my lost self, the self I had sold. My famous luminosity was fading fast. At any moment the light could gutter and go out.

*

Marilyn Fox's life was a constant war against dirt. She was a short, skinny woman with a pinched face and dark hair streaked an unconvincing blond. She worked as a cleaner for several professional families. Sometimes, on Saturday nights, when she and Ted went down the social club, she sang. She had a voice like Connie Francis, a gutsy voice with a sudden catch in it. She belted out all those songs of love and betrayal: 'Who's Sorry Now?', 'Carolina Moon', 'Lipstick on Your Collar'. Every morning, she put on her pink nylon overall and set off to clean other people's houses, and in the afternoons she cleaned her own with obsessive energy. She was terrified of dirt. The carpet and the three-piece suite in the front room were always covered in sheets of polythene. Shoes were discarded at the back door. Every surface was doused with bleach. All life forms were discouraged: the smallest and most inoffensive germ searching for a moist crack in which to breed was immediately sizzled to death in an acid bath of Domestos. She polished until the furniture glittered like ice. The bathroom was her passion. She struggled manfully to control her anxiety lest a smear of toothpaste should ruin the glassy perfection of her tiles, or a scattering of talcum powder fall on her peachy carpet. There was nowhere in that house where you could rest comfortably without feeling you were a source of contamination. Poor old Ted, yet another in the long British tradition of husbands swept like a panful of dust out of their own houses, retired to his shed, where he mended things, or to the Crown, which was warm and shabby. Every evening after tea, he leaned back in his chair and said, 'Well, love, I'll get out from under your feet, shall I?' Billy always sloped off after tea as well, to band practice. So I was left to help Marilyn with the washing-up. At first, I tried escaping like the men did, but I had nowhere to go except home. It was a two-bus journey across town to Andwall and another two buses back again – an hour each way. I hadn't got the energy to do it every night. So there I was trapped in a semi-detached temple of hygiene on the edge of the dual carriageway – what you might call a spectacular and unequivocal victory for God.

I was Mrs Sandra Fox now. I wore a ring on my finger to prove it, and for a week or two after I went back to work I allowed myself to bask in the envy of the other girls in the office. I had sprinted past them in the marriage stakes, I had reached the finishing tape while they were still pounding breathlessly along the track.

'So what's it like being married?' they asked, their eyes bright with desperation.

'Wonderful,' I said, because I know what lies people need to be told. But inside I was raging. I behaved at the Foxes' house like a trapped animal. I sneered at everything they did to make me feel welcome. A terrible trick had been played on me: I had grown up – oh, impossible! – to be unremittingly ordinary. My life had become dull, repetitive and instantly dismissible. Soon I would turn into a housewife and fuss around my kitchen cooking liver and onions, and expecting nothing more out of life (which I suppose is arguably a good thing since that's all there was ever likely to be).

Liver and onions was Ted's favourite meal. We had it at least twice a week because Marilyn said the iron in liver was good for growing babies.

'You cut the meat up, love,' she said. 'I'll do the onions.'

The slab of purple meat squelched on the draining-board. I peeled off the stringy bits and cut away the branching veins. Sometimes lumps of it slipped through my fingers on to the floor. It looked like afterbirth. My hands were dark with blood.

Marriage did nothing to change Billy's life. The only minor differences he experienced were as follows –
1. He moved bedrooms.
2. He slept in a bigger bed which he had to share with another person.
3. He had sex on tap (which was no real change for him, except this sex was sanctioned and in a bed).

Apart from that, everything went on exactly as before. He came and went as he pleased. He made no attempt to alter his life to accommodate me, although to be fair to him – which is not something I am often inclined to be – I can't imagine what changes I would have wanted him to make.

My first mistake was to assume that things would stay the same for me as well. I assumed, for example, that I'd still go with him to Quags on Saturday nights, but he wasn't keen. A wife was bad for his image, he said. A pregnant wife was worse. We had a fierce argument about this. I said I was sodding well coming and he couldn't stop me. He said, Oh yes he could. I said, How? Go on, show me. How?

He showed me how. It was very painful.

I fell against the wall, my jaw ringing with the impact of his fist. I fell so hard I made a bloody mark on Marilyn's pink wallpaper, a long bright smear from the point where I first made contact all the way down to the floor where I collapsed and for a second or two lost consciousness.

'You all right upstairs?' Ted called.

'It's that frigging wardrobe door sticking again,' Billy shouted back. 'It's just caught Sand a whack across the face.'

'I'll have a look at it after tea, son,' said Ted.

'You do that to me again,' I threatened, 'and I walk out of here for good.'

I should have left him there and then, but I was too embarrassed to admit that my husband had hit me in the jaw after only two weeks of marriage, and as the plausible lie about the wardrobe door had already been established I went along with it. I lied to Ted and Marilyn, I lied at work, and I didn't go back home until the last bruise faded. I was too proud to tell my Mum and Dad the truth, and too ashamed to lie to them. I wiped down Marilyn's wallpaper with my flannel and pushed the wardrobe slightly to the left so that the stain was hidden.

Billy swaggered round the bedroom putting on his

leathers and his aftershave, and went out to Quags without me. Ted sorted out the wardrobe door before he went down the Crown. Marilyn bathed my wound in Dettol.

'We'll have a nice quiet evening in, Sand,' she said. 'Just you and me.'

We sat together in the back room with our slippers on in case we marked the carpet, and watched television. Marilyn knitted and sang along with Tom Jones, and I seethed with anger.

'This is cosy, isn't it?' she said. 'I tell you what we'll do, next time, Sand, love, we'll get a couple of milk stouts in. That'll be nice. It's supposed to be good for you when you're pregnant, stout. Full of iron.'

I was eating so much iron the thing inside me was growing metal plates instead of skin. I visualized it as a kind of lizard, or a small dinosaur, something hideously reptilian with articulated steel scales. I willed it to die. I willed it to shrivel up inside me and die, but it knew nothing about me or my will. It cared only about itself, and went on growing with blind, insistent selfishness. It thrived on the liver and the Guinness which Marilyn poured down my throat. It lay curled in my stomach, feasting on blood and iron and growing bigger by the minute.

At two in the morning Billy came back flushed with the triumphs of the night, and climbed into bed. He seemed to have forgotten about hitting me. He wanted sex. I reminded him about my jaw. I told him he was dead lucky he hadn't broken it. I told him that I was in no mood ever to speak to him again, and as for sex – forget it. No one treated me like that and got away with it. No one.

But, of course, he did get away with it. He kissed the cut, he cried, he begged. He said it would never happen again. The problem, he said, was that he couldn't stand all those other guys at Quags leering at me. It was jealousy, that's all, he couldn't help it, he was so jealous. And he couldn't bear to think that he'd hurt me, he never wanted to hurt me, please, Sand, please, oh God, Sand, you're beautiful – all of which I believed because it gave me the illusion of power again. So I made him beg and when I thought he was suitably sorry for what he'd done, I put my arms round him and comforted him and let him into the warm places which his mouth and his fingers were groping for.

About three months before the reptile was born, a sudden and quite unexpected change came over me. I was sitting on the top deck of a number 63 bus at the time. I think perhaps it was something to do with being so high up. I was squinting through a damp hole I'd cleared in the steamy condensation. Below were sodden suburban gardens and flat garage roofs. I was thinking how small everything was, how cramped, how closely the suburbs resembled a rabbit warren full of crowded burrows: warm, smelly nests where human animals grunt and scratch and snuffle and breed. And then something very odd happened, something physical. Without any warning, a connection in my head came apart. It was like a hook slipping out of an eye. I could feel it happen. I could hear the click. I was aware of this disconnected part of my mind drifting away like a balloon to a point from which I could look down on myself; from where I could see a small, furious, distressed creature who, like the saints of whom I had complained to Sister Ambrose, had lost all sense of perspective. I felt mildly sad for her, but I couldn't see what it was she was so mad about. All she had to do was to wait until the iron monster was born and then she'd be free again. There were no chains holding her, so why, I wondered, was she pretending there were?

This cool disconnection stayed with me the whole of the bus journey and was still there when I got off. It stayed with me all through tea. It grew stronger. With detached boredom, I watched Marilyn serve up shepherd's pie.

'I put a nice bit of kidney in there,' she said. Kidney was, of course, full of iron. After tea she said, 'You're looking tired, love. I'll do the dishes. You go and sit down.'

So I sat in the back room with my feet on a strip of

plastic and my lungs scorched by the smell of neat bleach, and I watched the news on television. By this time I was so distant I was able to accept Marilyn's kindness with a sweet and passive grace.

'Our Sand looks a bit more cheerful tonight,' Ted commented.

Marilyn said, 'Well, it gets easier towards the end, doesn't it, love?' She reached over and squeezed my hand. She was obviously prepared to dismiss my raging ingratitude to them both as one of the more exotic symptoms of pregnancy.

July came. 'It's a boy,' my Mum said. 'You can tell from the way she's carrying.'

Marilyn Fox said it was a boy as well. I was the only one who knew it was an armour-plated lizard.

I grew huge. At night Billy Fox lay with his arms round my belly in bed. He liked me pregnant. He loved my vast, swollen, veiny breasts with the obscenely enlarged nipples. 'You're so big, girl,' he said, his voice thick with pleasure, and he twined his skinny white limbs round me as if he were an infant kangaroo trying to burrow back into the pouch. The huger I grew, the more he wanted me. 'When will the milk come?' he asked. And the bigger I grew, the calmer I became. I lay in bed, after Billy had fallen asleep, feeling the reptile stir and lash its steely tail.

Now that I had a proper perspective on things I could see that Billy Fox was not and never had been my destiny. He was a bauble God had tossed in my way, and like a brainless jackdaw I had swooped on him, assuming that because he glittered like a jewel, he must be one. My mistake. He was, of course, only a ring-pull off a beer can. He was never going to amount to anything. His endless blag about going to London and making it big was all a fantasy. He was too scared even to move out of his parents' house, let alone catch the train to a strange city. I kept telling him to ring up a record company and get an A & R man up to see the band, but he never did. His vision stretched no further than Garsditch in one direction and Quags in the other. London was too big a risk. Here he had a steady job and enough celebrity to keep his ego satisfied. The trouble with Billy was that he posed big but he thought small. The more I looked at him, the smaller he grew. His arms were like sticks of spaghetti. His torso was as smooth and as bony as a child's. Poor little Billy Fox, I thought, poor, slightly disgusting little Billy Fox.

Keith (Richards) Eric (Clapton) Fox was born three weeks before he was due. He weighed 5lb 12oz. He was a boy (obviously), he was nineteen and a half inches long and his hair was black. I can't think what else to say about him. I can't remember now what it is that interests people about babies.

'Here you are,' said the midwife, with as much pleasure as if she were offering me an expensive Christmas present. 'Here's your little boy, Mummy,' and she dumped him, a grey thing covered in fatty slime and blood-streaked mucus, on to my chest. He was as small and meaningless as Billy Fox. At some point in the birth process his iron scales had been scraped off him. He looked like a tortoise that had lost its shell. His withered skin hung in empty creases. His head moved feebly on the wrinkled stem of his neck.

'Come along, Mummy,' said the midwife. 'Give baby Fox a little cuddle.'

*Cuddle* him? It was no good her looking at me like that. I could hardly bring myself to prod him with a finger let alone cuddle him. I was exhausted and trembling with shock. The whole process had been a personal outrage, which could not, as she seemed to imagine, be put right with a cup of strong, sweet tea. I immediately vomited the clay-coloured liquid all down her front, and serve her right.

The worst shock was the pain. No one had told me about that. But then, to be fair, how could they? What words could they use? There are none. You can say, 'I'm being torn apart', 'the bones of my legs are being ripped out of their sockets', but this is way off the mark, and nobody pays any attention to you anyway. Childbirth needs huge words, cosmological words, words like 'tectonic plates' and 'tidal flow' and 'gravitational pull'. The fact is that there is no language in which to describe the most basic and powerful of human experiences. No words. I find that a bit disturbing. I might mention it to Mr Rick Thomas and see what he says. He is supposed to be a psychiatrist (or possibly psychologist) so presumably he knows about these things.

I suppose it's too late to start inventing a language now.

I looked at the other women on the ward with stunned respect. My Mum came to see me at visiting time and I was so moved by my newly acquired knowledge of what she'd been through not just once but *three* times, that I wept speechlessly until the bell went. 'It's all right, love,' she said. 'It's postnatal depression. It happens to everyone.'

Don't imagine I was a cruel mother or even a neglectful one. I fed the baby, I kept him clean, I dressed him in the lemon and white jackets Marilyn knitted for him. I pushed him out in his pram. I even grew quite fond of him, particularly when he filled out a little and turned pink and lost the last physical traces of his reptilian origins.

Marilyn adored him. She wiped his face and adjusted his buttons with an intimate, tender, proprietorial smile. After his bath, she buried her face in his powdery, sickly smelling stomach, and he drew up his fat legs and made noises which she interpreted as pleasure. Her sensual delight in him far surpassed anything she felt for Ted. 'Oooh, who's my little love, my little sweetheart, who smells so sweet for his Nan, then?' she whispered into the folds of his flesh, and she drew in great breaths of him and nibbled at the bracelets of fat round his wrists and sucked his tiny fingers. If Ted had asked her to nibble the skin on his wrists, or indeed anywhere else, she would unquestionably have shrieked with nervous horror and refused on the grounds that it wasn't hygienic. But Keith was different: in Marilyn's philosophy babies were innocent of any kind of earthly contamination.

Billy was self-consciously besotted by his son. Babies were women's work so he divorced himself from the details. He complained about disturbed nights, and said the usual things like 'Can't you shut him up?' But he liked to watch me feed Keith, and I often caught him talking to him in the pram and addressing him as 'son'.

All through the summer and the autumn nappies soaked in buckets of Napisan, and hung on the maiden in the hall overnight to air. Marilyn sang as she knitted larger-sized bootees. Ted spent his evenings in the shed making his grandson a wooden train on wheels. As soon as Keith learned to crawl, the house reeled under renewed onslaughts of bleach. 'We don't want him picking up any germs,' Marilyn said. She breathed in lungfuls of noxious air and exhaled blissfully, 'Doesn't it smell lovely and fresh in here?'

He was a happy child, Keith Eric Fox. He inherited my smile. It had the effect of turning everyone immediately into his slave. In turn, he adored everybody. He lifted his arms to be picked up by complete strangers. His face broke into radiant grins whenever anyone approached. But sometimes, mostly when I was feeding him, I caught him looking up at me, and behind the disguise of untouched innocence, behind his blue, unblinking eyes, lived something that was centuries old. I hated that look. It made me uncomfortable.

I gave up the office job because there was no one else to look after Keith in the mornings when Marilyn was out cleaning. Instead I got work testing light bulbs on the two to six shift at the factory on the industrial estate two roads back from the Foxes'. I sat at a bench in a white overall and watched filaments light up. It was a mindless job, but I liked it. It was only to fill in time until the next thing happened. It was like watching small lives, small potentials, briefly make contact with the source of energy, light up for an instant and snuff out again.

Christmas came and went, and then another Christmas. I was growing very restless. Keith was fifteen months old and staggering about on fat, mottled legs. Marilyn bought little baseball boots for him and denim trousers from C & A, and taught him to say 'Keefy loves Nan' and 'puffatrain'.

Billy came back one day from the studio and said, 'There's this kind of party thing at work.'

I didn't really want to go, but Marilyn insisted it would do us good to have an evening out together. I don't know on what grounds she based this extraordinary belief. I seldom saw Billy these days. He said he was busy writing songs. He spent every evening with the band and the simpering girls who hung round them. This suited me fine. I had completely forgotten what it was I had once found attractive in him. I could hardly bear him to touch me. By the time Keith was weaned and my monumental, veined motherliness had shrunk back again to human proportions, he had lost interest in me as well. We had sex occasionally in the dark, a sudden lazy desire on his part and total indifference on mine. The last thing on earth I wanted was to spend a whole evening with him, but I overheard him tell Marilyn that Alisdair Duff had invited the boss of a northern-based model agency for whom he had done some work in the past, and because in my head I was getting ready now to move on, I thought this might be a useful contact.

I rinsed my hair in vinegar so that the copper in it blazed. I wore a black T-shirt, an old black miniskirt and one of Billy's silver-buckled, death's-head belts. I spent fifty pence on a pair of huge orange plastic earrings. Before we left, Marilyn said nervously, 'Don't you have a proper dress, love? I could probably lend you something only I don't suppose it would fit.' I smiled kindly at her: I could afford to be kind because I knew I was leaving soon, and because it wasn't her fault she didn't understand how extraordinary I looked.

In the van on the way to Wellington Street, Billy said: 'You're making a show of yourself in that skirt.' But Alisdair Duff, who seemed to be the only person who appreciated my originality, said, 'Sandra, my dear, you grow more and more stunning with every passing moment. What inspired earrings,' and kissed my hand in a skittishly flirtatious way.

The studio was full of people holding glasses. Alisdair Duff introduced me to two other photographers, the woman who ran a sandwich bar down the road, a couple of reporters from the local paper, someone he said was a lecturer in something or other at the art college, a man who was a writer and who was apparently quite famous although I'd never heard of him (this was long before I'd read anything at all), and a sparrow-boned woman with a beaky face called Ailsa who turned out to be the boss of the model agency. She gave me a cursory look and started talking about a house she was buying somewhere near Leeds.

'Sandra's a model,' Alisdair Duff remarked after the sparrow-boned woman had delivered a monologue about the horrors of solicitors' bills.

'Really?' Her thin, scarlet lips stretched into a smile of bored incredulity.

'Yes,' I said. 'Excuse me. I have business to discuss.' And I smiled coldly and walked away. I wasn't going to put myself in the humiliating position of begging this stick-woman to take me on to her books. So I drifted about looking for a group to which I could attach myself. Billy was cruising the room with two bottles of wine filling up people's glasses. I held out my glass to him. 'How many have you had?' he said under his breath. 'You get pissed and show me up . . .'

'Oh, get lost,' I spat in his ear. I wandered off and joined Alisdair Duff who was hovering between groups.

'It's going rather well, don't you think?' He looked round the room with professional satisfaction. 'Who would you like me to introduce you to now?'

'Who else is there?'

He considered this for a moment. He was wearing a red velvet waistcoat with a dark green silky shirt.

'You look like a holly berry,' I said. Perhaps I *was* a bit drunk. I smiled down at his bald patch. Under the thin puff of hair above his right ear I noticed a dark, pulpy mole.

'What did you say to Ailsa?' he asked.

I told him what I thought about Ailsa.

He sighed. 'Sandra,' he said, 'it doesn't matter whether you like these people or not. It's whether they like you. She could be very useful to you.'

'I doubt it,' I said with a grand and dismissive gesture that sent a slurp of wine over my shoulder. 'Anyway, I'm not interested in Leeds and Manchester. I'm only interested in London.'

Alisdair Duff laughed. His laugh rumbled round his puffed red velvety chest. 'I wish you'd let me photograph you again,' he said. 'No charge. What did you think of the other ones I did? For your portfolio. You didn't like them, did you?'

'I did quite.'

'You never had any of them enlarged.'

'I would've done if I hadn't got pregnant.'

'Come upstairs a minute,' he said. 'Let's have a look at them again.'

I hadn't realized there was an upstairs. We went through into the shop. A door at the back which I'd never even noticed opened into a damp, flaking passage. I followed Alisdair Duff up some wooden stairs.

'I never knew you had a room up here,' I said.

'So where did you think we did all our developing, then?' he asked.

I shrugged. It always surprised me the way people asked questions that assumed I was interested enough in them to have actually given their lives serious thought.

'That's the darkroom,' he said. 'And this,' he opened a door and switched the light on, 'this is where we store stuff we want to keep.'

It was very cold up there. Under the feeble light, I saw shadowy stacks of metal shelving crammed with folders and files.

'What I'd really like to do is to take some serious photos of you,' Alisdair Duff said.

Far away below us I could hear Nat King Cole whining on about something or other – love, I suppose – and the drone of party chat.

'There's an electric fire somewhere,' Alisdair Duff said, scuffling under dusty piles of dog-eared brown envelopes. 'Are you cold?'

He unearthed an ancient, single-bar electric fire and plugged it in.

'Now then, how's that?' He rubbed his hands together. 'You sit down there and get yourself warm, and I'll have a look for these contact prints.'

The element glowed a fierce orange in the middle. I watched Alisdair Duff pretend to look through the Bs on the first stack. His small fleshy fingers flipped along the folders on the shelf. 'Babcock, Badlands, Badworth,' he muttered. 'Balder. Missed it. Maybe it's filed under Fox.' He looked across at me. 'Are you warmer? Is that fire working properly?' He came across to check, and squatted to adjust its position. 'Let me feel your hands,' he said.

My hands were bigger than his and bonier and very cold. 'Warm heart,' he said. Suddenly, he pressed both of them hard into his cheeks and kissed each palm in turn in a furtive, apologetic way. His lips were dry. He was blushing. He swallowed noisily and let go of my hands.

I saw the hopeless adoration in his eyes and was grateful for it. I felt it deserved some reward. 'Do you want to sleep with me?' I asked.

After the long paralysis of shock, he laughed: a high, feminine, hysterical laugh.

'I dream about it all the time,' he said. His voice was choked with longing. 'God, you don't know. I think about nothing else.'

If I ever mention this incident to Mr R. Thomas, which I don't intend to but you never know what these psychiatrist people will trick you into revealing, I must remember to explain that I was motivated by gratitude. I must make it clear that I don't usually ask such blunt and unequivocal questions.

I go to see Mr Thomas once a week now, on Thursday afternoons. It's a regular appointment, like going to the hairdresser. I spend an hour with him. I am supposed to do all the talking. It's a long time to fill.

Mr Rick Thomas's office is a small, stuffy room, an oddly shaped afterthought of a room, like a large cupboard, at the end of a corridor. He sits with his feet on the radiator and a quizzical look on his face. He asks a lot of questions. I have to think fast: I do not want to give anything of substance away. He twiddles a pencil while he thinks. Sometimes he pokes it down his collar and scratches his back. There is always the smell of baking shoe leather and a faint, rancid, cheesy whiff of toasted sock.

So as I said, it was a matter of gratitude, a small gift in recognition of Alisdair Duff's discernment. He was the one person left who could still glimpse the last flickers of my dying luminosity.

I unbuckled my belt. He gave a breathy gasp, and flicked his tongue over his lips like a snake. I pulled off my T-shirt. Underneath I was wearing a very old and not very clean bra. 'Oh God,' he groaned. Immediately the familiar magic streaked through my veins. I was invincible again. I was Circe. I was rich with power.

'No, please, please. Let me do that.' He turned me round and undid the bra hooks. He slipped the straps off my shoulders. His face was on a level with my breasts. They bounced out of their grubby confinement. The sight of them seemed to be too much for him. He reached out and touched them. His fingers were trembling. To be honest I was knocked a little off-balance by the sweetness of his touch. 'Lie down,' he said. He sounded as if his throat was stuffed with feathers. He eased the length of me on to the floor in front of the fire, and knelt beside me, staring humbly at my revealed nakedness. Tears oozed into his eyes. He brushed them away with the back of his hand and started reciting a poem about 'World Enough and Time'. I wasn't sure whether a bald dwarf reciting poetry over me was deeply romantic or just comical. Get a move on, I thought. Get on with it.

To hurry him up I started to unbutton his waistcoat. His chest was white and fleshy. A flurry of black hairs skittered down the cleavage between his breasts. An appendix scar was gathered into a flabby pucker on the right-hand side of his belly. I closed my eyes. It was all over in less than a minute. He came while I was still trying to adjust my position on the floorboards. He was very apologetic. I had no idea what he was so sorry about. I was delighted to be finished so quickly, particularly since for a second or two, when his fingers had touched my skin, I had felt this odd pang, this sudden sharp ache, which unnerved me because it seemed like the first sign of a possible weakness. I had no desire whatever to be reduced to the state of abject and humiliating weakness to which sexual pleasure had reduced both the men of whom I'd so far had experience. I preferred to keep my power. So when Alisdair Duff asked what he could do for me, I didn't understand the question and pushed him away.

'We should go,' I said.

He looked absurd hopping about in his underpants, pulling up his trousers, buttoning his waistcoat over his blubbery belly. I was disgusted with myself, not on moral but on aesthetic grounds. On the other hand – let me try to be honest about this – there was something very exciting about his physical repulsiveness. I felt like a nymph who has unexpectedly been ravished by a wart-hog.

'So where did you and old Duffy disappear to?' Billy asked as we lay side by side in bed in the early hours of the morning.

'The storeroom,' I said, remembering the tears in Alisdair Duff's eyes. 'We were looking at contact prints.'

Billy laughed. 'He's always had an eye for you,' he said.

He ran his hand along my thigh but I turned over and pretended I'd dropped off to sleep. The idea of me and Alisdair Duff was obviously as ludicrous to Billy as it was to me; so ludicrous that he wasn't even jealous. It *was* ludicrous. Duffy was seven inches shorter than I was and nearly twenty years older. All the same, his breath was sweet and his small hands were soft on my skin, and no one had ever recited poetry to me before nor worshipped quite so reverently.

I started going to his flat in the evenings instead of staying in with Marilyn. I told her I was going to see my Mum and Dad. She was surprised I didn't want to take Keith with me, but I said what was the point in dragging him back and forth from Andwall when he ought to be sleeping.

This arrangement worked brilliantly until one day Keith developed earache. His temperature shot up. Marilyn suspected an abscess. She rang Belmont Road in a panic and discovered that I wasn't there. By the time I got home, Keith had been rushed to Casualty and everybody was too anxious about him to bother much about me. I rapidly invented a friend from the office where I'd worked before Keith was born. I called her Andrea. When the panic was over, I affected an expression of pained amazement that they could have so completely forgotten what I'd told them earlier. 'But I was at Andrea's,' I said. 'I told you I was going to Andrea's.'

'I thought you were at your Mum's,' said Marilyn. 'I don't remember you saying anything about this Andrea.'

I did a good line in controlled exasperation. 'Well, I did tell you,' I said. 'Several times. I *knew* you weren't listening.'

After that, I went to 'Andrea's' two or three times a week.

Alisdair Duff lived in a garden flat in one of those big Victorian houses off the park. His flat was full of books. Framed photographs of weird things like bicycle wheels and ugly women sitting on the sea front hung on the walls. His curtains went all the way down to the floor. Instead of proper carpets he had skimpy mats on bare polished wood. Large plants like trees stood in the bay window. Every surface was covered in clutter: unframed photos, piles of stones Duffy had picked up from a beach in Crete, record sleeves, pencils, feathers in glass jars – all sorts of rubbish. The high walls were painted white. All the woodwork was chipped. His kitchen led out into a cobwebby conservatory piled with musty cushions and rotting magazines. The cooker would have furnished Marilyn with a month's supply of nightmares. I loved Duffy's flat with the kind of passion that a Victorian Englishman must have felt for the exotic cultural mysteries of the Indian Raj.

He liked to have a bath as soon as he got in from work. Sometimes I arrived at his front door when he was in mid-soak, and he opened the door to me holding a glass of wine in one hand and clutching a towel round his middle with the other, his pink plumpness fuzzy with steam.

Sometimes he wanted me to get into the bath as well. He liked washing me. I was very clean that winter. His bathroom was tiny. It was crowded with tall ferns and dark-leafed plants. On the shelves were bottles and tubes of mysterious masculine things. He made me stand in his bath – an old white tub with claw feet – while he soaped me down. I had to bend my knees so he could reach the vast span of my shoulders. It made me feel awkward and clumsy, like an elephant being hosed down by its keeper.

After he'd eaten – and he ate very strange things in even

stranger combinations: sardines with pickled cabbage, tinned custard poured over chocolate éclairs – we sat on the floor drinking more wine and coffee and listening to music. Sometimes we shared a joint, although I never really liked it. I never liked the sex much either, and yet I spent long afternoons in the light-bulb factory fantasizing about it, remembering the suction slaps as his stomach squelched off mine, and the curious comfort of his fatness.

It was odd, this obsession of mine with Alisdair Duff. I would like to say that it was founded on a longing for self-improvement, a desire to learn, a hunger for art, but it wasn't. This, if pressed, is what I shall tell Mr Rick Thomas, and he will believe it because it makes perfect sense. It just happens not to be true. I seldom if ever listened to what Duffy said, not properly, certainly not with any thirst for knowledge. Most of what he told me about art or jazz or poetry dripped through my consciousness like water through a cracked gutter. My obsession with him was about something quite different, something shameful and slightly perverted. The things that most excited me about him were the things that also most repelled me. His fingers, for example, which touched me with such concentrated adoration, made me shudder when I inadvertently caught sight of them sliding over my skin: they were like nests of fat white slugs. And yet the very nastiness of them gave me a secret, dirty pleasure.

But all this was a long time ago. Best, I think, not to look into these things too deeply.

Two of the photographs he took of me that winter have become classics. You probably know them. There's one where I am lying on bare floorboards in front of the fire with my back to the camera. I am a series of planes. First you see nothing but a grey line, grey against grey, like a dawn horizon in the desert. And then you see that it's a peak, or perhaps a sand dune, descending gradually into a valley on the far side of which rises a smooth hill. This in turn falls away into a long slow descent. It's an image of such purity, such perfection, that it takes a moment or two to realize that what you're looking at is not a desert landscape at all but the outline of a reclining human female from shoulder to mid thigh. And only then do you start to see the texture of the skin and the satisfying geometry caused by the shadows catching bones and muscle. It's called 'Surfaces II'. (There were ten in the series.) You must have seen it.

Then there's another one where I am standing in the bath. Not surprisingly, this one is called 'Woman in the Bath'. I am holding up one arm and soaping it. I find that one embarrassing because of the jungle ferns casting jagged shadows across my body, and because I look so heavy and have this absorbed, stupid expression on my face, and because my armpits are hairy. But it's the photo that won Duffy loads of prizes and it's reproduced everywhere. I saw it quite recently on a poster advertising an exhibition at the Museum of Modern Art in New York.

It was also the photograph a reproduction of which Dysart had bought and hung in the room with bare walls.

I didn't plan what happened next. I didn't sit down and coldly work out what I was going to do, but obviously I'd been working on it subconsciously ever since the experience in the bus when I became unhooked from things. And so, when the moment came, I recognized it as such, and did what I had to do without any dithering or second thoughts. It was a matter of survival.

Early one Friday I woke up knowing that this was the day. There were no obvious signs to alert me to this fact: I just knew. The sudden excitement of knowing, the necessity for action after months of vegetating, made me feel sick. I couldn't eat any breakfast. Marilyn looked at me with speculative interest. I spent all morning packing my things into a series of carrier bags which I hid at the bottom of the wardrobe.

After my shift at the light-bulb factory, I told the

forewoman I was packing in the job. I collected my pay packet and my cards from the office. I walked back to the Foxes'. Marilyn was in the kitchen frying chips.

'I shan't want any tea,' I said.

She glanced at me. 'Are you all right, love?'

'I'm fine,' I said.

In fact I felt rather odd. I had no sense of being Sandra Bagnall at all. Or Sandra Fox. Or anyone.

'It's just that I have to go out,' I explained in a surprisingly high-pitched voice. 'Is Billy back yet?'

He wasn't. I went upstairs and collected the carrier bags from the wardrobe. I dumped everything on the bed, on the vile, peach nylon cover, and paused to wallow in two minutes of pure loathing for this room, for this disinfected symphony of pink in which I'd trapped myself. That was when Billy walked in.

'What are you doing?' he said.

The plan, such as it was, was to be out of there before he got home, so I hadn't got any dialogue ready. 'I'm leaving,' I said.

His hair was limp with grease. The streaks needed re-colouring. He might fill out a little as he grew older, but apart from that he would never amount to anything more than he already was. I felt no guilt at leaving him. I deserved better.

He didn't know whether to believe me or not. 'What do you mean "leaving"?' he said.

'I'm going to my Mum's,' I told him.

He stuck out both his arms so that he was completely blocking the doorway. 'Mam!' he yelled. 'Mam, come here. Our Sandra's walking out on me.'

'Oh, that's right,' I said. 'Get your Mum to sort it out.'

'You what, love?' Marilyn called back.

'She's packed her bags. She's friggin' leaving me.'

I tried to push past him, but he wouldn't budge. His face was as vicious as a ferret's. I was calculating whether or not I could dodge under his arm, when Marilyn, who was pounding up the stairs in her fluffy slippers, arrived to block the gap.

'What's going on, love?' she said, peering over Billy's arm.

'I'm leaving. I'm all packed. I just want to get out through this door.'

She shrieked downstairs for Ted. 'Ted! Come here. It's our Sand.'

So then they were all three in the doorway and my escape route was completely blocked.

'Tell us what the matter is, love,' Marilyn said. 'If our Billy's done something to upset you, then I know he's sorry.' She thumped him in the chest with her elbow. 'Aren't you, son? And he won't do it again. Will you? You tell her you're sorry. Apologize to her nicely.'

'It's not me, it's her,' Billy sulked.

Marilyn's eye was distracted by the mess I'd made of the coverlet. It was rucked up where I'd dumped the carrier bags. She tutted and smoothed and gathered up bits of imaginary debris.

'Excuse me, please, I want to get past,' I said to Billy and Ted, but they had closed ranks again across the doorway. They were a solid wall of masculine disapproval.

'What about our Keith?' said Ted.

Marilyn looked up in alarm. 'You're not taking Keith?'

There was such defenceless fear in her eyes that I saw immediately how I could get past them.

'Yes, of course I am,' I said. 'I'm his mother,' although never for one minute had the idea of taking Keith with me even crossed my mind. Keith was theirs. I'd mistakenly managed to hatch him out, but that was our only connection. He belonged entirely to them.

The colour had drained out of Marilyn's face leaving a cracked, dry, orange mask of foundation cream. 'No, Sand,' she begged, 'you can't. You can't take our Keith.'

I pretended for a while, until Marilyn was hysterical with panic, that I had no other option. I refused even to contemplate abandoning my child. Within ten minutes she was so distraught she was ready to agree to anything. I strung it out a little longer and then allowed myself to give in graciously. I made a bargain with them.

It was one of my more successful bargains. The doorway cleared.

The fear in the house must have seeped under the lounge door like a dense, creeping gas. It curled through the bars of Keith's play-pen and filled his lungs. He started screaming. Marilyn flew downstairs to pick him up. She refused to let me say goodbye to him. She said it would only unsettle him more. She stood at the far end of the hall, jigging him up and down in her arms. His face was buried in her neck, and his fat hands clutched at her hair. She held his head so that he couldn't turn it and catch a last glimpse of me. He was rigid with fright. I turned my back on them and opened the front door. Billy yelled a few predictable insults after me, but I could tell it was all show, his heart wasn't in it.

The truth was that they were as glad to see the back of me as I was to go. I'd been a very uncomfortable cuckoo in their nest. The only good thing they could say about me was that I'd done my bit: I'd provided them with Keith. Now I was just a nuisance. It would be a relief to get back to their comfortable ways, just the four of them, Nanna, Gramps, our Billy and baby Keith. And eventually, God willing, Billy would find a proper wife, a nice quiet girl who fitted in and liked the smell of bleach and who had no dreams beyond a leather three-piece suite and the occasional night out with the girls. So I doubt if they wasted much more than half an hour on me after I'd gone. Good riddance to bad rubbish, they said. Don't you worry there, son, better off without her, unnatural cow, can you believe a woman walking out on her kiddie like that?

And I bet when the pleasure of eviscerating me was thoroughly exhausted, they sat in front of the television with a cup of tea and a nice fry-up – bigger portions than expected – and a feeling of being washed clean, of fresh starts; the exhilarating feeling of having undergone a titanic struggle from which they had emerged triumphant.

And upstairs their Keith slept peacefully in his cot, and no one was ever going to take him away from them.

I went to Duffy's first. I rang his bell and waited on his doorstep. It was trying to snow. Pinheads of sleet spiralled in the spillage from the street light. My breath streamed out of my mouth like the visible puffs from the fat lips of baby cherubs. Duffy was surprised to see me. I told him I had come to say goodbye. He pulled me into the warmth of the hall and told me I looked terrible. I glanced at myself in the mirror above the telephone table. I did look odd. I had a yellow, pinched look. 'Come in and get warm,' he said.

'I can't,' I said. 'I'm going to London.'

'Not tonight. Go tomorrow.'

This was what I'd hoped he'd say. I'd been counting on him letting me stay the night, but you can never rely on people behaving the way you calculate they will, so it was good to know that he was as predictable as I thought.

I followed him into his living-room, where the gas fire was burning. The wooden floor glowed with heat. There was a bowl of tangerines on the table.

'What have you done to yourself?' Duffy said. Under the weight of my shoes, the handles of the carrier bags had twisted themselves into thin wires which cut into my skin. He untangled me and rubbed my wrists to get the blood flowing again.

'I've left Billy,' I told him.

He asked a string of practical questions. Had I got any money? Had I had anything to eat? He ran a hot bath for me and undressed me as if I were a small child, and made me lie in the steaming water while he opened a tin of soup. There was a long mirror in the bathroom. I stood up in the bath, wiped the streaming condensation off it, and looked at the reflection of my liquefactious, trickling body. I was completely out of touch with the part of me where feelings happened. I couldn't feel anything, not pain nor the lack of it, not cold, not heat, not hunger, not satisfaction. I was quite surprised to see any reflection at all in the mirror, so absent did I feel.

This afternoon I tell a version of that story to Mr Rick Thomas. He has noticed on some official form that I have one child, so I am more or less obliged to tell him something. He listens, picking idly at his nose. He has remarkably thick hairs in his nostrils. I wonder how he manages to breathe through such a growth. It's like those bristly draught excluders on the bottom of doors.

I am surprised at how much weight Mr Thomas places on this incident, but apparently he is very keen on motherhood as some kind of psychological imperative for women. He believes that for a woman to deny her motherhood is to deny her true self, or some such crap. He thinks that 'abandoning' Keith has marked me for life.

It always amazes me the way men make statements like this. What do they know about it? He asks if I have read *Anna Karenina*. '*Anna Karenina*?' I ask. 'Is that by Shakespeare?' I know, of course, that it isn't. I saw the film. But it amuses me to pretend to be more of a cultural ignoramus than I am.

Personally, I count abandoning Keith as one of my few acts of selfless generosity.

It's very noisy in here tonight. I can't sleep. The radiators click. It's too hot. Women cough and mumble madly to themselves. In other circumstances I could go downstairs and make myself a cup of tea. This particular freedom is the one real loss I can think of so far.

Now someone is laughing, a sharp-edged bark which ends in a kind of sob. The noises in this place are inexplicable. No one seems to hear them but me. Certainly no one ever mentions them.

This is a good time for writing, for jotting down the odd observation. I write in the semi-dark, in the low wattage of night, like a blind man. In the morning I find all the lines have run into one another.

\*

Where was I? Yes – in the bath. On the night I left Billy Fox.

Duffy came into the bathroom and said the soup was ready. I was standing up staring at myself in the mirror and idly patting at my armpit with a flannel.

'That's it,' he said. 'Perfect.'

He set up some lights and put some more hot water in the bath and moved the plants about and took a series of shots one of which, of course, was the famous one, the one Dysart found.

Afterwards, he rubbed me dry and wrapped me in a duvet and sat me by the fire where he fed me soup and whisky. If he had not been so repulsive, I might have loved him.

The warmth, the soup, the whisky combined to knock me out. I was so exhausted that my insides trembled with fatigue and my eyelids wouldn't stay open. Disconnected images tumbled into my head to fill the vacuum of unconsciousness. Duffy hauled me on to my feet and guided me into the bedroom like a small tug piloting a steamship. I fell asleep while he was readjusting the pillows. In the night I woke briefly to feel a body beside me, and confused it for an instant with Billy's. But this body was shorter and softer, the bed I was lying in was deeper, and the room smelt of something rich like garlic frying in butter, of burnt biscuits, not of bleach and traffic fumes. So I burrowed down again into the dark pleasure of sleep. I felt as though I had passed through some great drama of hushed voices and extravagant weeping and shaded lights, and by the skin of my teeth had survived.

In the morning Duffy brought me a bowl of cornflakes and a cup of tea.

'Don't go till I get back,' he said.

I lay in bed for hours when he'd gone to work, pretending that the flat was mine. In the afternoon I went for a walk in the park, muffling my face with one of Duffy's scarves in case anybody recognized me.

When he came back, he was full of gossip. Billy had come into work, he said, mouthing off about what a cow I was and what a relief it was to get shot of me. He said his mother had never liked me, that she'd begged Billy not to go through with the wedding, which, considering the pressure she'd put on me to get married, was an amazingly distorted feat of memory.

Duffy said that I ought to ring my parents at once and let them know where I was because Billy and the Foxes thought I'd gone home to Belmont Road.

'I'll ring them from London,' I told him. 'Tomorrow.'

But Duffy said Sunday wasn't a good day for travelling by train. It took hours. So I spent most of Sunday lying in his bed looking though his books of photographs and listening to the radio. On Monday I woke up with every intention of getting off to the station, but my throat was sore and I started sneezing. I felt too ill to get up. I stayed in bed for another couple of days.

On the Wednesday, Duffy reported more gossip from Billy. Apparently Marilyn had rung Belmont Road to tell me that I'd left a mac in the cupboard under the stairs, and that Keith was all right. My Mum answered the phone. She was at a loss to know why Marilyn was ringing her. Marilyn was at a loss to know why my Mum was at a loss. When they both grasped that neither of them knew where I was, accusations and counter-accusations were hurled across the city from Garsditch to Andwall and back again. Marilyn accused me of unnatural behaviour, of failing to appreciate her son, of refusing to knuckle down. My Mum accused Marilyn of driving me away. She implied that if I was found floating in the river, or discovered wrapped in blood-soaked sacking and dumped in a skip, then she would hold the Foxes responsible.

'Ring your Mum now,' Duffy said. He lifted the phone off the receiver. I considered dialling a false number but then what would I do if someone answered?

'Go on,' said Duffy.

I dialled. As soon as the phone in my Mum's hall started to ring, I slammed Duffy's receiver back on to the hook.

'I can't,' I said. 'I'll go and see them. I'll tell them face to face. I promise.'

Duffy was implacable. 'Go now,' he said.

He gave me the money for a taxi. He even offered to come with me, but I wasn't having that. I couldn't possibly admit in public that I had fallen so low, that Sandra Bagnall, *the* Sandra Bagnall, was now reduced to living with a dwarfish, scrofulous, pot-bellied hog, even if he was quite a good photographer.

I made the taxi driver stop at the cemetery gates. It was two years since I'd left Belmont Road, and although I'd come home for occasional visits, it already looked foreign to me. The houses appeared to move closer together every month. At this rate, it would be a terraced street within two years. I strolled along the pavement on the cemetery wall side, looking across the road at wind-bitten clumps of budding daffodils in identical flower-beds under identical bay windows. Cars cluttered the kerb on both sides of the road. It no longer felt like home. There was a cramped, shabby feel about it. A cold wind sliced into the skin of my cheeks and made my eyes ache. The closer I got to number 22, the less certain I became of what I was going to say. I stopped and leant against the wall in the shadow of the telephone box. It would be easy enough to explain why I'd left Billy, but in the bleak, moral light of Belmont Road – the cemetery on one hand and my parents' house on the other – walking out on Keith no longer looked forgivable. You could leave a husband if you had to, but under no circumstances could you abandon a child.

I was hovering uncertainly by the telephone box when I saw two women walking along the pavement on the opposite side of the road. They were coming towards me. They walked in a familiar way. I'd recognize my Mum's walk anywhere. Her face was covered with a headscarf. She was pulling it tight across her cheeks to protect her from the wind. My sister Beverley was in her school uniform. They had their heads down and were struggling to make progress. Beverley was almost exactly the same shape as my mother now, but a little taller and more solid. Her face was puggier than ever. Her eyes bulged. Her nose was as flat as a Pekinese's. I laughed to see how ugly she was growing.

They were turning into the drive of number 22. I could have run across the road and caught up with them. I could have seen my Mum turn, and watched the relief, the surprise, the condemnation tangle themselves hopelessly on her translucent face. They were laughing together about the wind as they staggered up to the front door. My Mum pulled off her headscarf. Her hair was a duller colour than I remembered, as if it was starting to rust. I hated to think of her getting older. I put my hands in my pockets and turned away so I wouldn't be seen. I'd already inflicted too much pain on her; it was better, I thought, to stay absent, better to stick to defined roles. I would be the beautiful, the absent daughter, Beverley would be the boring, sensible one, and Joanne would be the idealized memory who could never grow old and never disappoint.

I was very cold. The ends of my fingers had gone waxy. I opened the door of the telephone box, found some money in my pocket and dialled.

Beverley answered the phone. 'Oh, it's you,' she snapped. 'At last. Where the hell have you been? Me Mum's been worried sick.'

'Can I talk to her?'

I heard her yell, 'Mum. It's our Sand on the phone.'

My Mum snatched the phone off her. 'Sand?' she said. 'Is that you? Where are you?'

'In London,' I said.

'London? Where? Where in London?'

I couldn't think of anywhere in London. 'A guesthouse,' I said, and realized at once what a mistake this was. 'It's only temporary,' I said, 'and it's not on the phone either. This is a phone box. I'll send you my address as soon as I've got work.'

'Are you all right, love?' Now she knew I was two hundred miles away, my Mum had raised her voice proportionately. If I'd opened the kiosk door the phone would probably have been redundant.

'I'm fine.'

'What kind of a guest-house?'

'Just a bed and breakfast place.'

'You be careful, love. There are some funny places in London.'

'Don't worry,' I said. 'I'm fine. I'll ring you again in a week or two.'

'Hang on. Wait a minute . . .'

'I'll have to go now, Mum. Give my love to Dad.'

'Why didn't you let us know? Why didn't you tell us you were thinking of leaving Billy?'

'Well, I . . .'

'Sand, love, if you couldn't stand it at the Foxes', you should've come home. And what about Keith?'

'Keith's better off with his Dad,' I said, tracing a grid pattern in the steamed-up glass.

I heard Bev say, 'She'd dump anyone if they didn't suit.'

My Mum must have put her hand over the receiver because what sounded like a heated snap between them was suddenly cut off. Then Mum said, 'Ring us this evening, love. Your Dad'll want to talk to you. We've got to sort things out.'

'It's difficult in the evenings,' I said.

'Well, as soon as you can, eh? Are you eating properly? Have you got enough money?'

'I'm all right, Mum. Don't fuss. Listen, I've got to go now. There's someone waiting for the phone,' and I put the receiver down before the conversation got any trickier.

My fingers were bloodless and numb. I ran to the end of the road. I ran until sweat broke out all down my back, and I was deafened by the dark roaring of my heart.

\*

That night there was a heavy frost. The road outside was like iron. The air scraped your lungs raw. Duffy turned up the central heating and lit the gas fire. He took off all my clothes and made me lie on the bare wood. He took the 'Surfaces' series, which, according to a catalogue I read years later, are all about the body as landscape. The most famous one is 'Surfaces II', the one I've already described. In some I look like a desert, in some like a bleak, treeless plain or the crust of the moon, in some like a range of snow-capped hills. The whole series is immensely cold. This is odd, because never mind what the catalogue says, I happen to know that Duffy was trying to capture the effects of warmth and light on human skin. He took a whole film just of my bare stomach barred by the light of the gas fire, but everything he tried fell short in some way I didn't understand. He grew increasingly dissatisfied and frustrated.

I got bored and fell asleep.

The next day was too cold to travel. The points were frozen, heating failed, power lines were down. After that it was Sunday again. And so time went by, day after day, one week and then another, and I was still at Duffy's. It was a transitional time, I told myself. I would move on when I was ready.

Billy was seeing a girl called Debs. 'He's been out with her twice,' Duffy told me.

'He didn't waste any time, then,' I said. 'What does she look like?'

Duffy said she was small and thin with straight blond hair. A small, pale girl was probably as much as Billy could handle.

At the end of the week, I went back to Andwall. I don't know why. I could have phoned from anywhere. I got off the bus at the cemetery gates and walked to the phone box. I kept my collar pulled up, and my face muffled behind a scarf. I didn't want anyone telling my Mum they'd seen me. On the other hand, the possibility that someone *might* see me added an invigorating edge of danger.

I dialled home.

'It's Sandra,' I said. 'I'm phoning from London again.' I spoke fast so no one could interrupt me.

I could hear my Mum's panic. 'Have you got a job yet? Have you signed on? What are you living on?'

'Sorry, Mum, must dash. No more change. I'll phone again next week.'

On a sudden impulse I decided to walk back through the cemetery. It was a reckless thing to do. I even let my scarf hang free as if I *wanted* to be spotted. I liked the idea of a neighbour saying to my Dad, 'Saw your Sandra this afternoon,' and my Dad saying that he couldn't have done because Sandra was in London. I liked the thought of the puzzled neighbour wondering whether his mind was going, or whether what he'd seen must have been some kind of ghost.

I suppose the real reason I decided to walk through the cemetery was to look at Joanne's grave again. I couldn't remember where it was. All the rows looked the same. I walked up and down identical rows of the dead until finally I found the small stone that marked her grave. It had begun to weather. Rust-fringed lichen had softened the inscription:

> Joanne Maria
> beloved daughter
> of
> Francis and Eileen Bagnall
>
> 1960–1968

She was down there below me in the frozen earth. By now she must be almost entirely free from herself, although not from her involvement with the world. Even as dust she was still part of all that. I squatted down by the headstone and whispered things to her. Not apologies. Not justifications, nothing so concrete. Meaningless things really, silent things. I rested my ear on the gravestone. All I could hear was reciprocal silence and the ticking of my heart and the distant sound of traffic on the inner ring road.

Today Rick Thomas asked me about my relationship with my sisters. He is becoming my chief source of entertainment here. I lie in my narrow bed devising new ways to confuse and confound him. I concoct delicious surprises for our next session. A fat nut of incest, for example, floating in a creamy fudge of total denial. Or a little whipped chocolate tease of repressed sexual fantasies. He laps it all up, smacking his lips and salivating in anticipation of the next revelation. He writes reams of notes which I read upside down. He is very excited by me. He thinks he is digging deeper and deeper. He thinks he is beginning to uncover the root.

I spend half an hour telling him about Beverley. The air steams with a thick, delicious stew of bitchiness. I describe her in vituperative detail. I describe her detached mock Tudor house with the Georgian pillars at the front and the Victorian conservatory at the back. I describe her white carpets, her gold taps, her swimming-pool and her fat-faced, dull, piggy children.

'And what about your other sister?' says Rick.

Suddenly, and without any of the usual warnings, I burst into tears. They pour down my cheeks in hot, salty streams. I try to speak but I've lost control of my voice. I have lost control of my throat. I rest my head on Mr Rick Thomas's desk and sob.

He makes no attempt to comfort me. He doesn't even offer a handkerchief. He just sits in his swivel chair watching me weep, with what he probably imagines is a look of tactful withdrawal on his face. I wipe my nose across the back of my hand and a long stream of mucus dangles from my nostrils.

'I need a tissue,' I tell him.

He searches in the desk drawers for one, which gives me time to think up an explanation for my sudden loss of control. I am like a zoo keeper whose leg is caught in the jaws of a starving lion. I must distract the beast, I must throw him a hunk of meat to satisfy his lust for flesh. I must give him something which will stop him chewing off my leg. The bloody hunk of meat I throw Mr Thomas, between shuddering sobs and gelatinous nose blowings, is a half story. It is almost the truth.

I tell him that my other sister, my sister Joanne, was decapitated by a train and that I was there when it happened. I think that is enough to keep him fed.

He listens with greedy attention. After a moment of rapt silence, during which he presses his pencil hard against his pursed lips, he talks to me in a grave, hushed voice about guilt. Guilt, he says, is at the heart of everything.

Guilt seems to be one of his specialities. He is unstoppable on the subject. Could I have saved my sister, he asks? Was there ever any possibility of my preventing the accident, of my pulling her to safety? I open my mouth to answer, but apparently it doesn't matter whether or not I could have saved her, that was a rhetorical question, the point is, he says, that I am eaten up with guilt because I *didn't*. And this, he argues, as excited as a dog after a rat, is the reason I abandoned my child: because I was afraid that I would fail him, as I have always believed I failed my sister. 'I see it so often,' he says jubilantly. 'This endless cycle of guilt.'

'What guilt?' I say. 'I don't feel any guilt.'

'No, of course not,' he says, 'because you're still suppressing it.' He leans back in his chair and pokes his pencil through his beard.

Personally, I think theories like this are too neat. People are not neat. He is not a stupid man, he must know that. He must know that people are not to be so easily grasped. I think I will remind him of this. I open my eyes slowly. I lean forward.

'Do you believe in original sin?' I ask him. 'Because,' I say, 'I think I ought to explain to you that I was born evil. So I've never been susceptible to guilt. It's one of a number of things that don't apply to me.'

I let my tongue flick across my lips to moisten them. 'Once,' I say, 'when I was very young, I had exalted ambitions. I wanted to be a saint.'

I knew that would excite him.

'But unfortunately,' I explain, 'I was marred from birth.' I lean further forward so my head is almost in his lap, and part my hair with my hands. 'Feel the scar.'

'What scar?'

'The scar where the worm bored his way in through the bone. Feel it.' I take his hand and place it on my head.

'The worm?' he says. His voice is shaking with excitement. Or possibly lust. I hold his hand on my head and make his fingers rake gently through my hair.

'Of original sin,' I explain. I let his hand go and sit up, tossing my hair back so that he can smell the clean tang of shampoo.

Oh, this is fun, this is far more entertaining than reading the next chapter of *Anna Karenina*, which I have taken out of the library, and which – there's no point in pretending – is very tedious. I have lost patience with the woman already. She is immensely stupid. I don't believe in her for a moment.

Mr Man-eating Lion Thomas is on to the scent now. Sniff, sniff, sniff. 'You believe that you have been penetrated by a worm?' he says.

I nod. 'I know I have.'

He gasps. Truly, he does. He gasps.

Oh, Mr Rick Thomas, what a joy I am to you, what infinite pleasure I bring you. And I am glad to do it, too. Really, I am. I'm enjoying it as much as you are. I am probably the most exciting thing that has ever happened to you. I may even make your name. And I can do it. Believe me. I've done it before. I made Duffy's name for him. I made him famous. Write a book about me, construct a theory, compose a learned paper. Enjoy me, Rick Thomas, because I am probably your best chance of immortality.

\*

How long did I stay at Duffy's?

I am trying to think. A long time. Much longer than I meant.

Every week I rang my Mum. 'What's the weather like down there?' she asked. She always asked that and I always told her the opposite to whatever was happening outside the phone box. If it was raining I said, 'Sunny.'

She tutted. 'You're lucky. It's chucking it down up here.'

I managed to avoid giving her an address or a phone number. I said I was on the move. I might not even stay in London, I said, Paris is where all the best fashion houses are. I might be going to Paris or even Rome. I'd let them know. Lies leapt easily out of my mouth. No, I wasn't at the guest-house now. I was staying temporarily with a girl I'd met, another model. No, she wasn't on the phone, she was waiting to be connected. No, there was no point in writing to me because by the time the letter arrived, I'd probably have moved on. It would be much easier if I contacted them.

Do you know a photograph called 'Machismo'? It's quite famous. It was used as the cover for an album of the same name in the late seventies by a cult band called X-Ternal. You must remember it. It's a picture of a naked woman with her head tied up in a scarf, an Oldham Athletic supporters' scarf which I found under a heap of coats on the pegs by the back door. Duffy denied all knowledge of it: he said he'd never seen it before. It was the scarf I used to muffle my face as I walked across the park. That year winter got a stranglehold on spring. In late March the daffodils were frozen. Sleet blew in from across the river. It was hard work keeping warm.

One night when I was walking about his flat naked except for my football scarf wrapped round my neck, he started taking quick snaps using the flash gun. I was getting very used to this. I posed for him jokily. I allowed the scarf to take all kinds of intimate liberties.

Just stand still, he said. Be natural. He set up lights. He wrapped the scarf round my head like a bandage. It was a shock to me, this sudden blindness, this hot stifling. In the photograph I am standing there quite naked and exposed, with my hands twisting awkwardly at the level of my pubic bone. You can see that I suddenly have no idea what to do, or what is happening. I am entirely faceless.

It still seems to me a strange thing for Duffy to have done. All the other photos he took of me were celebrations. This was a denial. I have never admitted to anyone that the naked woman on the 'Machismo' cover was me.

'Get this thing off me,' I said, furiously unwrapping my head. There were bits of wool in my mouth. My face was scarlet and sweating. 'I could have suffocated,' I accused him, because I knew I had cause to accuse him of something but I didn't then know what it was.

In reply he said, 'I love you.' He regretted it immediately. 'I'm sorry,' he mumbled. 'I didn't mean to say that. God, Sandra, what are we going to do?'

I looked at him in surprise. It was very odd timing. 'About what?' I said, picking bits of fluff off my tongue.

'About this. The whole situation. Us.'

'What do you mean "do"?' I said. I couldn't see the connection. Why should wrapping my head up in a woollen bandage and photographing my faceless body have inspired a declaration of love? And phrases like 'What are we going to do about it?' made me nervous. 'Why do we have to do anything?' I said. 'Isn't it fine just like this?'

'No,' he said, 'no, it isn't fine. It's driving me crazy. I want you all the time. I want to marry you. I'll pay for the divorce. I'll find a good solicitor . . .'

The idea of marrying Alisdair Duff was so absurd that I burst out laughing. I saw myself sailing up to the altar in a voluminous white dress with Duffy tucked under my arm like a podgy lap dog.

He winced. He went white.

'I'm sorry,' I said. 'No, really, I'm sorry. I didn't mean it.' But I couldn't stop myself. Cataracts of laughter poured out of my throat.

Duffy turned and walked away. Even trapped in my

paroxysm of hysteria I could see that his eyes were damp. He blinked hard. He shut the door quietly behind him.

I forgot to mention Rick Thomas's theory, didn't I? It's quite a good one too, as theories go. He says that witnessing Joanne's death gave me a kind of celebrity which I then took to be my due. It's possible, he suggests, that the subsequent events of my life have largely been triggered by the pursuit of renewed celebrity.

I say to him cheerfully, 'You're almost as good at inventing theories as I am at telling lies.'

He laughs.

'So all that about the worm of original sin was a lie, was it?' he asks.

'Oh no,' I say. 'That was the truth.'

For a short while, I am quite impressed by his theory, at least until I think about it more deeply. Then, of course, I reject it at once because the fact is that I have *always* taken celebrity to be my due. It was an assumption I made from the moment I slid into the midwife's hands.

Later that day I stole twenty pounds from Duffy's wallet. He always had extra over the weekend because he brought home the studio takings on Saturday nights.

I also stole a suitcase.

It was kinder to make a clean break. He must have known it wasn't going to last. Nineteen-year-old girls with long, golden bodies and coppery hair do not marry plump, thirty-seven-year-old dwarfs, not unless there is a great deal of money involved.

The morning after Duffy proposed, I walked out of his flat as soon as he'd left for work. I didn't leave a note. He had plenty of photographs of me to fill the gap. Besides, I didn't intend to lose touch. Once he'd recovered from the theft of his twenty quid, I'd ring him.

So one Monday morning, early in April, I stood on the concourse at the main railway station waiting for the

London train. In my hand was a stolen suitcase, and in my pocket some stolen money.

And what about my quarrel with God? Don't imagine I'd forgotten about it. I hadn't. But it seemed to me that if he was a fair God then he must know how heavily I'd paid for my ill-judged attempt to bargain with him. I reckoned we were now quits. The slate was clean. So I walked through the ticket barrier on to the platform confident that finally I was in charge of my own destiny.

*TWO*

I've been here almost a month now. I have no complaints.

It's better than I expected. I thought it would be like Holloway only worse: stone floors, dripping walls, a wooden pallet to sleep on, a bucket in the corner, a cockroach or a rat with whom to strike up an intense relationship in the dark hours when the place reeks of grief and loneliness.

In fact, it's very civilized.

I am in the new wing. The other prisoners complain that the corridors smell of raw bleach, but I am not disturbed by that, not after my nineteen months in Marilyn Fox's house. No, I have adjusted well. I am very comfortable. It could easily be a convent. Or possibly a whorehouse. I understand these institutions: houses of women contained by a set of rules devised by men. I'm not knocking it: it's a comfortably familiar regime. We are wrapped up in rules, tight as bandages, like being mummified. Some of the women, of course, are by definition particularly unsuited to this regime. Rules are as alien to them as they once were to me, but I think I must be getting better at them. The structure they provide exempts me from any responsibility. Those of us who fall as easily as I have into this life are free to read and think and live entirely secret lives in our heads. Some think too much. Some manufacture artificial dramas and crises to amuse themselves, which is noisy and irritating, but keeps them occupied. Fortunately, I am still kept largely separate from the others.

I am not unhappy. Truly I am not. I have no right to be

either happy or unhappy. I read. I write. I look at the wall. If the food were better, I could fool myself that I was taking a health cure in some rigorous German hotel.

One small complaint: I miss a glass or two of wine with my evening meal.

If you were to ask me what I miss most I think I would say the smell of raw air. In here the air is endlessly recycled. It has passed through countless lungs and emerges pure essence of female breath, of sadness, of sour saliva. But apart from this tired air, and also the lack of wine, I really have nothing serious to complain about.

I am reading *Little Dorrit* now. It seems to be about someone in prison. I thought it might be useful. I gave up on *Anna Karenina*. She was too silly to waste time on. I lost my temper with her and threw the book across the room. The spine broke.

The governor is pleased that I am making use of the library. I am allowed to borrow books once a week. I am escorted there by a prison officer. They choose a time when there is no one else around, except the librarian, who is also a prisoner. Have I mentioned the governor yet? He is a shiny-skinned young man – younger than I am anyway – with receding hair. He believes in education and sweats a lot.

The governor is afraid of me. He treats me with scrupulous politeness, but he dare not look me in the eye. The poor man has never had to deal with such a high-profile prisoner before. According to the girl who works in the library – and who is in for fraud – the press have recently discovered where I am. She says they hang round the gates trying to get gossip about me from newly released prisoners. This apparently has caused the governor a lot of problems. He is not at all sure what to do with me.

The other women here have no time for him. They speak of him as though he were a pleasant but slightly dim schoolboy. This is what the librarian says anyway. But I feel quite sorry for him. What a fearful job for a young man: to be in charge of a cageful of women, half of them old enough to be his mother. No wonder he sweats so much. No wonder he looks so uncomfortable.

What I wrote just now is not true. What I miss most is not the smell of raw air. It's flowers. That's what I really miss. Flowers in gardens. Not that I know much about them, but I was going to learn. I was saving up gardens for when I was older.

You probably thought I was going to say that freedom is what I miss most. It's true that I miss having a bath when I want or making a cup of tea in the middle of the night, but you soon get used to things like that. Freedom is a relative thing. Flowers aren't.

No, I really think it's flowers I miss most.

So, anyway, I was on the train down to Euston.

I was not impressed by London. The long run in put me off: a flat wasteland of railway tracks and crumbling warehouses. In the tired, watery light of an April afternoon it is infinitely depressing. I thought London would be a dazzling white city like the Nash terraces in a book of photographs Duffy had. I imagined square after square of elegant, glittering iceberg houses with communal gardens in the middle, and elaborate gateways into one of the big parks at one end. Obviously I had been deceived.

I walked out of Euston station. A cold wind nipped at my exposed skin. Litter blustered across the forecourt. A man whose coat was tied up with string and who wore greasy fingerless gloves lay slumped against a bench. It was exactly like the cheap shopping precincts back home. It was a grey concrete space designed for debris of all sorts to blow about in.

I started to walk. The wind gusted along the Euston Road. I wandered off down side streets looking for something which would fulfil my expectations of London, and also for somewhere to stay, but I seemed to be wandering deeper into the wasteland I'd seen from the train. Blackened railway bridges arched above half-derelict shops selling furniture. Boarded-up newsagents bulged with damp, yellowing porno magazines and boxes of crisps. The houses grew meaner, windows dirtier. Sweet wrappers and fag packets jostled in the gutters. The air was edgy with aggression. I kept finding myself walking so fast that I was short of breath.

I walked and walked until it started to grow dark. A woman came hurrying towards me.

'Excuse me, where is this?' I asked.

She was some kind of foreigner. Her eyes darted about in panic. 'No, no, no,' she said.

'I'm looking for a hotel,' I said, speaking slowly.

The word hotel was one she recognized. 'Hotel,' she repeated. 'Many hotel. Up road. Go left. Go left. Many hotel.'

She bent her head against the wind and hurried off.

I walked up the road and took the first left. There were several empty shops but no hotels. I turned left again into a street in which almost every house seemed to be a hotel. Above each door was a dingy lighted sign: The Sheridan, The Sussex, The Clarendon, The Lancaster. Some had the name written in an arc on the glass fanlight. They looked respectable enough. The outsides were freshly painted, although the paint was suspiciously thick, as if it was holding the window frames together. I chose the Astoria because there was a yellow card in the window saying 'Vacancies'. Propped beside the card was a price list made of interchangeable black plastic letters and numerals.

I pushed open the door and walked into a narrow hall. It smelled of cooking fat and old clothes. There was a thickly patterned crimson carpet on the floor. The walls were papered in crimson flock. On the right was a reception desk that looked like a bar. The front was made of grooved beige plastic panels, one of which had broken and fallen sideways. It was trapped between two plywood battens. There was a vase of mauve plastic gladioli on the desk and an electric bell. I pressed it. After a few minutes I rang again. An elderly man appeared from the far end of the corridor. He was wearing slippers and a Crimplene cardigan. An overweight Labrador with one blind, milky eye followed him. 'Good evening,' he said shuffling towards the reception desk.

I said I wanted a room. For about a week, I said. I thought it would probably take me about a week to find work. I calculated that I could easily last out a week with what remained of Duffy's twenty pounds.

He looked at me suspiciously. 'You English?' he asked.

'Yes,' I said.

'You don't look English to me.' He pushed across a registration form. His hands were dappled with liver spots. He looked as if he was wearing jungle camouflage on them.

On the registration form, I put my name down as Sandra Elizabeth Bagnall. I gave Duffy's address. Under 'Nationality' I wrote BRITISH in capital letters.

The man pushed a key over the desk. 'Room 11,' he said. 'Third floor. Breakfast between seven and nine. Bathroom and WC along the landing.'

Room 11 was a small high-ceilinged room. There was no bulb in the bedside light. The candlewick bedspread looked as if it had been boiled to death. In the bald bits between where the tufted ridges should have been were several neat cigarette burns. The window looked out on to a damp, black well which plunged down to the basement. At the bottom, some kind of weed was growing. I liked its optimistic aggression. I counted it as a good omen. Behind the door was a yellowing notice about fire regulations which I read from beginning to end. It was signed 'Leonard Haskin. Proprietor'. There was no television and no radio. The notice on the back of the door was the only entertainment on offer. I sat down on the bed and wondered what to do next.

Somewhere outside, I thought, life would be starting up soon: restaurants would be opening, theatres filling, roadies doing final sound checks, orchestras tuning up, people streaming along the streets in search of excitement. That's what I had come to London to be a part of, but

I didn't know where to find it. I sat on the boiled candlewick under a forty-watt light and wondered what to do next.

People came and went, up and down the stairs. I heard the sound of movement in other rooms. A smell of smoked haddock drifted up the well and seeped through the rotten woodwork of my window. I was beginning to feel hungry and I *still* hadn't found London, so I decided to go out. I walked down the road in search of somewhere to eat, and after ten minutes or so of turning left or right at random came fortuitously to a main road. Opposite me was a brightly lit place where people were eating. It turned out to be one of these American places with plastic, garishly photographed menus. You could eat fried potato skins and sour cream, and stuff I'd never heard of like enchiladas. I had a large slice of pizza with a baked potato and a bowl of side salad which I filled from the salad bar with such cunning that I managed to get at least twice as much in the bowl as it was designed to hold. After that I had Mom's Deep Southern Apple Pie and American ice cream – which tasted much the same to me as any other kind of ice cream.

The cheese dripped off the pizza in long pale strings. There was a salty black olive on top and rings of spicy sausage with burnt edges. I remember the syrupy lumps of apple in the pie. I remember the pleasure of hot pastry and cold ice cream in my mouth at the same time.

What did I write that for? Now I can't stop thinking about food. I can taste it – cheese and garlic on my tongue, floury baked potato melting in my cheeks.

What I would like now is something lighter: slices of ripe Italian tomato and mozzarella drizzled with olive oil and sweetened with basil leaves. And some bread to wipe up the juices. And a bottle perhaps of Chianti Classico. And then after that . . .

No, this is torture. I must stop this.

\*

After two coffees, I paid the bill and walked a little further along the main road to see what else there was. I came to a cinema. People were queuing for the late showing of a film. I thought this was exactly the sort of thing I had come to London for, so I joined on the end.

It was a foreign film and very strange. I fell asleep halfway through. When I woke up I'd lost track of the plot. In fact it may have been another film altogether because it was in black and white now and before I fell asleep it had been in colour. For a while it seemed to be about someone like me. A young woman in a pale trench coat walked through the wet, deserted monochrome streets of some European city, stalked by an unspecified menace and an invisible modern jazz combo. I stayed until the end because I didn't want to waste my money, and because I was interested to find out what this menace was, but either I missed the point or it was never made clear, because the film finished and I was still none the wiser.

Away from the lights of the main road, the streets were dark and silent. My high heels made a sharp metallic ring on the pavement. When I stopped to cross a road I saw that a man was following me. He wore jeans and soft-soled shoes which made no sound at all. I walked faster. But when I surreptitiously checked again at the next corner, he had gone.

The front door of the Astoria was locked. This threw me. My sparse knowledge of hotels, gleaned entirely from films and television, had led me to believe that hotel doors stayed open all night. I rang the electric bell. After a while a dark skinned young man who managed to look both powerful and delicate at the same time, opened the door for me.

'You want room?' he asked.

I explained that I'd already got one. I held up my key to prove it.

'No,' he said. 'You leave that here.'

'Why?' I said. 'I need it. I can't get in without it.'

He shook his head. 'No, no, you leave key here. You go, you leave key here.'

I thought for a moment he meant that I had to leave. 'That's not fair,' I protested. 'I've left all my things in there.'

He waved his hands about in exasperation. 'No, no, no . . . you go out to eat, you go out to shop, you leave key at reception.'

'Oh,' I said. 'Oh, I see.'

'So you not lose,' he explained. He pointed to the board of key hooks. 'I hang up here,' he said. 'Good night.'

I went upstairs to bed. The room still reeked of haddock.

In the morning, it reeked of bacon: bacon with a subtle base note of fish.

Breakfast was served in an airless basement room. I sat at a table laid for one. The tablecloths were plastic lace. Two Indian men in suits were eating Shredded Wheat at another table. After a while the man who booked me in, the elderly one in the Crimplene cardigan, appeared with a plate of toast for the two Indians. He shuffled over to my table to take my order. I decided to have everything so that I could manage without lunch. I ate cornflakes, a plate of bacon swimming in water, two fried eggs with grease caught in the undulations of the whites, tinned tomatoes, baked beans, mushrooms, sausage and fried bread. I also ate my way through a rackful of toast and drank several cups of warm muddy water which came in a coffee pot.

The dark-skinned youth who had opened the front door to me in the early hours of the morning brought me extra butter. He seemed impressed by how much I had eaten. 'You not get fat?' he asked.

'I can't afford to,' I explained. 'I'm a model.'

This was now only a very slight distortion of the truth, because by the end of the day I *would* be a model. I had no doubt about this at all. In my pocket I had a list of all the agencies I was going to interview.

At twenty to nine I was bouncing along the main road,

past the place I had eaten last night, past the cinema, on my way to find a tube station. My skin glowed in the cool April sunshine, my hair crackled and sparked in clean, snaky ripples. My eyes were as fresh as peeled grapes. I was in London. I was about to start my dazzling career. I beamed, I oozed, I radiated confidence. People stopped in the street to stare. Workmen whistled. Old women smiled with indulgent nostalgia.

I strode across streets without even bothering to look. I thought myself invincible.

Mr Rick Thomas has a wife. Well, of course he has. If I'd bothered to think about him at all, if I had ever imagined his life beyond these sessions with me, then I would have known he had a wife. Men like him always do.

I discover the existence of this wife because this morning his eyes are bloodshot and he looks rough.

'I may not be a hundred per cent on the ball this morning,' he says. 'Les had a bad night.'

I am considering who Les can be, when he says, 'She's due at the end of the month.'

So Les is a she.

'We're hoping for a girl this time,' he says.

Which means that he and Les must already have at least one son together.

It turns out, in fact, that he and Les (trust him to have a wife with a thoroughly manly name) have two sons. I have discovered that unearthing his private life is quite a useful diversionary tactic. I keep him talking on the subject of himself, his wife, his sons, his wife's pregnancy and their recent acrimonious break with the Caravan Club for the whole session. This suits me very well, because I have decided not to tell him what happened to me in London. I will not have the things that happened to me raked over by a man who has the gall to entertain theories about motherhood.

The truth is I have never spoken of those eighteen months to anyone, to no one in the world, not even

Dysart, and I do not intend to dig them up now and offer them for examination to this professional stranger. So it suits me to prevaricate. I slip subtle, bland questions under his guard, and because he is tired he appears not to notice what I am doing. He makes us coffee, he sticks his feet up on the radiator, he chats.

Lesley, he tells me, is his second wife. His first marriage was very brief and a mistake.

'Mine too,' I say.

Lesley teaches physics at the local sixth-form college. This is tough for me to imagine. I can accept Rick Thomas marrying a physics teacher, that's perfectly feasible, but what I can't grasp is that anyone should actually *choose* to teach physics. What can such a person possibly be like?

He shows me a photograph of her. She has short dark hair and is pretty in a boyish, sensible way. She reminds me of a healthy dog, full of energy and bounce. Her hair shines, her teeth are strong. She looks like the sort of woman who enjoys camping in a wet field in Scotland, and who plays Monopoly for fun.

The boys are called Harry and Greg. He has a photograph of them as well. They both have dark hair and thick wet lips, and pant eagerly at the camera in the hope, I suppose, that someone will soon throw a stick for them.

The new baby is already dying to get out and start being part of this jolly family. She is so eager to join, she nearly made a premature appearance during the night. This is why Mr Thomas is too tired to notice that the session has not progressed an inch beyond the point where we left it last time.

While he talks about Les and Harry and Greg, I am calculating what version of the truth I can tell him that will satisfy both of us. Perhaps I will simply cut eighteen months cleanly out of my life.

What follows is the truth. This is the story I shall not, under any circumstances, tell Rick Thomas.

Imagine me. I am nineteen years old and five foot ten in

bare feet. I am striding along the streets of Mayfair on my way to the first agency on my list. I have no doubts. I do not even have the sense to be nervous.

I went to them all, all seven of them. I pushed through revolving doors into reception areas full of steel and glass and muted beige. I swooped up in lifts to tenth floors. I climbed stairs carpeted in unstained, pure wool, and less elegant uncarpeted stairs to attic offices, but inevitably I landed up in exactly the same place. The same girl sat at the same reception desk. Sometimes she had smooth blond hair, sometimes it was dark, but invariably she had drawn the same features on to her face, invariably she wore a long black skirt and jangled with expensive gold bracelets. She was called by a variety of names: Arabella, Caroline, Harriet – but she had the same voice and the same cold, incredulous eyes.

'Do you have an appointment?' she asked.

This was a particularly silly question because she always had the empty appointment book in front of her, so she must have known I hadn't.

'No,' I said, 'but I'm sure Miss X or Mr Y will see me.'

'Do you have a portfolio?'

I handed over the original shots Duffy had taken of me.

Arabella/Caroline/Harriet glanced at them briefly, handed them back and said to ring later in the week to make an appointment.

After the first few exchanges along these lines, I felt inclined to answer back. It did me no good at all. Either way, Miss X was always in a meeting. She saw no one without an appointment.

In the lift on my way to agency number seven, I caught a glimpse of myself in a strip of mirror. I was pinioned to the wall by the merciless dull glare of neon. I looked damp and heavy. My face was dull. My eyes glittered with the brightness of desperation.

The lift arrived at the tenth floor. I was at the same place yet again. At a vast desk sat Arabella/Caroline/

Harriet, who this time was called Kate. I knew this because there was a little plastic name thing on the edge of the desk which said Kate Capstick-Jones. She seemed friendlier than most. She looked up and bared her teeth, which showed (a) how perfect her teeth were, and (b) how exquisitely applied was her lipstick.

'Hi,' she said, 'I'm Kate.'

She must have been expecting someone else, because when I said, 'Sandra, Sandra Bagnall,' her smile froze into a display of dental perfection, and her eyes glazed.

'I'd like to see Miss X,' I said.

'Do you have an appointment?' she asked.

I was tired of this question. 'Well, let's see, shall we?' I said. 'Let's check. Is my name written down in your appointments book?'

'No,' she said coldly.

'No, well then obviously I don't have an appointment, do I?' I handed her my photos. 'Could you tell Miss X I'm here.'

She glanced through the photos. 'Miss X is in a meeting,' she said.

It was nearly the end of the working day, so I calculated Miss X couldn't continue in her meeting for much longer. I sat down on a cream linen settee to wait. To tell the truth, that wasn't the only reason I sat down. I was feeling a bit dizzy as well. It was a relief to sink back into the cushions. There was a nasty dryness in my throat. I thought it was something to do with not having had anything to drink since breakfast.

'I'll wait,' I said.

This threw her completely. 'You can't.'

'Why not? I'm not in your way, am I?'

She looked at me in exasperation, picked up a pile of papers so that she could slam them tellingly back on the desk and got up. She snatched up my photographs and marched away with them towards some distant door. I was pleased to see that she had thick ankles.

It was comfortable swallowed up in the creamy fabric

of the settee. I closed my eyes and imagined a glass of cool water.

When Kate Capstick-Jones came back she was looking hot and pink. She was in a very sharp mood.

'Miss X will give you five minutes,' she snapped. 'This way.'

I followed her along a pale mushroom carpet, past a lot of bleached wood panelling. She paused at a set of double doors and tapped deferentially. 'Miss Bagnall to see you,' she said.

Miss X was a small woman in her fifties with white hair and eyes the colour of smoke from burning rubber. Her nose was crooked both on the horizontal and the vertical plane. She was one of those women who are so odd and so ugly that they surpass all normal rules of beauty. I admired her immediately. She stood up to shake my hand and her burning-tyre eyes looked at me critically.

'Sit,' she said.

I sat.

She turned her attention to my photographs. She examined each one minutely, holding it up so that the light from the window didn't obscure it, so that she could compare the picture with the reality sitting opposite her. I stared round at the room. The walls were smothered in photographs of vapid doe-eyed blondes and pin-thin schoolgirls in flowered smocks.

'Well, Miss Bagnall . . .' she said finally.

'Sandra.'

'There's no doubt at all that you're extremely photogenic.'

I sat back in the chair. A sudden dampness erupted in my armpits.

'And very striking. I can't think of anyone on my books – or indeed on anyone else's books – with whom I could easily compare you. You fall into no obvious category.'

I took this as a compliment. I nodded.

'And that, I'm afraid,' she said, tidying the photographs back into their folder, 'is the problem.'

It didn't seem much of a problem to me: it seemed like an advantage. I said so.

'I regret not, Miss Bagnall,' she said. 'The times are against you. I'm afraid that presently we require our models to fit into very clearly defined categories. Occasionally we "discover" a so-called "new look", but it's only a variation on the usual well-worn and eternal themes from waif to vamp.' She waved her arm round the massed photos on the walls to illustrate her point. 'You, Miss Bagnall, are an original. Which would be fine if the industry wasn't locked into such a limited view of beauty. And besides,' – she smiled; her teeth were engagingly crooked – 'we want our models to *sell* the clothes, not upstage them.'

This was not happening the way I'd expected. I must have looked as shocked as I felt, because she sighed and pushed against her desk so that her chair wheeled away over the pristine carpet. 'Look, Sarah . . .'

'Sandra.'

'I could be kind and say you're ten years ahead of the times – which is probably the truth but very little comfort. Or I could be brutal and tell you a more unpalatable truth, which is that in the present climate you'll never make a model. You'd have to swap your bones for a more delicate set, have a nose job and lose your bust.'

Her voice seemed to be coming from further and further away. A hot pulse had started to beat in my neck. Suddenly her face twisted out of shape until it was a jumble of teeth and a dark scarlet slash of lips. I had to blink hard to make it revert to normal.

I stood up. 'I do have other agencies on my list,' I said.

She smiled. 'Any reputable agency will tell you the same.'

Standing up made me dizzy again. Miss X's face swam anxiously into focus. 'Are you all right, Miss Bagnall?' she asked.

'It's very hot in here,' I said and stumbled towards the door.

I remember saying, 'Thank you for your time.' I remember floating into the reception area and smiling coldly at Kate Capstick-Smith, or whatever her name was. I remember shooting downwards in a lift. The mirrors reflected back a big-boned, top-heavy lump of flesh with tangled hair, a powerful nose and burning cheeks. I vaguely remember walking through a vast blue place and hearing my name called out, but refusing to turn round. I kept on walking, across a marble plain, and out through the revolving doors where I was immediately caught up in a flash-flood of rush-hour pedestrians. There was an ache in my throat like the ache of wanting to cry, but my eyes were as dry as ashes.

At some point I landed up in Piccadilly Circus. I recognized it from the films, although it was smaller and dirtier than it looked on celluloid, and much too insignificant ever to have been thought of as the hub of the universe. I stood in a crowd of people waiting to cross a wide street. The lights changed. The people moved, but I stayed there, stuck on the edge of the pavement like a boulder in the middle of a swollen river. I had just remembered that I'd left my photographs in Miss X's office, which must have been why they were paging me.

'Come on, duck. Give us an arm,' said a woman whose orange hair was sprouting through the holes of a crocheted hat. She was old and blind. She linked my arm and dragged me across the road.

And so it was that I, Sandra Elizabeth Bagnall, stormed the world of fashion.

I didn't go back for my photographs. There was no point. I knew Miss X was telling the truth. She was right: I *was* too extraordinary. I always have been.

On the far side of the road the crowd swept me along and down into the Underground. I remember a sulphurous smell. I remember sitting in a hectic rattling tube of light, while people with pale, nodding faces pushed against me. I was thinking: what will I do now? How will I ever make any mark? But already I was feeling too ill to think clearly. I must be suffering from shock, I thought. It felt like shock. Or maybe a kind of grief. On the outside I was numbingly cold; on the inside a hot, deep, miserable pain had taken hold. My throat seemed to have seized up. Vast letters swam up against the glass opposite. Dumbly, thick-headedly, I recognized my station. A sepulchral voice warned me to 'Mind the Gap'. In a slow stream of tedium-drugged commuters I stumbled up flights of steps and staggered out into blistering sunlight.

It was a miracle that I managed to find the Astoria again. Room 11 seemed like paradise. I collapsed on to my bed. I had a whole lost life, a dazzling career to weep for, but when I tried to cry nothing came. The stems of my eyes ached. Under my eyelids things lurked. Liver-coloured shapes and yellow blobs formed and re-formed themselves like sinister bacteria caught under the microscope. I opened my eyes to get rid of them, but somehow they managed to escape into the room and rearranged themselves in the form of four strange shapes, four incubi, who danced in a ring just below the ceiling, a slow, solemn, terrible dance, a dance of mocking deference. They turned their vile, heavy heads as they circled so that they were constantly watching me. On their faces were fixed smiles of pure evil.

(From what do we form our images of evil? How do we know it with such instinctive terror when we see it?)

Size spun out of control. The demonic four, engaged in their foul and solemn prancing, had shrunk to the size of flies, and as they shrank so their evil became more concentrated. At the same time the walls of the room floated away into the menacing distance. The floor undulated, the ceiling flew off into a dark starry mass.

Years later, Dysart took me to an exhibition of German Expressionism in New York. It was perfectly clear to me that the Expressionists had all at some time suffered from the delirium of high fever. I suspect they all had TB. I said as much to Dysart. He said no. He said that their work was an expression of a wider delirium with strong political references, and reflected rather what was happening in Germany in the twenties and thirties.

But what I think is where did they find the images to express this wider delirium if not from their memories of fever?

The night stretched into darkness and pulsing pain. Sometimes I drifted into unconsciousness. Hours passed in long, gathering seconds, like the drip of a tap.

In the end, when the night had dragged itself through to early morning, I slept. Then the dreams came. Old, familiar dreams that I had not allowed for years, dreams that I had banished to the far-flung prison colonies of my unconscious. Now, seeing a weakness, they had staged a mass break-out, now they ran amok. I dreamed of the relentless perspective of railway lines, of shuddering branches, of a tree swarming with snakes which flew into the air. I dreamed of throwing a ball back and forth against the side of the house in Belmont Road, only it was not a ball. I looked down into my hands and saw it was a head, a severed head, with flapping bloody hanks of hair.

This was when Joanne came.

I heard her voice first. It woke me up. It stopped the dreams. It wasn't a child's voice. It wasn't the voice of Joanne at the age when she had died. But I knew who it was immediately. I could hear her clearly. It sounded as if she was a long way away. She was calling my name.

'Where are you?' I asked.

I don't think I can have said it out loud because my throat was too raw, too swollen to let any sound through, but she seemed to hear me.

'Down here,' she said.

I swung my legs off the bed and stood up. Though I could feel my own solid weight and the lumpen pain in my throat, I seemed to float across the room to the window. I pushed back the curtains and looked out. A white moon, as thin as a smile, slid from behind the roof. I could see her there at the bottom of the well in the murky light of dawn.

'What are you doing down there?' I asked.

Her face, looking up to me from the pit of the well, was peaceful and completely untouched by slugs or maggots. A cold draught rattled the ill-fitting window against its frame.

'Go to sleep,' she said.

I explained to her that I couldn't sleep. If I slept I had nightmares, if I stayed awake I had visions.

'Well, of course you do,' she said. 'You've got a fever. You're very ill.'

The moment she said that, the moment she said the word 'ill', everything slid back into its proper perspective.

'None of it is real,' she said. 'Sleep.'

So I climbed back on to the bed and slept, curled up in my own dark, warm biscuity smells.

I woke to hear the whine of a vacuum cleaner. It stopped. Someone rattled at the door. Then there were voices outside; a woman was complaining. She said something about not stopping beyond midday, she had shopping to do; if he wanted her to stop beyond midday he'd have to pay overtime. A man's voice muttered the words 'pass key'. There was a long pause. I was almost asleep again when the woman's voice said in an awed whisper, 'Suppose someone's been murdered in there?'

I heard Joanne laugh. I opened my eyes. She was sitting in the chair where I'd thrown my coat. I don't know how she'd managed to get into the room. But when I focused my eyes properly, she wasn't there any more. Maybe she slipped silently out of the door like the shadow of a cat when Mr Haskin opened it with the pass key.

The effort of focusing exhausted me. Painfully, I slipped back into delirium.

\*

I still don't know what illness I had. No one put a name to it. At the time I thought it was tonsillitis or some kind of septic throat.

I once told this story at a drinks party. One of the guests was a doctor. He said it could have been a dose of diphtheria. There were, he said, occasional localized outbreaks of the disease. Or even, he suggested, pneumococcal meningitis. 'Were you unconscious for long periods of time?' he asked.

I was. Sometimes I woke to a sort of half-consciousness, like a dim light. My face was pressed into a green cardigan that smelt of dog, and I was clinging to this cardigan as I squatted over a china pot on the floor. I remember the confusion of missing, the shame as a striated stream of dark yellow pee spattered over the carpet.

Sometimes I was being supported against the smelly cardigan while a spoon brought soup to my mouth. Sometimes a straw was inserted between my lips, and then there was a sudden rush of cool, sharp orange juice which I allowed to slide in minuscule drips past the agony snarling like a guard dog in my throat.

Sometimes, a grey jowled face hung over me, and the edges of the green cardigan flapped against bare flesh while something wet, a sponge or a flannel, wiped me down. I tried to move my head to find out just exactly how much of my flesh was bare, but the effort required was out of all proportion to the amount I cared. It was babyishly pleasurable lying there in the intimate light of a forty-watt bulb, while my arms and legs, my chest and stomach, were washed and patted dry, and sprinkled with a spicy talcum powder.

Sometimes Joanne appeared while the sponge was stroking my back in soft hypnotic circles. She stood in the corner by the chair. 'Dirty old bastard,' she said.

Most bizarre of all, sometimes I woke to hear a strange chanting noise round the bed. Once or twice I managed to force my eyes open and saw above me a ring of disembodied faces, with closed eyes and flapping mouths. I thought maybe it was a kind of witches' coven and that I was their sacrifice. But I really wasn't bothered about any of these curious things. I just wanted to sleep. Everything was so strange that I dismissed all of it as yet another manifestation of the fever.

One morning, very early – I knew it was very early by the quality of the silence and the hushed burbling of pigeons which roosted in the holes under the guttering – I woke up and realized that I was aware of these things. I was cool. When I swallowed there was only the ghost of pain left in my throat. I was not only aware, but aware of being aware, which is to be truly conscious again.

I tried to sit up, and dislodged a sediment of floating iron filings in my head. 'Joanne?' I called, but there was no answer. I fell back on to the pillows. The curtains blew quietly at the window. On the brick wall opposite was a wedge of clean morning sunlight. I could smell the dry astringency of urban pavements heating up.

Eventually someone came.

It was Mr Haskin. His dog sneaked in beside him, cringing watchfully as if she felt she ought to be following at a more respectful distance. When he saw that I was properly awake, Mr Haskin's face drooped.

'Oh,' he said. His Adam's apple leapt about in the wattle of skin under his jaw. He cleared his throat. 'Ah. You're awake.'

I said I was feeling much better.

'Good,' he said. 'Excellent.' But his face had turned a dull purplish colour and his cheeks collapsed in mournful folds.

I told him that I'd just tried to sit up, but had been defeated by faintness.

'I expect so,' he said. 'Yes, indeed. You'll be weak for a while yet.'

'Mr Haskin,' I said, 'I would like to apologize for causing so much inconvenience. And I would like to thank you for everything you've done for me.'

The purple flush spread down into the flaps under his chin where the erect hair follicles turned livid yellow as if full of pus.

'Nonsense,' he said. 'I've done nothing at all. Nothing. Except occasionally bring you a drink or some soup. That's all. Nothing else.'

'Oh,' I said.

'You were feverish. Anything you may think you remember was just . . . you were hallucinating.'

'I don't remember anything,' I said.

'Well, if you did . . .' he said.

'I don't.'

'No, but if there was anything you thought maybe you'd imagined . . . well, it was just . . . let me assure you it was just delirium.'

'How long have I been ill?' I asked.

'Eight days. But you mustn't worry. You were well cared for. The ladies of our little group took it in turns to . . .' he started pulling nervously at the lobe of his left ear, 'to . . . do the necessary.'

'Oh, I see,' I said.

He coughed. 'You have no memory of being washed, or um . . .?'

'No,' I lied. 'None at all.'

He breathed out. The purple flush started to fade.

'Well, you see, Miss Bagnall,' he said, daring to look at me briefly, 'we have this little prayer group. You may have heard us praying for your recovery. And praise be, yet again God has heard our prayers.'

'He certainly has,' I said flippantly, but Mr Haskin was still too anxious about setting the record straight to notice.

'No,' he said, 'no, you really mustn't worry, Miss Bagnall. The ladies from our prayer group attended to all your personal needs.' He tweaked at his ear and mumbled, 'You will find a chamber pot under the bed if you need it.'

\*

The prayer group was called something like the Church of the Sinful Children of God. Mr Haskin was a prominent member.

'You made that up,' says Rick Thomas. He laughs. There is a damp red hole in the brown luxuriance of his beard. 'The Church of the Sinful Children of God? No, you made that up. Come on. How much of this am I supposed to believe?'

Well, very little of it, of course, because I am telling him a neatly curtailed version of the truth. I have told him nothing about my humiliating trek round the agencies, nor about my illness.

'The Sinful Children of God?' he scoffs. 'I don't believe it.'

The more I think about it, the more convinced I am that my memory of it *is* right. That *is* what they called themselves.

Or perhaps not. I can't remember. Anyway, it's a good-enough name for now.

The Camden branch of the Church of the Sinful Children met twice a week, mostly in Leonard Haskin's bedsitting room in the hotel basement. It smelt of boiled cabbage and dirty sheets. The chairs were covered with dog hairs. There were twelve or thirteen members. God knows where they came from, from what small flats and cramped lodgings they scuttled out into the night streets, keeping their heads bowed and their eyes alert for danger. They arrived, blinking in the light of the Astoria's entry hall, undoing headscarves and unbuttoning ancient tweed coats. They were as timid as mice, and had the same musty smell, a smell of damp wood shavings and something earthy and frightened. Their mouths chewed anxiously as they mumbled their breathless prayers. Their teeth were yellow and sharp. They nibbled on digestive biscuits and drank milky sweet tea in the interval between the readings. It was difficult to imagine the precise nature of their individual sinfulness. Was this a group of rapists, adulterers, thieves, con men, killers, child abusers?

I got to know them quite well. Mr Webster – George – with his sad moustache and his sadder eyes; Miss Gough, with her lacy knitted jumper and her face like rice-paper; Mrs Todd, who was six foot two and had short wiry hair like an RAF officer in a 1950s film, and whose left cheek was obscured by a squashy purple birthmark. Then there was Mr Noble, who had the features of a water vole, and who couldn't close his mouth over his two prominent, tobacco-stained teeth. He could never meet anyone's eyes. He spoke in an apologetic mumble, his head averted, so that every remark was addressed to a point somewhere between his left shoulder and his left elbow.

They crowded shyly into my room a couple of days after the fever broke. Mr Haskin warned me they were coming. He said they wanted to congratulate me and to share with me a word or two of thanks to God that their prayers had brought about such a quick recovery.

I was tempted to say that a course of antibiotics might have done the trick equally efficiently, and probably twice as fast. I might also have mentioned that I was young and strong, and that I'd have got better anyway, without the help either of antibiotics or prayers. But I kept my mouth shut, not from any sense of discretion, but because talking took a lot of energy and I had none.

'One other thing,' Mr Haskin said, twisting his liver-spotted hands together. 'I think it would be better if you didn't mention anything to the ladies.'

'What kind of anything?' I asked disingenuously.

'About . . . well, about the arrangements for your ablutions.' He swallowed loudly as if a pill were stuck in his throat. 'The fact is, Miss Bagnall, the ladies are very shy . . .'

'But I *must* thank them for looking after me while I was ill,' I protested. Oh, how wicked . . . how cruel of me to keep on about it. 'They'll think I'm so rude if I don't.'

'Well, that's just it, you see,' he said, his eyes sliding about in damp panic. 'They won't. They really would prefer you to say nothing. They don't expect thanks, so I'm afraid it might embarrass them. They're very modest ladies. Very easily embarrassed. Better not to mention it. Or rather, I tell you what, Miss Bagnall, perhaps it would be better if *I* did it . . . in a generalized sort of way.'

The Sinful Children of God gathered round my bed smiling shyly and nodding at me.

Mr Haskin said, 'I know Miss Bagnall would like to thank each and every one of you for your prayers. So shall we clasp hands and offer our sincere praise to God for giving her back her health and strength.'

There were little cries of pleasure and consent, and a sudden silliness in the air as if we were all going to pull a cracker and couldn't work out which way to cross our hands. It took several seconds before we were all properly linked. Mr Haskin clasped my right hand and Miss Gough my left.

'Thank you, Lord, that in your infinite mercy you have listened to the prayers of us miserable sinners . . .' they muttered happily. They prayed that I would continue daily to gain strength and health. They prayed that I would soon be restored to full working order as one of the miracles of God's creation.

Certainly, even in my weakened state, I was more of a miracle of creation than any of them were. I looked up into their absorbed, quietly rapturous faces, and thought that they all, all of them, looked more like God's mistakes than his miracles. They were all old, or sad, or deformed, or disfigured, or chronically and endemically unloved. I couldn't seriously believe any of them were sinners. Perhaps they felt that having fallen so far below the ideal of God's miraculous creation was in itself a sin.

'What do you think sin is?' I ask the manly Rick Thomas.

He is not concentrating at all today. Last night, Les was taken into hospital. Her waters have broken, but since then nothing has happened. She has sent him into work, because, of course, she is a sensible no-nonsense sort of lady and is not going to make a fuss about a natural process. He sits eating a biro, and waiting for the phone to ring.

'Don't ask me,' he says. 'You're the Catholic.'

'No, go on. Define sin.'

He thinks for a moment. 'Well, the Ten Commandments, I suppose. Or the seven deadly sins, whatever they are. Can't remember.'

We make a list. I manage without too much trouble to name all ten commandments and all seven deadly sins. My time at the Sacred Heart Grammar School was not entirely wasted.

'I suppose,' he says, looking at the list, 'I suppose, in essence, a sin is any kind of behaviour which militates against the smooth running of a society. Or which might hinder the procreation of the species. Or, looking at this lot,' he examines the list, 'to do with ownership, the distribution of property, inheritance, that kind of stuff.'

'Do you think it's a sin to be one of society's rejects?' I ask him. 'Old? Or deformed? Or disfigured? Are those sins?'

'Not sins, no,' he says. 'No, of course not.'

'Why aren't they?' I say. I point out to him that in the wild, nature has very little mercy on the old, the ill or the disfigured. Nature abhors a weakness. So does society.

'No, no,' he says, 'that's the point of society: it should be a sufficiently cohesive and stable force to be able to accept and support even the weakest individuals.'

He is a decent if rather boring man.

'After all,' he says, 'we are not animals.'

Aren't we?

'So what are we then?' I ask. 'Machines? Chemical machines?'

He speaks as if he is explaining a simple and self-explanatory scientific fact to a child. 'Well, yes, physiologically we're animals, of course we are. But that's as far as it goes. Beyond that we've got an intellectual and spiritual dimension that raises us above mere animals.'

What an arrogant attitude. This is 'Man is Lord of the Universe' theory. This is exactly how Dysart perceived the world. This is how he saw himself in relationship to it.

But when he bled, he bled like a pig.

As soon as the prayer was over, the Sinful Children of God left me to rest, but they each wanted to say a little personal something and to press my hand. I whispered 'Thank you' until my throat felt hoarse again. Mr Haskin hurried the ladies away before I could say anything more to them. 'We're going downstairs for the reading now,' he said. 'I'll get Jordi to bring you up some cocoa later.'

Jordi was the Spanish lad who had been on the desk when I got in late my first night there, and who had been so impressed by my appetite. He was illegal, so he was very cheap. He came upstairs later with the promised mug of cocoa, a drink in which Mr Haskin had great faith. He said it would strengthen me. It was rich in iron, he said. He obviously shared Marilyn Fox's curious lust to fill me with ferrous metals.

Sometimes, lying up there in room 11 with nothing to do and no energy even to hold a book, I imagined odd things. I imagined, for example, that a vampire had flown in through the window and bitten my neck with its tiny, poisonous teeth. This would explain why my throat had gone septic and why I was still so drained of energy.

Mr Haskin gave me an old Bible to read. The cover was water-stained. The print was so small and so dense that even had I discovered in myself a great urge to read it – which I didn't – I doubt I could have managed more than a few verses without eye strain. At the same time he brought me an equally water-stained paperback about submarine commandos. On the inside cover was written, in faded pen, Leonard Haskin, 42 Abney Road, Stoke Newington. December 25th 1952.

'I thought you might like something to read,' he said.

Jordi brought me up some out-of-date women's magazines. Because I was still so weak, these simple kindnesses made me maudlin. I lay feebly flipping through the unreadable paperback, the unreadable holy book, and a pile of *Woman's Realm*s, and dripped tears on to them.

Days sifted past, each filled with long empty spells of sleep and longer emptier spells of simply lying staring at the window and the opposite wall. Mr Haskin and his one-eyed dog (who was called Phyllis), brought meals up to me. Mr Haskin believed that invalids should be fed a diet of cod poached in milk served with watery and unseasoned mashed potato. He was a keen devotee of milk puddings. I don't think he knew about any other sort. I preferred it when Jordi cooked. Then I got my fish grilled with dots of butter on top, or sometimes an omelette.

I was very peaceful. It was a little bit like being dead. I didn't really want to get up and have to start living again. The extent of my ambition now was to stagger to and from the bathroom. Sometimes I slept so much during the day, I spent hours awake at night listening to the odd whisperings and murmurings you sometimes hear in the stillness before dawn, as if there are people living some kind of secret parallel life in the walls.

And I thought that if I *had* been bitten by a vampire, then during this long, lazy period of recuperation I must slowly be turning into a vampire myself. This was how it worked in films. It was like a kind of infection. Soon I would be able to transform myself at will into a bat and fly out of the window, up over the shiny roofs until I found a victim, a vagrant perhaps, or some careless woman sleeping with her window open, into whose throat I would plunge my teeth, and whose energy I would suck dry with fierce greedy laps of my guzzling tongue.

I was lying in the darkness thinking about this, when a curious fact which I remembered from somewhere or other popped suddenly into my head. I remembered reading that bats are one of the few species of mammals, other than *Homo sapiens*, who menstruate. The females, that is. This struck me when I first read about it as very bizarre. You could be walking along a country lane at night, for example, and be totally unaware that a menstruating bat had just flown over your head. You might feel a sudden trickling wetness on your cheek and put your hand to it, and then, in the dim light, see that inexplicably your fingers were smeared with blood.

Now, however, this curious fact set off an entirely different train of thought.

When had *I* last had a period?

I've never been very good at dates. The idea of bleeding in rhythm with the cycle of the moon has always struck me as even more bizarre than turning into a vampire, and was yet another in the long list of things that surely didn't apply to me. When a period came – which it never did with the kind of clockwork regularity medical articles seemed to suppose – I was always taken by surprise. So I never really thought about them, or expected them, or had any noticeable symptoms beforehand which might lead me to believe that one was on its way. Unless I had bled at the height of my illness, while I was largely unconscious, then it seemed like an awfully long time since I'd last had a period. Longer than was natural.

By an exhausting effort of thought I managed to work out that I had bled in the week before I had left Billy, which was now nearly two months ago. Counting on my fingers, I deduced that give or take a couple of days I ought to have started round about the time I came to London.

I sat up in bed. A sudden nausea hit me. I told myself I was imagining it. I turned on the light so that I could examine myself. I found an ancient tampon at the bottom of my bag and inserted it to check whether there was even a minuscule drop of blood to stain its virginal whiteness.

The tampon emerged as pure as it had gone in.

Mr Haskin brought my breakfast every morning at about seven, just before the rush of the guests' breakfasts and before the smell of frying swamped my room. He brought me tea, orange or grapefruit juice, a boiled egg, several triangles of toast and a vitamin pill. The egg sat like a fat white symbol of fertility in its plastic eggcup. There was no avoiding it.

'Mr Haskin,' I said. I had to know. 'Can I ask you something? When I was ill and . . .' – this had to be phrased carefully – 'somebody washed me . . .'

'One of the ladies.'

'Yes,' I said. 'One of the ladies. Was I . . .?' I found that I couldn't ask him straight out. I doubted if his embarrassment threshold could stand it. So I approached the subject obliquely. 'The thing is, Mr Haskin, I need to speak to one of those ladies urgently.'

His grey jowls trembled slightly. 'I'm afraid . . .' he said. 'The problem is . . . Unfortunately . . .'

'There's something very important I need to ask them,' I said.

He was shuffling nervously backwards towards the door. He tripped over the dog and trod on her foot. She yelped. 'Perhaps you should write it down,' he suggested. 'This important question. I could fetch you a piece of paper and an envelope, and then I could hand it over to one of the ladies who dealt with . . . who . . . with your . . .'

'Personal hygiene,' I said.

He blushed a dark, distressed purple.

'Precisely,' he mumbled.

Later he appeared in my room with a piece of lined notepaper, an envelope and a biro.

I wrote, 'When I was ill and you washed me, was I having a period?'

I held my arm curved round what I was writing in a pretence of modesty. Then I folded the paper, slid it into the envelope, sealed it, and handed it back to him. Later in the day, when he brought up my cod, mashed potato and semolina pudding – a meal of such whiteness, like the white of egg, like the clean rounded end of the tampon, a meal aching for the brilliant red splash of a tomato, or a bright circle of strawberry jam – there was an identical envelope hidden underneath the plate. I didn't find it until he'd gone. I slit it open with the knife. Inside was another piece of Mr Haskin's lined notepaper. It had only one word written on it. 'No.'

Nothing was said about this farcical correspondence when he came to collect my tray. I had eaten very little. I was too anxious. The long days of peaceful dreaming were over.

'You've hardly eaten anything,' he said, his face lugubriously reproachful.

'I'm not hungry.'

He stood in the doorway for a moment. His dog, Phyllis, searched his face earnestly and myopically for some clue as to whether they were stopping, and she could lie down, or whether they were on their way downstairs.

He opened his mouth to speak. 'I . . . um . . . I must remember to bring you up a bulb for that bedside light.'

He took a large handkerchief out of his pocket and blew his nose.

'Though from what I understand,' he said, obscurely starting in the middle of a conversation we were not having, '. . . from what I understand, these things are very delicate.'

*Light bulbs?*

'Very delicate,' he repeated. He was still holding his handkerchief to his nose so that most of his face was obscured. 'Very . . . um . . . very easily put off their stroke, as it were. So to speak. By all sorts of things. Emotional problems. Illness. Particularly illness. I should think that's probably all it is.'

The knotted ball of panic inside me melted into warm relief. He was right. Of course that's what it was. Temporary . . . that medical term beginning with 'a' you read about in magazines.

Amenorrhoea. Temporary amenorrhoea.

*

I started to get up, for short periods at first, and then for whole afternoons. I got myself dressed and sat feebly in the chair like an old woman, and read the magazines Jordi brought me. But my strength increased every day. Soon I was going downstairs for breakfast. A week after that and I started taking short walks in the sunshine. It was early June. Suddenly it had got warm. In the window-boxes, flowers whose blossoming I had missed altogether were turning papery brown, like old skin. As I got stronger, I bought sandwiches from a bar near the tube station and ate them sitting on a bench in a small garden near the Astoria. I told Mr Haskin that I wouldn't be needing any more meals.

'You're on the mend, then,' he observed mournfully. He seemed to like me better when I was ill.

On one of my walks, when I had begun to feel almost normal and was beginning to explore beyond the narrow network of streets close to the Astoria, I passed the unequivocal scarlet of a phone box and thought two things.

The first thing I thought was that I *still* hadn't started bleeding. But after a second or two of irrational terror, this thought slipped blithely out of my head again. I was full of reassurances to myself. It would be a long time yet, I said, before my body was fully recovered from the trauma of whatever illness I had had.

The second thing I thought was that I hadn't rung my Mum and Dad for over a month.

The temptation was to let this thought slip blithely out of my head as well. I argued that I was not strong enough to face explanations and reproaches. But if I didn't do it soon, then a time would come when I could never do it again. I struggled weakly to open the phone-box door and dialled home. My Dad answered the phone. This made it worse. I needed to talk to my Mum. Only by listening to the tone of my Mum's voice would I know whether it was all right or not, whether or not they were seriously angry with me.

'Hello,' he said, from two hundred miles away. I knew

exactly where he was standing. I could see him leaning back against the cream anaglypta.

'Dad?'

Silence. Then: 'Sand?' Then again, when I didn't contradict him: 'Sandra?'

'Hi, Dad.'

More silence, as if he was winded. Then a torrent of questions and recriminations. 'Where *are* you? Why haven't you rung? Your Mum's been worried out of her mind. Are you still in Paris? We didn't know whether to contact the police or not.'

I told him the truth. I told him that I'd been ill for weeks.

It wasn't a good enough excuse. Now I'd worried him even more. His voice shook. 'Who was looking after you? They should have rung us.'

All this was true. I should have asked Mr Haskin to ring them. I could hear my Mum chipping in. 'Is she in hospital? Has she seen a doctor? Where is she?'

'In Paris,' Dad said.

I cut all this short. I told them I was fine. I said I'd had a very rough few weeks, some kind of throat infection, but that I'd been well looked after and that I was completely back to normal now.

'Tell her to come home,' my Mum said.

'Your Mum says . . .'

'Yes, I heard.'

'What's she living on? Is she all right for money?'

I said I couldn't come home because I'd got work.

My Mum said, 'Get her address. What's your address, love? Where's a pen?'

'Sorry, Dad,' I said. 'Got to go.' I used the old stand-by. 'Money's running out. I'll ring you next week.'

As I put the receiver back, I heard my Mum say, 'Get her phone number. Quick!'

After that I went straight into a café and had a mug of coffee and two large sticky Danish pastries.

I find that the rapid intake of carbohydrate is the best

way of subduing an uneasy conscience. Danish pastries I find particularly effective in this respect.

On my way into the Astoria, Jordi stopped me. He was behind the reception desk. He said there was an envelope for me.

'A letter?' I said, assuming that my mother, by some feat of maternal telepathy, had divined my address and had managed to get a letter to me in less than an hour.

'No, no,' he said, handing me a long brown envelope. 'Not letter. Bill.'

I took it upstairs and opened it in my room. It was, as he said, a bill. It was written on a piece of Mr Haskin's lined notepaper, with a smudged logo stamped on the top. What I owed was itemized in careful writing. Thirty-three nights' rent on the room plus 'additional extras' such as food. Total: a couple of quid short of one hundred and thirty pounds.

I marched down to the basement. I knocked on Mr Haskin's door. On the other side I heard someone ejecting bronchial phlegm from their lungs. I knocked again. There was silence for a moment, then the distinctive shuffle of Mr Haskin's slippers on linoleum.

'I've come about this bill,' I said when the door opened.

He smiled vaguely. His wet purple underlip quivered. 'You'll find it's all correct,' he said. 'I can go through it with you, if you like. I have, of course, only charged you a nominal sum for the extra meals. And naturally, I have added nothing at all for . . .' he swallowed twice, 'for anything in the way of nursing. So to speak.'

There was a long pause. The dog, scudding along on her bottom, had edged herself between me and the door. She pushed her wet nose into my hand. The room stank of her, of old dog, old man, old tobacco.

'I haven't got a hundred and twenty-eight pounds,' I said. I opened my purse and counted out what little I had left from the money I'd stolen from Duffy. Together with a couple of pounds of my own, I had approximately thirteen quid.

He took it well. He seemed almost pleased. His only reaction was a spasm of blinking. His eyelids were rimmed with red as if he had a permanent dose of conjunctivitis. He didn't appear to have any eyelashes at all. Perhaps disease had rotted them away. Certainly the hair on his head was very thin. He asked if I had a bank account or any post office savings.

I said no.

'No savings at all?'

'Nothing.'

'What about something you could sell?'

Silently I ran through the meagre list of my possessions, but I could think of nothing. Nothing that was worth whatever a hundred and twenty-eight minus thirteen is. A hundred and fifteen. Nothing worth a hundred and fifteen pounds.

There was another long pause.

'So what am I going to do?' I said.

He shook his head.

'Are you going to call the police?'

Water was dribbling from one inflamed eye. He took out his handkerchief and mopped it. 'The police?' he said, as if I were talking about some alien race.

'Well, I can't pay you. I haven't got it. So what else can you do?'

'There is one obvious solution,' he said. 'You could work the debt off at a fixed rate per week.'

'But I haven't got a job.'

'I should have thought it would be easy enough for a young girl like you to get work,' he said.

The bleakness of the word 'work' as he meant it, the necessity to waste days of my life sitting in a factory watching things pass by on a conveyor belt, or of filing useless bits of paper into alphabetical order, or standing behind a counter all day, brought tears to my eyes. They spilled over. Mr Haskin offered me his handkerchief. I shook my head, and used my sleeve instead.

I didn't want 'work'. I wanted to be extraordinary.

This was God's doing again, of course. He was determined to grind my life down to the common condition of irredeemable ordinariness. I would never be a saint now, I would never be a model. Neither my name nor my face would ever make a mark. I was condemned to insignificance.

Phyllis, who was staring up at me with damp, bloodshot eyes, expressed her sympathy for my evident despair by flopping down heavily on my feet.

'Oh, come now, Miss Bagnall . . . please.' Mr Haskin grabbed the dog by the collar. 'No, Phyllis, get off. Bad dog. Off.' He hauled her away. 'I'm sure it isn't as bad as all that. I'm sure we can find a way round the problem. Prayer,' he said, 'generally provides us with an answer.'

He helped me into his armchair.

'Shall we pause for a moment and say a quick prayer for guidance?' he suggested.

'I'm a Catholic,' I sniffed, as if this exempted me from anything so bizarre as praying at half-past eleven in the morning in an elderly hotelier's bedsitting room. *My* God, my powerful and vengeful God, my ancient enemy, was not likely to be appeased by such simple-minded mumblings.

Mr Haskin closed his eyes. He clasped his hands like a child. His loose damp lips muttered silently.

I wasn't sure whether I was supposed to close my eyes as well. I took the opportunity of his temporary blindness to wipe my nose on the underside of my skirt.

After a while he stopped mumbling. He looked up. 'You see,' he said. 'It always works. God has suggested to me a very possible solution.' He nodded briskly for no reason at all, unless he was responding to some further suggestion from God. 'Yes,' he said, and nodded again. Then he turned his attention back to me. 'Suppose you were to work here, Miss Bagnall? For me. Until the debt is paid off.'

The suggestion floored me slightly. 'As what?' I asked.

'Well,' he said, 'I am thinking of sacking my present cleaner. She's not as honest as she might be. Guests have reported losses.'

'You want me to clean your rooms?' I said. 'You want me to be a *cleaning lady*?'

Laughter exploded from my mouth like a round of machine-gun fire into the refined and odorous silence of Mr Haskin's room.

He sat upright, his legs together, his liver-pocked hands like two diseased lobsters hanging over his knees. His face trembled gently as he spoke.

'That or the police, Miss Bagnall,' he said. 'Your decision.'

Which is how I, Sandra Bagnall, ex-saint, ex-model, defeated and humiliated warrior, landed up working as a cleaner in a crumbling, twenty-room hotel in Camden.

Maybe they will put a blue plaque up there one day. I wouldn't be at all surprised. It will say:

Sandra Stevens
lived here
1976–1977

Such a pity I finally achieved fame under the name of Stevens. I always think Sandra Stevens sounds a bit like one of those blond Hollywood starlets in the fifties who never quite made it. It sounds trivial to me: it doesn't have quite the same solid ring as Sandra Bagnall. Still, a blue plaque is a blue plaque. And one thing is sure: they don't put them up for fashion models. In future years art historians will make pilgrimages to the Astoria. People passing by will look up at the plaque and experience a delicious frisson. Good God, they'll think, did *she* live there? And they will be irked by the intransigence of time which will not allow them to pass back into 1976 and speak to me. They will think, if I could only get back there for five minutes I could save her from the future.

Would I listen, though? Would I want to be saved?

*

My solicitor came to see me today.

I receive people here with regal graciousness. I choose whom I wish to see. I send them visiting orders which are the equivalent of royal summonses. My affairs are conducted in a council chamber to which I am escorted by my attendants.

We sit facing each other across a table, my solicitor and I. His name is Philip Roebuck. Already, at thirty something, he is a senior partner in a distinguished city law firm. The thing that interests me about him is how unnaturally clean he is. His shirts are a blistering white. His neck is tanned and smooth. There is no hint of a blackhead or a boil, no grime on the pristine whiteness of his collar. He must shower at least three times a day.

As he talks, I make him take off his glasses, and toss his shirt on to the floor. I make him drop his trousers and step into the shower cubicle. I make him lather himself all over, slowly and soapily, rubbing his hands in circles over his skin. But whatever I make him do, the image, which ought to be an erotic one, remains obstinately sanitized.

'How clean you are, Mr Roebuck,' I say to him. 'How do you do it?'

He smiles politely and ignores me. He doesn't like the impromptu expression of a stray thought. He himself never suffers from stray thoughts. His mind is as crisp as his shirts.

He has come to talk about my appeal. He's not hopeful. 'You have to understand,' he says, 'that public opinion is still running very high against you.'

I have never tried any tricks on this man. He is immune to me. We speak to each other strictly on a business footing.

'Well,' I say, 'at least they can't hang me.'

He makes a nervous bleating sound which I take to be a laugh. His tongue is very healthy and pink. He opens his briefcase and gets out the thick file of papers.

He says, 'So shall we get down to business?'

I forget what the point of this appeal is. I know, of

course, the grounds on which we are appealing, but I can't remember now why we're bothering. He's right: there's very little chance we'll win. Our main argument is that the judge, Lord Justice Carey, misdirected the jury. We claim he showed himself to have been unduly influenced by the media. Personally I think it's a waste of time and money. Mr Roebuck can argue till the cows come home that the judge was unduly swayed, or that the jury were out for blood, but nothing will change. A scapegoat is needed, and I have been cast in the role. From time to time, when the established order becomes dangerously disturbed, a living sacrifice is needed to bring the rest back into line again. This is the function I have been chosen to fulfil.

I moved out of room 11 into a smaller room in the basement. It was next door to the kitchen. There was a bookcase in my new room sparsely filled with a few ancient hardbacks: Dornford Yates, Edgar Wallace, Dennis Wheatley and a pile of *National Geographic* magazines. There was a bulb both in the overhead light *and* the bedside light. The floor was covered in curling green lino and two balding rugs. The window in this new room also looked out over the well, but I was right at the bottom of it now, I was even a little lower than the bottom, because the floor of the well was on a level with my window-sill.

Between my room and Jordi's was a small bathroom which we were supposed to share. It was infested with silverfish. The floor was squashy and permanently damp. There was one toilet and one wash-basin with a gas geyser above it. If we wanted a bath we had to use a guest bathroom.

At six thirty every morning, when Jordi had finished in the bathroom, he banged on the adjoining wall to wake me. He was always up early to start the breakfasts except on Mondays when he had the morning off and I had to do them. I got up at about seven thirty, helped myself to toast in the kitchen, and then collected the cleaning things and started on the rooms. I had to change sheets, remake beds, hoover, polish, dust, scrub the one bathroom per landing, bundle up the day's washing and do the paperwork connected with it, clean the landings, the stairs, the reception area and the dining-room. Jordi cleaned the kitchen.

The previous cleaner had somehow managed to do all this by midday. It took me at least twice as long. I wasn't used to cleaning things. But after a while I learned short cuts. It was not an establishment with any pretensions to class. There were no en suite bathrooms, no delicate cakes of scented soap, no generous piles of thick white towels to change daily. What little furniture there was I seldom bothered to polish. A quick squirt of Pledge and the room smelled clean. If you tried to wash the paintwork, flaky bits came away on the cloth, so I gave up that idea, although Mr Haskin had instructed me to do the windows and skirting-boards daily. Hoovering was all I really bothered with.

For this work I got bed and board. I made my own lunches and evening meals from whatever I could find in the kitchen. Sometimes, in the evening, Jordi cooked something exotic: chicken with rice and peppers, or a pan of fried sardines, and shared it with me.

At the end of the first week Mr Haskin gave me a small brown envelope. In it were two pound notes and a piece of paper on which was written: 'One hundred and fifteen pounds minus four pounds. Debt currently stands at one hundred and eleven pounds.'

At this rate I calculated I would be free in about six months.

I was not unhappy. I didn't yet have enough energy to be seriously unhappy. It seemed to be yet another time of waiting, and I could see that times of waiting had a value, particularly when you had no idea what route to take next, so I was quite glad of this hiatus. It gave me time to readjust to the radical setback in my plans and to work out an alternative.

The trouble was I had no talent except my looks. I

hadn't needed one. I didn't even have a proper education, and I wasn't going to start getting one now. Education was too much like hard work. Anyway, I had the attention span of a dragonfly. What else could I do? I couldn't sing. I couldn't dance. Perhaps I could act.

I asked Jordi's opinion.

'I speak to friend for you,' he said. 'He is actor.'

Jordi had a number of friends, all of them young men, whom he smuggled into the Astoria when Mr Haskin wasn't looking. It took me a long time to understand the nature of Jordi's friendships with this stream of well-muscled young men, all of whom had perfect teeth and dark moustaches.

Jordi's actor friend was called Dom. Dom suggested I should try out my vocation by joining an amateur dramatic society. It seemed a ludicrous idea to me. I didn't want to join a group of secretaries and bank clerks indulging in fantasies of stardom in a dusty scout hut twice a week. I wasn't interested in the fantasy. I just wanted the stardom.

Dom talked about acting in a depressingly serious way. He said it required years of dedication. He himself, he said, had done three years at drama school and worked fairly regularly since, but had hardly started learning his craft yet. He was, he said, daily humbled by his own ignorance. Jordi, whose grasp of English never advanced in the time I knew him, nodded happily and smiled.

'So what exactly is there to learn?' I asked.

The answer was bewildering. It seemed that acting was a kind of spiritual philosophy which involved knowing the self, tearing away the layers until the naked vulnerable soul is exposed like a layer of quivering fat. Only then, apparently, was any real artistic truth, any real integrity possible.

'I thought you just got up and did it,' I said.

He shook his head at the touching ignorance of the general public. 'It's a fuck of a job,' he said. 'I wouldn't advise anyone to take it up.' He started talking about the tortures of being out of work, the meagre pay, the indolence of agents, the perfidy of casting departments, the agony of auditions, the nightmare of seeing the talentless succeed while the talented – himself, for example – got cast endlessly as bit-part policemen and swimming-pool attendants.

'I tell you what though,' he said. 'I know an actor, a friend of mine, who does a little modelling for this photographer guy. It's not exactly acting, but it's very well paid. You're probably the sort of girl this guy's looking for. I can get his telephone number for you, if you like.'

A couple of days later, when I went into the kitchen to make myself beans on toast, Jordi pressed a piece of paper into my hand.

'Phone number,' he said. 'Dom give. For you.'

I put it in my pocket and later slipped it into one of the folds in my purse. I had a pretty good idea what sort of modelling it would be, but it was worth keeping the number: it was a kind of insurance policy if all else failed.

On Tuesdays and Fridays the Sinful Children of God met at the Astoria. They arrived in dribs and drabs from seven o'clock onwards, shaking umbrellas and twittering about the weather, a gathering of the disenfranchised and the disfigured, like a coach party on the way to Lourdes.

Part of my duties on prayer-meeting days was to bring in the refreshments. At half-past eight I took through a tray of tea, sandwiches and biscuits. I liked making the sandwiches. The bread was soft and moist. I liked cutting it into little triangles and slicing off the crusts which I ate. I was permanently hungry. I also stole all the Bourbons from the selection of biscuits. I had developed an inexplicable craving for Bourbons.

The Sinful Children were always pleased to see me, not just because my arrival signalled a break in the proceedings and I brought refreshments with me, but because I had become special to them. I was their mascot. I was a walking testimony to their efficacy as a group. They had saved me. And having saved my body they were now quite keen on saving my soul. I was welcomed with shy little noises of pleasure, and pressed to stay for the second half of their meeting, which I usually did. Well, I had nothing better to do. Jordi was locked in his room involved in mysterious sexual practices with one of his well-muscled friends, I had read all the books and the *National Geographic*s in my bookcase, and there was no television lounge. So I stayed to listen to the readings, and slowly ate my way through the bulk of the sandwiches.

The Sinful Children of God were working through the entire epistolary output of St Paul. It was all good Christian stuff, although the more we read, the more surprised I was by the state of St Paul's mental health. After the readings, we had more prayers. It was pleasantly tedious to sit there listening to the mumbling voices and munching biscuits.

I *still* couldn't work out what terrible sins these humble, timid people smelling of mice and damp wool and mothballs could possibly imagine they had committed. During the prayers, I invented sins for them. Mr Webster, with his drooping moustache, was undoubtedly a wife murderer. He probably had three stashed away under the floorboards. Perhaps he made soup out of their tender parts, with a little chopped onion and carrot, and a sprinkling of parsley from the window-box. Miss Gough clearly ran a brothel. Mr Noble, the one who could never meet your eye, was, like the Romans and the Corinthians, an obsessive self-abuser. Mrs Todd spent her afternoons whipping Members of Parliament and handcuffing them to beds.

I knew what Mr Haskin did. I didn't have to invent a sin for him. I could remember the long, slow, lascivious wipes of his flannelled hand.

Sometimes, while the Sinful Children prayed, I considered the niggling problem of God whose vengefulness towards me seemed to be out of all proportion. I wanted him to be another sort of God altogether, the sort of God the Sinful Children had imagined for themselves, a mild and indulgent God, a kindly old gent whom I could easily fool, whom I could twist round my little finger: someone, in short, pretty much like my Dad, only older (and probably not black), someone who would forgive me and who would go on forgiving me however bad I was. That was the kind of God I could cope with. Not an irrational, malevolent, warmongering patriarch.

One evening, Mrs Todd was reading from Corinthians, Chapter 11. It was a very odd piece. It started off about hair. 'Doth not nature teach you that if a man have long hair it is a shame unto him, but if a woman have long hair it is a glory to her, for her hair is given her for a covering.'

*Where*, I thought, does nature teach us this? It sounded to me very much on an intellectual par with the nuns' strictures against walking on the left-hand side of corridors. After this curious opening, St Paul continued by stating without any qualms or qualifications that man is higher up in the divine hierarchy than woman. His argument to prove this is as follows: 'For the man is not of the woman, but the woman of the man, neither was the man created for the woman but the woman for the man.'

This struck me as so outrageous I snorted. So who gives birth to all these men, then? Good old blokish St Paul, taking every opportunity to bolster up the status quo.

'I don't think you should be reading silly stuff like that,' I said, interrupting Mrs Todd in mid-flow. I couldn't stop myself.

They stared at me, their mouths open with shock. Nobody had ever interrupted a reading before. But I couldn't help it. Well, for goodness' sake, how could I let such rubbish pass? I only had to look at the examples of manhood we had in the room – Mr Haskin, Mr Webster, Mr Noble – to see how absurd it was.

Miss Gough broke the embarrassed silence with a few inarticulate squeaks of distress. The Sinful Children stared at me reproachfully.

'Well,' I said, 'I'm sorry, but I find stuff like that very

offensive. I don't know how you can bring yourself to read it.'

Mrs Todd said: 'Miss Bagnall, dear, we can't just ignore the bits of the Bible we don't like.'

'It would be very convenient if we could, I'm sure,' Mr Noble remarked to his left shoulder, 'but I'm afraid we either have to accept all of it or none at all.'

Miss Gough nodded. 'Mr Noble is right. We can't pick and choose.'

There were soft pigeon burblings of assent.

'So you *don't* like it, then?' I said.

They all looked at me blankly.

'Well, to be honest,' said Mrs Todd, 'I hadn't really thought about it. But now you mention it, no, I can't say I do like it very much. On the other hand, it's not up to us to doubt the word of God.'

'But it *isn't* the word of God. It's the word of some screwed-up, neurotic, first-century Roman who should have been under observation in a psychiatric ward.'

There was general consternation at this description of St Paul. Several of the Sinful Children were uncertain precisely what 'screwed-up' meant and had to consult each other.

'Well, anyway, I think it's evil. I think it ought to be banned,' I said, and I burst into tears – I seemed to be doing a lot of that recently – at the thought of centuries of injustice sanctioned and perpetuated by the chief religious book of Western culture.

Mr Haskin and his fellow sinners were at a loss. They had no idea what I was so upset about. They hovered round me, twittering with kindly incomprehension.

'Oh, Miss Bagnall, dear, I'm sure God wouldn't want you to distress yourself,' Miss Gough murmured.

I didn't actually share her certainty.

'You mustn't take it personally, you know,' said Janice, who was the youngest of the sinners and who worked in the tax office. 'God values all his servants equally, male and female. He wouldn't want . . .'

'Yes, and that's another thing,' I sobbed. 'It's always "he", isn't it? Why? Why should it always be "he"?'

This baffled them so completely they assumed I was sickening for something, and sent me to bed with a cup of hot milk, three aspirins and the promise that they would pray for me.

I lay in bed, trying to fish the skin off the milk, and thought how arrogant it was of men to assume that God must inevitably be formed in their image. In comparison with that, my arrogance looked pretty pathetic.

Don't imagine from this that I am some kind of ardent feminist. I am an ardent nothing that ends in '-ist'. In fact, on several occasions I have been reviled in the press by eminent spokespersons for the feminist movement. At one time I was the symbol, the archetype, of anti-feminism. No, what upset me so much about Corinthians 11 and other similar utterances, was that if St Paul *had* got some sort of line through to divine thinking, then obviously God didn't rate the female side of his creation very highly, which might explain why he was trying so hard to smack me down. On the other hand, it seemed more likely that St Paul was just a misogynistic old bigot. Either way, it hurt. Either way, I took it very personally.

I wrote somewhere – all these pages are in a muddle now, so I can't find it – that I have a needle-sharp eye for the truth. This doesn't, as you will have noticed, mean that I always tell it – I seldom do that – or even that I choose to acknowledge it, just that I am quite good at seeing it, which is a rarer gift than you might imagine. I knew, for example, from the moment I thought about menstruating bats, that I was pregnant, though for weeks I pretended I wasn't. When July came and I still hadn't had a period, I wondered if I ought to get a pregnancy test, but I preferred to go on pretending. So I drifted on from day to day in a state of quiet suspension, avoiding any kind of action. I spent the afternoons walking, or drinking cheap wine with

Jordi and his latest lover. Sometimes in the evenings I went to the pictures, sometimes I attended prayer meetings.

I had grown fond of the Sinful Children. I studied them in detail because I wanted to know how it was possible to grow old without ever having been of any significance whatever in the world.

After my outburst, I had become doubly special to them. Now I was their pet intellectual prod. The evenings consisted now not just of prayers and readings, but of a good argument as well. The Sinful Children defended their corner with gusto, but their arguments tended to drift away into irrelevancies or get beached on the sandbanks of semantics. Mr Webster, for example, who was an instinctive peacemaker, would say something like: 'Well it rather depends on what you mean by Faith [or Hell, or Death, or Covetousness, or Miracles, or whatever was the subject of the argument].' After which the conversation would deteriorate on roughly the following lines:

'Well, I should imagine we all mean exactly the same thing, don't we?' Mrs Todd would maintain stoutly.

'But how can we ever know that?' said Miss Gough, who liked vagueness and had a natural bent for philosophy. 'How can we be certain that what I mean is what you mean? Blue, for example. How do I know that what I call blue is the same as what you call blue?'

'Because,' said Mrs Todd with crushing logic, 'blue is always blue.'

'Yes, but what *is* blue?' Miss Gough persisted, clutching the beads round her throat in her excitement.

Mrs Todd said, 'Blue is the colour of Mr Noble's cardigan. You're surely not going to pretend Mr Noble's cardigan is yellow? Or purple?'

'No, no, it's blue. *I* call it blue, *you* call it blue. But we don't know, do we, and we can't prove that we're both seeing the same thing.'

'This is very interesting, you know. Very interesting indeed,' said Mr Noble, examining his cardigan. 'Because I would call this colour turquoise.'

'Oh, Sandra, my dear,' said Miss Gough, laughing happily, 'you've started something now.'

I certainly brought a bit of excitement into their lives.

At one meeting Janice said to me, 'Are you putting on weight, Sandra?'

I was. I was putting on weight all over but particularly round the middle. I was always hungry. I had taken to munching the leftover scraps on the guests' breakfast plates. One afternoon I ate a whole sliced loaf with butter and blackcurrant jam. I sat on the floor in my room and slowly chewed it, all twenty-six slices from crust to crust. It took an hour and a half. It was delicious.

'Yes,' I said, wolfing down a tuna-fish sandwich. 'I shall have to start slimming.'

It was surprisingly easy to ignore the truth. I didn't suffer from any of the usual things like sickness or heartburn. My breasts got bigger and veined and started to prick in a familiar way, but I simply pretended it wasn't happening. I felt very comfortable, as if I and not the baby was the one floating safely and dreamily in a sea of amniotic fluid.

Mrs Nightingale, who is one of the screws on this wing, has just come in to say that my session tomorrow with Mr Thomas will be cancelled. Would I like to help the librarian for an hour or two instead, she asks?

I am perfectly happy to work in the library instead of warding off Mr Rick Thomas's psychological intrusions.

'Good,' she says. She seems relieved. Obviously she expected me to be difficult about it. They still treat me here with wary deference as if I am a famous and temperamental diva with a reputation for eating people.

Miss Gough worked in a library. I'd forgotten that. It's just come back to me. At the library on the High Street. It was a job that ideally suited her: it was the acme of genteel invisibility. Her chief qualification was a naturally quiet voice. She pottered up and down the shelves pushing a little trolley of returned books which she replaced in their precise slots. She told me once how much she loved using the date stamp. From childhood, she said, she had nursed the ambition to get a job which required her to use a date stamp. 'I always loved those little black inky pads,' she confessed. I suppose, therefore, hers was a supremely fulfilled life. Blessed are they who want so little and are never consumed by the raging fires of ambition, for they will be easily satisfied.

It's very kind of them to let me work in the library, although actually, given the choice, I would have preferred the kitchen. I would like to get my hands on a raw carrot. Here they cook them until they've reduced them to a mound of slimy orange discs.

The reason Mr Thomas is away this week is because the lovely Les has finally given birth.

'What is it?' I ask Mrs Nightingale.

'A boy,' she says. 'Another boy.'

A boy. Good.

I never for one moment considered an abortion. This was not a consequence of any moral conviction on my part, nor was it because by the time I was forced to admit I was pregnant it was too late for an abortion anyway, but because this baby was quite different from Keith Eric Fox. It was never an invasive growth. It never imposed its will on me. It was more like a luxurious sleepiness. It seemed to radiate a sort of warm, sweet languor. Even while I was pretending that it wasn't happening, we were already deeply entwined, this baby and me. We were already involved in a complex and silent conversation.

'Miss Bagnall,' said Mr Haskin as I was manoeuvring the long tubes of the vacuum cleaner out of the cupboard. His face hung in sad, doggy folds. He had a little egg yolk caught in the corners of his mouth like dried scabs.

'Yes, Mr Haskin?'

'Miss Bagnall, I don't want to pry into the private affairs of my employees, but according to my calculations our agreement does not end until the last week of November.'

'Are you talking about the debt, Mr Haskin?'

'Yes, indeed. The debt. I am just a little concerned that circumstances will prevent you from fulfilling our contract.' His eyes dropped to my stomach and looked rapidly away again. 'Perhaps you could let me know for how long you anticipate being able to continue in employment.'

I smiled vaguely at him. 'I'm afraid I've no idea,' I said.

'But I am right, am I not,' he said, staring at the top of the cupboard door, 'in assuming that you . . . that you are . . .?'

'Yes, Mr Haskin,' I said. 'I do seem to be.'

He cleared his throat. 'Well, Miss Bagnall,' he said, 'if you could make some kind of guess as to when you're . . .'

'Possibly December,' I said, counting nine months on from April.

'Have you seen a doctor?' he asked.

'No.'

'I think you should. I will give you the name of my GP. You will need, I believe, to have your blood pressure checked. And presumably other things as well. And where do you plan to have the baby?'

'I don't know.'

'I see. Well, Mrs Todd informs me that you need to book a hospital bed. I think you should speak to the doctor about that. And what plans do you have for after the baby is born?'

None. No plans at all. I couldn't imagine the warm sleepiness inside me as ever having an existence separate from mine. It was like an alternative self, a cherished encapsulated self who would never have to face the outside world, who would never grow tough-skinned and bruised and old, who would lie for ever in its shell of perfect protection like a pearl inside an oyster.

Mr Haskin said, 'I take it the father has refused to marry you?'

The father question was a bit of a problem. I was pretty

certain that the baby couldn't be Billy's because we hadn't had any sort of sex for at least a month before I left him. This meant that it must be Duffy's, although even that was doubtful: he'd always been so careful. Still, who else was there?

'I am not making any kind of judgement,' said Mr Haskin. 'I do hope you understand that, Miss Bagnall. I just wanted to get certain practical matters cleared up. We are all of us sinners. None of us has the right to condemn our fellow man. Or woman. My point being, Miss Bagnall, that if you wish to stay on here . . . under the same terms as present, of course . . . you, and the child, will be very welcome.'

The Sinful Children of God were thrilled by my pregnancy, which Mr Haskin announced at the next meeting. They beamed shy smiles at me as I passed round the plates of sandwiches. They were full of eager questions. They wanted to touch me. Their hands rested gently on my arm, or brushed my shoulder. They cooed and clucked. They nibbled biscuits and sipped tea with their eyes fixed wonderingly on my stomach as if I were the Virgin Mary come amongst them.

Miss Gough offered to knit some cardigans. Janice said she would like to make a patchwork quilt for the cot; she was keen on patchwork and did a lot of it in the evenings. Mr Webster said his nephew worked in a second-hand shop so that if I wanted he would ask him to look out for a pram for me.

Their faces shone with joy. At last they had in their midst a real sinner, an acknowledged fornicator, their very own unmarried mother. (I decided not to spoil their fun by admitting that actually I was married.) What a thorough pleasure I was to them. How joyfully they took over my life. If I still believed in heaven I could be confident that I had earned my place there on the strength of my services to the Sinful Children alone.

Janice asked me if I'd seen a doctor yet. When I said no,

she offered to take an afternoon off work to go with me. She sat like a small hamster in the waiting-room, chewing nervously on her bottom lip.

'I hate anything medical,' she whispered, which was clearly true and made her gesture all the more noble.

The doctor examined me and said that at a rough guess he would say I was due mid to late December. He gave me the inevitable iron tablets on the basis that it wouldn't do any harm to take a mild dose until the results of the blood tests came through. He also gave me a diet sheet on the basis that I was overweight. Otherwise, he said, I was doing fine. He arranged to book a bed for me at the local hospital.

'Well, that wasn't so bad, then, was it?' said Janice as we walked home.

In the weeks that followed the Sinful Children kept an eager watch on my haemoglobin levels, my blood pressure, the normality of my urine and my poundage. The evening meetings frequently involved passing round my antenatal card so that they could all see how well I was doing. Miss Gough had found some books in her library about breathing exercises which she insisted on lending to me. As a group they prayed for me with devout and passionate concentration. I enjoyed the attention. To be the *raison d'être* even of the Sinful Children of God is better than not to be a *raison d'être* at all. In this bizarre circle I had become a star.

She was born on 21 December.

This is what happened:

The Sinful Children were having a Christmas get-together. They had three bottles of sweet sherry and some fizzy white wine, which allowed them to feel dangerously wicked, because although they could not condemn alcohol – Jesus himself drank wine – they were very wary of it. I made turkey-roll sandwiches and heated up some mince pies. The party got off to a cheerful start. Miss Gough opened the proceedings by remarking that she thought the dog must have eczema because it was scratching so much. Mrs Todd suggested that it could be fleas but Janice said it was too late in the year for fleas. Mr Webster, perched anxiously on the edge of a grease-stained chair clutching his glass of sherry, said that he had suffered badly from eczema from childhood and had only been cured by prayer in early middle age. Mrs Todd remarked that eczema and asthma often went together. Janice said her uncle had psoriasis and sometimes it was so bad he ripped his skin off with his nails. Miss Gough said that at the next prayer meeting they must pray for Janice's uncle.

After this lively discussion on skin diseases it was time for carols.

I was so big now I filled every room I went into. Inside me the baby grew like a flower, unfolding petal after petal; and with each unfolding, a heavy waft of sweetness was released, like a drug, so that for the last weeks of pregnancy I lumbered about in a dim narcotic dream. It was in this state that I passed round the turkey sandwiches and mince pies, knocking over small pieces of furniture in my wake, and smiling in a spaced-out way at all these kindly, carol-singing religious cranks.

'Doesn't Sandra look wonderful,' said Miss Gough, clasping her hands together in childish joy.

Mr Webster and Mr Noble nodded and gallantly agreed that I looked splendid.

Mrs Todd said that she thought I ought to be the one to bring the evening's jollities to a climax by reading to them from the Gospel of St Luke, Chapter 2. She found the place for me. I stood up, vast as a mythical giantess. 'And it came to pass,' I read, 'that in those days there went out a decree from Caesar Augustus that all the world should be taxed . . .'

The words were familiar and comforting, though only comforting *because* of their familiarity. Looked at objectively it wasn't a comforting story at all, particularly not for poor Mary. She must have felt like I did when I was pregnant with Keith: that she was carrying something alien, some kind of monster, and that in the process she had become an irrelevance.

I came to the final verse – 'But Mary kept all these things and pondered them in her heart.' There was a soft murmur of satisfaction. The Sinful Children breathed out, they smiled. My eye had flipped forward to a verse in brackets – 'As it is written in the law of the Lord, Every male that openeth the womb shall be called holy to the Lord.'

Outraged, I jabbed my finger on the offending verse and was just opening my mouth to tell them that I had found yet another offensive piece of garbage, and to ask just exactly who it was who had written this so-called 'law of the Lord', not a woman that's for sure, when a sharp pain clutched my gut, and I was paralysed.

'Are you all right, dear?' Miss Gough asked, taking the Bible from my hand.

The pain reached its peak. I grabbed hold of the back of Mr Haskin's chair.

Mrs Todd said, 'Is it . . .? Should we . . .?'

Janice said, turning pale, 'Someone ring for an ambulance.'

But after two or three seconds of agony, the pain faded into a long and mercifully silent fart. 'No,' I said, moving as fast as my bulk would allow away from the gaseous fumes for which I didn't want to be held responsible, not if they were as fierce as I suspected. 'It's OK. Just a touch of indigestion.'

At ten o'clock the party broke up, with the exchange of cards and little gifts. I went to bed carrying half a bottle of sweet sherry which I had managed to hide before it all got drunk, and a plate of leftovers. I sat propped up against my pillows swigging sherry, eating mince pies and re-reading one of the *National Geographic* magazines. Outside it was pouring with rain. I could hear it gurgling down the drain in the well. The soft, relentless beat of rain, the sweet sherry and an article about longhouses in Borneo made a pleasantly soporific combination. I fell asleep with the light on.

I was woken at the peak of a second pain. It was so violent it robbed me of all capacity. I couldn't think, or speak, or move. My skin broke out in a dank, oily sweat. The pain took me to a point where I was squeezed into unconsciousness. Time fell apart. Ten seconds might have passed, ten minutes or ten hours. Then, as the merciless, white-hot grip of the pincers began to ease, a rush of warmth spurted from between my legs. I lifted up the cover and saw blood-streaked liquid soaking into the sheet. I panicked. I tried to stand up, but the pain sucked itself up again like a wave, a vast breaker, and crashed over my head. I was knocked to my knees. I crawled, dripping like a half-drowned animal across the lino and out into the passage before the next pain washed me away. I was battling to stay afloat, to keep my head above water, to keep breathing, when I felt hands grip me under the armpits and haul me up on to the shingle where I lay exhausted and soaked. I opened my mouth to shout that yet another, yet a bigger wave was rearing itself to attack, to obliterate me, when she slid quietly out of me. It took no effort at all on my part. I hardly knew it had happened. The gathering wave crashed and spent itself somewhere beyond my feet. A light was suddenly turned on. I lifted my head and saw her lying there between my legs on the carpet.

'Good thing it's a red carpet,' I said weakly. That was the first thing I said. I had made a dreadful mess of it, but perhaps when it was dry red on red wouldn't show.

Mr Haskin was wearing beige-striped pyjamas. The flies sagged open. He said he was going to find some scissors so he could cut the umbilical cord.

Between my legs the tiny girl opened her eyes and looked at me. Her eyes were a deep blue, the colour of irises, the colour of delphiniums, the colour of the sky on a hot day in July. I took off the T-shirt I was wearing and wrapped her up in it, so that when Mr Haskin came back with a saucepan of boiling water in which lay the kitchen scissors, I was sitting there on the stained carpet, quite naked, staring into the bottomless eyes of my daughter.

Mr Haskin had put on an oven glove because the scissors were too hot to hold. He tied some cotton round the cord and then cut it, closing his eyes in squeamish horror as the blades squeezed shut. Fortunately there was just time for him to get some newspapers on the floor before the placenta slid out.

'You must be frozen,' he said, bundling up the afterbirth in pages of the *Daily Mail*.

As soon as he said the word 'frozen' some sort of reaction set in and I started to shake. He fetched a blanket and wrapped it round me and helped me back to bed. I had to ask him for some old towels which I held clamped between my legs as I waddled down the passage.

Soon after this a doctor arrived and checked me over. He looked at the baby and said she was fine. Tomorrow, he said, a health visitor would call and weigh her. 'What a beautiful child,' he said, looking at her lying in the crook of my arm. It was not a routine politeness. He was stating a fact.

When he had gone Mr Haskin brought me a bowl of water, a flannel and some soap so that I could wash myself and also the baby. Later he brought me a cup of tea and two hot-water bottles, for which I was very grateful because I was suffering from afterpains as powerful as the aftershocks of an earthquake. He had made a cot out of a suitcase which he rested on a luggage stand. She looked very comfortable there, with a pillow for a mattress and some pillowcases for sheets. Her skin was the colour of a ripening peach. Seven or eight threads of pure gold grew out of her scalp. I watched her for hours as she breathed. I watched her eyelids droop. I watched her fall asleep and later wake up again and smile in unfocused bliss. She was more beautiful than anything I had ever seen.

I decided to call her Jenny.

In the cold, dim hours of dawn I had considered the possibility of calling her Joanne, but the name didn't fit her. She was Jenny, not Joanne. She was entirely herself, so entirely herself that I could see nothing at all either of me or of Duffy or of anyone else in her. God alone knows where she came from.

'I'm calling her Jenny,' I told Mr Haskin when he arrived with a tray of breakfast. It was late. After ten. On the tray was a plate of scrambled eggs on toast surrounded by tinned tomatoes. He had been out shopping and bought two packets of jumbo-sized sanitary towels. They were wrapped up discreetly in brown paper. 'The doctor said you might need these,' he muttered, turning a dull red. He had also bought me a small bunch of flowers: some forced daffodils and a few freesias.

'Thank you,' I said.

I wanted to thank him as well for what he'd done during the night, but I wasn't sure how much he wanted to pretend that he hadn't. I found that I was embarrassed by my nakedness; not my physical nakedness – that was nothing new to him – but the ugly nakedness of pain, and by the mysteries of birth, which are not for sad, elderly bachelors to know.

'Jenny,' he said, poking a tentative thumb at her. She clutched it with her minute wrinkled fingers. 'Good heavens,' he said, 'what a remarkably pretty baby.'

Pretty? She was exquisite. She took my breath away. I couldn't stop looking at her. I wanted to touch her all the time. Feeding her was pure pleasure. She sucked gently and without greed, drawing off pain in a sweet flood of release. Her eyes stared up at me solemn, unblinking and dark. I loved her with a bottomless passion.

If this is beginning to sound sickeningly like a paean to motherhood, I apologize. I don't mean it to sound like that. I am not, as you know, the least bit sentimental about motherhood. But the way I loved Jenny was never maternal. I loved her like I might love a wild horse who had come to eat from my hand, or some priceless object which had been given me to hold for a moment.

Where had she come from, this extraordinary creature? She was the embodiment of beauty. Not a crude sort of beauty, like mine, not the sort that makes heads turn in the street, but a delicate beauty that is to do with absolute purity. It seemed impossible that together plump, balding Duffy and I could possibly have made this snippet of perfection.

What a pity it is that I can never tell Mr Rick Thomas about Jenny. 'The father, Rick?' I'd say. 'Oh, didn't I tell you. I was visited one night in Camden by a bat.'

And to be honest, although I knew Duffy was Jenny's father, it might just as well have been a bat. The question of fatherhood was irrelevant. She was a gift to *me*, that was the point. She was the sign I had been waiting for, the outward and visible proof that finally I had been forgiven.

In a week or so, I was back at work. I was happy to go on cleaning the Astoria for ever. I had temporarily lost all my ambitions. They seemed pointless now that I had Jenny. I carried her everywhere in a papoose which Janice had bought on the market. It folded her into my back and left my hands free to dust and hoover. She grew. She thrived. She seldom cried because she had nothing to cry about. When she did, it was in a slightly apologetic way as if she had no idea why she was making this noise but she felt it was something she ought to do occasionally. She was a happy baby, though not in the way Keith was happy. She wasn't ringed with sausages of dimpled fat. She didn't have Keith's wide happy grin. Her smile was so gentle and so subtle people failed sometimes to recognize it. 'What a serious little girl,' they said. 'Is she all right?' She didn't love people indiscriminately like Keith did. She stared at them with her deep blue eyes, deep as the sea, and weighed them up for a long, long time. Sometimes she dismissed them, sometimes, if she thought there was some answering echo from an equal depth, she gave one of her rare sweet smiles. Nothing flashy. Nothing promiscuous. Just an acknowledgement that she understood they were people of worth. I was the only one she smiled at freely. I was the only one she deemed worthy of her absolute trust.

The Sinful Children of God brought her presents. They looked on her as their baby. This was fine by me: it was nice for her to have this extended family and she found all of them worthy. She had stared deep into the soul of each one of them and given them the mark of her approval. She particularly liked Miss Gough and sometimes clutched at her pearls or at her spectacle chain.

The Sinful Children came to every meeting with extra little gifts. Mr Webster found a collapsible pram for her. Miss Gough continued to knit. Mrs Todd embroidered a dress, and bought her a pink nylon teddy bear from an Oxfam shop.

Every afternoon, when I had finished the cleaning, I wrapped Jenny up and wheeled her in her pram up and down the streets, partly for the air and partly to introduce her to the world. I liked explaining it all to her and showing her the things she needed to see.

At the corner of Berringer Street and Palatine Square was a telephone box. Every day I swore to myself that I would ring home and let them know about Jenny, but I never did. Mr Haskin had said that if ever I wanted to use the phone in reception I was welcome to do so as long as I didn't abuse the privilege, but it never occurred to me to use one of the phones in the hotel. I was in a state of permanent forgetfulness about them as if they were toy phones or as if they only connected with London and the South-East. It was the phone box at the corner of the square that made me so uneasy. I devised walks for us which avoided phone boxes and rang home only at very infrequent intervals. Dreadfully busy, I said. Always on the move. Shows in Rome and Milan. Don't worry if you don't hear from me.

I think of that time now as if it was splashed with gold. In my memory everything glows. I woke flushed with joy each morning as if the sun rose from our basement room, and we, Jenny and I, were at the source of the light. The feeling stayed with me all day. I never thought about the future. I never imagined Jenny at five years old or at ten or at thirty. I never considered what we would do or how we would live. Each day was contained perfection, and after it we slept curled together in a warm nest, her small body wrapped in the curve of my arm.

Odd how things happen.

At the clinic where I took Jenny to be weighed there was a tableful of magazines. I was looking through one of these on a day when Jenny was about two months old and we were waiting to see the health visitor. The magazine I picked up fell open at a page headed 'Art', and there in front of me was a reproduction of a photograph I knew well. The blurb underneath said, ' "Surfaces II" – Alisdair Duff, 1975.' There was a further short paragraph which read 'Catch this stunning exhibition of images from provincial photographers in Manchester, Liverpool, Leeds, Newcastle or Glasgow.'

Goodness knows how Duffy felt about being called a 'provincial' photographer. I bet he was livid.

On the next page was a kind of glossy gossip column with accompanying photographs of the rich and famous at some charity function. I stared at Mrs Gerald Whitely-Torrance and the Hon. Amanda Forsythe. Below this was a photo of a girl with bruised lips and a cascade of permed blond hair who was living exactly the kind of life I had imagined I would be living now. 'Melinda Brookes,' I read, 'international model, who has just signed a million-dollar contract with an American perfume company.' She was standing next to a man in a dinner-jacket. I looked at him without much interest. He had a thin, startling face. He was quite old, Duffy's sort of age or older, and therefore dismissible. (How weird the judgements of youth are: he was probably younger then than I am now.) 'Miss Brookes,' I read, 'seen here chatting with millionaire art collector, Dysart Stevens.'

It's strange, isn't it, the way you sometimes get offered a glimpse of your own future, and completely fail to recognize it as such.

I don't know how to write the next bit. Perhaps I won't. I will write something else instead.

I will write about the girl in the library. What can I say about her? She is called Faith and she is serving three years for fraud. She has a university degree and speaks, as my Mum would say, 'nicely'. I am cultivating her. I can see that there are several women here whose support will make life tolerable. Faith is one of them.

She is a quiet girl, thin-lipped and pale. Her hair is baby soft. When she's old it will turn pure white and her pink-skinned skull will gleam baldly through it. She's one of those women with a delicate, childish torso perched above massive hips as if half of her is an ancient fertility goddess, and half an untouched virgin. She believes herself to be innocent of the charge against her. It was her boyfriend who first tricked and then betrayed her. Whether this is true or not I can't tell because she is very dignified and reserved about what happened. She is also naturally suspicious of me, which I can quite understand. She's probably quite scared. So I am trying to be dignified and reserved as well.

We talk books. I explain that despite whatever she may have assumed about me, I am, in fact, an almost total ignoramus and have read nothing of substance.

'I tried a bit of Tolstoy recently,' I say. 'But I didn't like it.'

I tell her how annoyed I got with Anna Karenina. She laughs nervously. I tell her that *Little Dorrit*, which I have brought back almost untouched, is no better. In fact worse. What a wimp she is, Little Dorrit, I say, and what a stupid name. Goodness can be so nauseatingly unattractive, can't it, I say.

Faith insists it is worth persevering with *Little Dorrit*,

although to be honest – she confesses this uneasily as if she fears it might be heretical – she herself has always had a bit of a problem with Dickens. Do I know Hardy, she asks. In a burst of pink enthusiasm she presses on me a book called *Tess of the d'Urbervilles*.

I've heard of it. There was a film, I think, though I never saw it.

To reinforce the idea that I am a serious person, I accept the book and tuck it under the pile of comfortable trash I have chosen for myself.

Faith sets me a task. She gives me a pile of old hardbacks which are starting to fall apart, and sets me up with glue and Sellotape. I enjoy myself. I like mending things. After a while she makes a cup of coffee. She has access to an electric kettle. She fishes about at the back of a cupboard and produces a tin with KitKats in it. I haven't tasted a KitKat, or anything remotely like it, for months.

So all in all I have a very pleasant morning. I feel as if I'm at school and have been let off lessons to do a little job for the nuns.

She is a nice girl, Faith. Pity about the plastic glasses and the mammoth thighs.

It's dark now. I walk up and down the room twisting my hands like an anguished ghost. How can I do it? How can I write this thing?

Well, I won't. There's no compulsion.

On the other hand I want to. If I leave this out then nothing else makes sense.

Perhaps if I tell it so simply, so briefly, in less than a page, I will be able to bear it. I will just stick to the facts.

She was born in December. In January I floated in happiness, only slightly tempered by the continuing afterpains.

February was cold. It snowed, but we were warm. We glowed like twin suns. The snow melted under my feet. It fell on Jenny's face. She blinked and made little spitting noises with her mouth. There were snowdrops and crocuses in the park. She was two months old. Her hair grew in soft drifts, so pale it was almost white.

In March the daffodils bloomed. Sometimes it rained, sometimes the thin London air was full of wind-blown, nervy, jangling excitement. Jenny rolled about on the floor on her own and struggled to sit up. She could lift her head. I told her long stories. We both lay on our stomachs on the bed and I talked quietly to her about this and that.

In April I took her to the zoo. I showed her the animals. I showed her cherry blossom. I shook a branch over her pram so that she was showered in pink petals. Her laugh had a crack in it, a kind of gurgle that pierced some raw place inside me. She was growing a tooth. She loved music. I took her into record shops and sat her on my knee in the listening booths. She loved the pigeons who flew down the well and pecked for the crumbs from the kitchen.

Late in May the first roses bloomed. She copied me and buried her nose in them. Her face was covered with dew and pollen. You could see the beginnings of her real face now. She had a pointed chin and a straight nose. Her eyes were still dark blue. Above them her eyebrows were pale arched shadows. Her hair had darkened to the colour of primroses. She sang a lot. She wound her tiny arms round my neck and whispered damp wordless songs in my ear.

On 23 June I put her to sleep in the collapsible pram. There was a meeting of the Sinful Children, and I left her while I went to make the sandwiches. After the meeting I fed her and then we curled up together and slept. In the night she cried a little. I gave her some water but she didn't want it. I think a dream had disturbed her, or maybe a premonition. In a couple of minutes she fell asleep again.

When I woke up in the morning, she was dead.

I had woken as I always did, full of joy. I went to pull back the curtains so she could see the weeds at the foot of the well, the rosebay willowherbs, blossoming outside the window. 'It's a beautiful day,' I said. 'It's going to be hot.' I picked her up to show her.

She was limp, like a sparsely stuffed toy, limp and cold. Her head fell backwards with a sickening click. There was no breath in her. No life, no beating heart. Nothing.

Days of uncomprehending darkness.

A doctor came and signed something. They said I should register her death. I was very confused. I hadn't even registered her birth. I didn't know you had to.

The Sinful Children paid for her funeral. I didn't have enough money to do even that one last thing for her. She is buried in a small cemetery between the railway sidings and a jam factory. She has no headstone. What could I put on it? How could I bear such a solid proof of her death?

I asked Mr Haskin if he would plant some bulbs there.

I don't remember the funeral. I don't want to. For weeks I was in utter darkness at the bottom of a deep, deep pit. I have lost most of this time. The only clear memory I have is of that little patch of disturbed earth in the shadow of a factory wall. The bleakness of it makes me weep. Even now. Even now I am weeping.

Facts. Stick to facts.

It was described officially as a cot death. There was a post-mortem. The idea of her tiny body spread out on a slab like a frog pinned out for dissection was intolerable. I ignored the official letters Mr Haskin pushed under my door. I didn't work, I didn't eat, I didn't wash. My hair grew rank with grease. All day, all night I lay on my festering sheets and willed myself to die.

The guilt munched away inside me like a cancer. Oh, Mr Rick Thomas I lied to you, I lied when I said that I knew nothing about guilt. I know everything about guilt. I am as much an expert on the subject as you are. I was eaten alive by it. I was to blame; I was at fault. I had done something terribly wrong, or I had failed to do some obvious thing which I ought to have done. I was not worthy of her.

I tried praying. For the first time I understood my Mum's sudden religious obsession after Joanne died. Even an angry God, even a God with whom I was at war, was better than the alternative: that Jenny had been born randomly and equally randomly had died, and that there was neither meaning nor purpose behind it, nor anyone to hold responsible, neither a fierce, irrational, vengeful God nor a gentle old bloke who loves sinners. Nor even a combination of the two. Nothing.

The Sinful Children came tapping at my door to offer their condolences and their awkward comfort but I wouldn't speak to them. Their grief was like a knife turned in my heart. Miss Gough wept outside my door in the corridor but I covered my ears and refused to let her in.

This is what I did instead.

Before it was light, in the early hours of the day after the funeral – or maybe it was the day after that, I don't remember – I gathered up my bedding and dragged it into the kitchen. I stuffed one of my blankets against the gap under the door. I hung my sheet over the ill-fitting window. I turned on the gas and opened the double doors of the oven. The second blanket I arranged on the floor. I rolled up the other sheet to make a pillow which I stuffed inside the oven. I rested my head on my improvised pillow and breathed in deeply. It was not an unpleasant smell. It made me cough a little to start with. I tried to think of some facts about gas to keep my mind occupied until the time came when I no longer had a mind to worry about.

Facts about gas: gas is sometimes derived from coal which is formed from the fossilization of trees. That, in essence, was all I was doing – inhaling the concentrated perfumes of a prehistoric forest. Nothing more sinister. Drowsily I began to repeat the names of trees to myself:

sandalwood and cedar wood, mahogany, mountain ash, oak, sycamore. Soon Jenny and I were walking hand in hand along an earthy forest track. The sun skittered through the leaves. The bracken fronds were shoulder high. 'Look, Jenny,' I said, and we looked up into the veins of the branches and the glittering chiaroscuro (a Dysart word) of leaves. And then the sky clouded over, it grew dim, and the path we were walking on sloped away, the earth started to slither under my feet and then I was falling, tumbling, rolling, down and down . . .

(At this point one of those coincidences occurred which are so unbelievable it's hard not to think of them as the workings of fate.

Mr Haskin woke up and decided to make himself a cup of tea.

What are the odds against that? First against his waking, then against his thinking about a cup of tea, and longest odds of all, against his actually bothering to get up and do it?

Anyway, he did. He pushed open the kitchen door just in time to snatch me from the jaws of death. He said God must have woken him.)

Loose earth and dry leaves flew past me. My mouth was full of bitterness. Something caught me under the armpits. I shook myself free.

'Let go of me,' I said, 'I want to be sick.'

Acid liquid gushed into my mouth. My head was pounding. Above me a naked light bulb swung backwards and forwards. Shadows loomed and receded.

'Are you all right, Miss Bagnall?' a voice said.

I opened my eyes. I appeared to be lying on the red carpet with my face in a pool of brownish vomit.

'Oh dear,' I said. 'The carpet again.'

Mr Haskin yanked me up on to my feet. He slung my lifeless arm round his shoulder and half-dragged, half-carried me back to my room where he shoved and manoeuvred me until my back was to the bed. He was panting wildly from the exertion. His eyes bulged. When I fell back on to the bare mattress, he collapsed on top of me and lay there gasping for breath. I could feel his heart banging against my ribs. I thought what an irony it would be if having failed to kill myself, I killed him instead. Another death to add to my lengthening tally.

After a while, he disengaged himself. He apologized. 'I didn't hurt you, did I?' he said.

Since I wanted to be dead, the small matter of a few bruises seemed hardly worth mentioning.

'That was a very stupid thing to do, Miss Bagnall,' he said angrily. 'Don't you ever try a trick like that again. Killing yourself is no answer.'

I couldn't think of a better one.

'And not only that,' he said, 'not only is it no answer, Miss Bagnall, it's also a sin.'

My mouth felt disgusting, as if I had vomited lumps of bird shit.

I started work again, moving like a stunned and exhausted farm beast up and down the landings dragging the vacuum cleaner behind me. In my free time I walked about the streets, killing time. I wanted to suffocate and squeeze the life out of every minute. Often I found myself wandering into churches. I was very attracted to churches at this time. They were cool and smelled of dust, but I found nothing in them, nothing I was looking for. They seemed like sepulchres built to house a dead idea. All the same I was drawn by the emptiness in them. Emptiness is peaceful.

In the evenings I went to the cinema. I saw one film five times. I didn't care. The soundtrack drowned my thoughts. I sat watching the screen in dumb, fuddled pain. Anything was better than spending time in the room where Jenny had lived her short, perfect life. And it had been entirely perfect. She had died with her skin unbroken by any minor accident, and her mind untarnished by any less than generous thought. She had never known either unhappiness or evil.

The nights were worse than the days. Sometimes I fell easily into a dead sleep, but then the waking was so painful I swore I would never sleep again. Mostly I drifted off in short, confused, dream-riddled snatches.

The night when the relationship with Mr Haskin moved on to an entirely different footing, the noise of my own crying woke me. It broke through a dream of unbearable loss. The pillow under my cheek was damp. My nose was blocked. I was retching with grief. The sounds I made were so strange, so inhuman, I was impressed. I didn't know I was capable of such wild abandon, such depth of feeling. But then I grew frightened. Terrible noises came bellowing out of me, visceral noises, the mad, baffled roars of an animal wounded by gunshot. I lost all control. The last shavings of a civilized human veneer flaked away.

A voice said: 'Miss Bagnall?'

I opened a swollen eye. Mr Haskin stood by my bed in his dressing-gown.

'Miss Bagnall,' he said sternly, 'you must stop crying like that. You'll make yourself ill.'

I had gone now into uncontrollable spasms. Mr Haskin sat on the edge of the bed and put his hands on my shoulders to steady me, to hold me together.

'It's all right,' he said. 'It's all right,' although he didn't sound convinced about it. He pulled me up into a sitting position and held me tightly against his chest. His dressing-gown was rough against my cheek. It smelled of sick dog and stale tobacco. His arms were thin and bony, but they gripped hard, they allowed the spasms no space. His calm breathing next to mine soothed me; it gave me a human pattern to copy. Slowly, the juddering, muscle-tearing convulsions eased until they were reduced to limp hiccups interspersed with sudden trembling gasps for air.

'Lie down, Miss Bagnall,' he said at last, and he laid me gently back on the pillows.

Then – this is the strange bit – then he took off his dressing-gown and lay down beside me. His breath near my ear smelled quite pleasantly of toothpaste. We lay side by side like that for a long time, the silence between us broken only by the soft shudders as my breathing came slowly back under control.

'Are you all right now, Miss Bagnall?' he asked eventually.

I nodded.

His body beside me moved. I thought he must have decided I was calm enough now to leave. I thought he was going to climb over me to get back to his own room. Instead, he made a kind of choking, desperate noise and hauled himself on top of me. He was muttering something. I couldn't catch what he said, but I found his weight deeply comforting, like a heavy blanket. Then he hoisted himself up on to his arms and suggested I move my legs.

I let it happen. I don't really know why except that I needed comforting, and at the time it did feel like comfort. He was warm, he was heavy, he was human, and he was featureless: I couldn't see the empty swags of ageing skin or his thin yellow chest. So I put my arms round him and clung to him as if I was drowning and he was a piece of driftwood, and I let him get on with it.

Shortly afterwards I fell asleep, pinned safely to earth by his sprawling weight.

In the morning he was gone. He behaved as if nothing had happened. Perhaps it hadn't. Perhaps I'd dreamed it. Who knows what strange dreams a near-lethal dose of gas will induce? Except that the following night it happened again, and the night after that as well.

While it was happening I knew that it was real – a real thing was happening. A body slid into my bed under the cover of darkness. I never properly saw his face and no words were spoken. We simply gave and received comfort. It could have been anyone. It could have been a fantasy lover. The fact that I knew it was Mr Haskin made the silent anonymity of the coupling even odder, as if after midnight he turned into someone entirely different. Afterwards I slept for two or three hours, the pain eased by the solace of weight and warmth and human smells.

But when daylight came, when everything was back to normal, the idea that Mr Haskin had visited me in the night seemed so unlikely that I wondered if it might be some slightly shameful recurring dream. Neither of us ever mentioned these nightly visitations. Mr Haskin continued to treat me with his usual distant politeness. He continued to address me as 'Miss Bagnall'.

After about two weeks of this I went to a meeting of the Sinful Children. They were touchingly glad to see me, but afraid of my grief. They patted me as if I were a large sad dog.

When they prayed for forgiveness for their individual sins, I watched Mr Haskin. He kept his hands clasped and his eyes shut. His face was gloomily innocent. I thought how glad he must be that at last he had a real sin to confess, a sin sufficiently heinous to justify his calling himself a Sinful Child.

I felt that in this respect at least I had done him some small service in return for everything he had done for me.

It grew hot. I was as empty as a dried seed pod. The sun seemed like an insult. People wore sleeveless dresses and laughed and got on with lives that seemed to be packed with purpose and pleasure.

An infestation of ants marched through the Astoria's kitchen. They were large, and a glossy reddish brown. They were brilliantly organized. I watched a group of them combine to carry away a piece of solid fried egg-white which they found beside the cooker. It took about twelve of them to do it, staggering under the weight of their find, but bearing up. The others escorted them, offering encouragement and advice. They flowed like a stream of tea across the floor.

Late one night Mr Haskin sprayed them with an ant killer. I watched their self-confident certainty, their sense of purpose crumble. They panicked. They struggled to pull the dead back to their nest. They rushed about in confused circles.

'That's better,' said Mr Haskin, washing his hands.

One hot afternoon when the sweat was slimy under my armpits and my unwashed hair flopped greasily round my face, I was walking round the endless deserted back streets behind the Astoria when I came to a railway bridge. It was made of sheets of some sort of metal riveted together. The track was a surprisingly long way below. It seemed like an opportunity not to be missed. There was no one about. Across the road was a dilapidated-looking pub called The Greyhound, but it was closed, and I couldn't see anyone at any of the windows. A van drove along the road and over the bridge. I waited until it was out of sight, and then hauled myself up on to the black metal sheets. The top was quite wide, wide enough for my feet, but even so – and totally illogically since I intended to kill myself – I was scared of losing my balance. The drop was at least thirty foot. It made me dizzy. I remembered that tightrope walkers are instructed never to look down, so I tried staring ahead, and then very gingerly and with a lot of wobbling managed to straighten my legs until I was standing upright. I teetered there like Blondin about to cross the Niagara, my arms stretched out on either side. I told myself that I was now going to fly. I was pleased by the fortuitous discovery of such a fitting place. I took a small fierce breath in through my nose, shut my eyes and launched myself into space.

A millionth of a second later and I was regretting it. This wasn't how I wanted to die. If, indeed, I wanted to die at all, which I was suddenly no longer sure about. Anyway, I probably wouldn't die. I'd probably break my back, and land up still alive but paralysed. I was thinking all this even as I jumped, so that in a last-ditch recantation I tried to hurl my body to the right. The idea was to land halfway down the embankment, instead of crashing on to the rails.

The consequence of this attempt to save myself was ludicrous. I fell into a tree.

It was a large tree. I hadn't taken it into account at all. I hadn't really noticed it. I crashed through its branches and was well on the way to the rails below when the particularly ludicrous thing happened. My T-shirt caught on a stump of branch which had presumably been lopped off by British Rail in its annual prune. The T-shirt, which turned out to be as resilient as the stump, was hoicked up by the force of my fall so that the bulk of it was caught up round my armpits and my neck. It almost strangled me. I hung there in undignified suspension like a mad witch who had miscalculated her flight. No amount of kicking or wriggling could dislodge me.

This is how they found me. Someone crossing the bridge spotted me twirling listlessly in the tree. He ran into the pub and phoned for the emergency services.

A fire engine arrived. A fireman climbed into the tree and cut me down. They discovered, of course, that I hadn't hanged myself, that I was humiliatingly suspended there by my own T-shirt. I found I couldn't be bothered to explain how it had happened. Across my throat I had the equivalent of a rope burn which I clutched at as a way of explaining why I wasn't answering their questions, but the truth was that I hadn't got the energy to go through the whole story.

An ambulance arrived. I was helped into it and lay on a stretcher with a red blanket over me. My body was covered in long bloody scratches and there were more burn marks under my arms that had come up in angry red weals. My hair was a mass of twigs. It looked as if a magpie had built its nest on my head. A weird noise ripped through my throat like a rusty saw. It was meant to be a laugh. I was laughing at the absurdity of the afternoon, but the sound that came tearing out of me was a fiendish and unholy cackle.

*THREE*

It's visiting day today. In a spirit of idle malice I sent Beverley a visiting order. Surprisingly enough, she's come.

She sits opposite me doing a fine impression of a missionary's wife bringing a message of Christian charity to a colony of lepers. Her hands grip her Marks and Spencer's handbag, her eyes dart about in horror, she takes shallow little sniffs for fear of breathing in contamination.

'How are you, Sandra?' she asks. She's so stuffed full of moral superiority, it's a wonder her suit buttons don't burst open under the strain. This moment must be an exquisite triumph for her. I understand that. She has a lot to resent me for – more, actually, than she knows – so I am quite happy to let her enjoy her fifteen minutes of superiority.

'I'm very well, thank you, Beverley,' I say. 'How are you?'

'You certainly look well.' She sounds disappointed. People are not supposed to flourish in prison. They're supposed to grow pale and thin and wretched. It's in particularly bad taste for murderers to radiate such glowing health.

'How are the children?' I ask.

'Fine,' she says. 'Martin is doing his exams this year.'

She has three children. They are all equally repugnant.

'And what about Jenny?' I ask.

One of the small, painful ironies of life is that Beverley called her only daughter Jennifer. My Mum phoned me with the news. I was in Panama City at the time. I stood barefooted on the balcony of my hotel room in the liquid, dripping heat of mid afternoon, with the portable phone in my hand and the sun burning my shoulders, and listened to my mother rhapsodizing about her newborn granddaughter.

Fortunately Jenny Birtles – Beverley married a builder called Grahame Birtles – takes after her mother. She is one of those children who are born fat. She has grown from pudgy babyhood into a square, plump child with jowls and splayed legs. Her mottled thighs crash against each other when she walks. She whines and tells tales. She has nothing whatever to do with my Jenny.

I listen to Beverley ramble on about Jenny's new diet and how she has taken up horse riding, how Martin (the eldest) had a glowing report from school at the end of his fourth year, how Andrew (the youngest) is going to France on an exchange visit.

'And what about Grahame?' I say.

Grahame has made money. He drives a Jag. I thought he might drive her down in it.

Beverley looks at me sharply. 'There's no need to sneer,' she says.

'I wasn't sneering.'

'Yes, you were. Your voice always takes on that sniffy tone when you talk about Grahame.'

She moves on without pausing for breath to heavier stuff. I have broken Mum and Dad's hearts, she says, and destroyed their lives. She and Grahame are too ashamed to hold up their heads in the neighbourhood. Grahame is talking of resigning from Rotary and they may have to put the house up for sale. The scandal will probably destroy the business. The children's lives will be turned upside down. They may all have to change their names.

'Well, that at least will be a blessing,' I say.

Her face turns yellow with venom. She demands to know what is wrong with the name Birtles? It is a fine old Lancashire name, she says. Several mayors of Duckborough le Sands were Birtles.

There are things I could tell her about Grahame Birtles,

but I don't. I never will. I smile affectionately at her. 'Well, Beverley,' I say, when finally she runs out of steam, 'it's so nice of you to come all this way to see me.'

She stares at me in sullen silence. She suspects I am laughing at her. She wears a dull mustard suit which exactly matches her skin. It looks expensive, but it does nothing for her.

After a while she says, 'You don't change, do you? Once a cow always a cow.'

This I think a bit unfair, particularly since I have so meekly allowed her to crow over me and patronize me. Besides, she is wrong. I am always changing. I am in a continual state of metamorphosis. She is the one who never changes. But there's no point in starting an argument. Instead I say, surprising both of us, 'I'm sorry.'

This involuntary apology is so alien to our relationship that neither of us knows how to take it. We sit staring at each other. After a while we become embarrassed.

'Well,' she says briskly, and we both stand up anxious to end this before something even more disturbing happens. We lean awkwardly towards each other and kiss cheeks.

'You must bring Grahame next time,' I say.

Grahame, she says, is too busy to take time off at the moment. It's a matter of saving the business. 'There's a recession out here,' she says. The building trade's in big trouble. They've had to sell the second car. That's why she came down on the train. 'And the price of a Day Return,' she complains. 'I could have flown to Paris for that. Not that I begrudge it,' she adds hurriedly, 'I don't mean that at all.'

What she means is that the experience has come nowhere near justifying the cost of the ticket. If she had found me properly chastened, if my hair had turned white and my eyes were swollen and faded from constant weeping, then British Rail's exorbitant prices might have been worth paying. Poor Bev: I am afraid she is going home a disappointed woman.

I am quite sad when she's gone. I can't settle. I walk up and down, and watch deep indigo shadows slide across the brick wall. My skin feels uneasy.

It gets harder and harder, this writing business. I don't want to do it.

The odd thing is that I started at such a rollicking pace. I just wrote down whatever came into my head and it seemed to be all right. Now I have started thinking about it, and the result is that it has *stopped* being all right. The more I try to catch precisely what I mean in a net of words, the more the meaning slips through a hole and swims away.

But there is nothing else to do. I have read all my books, except *Tess of the d'Urbervilles*, which I had to abandon. A baby died. It was too painful.

Maybe I will write some more later.

I was just trying to remember if I had any visitors at the hospital to which I was taken when they pulled me out of the tree, but of course I can't have done because no one knew I was there.

I was taken first to some kind of casualty department. I sat in a cubicle with blue curtains while a nurse washed the scratches with disinfectant and pulled the twigs out of my hair. I said nothing. I didn't want to admit to anything. I was too tired to explain myself.

The hospital had problems identifying me. They searched my pockets and my bag, but all they could find was a screwed-up piece of paper with a telephone number on it. It was the number Jordi's actor friend had given me. A nurse took it away. She came back from the phone shaking her head.

They put a plastic bracelet round my wrist. It said 'Unknown'. They sat me down in a wheelchair and pushed me along wide passages, into a lift and along more passages until we came to a locked door. The nurse rang an electric bell and a young man in white trousers opened it. He looked like a baker. This is where I stayed, I think for three weeks, under the name 'Unknown'.

\*

Well, to tell you the truth this was a very bad time. I don't want to dwell on it.

Actually, I couldn't, even if I wanted to, because I remember so little. First they drugged me and then they electrocuted me. The fact that I wouldn't tell them my name and had been found in such bizarre circumstances, which they rightly interpreted as a failed suicide attempt, led them to a diagnosis of clinical depression, but what I don't understand is how they define the difference between clinical depression and just plain, ordinary, normal, everyday depression. I thought you were allowed to be depressed if you had good reason to be, which I certainly had. I didn't realize you could get electrocuted for it.

ECT shattered me into fragments like cracked ice on the surface of a pond, and then rearranged me in disturbing ways. My skull sizzled with blue flames. My eyes leapt out of their sockets. Sometimes, when I came to, the inside of my head was as clear as a glass of cold water. Other times I woke in a fug of dark confused mutterings and disconcerting fragments of lost memory. But as time went by, I woke more often in the first state than in the second.

One morning, I re-surfaced. I was so light that I had to keep checking the striped bed cover was firmly tucked in or I might have floated away. I stayed awake for hours. I stayed awake long enough to remember things.

I told the nurse my name. I told her I wanted to leave.

'Yes, dear,' she said. 'That's right. Tomorrow you're going to Quaffingham.'

Quaffingham Hall was a vast, rambling country house somewhere in Berkshire. It was built of a soapy-coloured yellow brick. The walls dripped with scarlet tendrils of Virginia creeper. Until the First World War Quaffingham had been a family home. Up the main staircase and along the landing were sepia-tinted photographs of young people playing tennis and croquet, and graciously entertaining the tenants to tea in the garden. Since then it had been a war hospital (twice), a girls' school (once) and council offices (once). Now it was some sort of psychiatric convalescent home.

When I arrived I had to write down my name and address as if it was a hotel I had come to and not a loony bin. I wrote 'Sandra Bagnall, c/o Astoria Hotel, London.'

'You don't have a permanent address, then?' the receptionist asked, peering at what I had written through her glasses, which she held up like a pair of lorgnettes.

'Not at the moment,' I said, 'no.'

'Well, I'm afraid there seems to have been some sort of error,' she said, running her finger down a piece of paper. 'We don't seem to have you down on the list.'

'Try "Name unknown",' I suggested.

She looked up, and then checked her list again. 'Why are you listed as "Unknown" if your name is Sandra Bagnall?' she asked suspiciously. She searched through several buff-coloured folders and removed a sheet of paper from the one she selected. 'Name unknown,' she read. 'Sex: Female. Age: Twenty to twenty-five.' She looked at me through her glasses to check. 'Height: Five foot ten. Weight: One hundred and forty-two pounds.'

'Yes,' I said. 'That sounds like me.'

She crossed out 'Name unknown' and wrote 'SANDRA BAGNALL' in capital letters on the front of the brown file.

'Good,' she said. 'Well, that clears that up.'

'I'd like to talk to somebody in charge,' I said.

I wanted to make it clear that I would not be stopping. I didn't like the look of the place. It looked to me like one of those private asylums you see on films where the doctors are systematically turning the patients into zombies for some not entirely convincing reason.

'Yes, of course, dear,' said the receptionist. 'Tomorrow. You'll see someone tomorrow morning. I'll put you down for nine o'clock.' She pencilled my name into a large diary.

'I'd like to see someone now,' I insisted.

'I don't think anybody is available at the moment,' she said. 'But if you'd like to wait in the lounge or go for a little stroll, I'll see what I can do for you.'

I chose a stroll.

It was late September. The garden was at the height of blowzy splendour. Huge, damp crimson and purple flowers hung in top-heavy sprays. I wandered between formal beds of standard roses and dying lavender. I walked along heavily perfumed box avenues, through an archway cut in a wall of yew trees and found myself among riotous herbaceous borders. Beyond the yew hedges was a walled herb garden with fruit trees espaliered up the bricks. One hidden space opened out into yet another. I found a square sunken pond with green slime and lily pads floating on top, and a grass path through thick shrubs where every so often I came across a mossy stone nymph in a clearing. I found a sundial. I was out there so long the receptionist assumed I had run away and a search party was sent to find me.

The next morning I had a long and interesting talk with a woman who looked like a games mistress. I didn't tell her about Jenny, I just said that I'd lost someone very close to me. By this time, the idea of staying on at Quaffingham for a couple of weeks didn't seem such a bad one. I had a pleasant room, the food was good and I had nothing better to do. The only problem was that all my clothes were still at the Astoria. The woman said I could send for them. In the meantime, she said, as soon as someone was free I'd be driven into town so I could fix myself up with a few essentials.

'What do I do until then?' I asked her.

'Whatever you like,' she said.

So I spent the rest of the morning wandering aimlessly about, not knowing where to put my arms now there was no small body to carry in them, not knowing what to do with time now there was no one to spend it on. I felt as if some vital organ had been cut out of me, and that although I had been cleverly sewn up again, and although curiously enough I was still alive, the essential part of me was missing.

The grounds were vast. At the back of the house, the cultivated gardens I'd explored the day before dipped down to an ornamental lake. Beyond was thick woodland which curved round the grounds in a rough horseshoe shape. At the front of the house, a long white drive divided two huge swathes of lawn, beyond which sheep grazed in acres of parkland. I walked about pretending that I owned it and that I was immensely rich. I didn't bother to explain to myself *how* I became immensely rich, I just did. Probably I married someone like Aristotle Onassis who conveniently was always away making more money while I stayed at home and spent it.

After an hour or so I realized two things. One was that I was quite enjoying myself. The other – less odd – was that I was hungry. I thought it might be lunchtime so I headed back for the house again and got lost. I took a path through the woods which I calculated would come out on the front lawn. It didn't. It emerged into a field full of flowers with paper hats on and spindly vines clinging to sticks. On the far side of the field were rows of seed-beds and cloches and three large greenhouses. Poking up above some trees in the distance I could see the tops of a cluster of yellow chimneys. I was halfway across the field, heading in the direction of the house, when a man came running out of one of the greenhouses. He was brandishing a hoe at me.

'Eh, you!' he shouted. 'Bugger off.'

His face was brick red. He was wearing army trousers, heavy boots and a vest.

'I'm trying to find my way back to the hall,' I said.

He glared at me. 'You a new member of staff or one of the patients?'

'One of the patients.'

'Well, you don't go this way. This way is private. Back through the woods, turn right, and straight on.'

'Why have those flowers got hats on?' I asked.

'Why d'you think? To protect the blooms.'

They looked like a mass of nodding babies in white woollen bonnets, a whole nurseryful of babies. 'What are they exactly?' I said.

'Chrysanths.'

'And what are the ones growing up sticks called?'

He made a noise halfway between a cough and a snort. 'Look, miss, I've asked you nicely. Now just clear off, will you? I haven't got time to stand here answering questions.'

'Are you the gardener?' I asked.

His tongue made muffled swiping movements under his lips as if he was readjusting his false teeth. '*Head* gardener,' he said. 'Jackson. And this is private land. You're trespassing.'

I don't suppose Quaffingham exists now. Not in the form it did then. It will have been sold off. Now it will be an expensive health farm, or a golf club, or the headquarters of some international drug company. I hope it refuses to conform to whatever it's supposed to be. It did then: it steadfastly refused to let itself be institutionalized. It insisted on retaining its past. I was always expecting to see the young unmarried daughters of the house in their shirt-waisters and long white skirts lobbing balls to each other on the tennis-court, or their mama in cream lace swinging in a hammock reading the latest Henry James.

In reality all I saw were deeply unhappy shadows flitting between rooms. They spoke in whispers and shrank against the walls as if afraid to take up too much space. Their lives had blown out of their grasp, like piles of dead leaves caught by the wind. In the days before such luxuries were cut, Quaffingham was supposed to give them time and space to regather themselves.

There were various treatments on offer but I can't remember whether any of them were prescribed for me. If they were I never took them. Nor was I pressurized into joining any of the various activities that were laid on daily. I could have played badminton or joined the art class. I could have done all sorts of things, but there was nothing I had the talent for, nothing I even had the energy to *want* to do. Nothing seemed worth the trouble.

The next time I met Mr Jackson he was working in one of the herbaceous borders.

'Hello,' I said.

He pretended not to have heard.

'Don't you remember me?' I said. 'By the greenhouses.'

He grunted.

'What are you doing?' I asked him.

He dug his fork into the ground. 'Look, miss,' he said, 'I've got work to do. I can't do it with you standing there jabbering at me. Nothing personal, but I go by the Good Book, Genesis, Chapter 2. I can tolerate women, as long as they don't touch nothing nor open their mouths.'

'Are you always this rude?' I asked him.

A crow flew out of a tree. Mr Jackson looked up. He ignored me. He shielded his eyes and watched the crow flap blackly against the sky, following its flight as if the direction it took was some kind of omen. Then he got on with his forking. I sat down on the spongy grass and rested my chin on my knees. 'I won't get in your way,' I said.

He took no notice. He was digging things out. As he worked he grumbled and muttered darkly to himself. 'Bloody bindweed,' he complained, teasing out long pale roots.

In the yew hedge a bird started to sing, a long, rich, throaty string of liquid sound. I could smell my soapy knees and the bruised sweetness of grass. A memory came back to me of rolling on the cemetery lawns, of the time before, the time I could never get back to. I thought of how I used to run across the graves, and how powerful I was then, how protected by the certainty of my own magic. I closed my eyes, and tried to slide back into the past, to visit it briefly like a foreign traveller on a package tour who observes strange landscapes through a coach window.

When I opened my eyes again, Mr Jackson had taken his wheelbarrow and moved on.

My new acquaintance, Faith, has a theory. She says that if you are in the right frame of mind – though she doesn't explain what that is – then you will always find the right book at the right time.

'What do you mean the right book?' I ask her.

I have just taken back *Tess of the d'Urbervilles*, which she snatches off me and clutches to her flat chest in a pink and flustered fit of embarrassment. 'I'm so sorry about that,' she mumbles. 'I never thought. It wasn't intentional.'

'That's all right,' I say, because I have no idea what she's talking about. 'Don't worry about it. I never actually got round to reading it.'

Now, of course, after this tantalizing display of panic and relief, I am quite curious about the book. What is it she did not want me to read? But she tucks it away firmly under a pile of other returned novels.

The good thing that's happened is that Faith has now asked if I can do a regular stint in the library: mending books, cataloguing them, that kind of thing. The governor has agreed to this, so from now on I shall do two hours every Friday morning. My social diary is beginning to fill up nicely – Mr Rick Thomas on Thursdays, the library on Fridays. Am I up to so much excitement, I wonder.

We try a silly experiment. I close my eyes and Faith pushes me round in circles until in theory I have lost my bearings. Then I stagger off to the nearest shelf and blindly pull out a book. It's supposed to be an entirely random choice. If I am properly receptive, she says – although she doesn't explain what that means either – then I will pick on something which will have a particular significance for me.

The experiment fails dismally. I pick out a German–

English dictionary. Nothing could have less significance.

Obviously, then, I am not properly receptive.

'Try again,' she says.

This time I pick an old copy of *Jane Eyre*. I'm a bit disappointed. I've seen the film.

Faith says I should stick with it: it's a good read, she says.

We suck the chocolate off fingers of KitKat and discuss her treacherous boyfriend, whose name is Jonathan. She met him, she says bitterly, at university. I find I am interested in her life. How strange it is, I say, that we should both, from such different beginnings, land up on this particular Friday morning in the late twentieth century sitting in a prison library eating chocolate bars, one of us serving time for fraud and the other doing life. What a curious collision of time and events, I say.

'It was obviously meant,' she says.

I ask her if she ever imagined anything like this for herself.

She says when she was very small she thought she would be an explorer. Or a ballet-dancer. Later she revised her ambitions along more realistic lines. 'I thought I'd get a degree,' she says, 'and then a job, possibly teaching, and then I'd marry a nice middle-class man and do all the normal sorts of things people usually do. What about you?'

I can hardly tell her that my sole ambition was to shine so brightly I would blind people.

'You're right, though. It *is* odd how things turn out,' she says.

For a moment or two we consider the particular oddness of it, and are both rather impressed by ourselves, by the dangerous characters we have become, so dangerous apparently that we have to be locked up. These ideas make us laugh nervously together.

I wonder if Faith's theory about books might also be applied to people. It might work better with people.

I am ashamed now to think of how I persecuted Mr Jackson. I made his life a misery. Well, there was nothing else to do and no one else to talk to, no one solid. The doctors were all busy, so were the domestic staff, and the patients were far too insubstantial. I craved human company, and Mr Jackson's was all that was available.

Thinking about it now, I am not sure whether it was me in particular he hated so much, or people in general. He certainly had no very high opinion of the species which he rated on a level with blackfly or earwigs: destructive pests.

'But, Mr Jackson,' I said to him, 'I thought the whole point of gardens was that people should enjoy them.'

'People?' he grunted. 'You look at your Bible, miss. Genesis. That's a very true story, that one. Gardens are wasted on people.'

I followed him round all day like a maddening lap-dog yapping at his heels. I asked him countless questions. He seldom answered any of them, but it didn't matter. His silence was enough for me. His silence was solid. He lopped and dug and hoed and did his best to ignore me. Sometimes he muttered to his plants, or cursed a weed. Sometimes he whistled. But most of the time he was as silent and unmovable as stone. His skin was scrubbed raw by wind and sun. Purple veins had burst in his cheeks. He must, I suppose, have been in his fifties, an indeterminate, toughened sort of age. His ears were thickly stuffed with gingery hog bristles. He smelt of bonfires and wet wool. Sometimes I made him so angry his fists clenched and he was forced to spit. He said I was driving him mad. After a few days, a haunted look began to hollow out his eyes. He started licking his lips like a nervous cat. A week of my leech-like attachment, and he put in an official complaint about me, but it did no good.

'Frigging useless,' he muttered. 'They says – can you believe it – they says, well, Jackson, they says, there's nothing we can do about that, is there? Because Quaffingham Hall is run for the benefit of the patients, not the staff.' He made a harrumphing noise of disbelief and speared the earth with his bulb planter.

\*

Two or three nights after I arrived at Quaffingham, I looked up from a plate of cod mornay and saw Joanne sitting at a table on the opposite side of the dining-room with her back to me.

It wasn't Joanne, of course. After the brief, painful lurch of muddled recognition, I was amazed to think I could have been so stupid. Apart from the fact that Joanne was dead and rotted now beyond all recognition, this girl, with her mass of black hair, who sat at a distant table confusingly like a scaled-up image of my eight-year-old sister on her go-kart, was in fact nothing like her. It was the foreign, withdrawn look that confused me, that small head held high on that long neck.

I stopped eating and stared at her. She bent to pick up her bag. When she stood up, she was surprisingly short-legged. I abandoned my cod mornay and ran out of the room in pursuit of her.

'Excuse me,' I said. I caught her on the stairs. Her eyes were dark with panic. 'I'm sorry,' I jabbered. 'It was just that I once had a sister who looked exactly like you. Almost exactly. Or might have done. If she'd lived.'

She shrank back against the curving banister and grasped at her throat as if she couldn't breathe. Afterwards, she told me that she had arrived at Quaffingham only that afternoon, and was convinced she had come to a place full of mad people. My approach had done nothing at all to reassure her.

Her name was Shura Khanamirian. She was part Iranian, part Russian, part Lebanese. She spent her time flitting between America and various European capitals in a cocoon of first-class travel, luxury flats, American Express cards and designer clothes. Personally I couldn't imagine a more congenial lifestyle, but it seemed to have done nothing whatever for her. She was the most deeply unhappy person I have ever met. I don't think her unhappiness was curable either. She talked obsessively about it. It was the one real, the one truly dependable thing in her life.

She said her family was to blame. Her father was unimaginably rich. He was something to do with oil. He lived mainly in New York and changed his wife on average every three years. His present model, wife number five, was twenty-two. Shura's mother whom he had divorced (a) for passing thirty and (b) for not providing him with a son, spent six months of the year drying out at the Betty Ford Clinic or losing weight at some ultra-expensive health hydro. The rest of the year she wandered about Europe spending vast sums on clothes which she then got too fat to wear.

Shura claimed that if she had been a son then her life would have been a sunlit plain of happiness. 'My father has never valued me, never,' she whined when she'd had a couple of whiskies. Apparently, he had sent her away to boarding-school in Switzerland at a pitifully early age and then forgotten all about her. 'He never came to see me,' she wept, moved to tears (as she was nightly) by the pity of her own story.

'The tragedy is, Sandra, that in the end, despite everything, I have nothing,' she wailed.

Nothing except a very rich father and an allowance generous enough to keep several families housed and fed in luxury. I could have wallowed joyfully in what she called 'nothing'. She was the only patient in the whole private wing at Quaffingham. Every night after dinner we went up to her room, which was a small suite with attached sitting-room and shower. She sat curled up in an armchair drinking whisky and elaborated on the subject of her unhappiness while I drank even more of her whisky than she did, rooted through her jewellery box, tried on all her clothes and stalked about the room in whatever I liked best.

After midnight, she became maudlin. She pressed gifts on me: a lipstick she didn't like, an Yves Saint Laurent jacket that she claimed made her look fat. I scooped them up, all her droppings, all her leavings, and laid them out on my bed to gloat over. 'Please,' she said, when I put on a hypocritical show of reluctance, 'no, please, no, I want you to take it. You must indulge me. You are my friend.'

And for a couple of weeks that was the truth: for a week or two we were friends. It was a unique relationship for me. I had never really had a friend before, not a girlfriend, not someone I tried on clothes with. There were friends at school, of course, but I was never involved in one of those intense schoolgirl relationships. Somehow I missed out on that.

'This is so nice, you know,' said Shura. 'I thought everyone here would be mad. I refused to come. I said, no, I will not, I will not go to that place full of crazy people. But they made me. And, you know, Sandra, I am so glad now, because I have found a friend.'

Shura was older than I was. She was twenty-four. Already her mass of dense hair had thin streaks of white in it. Heavy, stained, brownish purple eyelids drooped over her milky eyes, opaque as marbles. Her face was shockingly pale, as if she had rubbed chalk dust into her olive skin.

I never saw her during the day. Like a vampire she slept through the hours of daylight. She was good at sleeping. Her ashy, exhausted face looked as if she could never get enough. This suited me fine. All day I trailed round after Mr Jackson, and after dinner Shura and I spent the evening in her room getting mildly drunk like two teenagers.

Mr Jackson liked bonfires. He liked burning things. He had no mercy. He chopped back diseased wood, hacked out nettles and brambles, ripped up bedding plants, dug out things that were flowering in the wrong place or swamping something else and then burned whatever he couldn't compost. His ruthlessness interested me. I watched him set the match to the screwed-up balls of newspaper, I watched him stare into the flames, his face heavy with satisfaction as he forked piles of discarded and diseased green stuff on to the burning heap. The smoke rose in dense columns from these pyres, sometimes for days on end.

The weather changed. We had two nights of severe frost and then rain: endless, cold, dense rain. The seed pods hung empty and dripping, the late roses rotted, the herbaceous border turned black. Mr Jackson retired to the greenhouses. I followed him.

He panicked. 'You can't come in here,' he said. 'This part is strictly private. You just clear off now, miss, all right?'

The shelves were full of flowerpots with dead plants in them.

'Are you going to burn those?' I asked.

He snorted. 'What would I want to burn them for? They'll come again next year.' He stood in the entrance to the greenhouse, blocking the way in. 'Now look, miss,' he said, 'I've been very patient with you, I've done my best. I've had nearly three weeks now of you pestering me with all them daft questions of yours, and I've just about had a bellyful of it. So I'm asking you very politely now, miss, bugger off.'

'I don't know where to go,' I said.

'Anywhere,' he said. 'Anywhere except here.'

I stood there, uncertainly. The rain dripped off my hair and ran into my eyes. 'Couldn't I just sit and watch you?' I asked.

Mr Jackson tore off his woollen hat in a gesture of furious despair and threw it down on the floor. 'All right, then,' he shouted. Foaming spittle gathered at the corners of his mouth. 'All right,' he spat, 'I want this finished and done with. You just tell me what it is you want from me, miss, and I'll do it.'

'I don't want anything,' I said. 'Just to sit and watch.'

This was not entirely true. I wanted more than that. I wanted his silence, and the comfort of his indifference. No, that's not right either. God knows what I wanted.

Poor wretched man. He was tugging distractedly at his hair. 'All right then, miss, if that's how you want it.' He pulled me into the greenhouse, under the swimming sheets of glass. His dusty ginger hair stood up in demented tufts. He looked at me with fearful loathing. 'I tell you what, miss,' he said, 'I tell you what – there's something very wrong with you.'

'No there isn't,' I protested.

But there was. I see that now. I was shot through with wrongness.

'Then what did they send you here for? Tell me that, eh? Got to be some kind of loony before they send you here.'

'No you don't,' I said. 'People come here for all sorts of reasons. I came because someone died.' And as I said it, something swelled up inside me, something soft and airy – a lightness. 'Someone died,' I said again, testing the quality of this lightness, probing to see how much the phrase hurt me.

Mr Jackson snorted. 'Is that all?' he said. 'People die all the time.'

And the lightness was still there, like a warm soufflé, like a soft breeze. It filled the empty spaces. It was nothing substantial, nothing I could define, but it *was* something.

The next morning I woke early, still with this strange puff of lightness under my ribs. Mist lay in thick white drifts across the park, dense as snow. The sky, grey as a Whistler river-scape, was streaked with gold. I wandered out and waded knee deep in dampness across the lawns. Ahead of me the mist swirled and flurried. How silent it was – just the soft rasping brush of wet grass against my legs – a hushed, breathless silence as if for a moment everything was stunned by the contemplation of its own pallid beauty. And it occurred to me, as I passed between the yew hedges threaded with intricate spiders' webs, that this was where I would finally leave Jenny, here in the gardens at Quaffingham. Her small bones, hardly bigger than a cat's skeleton, lay in their wooden box in the shadow of the jam factory, but the memory of her would live here. When I think of her now – and I am seldom not thinking of her in some way – it is always running along the grass paths under the yew arches, climbing the trees, jumping over the railings, eating peaches, while Mr Jackson works stolidly on in silence, and the seasons come and go, and things bud and flower and fruit and die and rest and bud again.

On the last Saturday of the month there was a dance for the patients and the staff.

Shura treated this institutionalized get-together as if it were a glittering social occasion. She wore a Balenciaga, a stiff strapless cream number with a skirt like a tulip. I wore the discarded jacket she'd given me over one of her black skirts. She also lent me some jewellery.

'Choose something,' she said, pushing her jewellery case across. 'Anything you like.'

I chose a pair of earrings: long green drops cut into facets.

'They're nice, aren't they?' she said. 'Emeralds.'

'*Real* emeralds?'

'Yes, of course real. You think I would wear glass?'

With a tight, bitter laugh she told me that her father had completely forgotten her eighteenth birthday. When his memory was jogged, he had sent instructions via his secretary that she was to buy herself a little something in Tiffany's on his account. In revenge she had chosen a ruinously expensive emerald and diamond choker set. The earrings were a part of it.

Downstairs the dining-room had been decorated with garlands of dusty, crushed paper flowers. There was a local three-piece band playing ballroom music. Shura and I sat on chairs by the wall and watched patients shuffling round doing the veleta.

'What *is* this?' asked Shura fastidiously. 'What kind of dancing is it they do here?'

Dr Willis, the head doctor at Quaffingham, was performing his duty by partnering all the female patients at least once. By the time he got to me it was the Gay Gordons.

'You look much better,' he said, as he twirled me under his arm.

'Did I look ill, then?' I asked.

'No, not ill,' he said, galloping away with me. 'Wrong word. Sorry.'

'So what *did* I look like?'

He shrugged and laughed and said, 'Oh, you know, the way people do when they come here' – which was no help at all.

After that I did a clumsy jive with one of the ladies from the kitchen who had taken a fancy to me because I was always after food. But my heart wasn't in it. There was no one interesting there. I was bored. I felt a need for something unforgiving and unmovable, for hogs'-bristle hair and a stiff collar. 'Where's Mr Jackson?' I asked, scanning the room.

A student called Brian, a thin boy who'd had a nervous breakdown just before his finals in June, came shambling over to us. He wore wire glasses which he'd mended with sticking plaster. His one passion (apart from staring at me fixedly during meals with his fork halfway to his dangling mouth) was political theory. He asked me if I wanted to dance. I stood up, but the band started to play a foxtrot which neither of us knew how to do. We walked about for a bit, roughly in time to the rhythm, bumping knees and apologizing a lot, while he lectured me on the genius of Adam Smith. When he paused for breath, I said, 'You really ought to be telling this to Shura, not me. She's the one who's keen on politics.'

He blinked at me. His damp lips puckered. 'She'll be fascinated,' I assured him.

Shura took our arrival as a signal to start up yet another in-depth investigation of her own unhappiness, so I left them to it. Adam Smith versus Shura's despair. Neither of them seemed either to notice or care that the other wasn't listening.

Outside, the darkness was thick and wet. Drizzle blew

into my face. It clung to my hair. I cut across parkland and climbed over the railings on to the lane. Mr Jackson's cottage was a couple of hundred yards up a dirt track leading to a farm. There was a light on in the front room. I knocked at the door.

I could hear him grumbling as he pulled back the bolts.

When he saw who it was, he flinched. 'I ain't got nothing to say to you, miss,' he said, eyeing me warily round the door. 'Go back. Go away.'

'I just came to ask if you were coming up to the hall for the dance,' I said.

'I don't have nothing to do with dancing,' he said. He was wearing bald brown cord trousers and slippers with holes in. 'This is past a joke now, miss,' he said. 'This is my privacy, this is. You've gone too far this time.'

Beyond him I could see a tantalizing glimpse of his living-room. Firelight flickered on the walls.

'It's wet out here,' I hinted. Two guns were leaning against the wall just behind him. I could see the corner of a dresser. I was very curious about his house, and what kind of things he had in there. I wanted to sit with him for a bit in front of an ashy fire and drink tea and look at his furniture and smell the earthy mustiness of stone flags and old rag mats.

His weather-sore face swelled with horror. 'I can't ask you in here without a chaperone, miss,' he said.

I saw then – how could I have failed to see it before? – that he had misinterpreted everything. He thought I was after him. He thought I was a predatory female trying to trap him into some compromising liaison. This was such a ridiculous, such a sad, naked, embarrassing misreading of my intentions that a hot wash of shame flooded my face. Shame or rage. The two are often indistinguishable. What arrogance. Who did the man think he was? I considered a number of ways to punish him for his presumption. What fun it would be, I thought, to grasp his cheeks and kiss him hard on his thin, dry lips. That would teach him. How revolted he would be, how afraid. How he would hawk and spit, and smear the back of his hand repeatedly across his mouth to wipe the filth away.

'Do you kill things, Mr Jackson?' I asked him. 'What do you kill?'

'Rabbits,' he said. 'I shoot rabbits. Vermin. Magpies and stuff.'

'Do you believe in God?' I asked him. Goodness knows where that came from. It was the last thing I expected to say. I was expecting to ask some further question about his guns.

He wasn't half as surprised by the God question as I was. 'I just get on with my work, miss,' he said, as if that was any kind of answer.

I tried delaying tactics. 'Would you like to make me a cup of tea?' I asked him.

'No, miss,' he said. 'I wouldn't.'

It was cold and wet on his doorstep and I could see I was wasting my time: there was no way he was ever going to ask me in. 'I'd better be off, then,' I said. I offered him my hand. I watched him wonder whether this was yet another of my tricks. Then he wiped his palm down the front of his trouser leg and we shook hands briefly and limply.

As I walked down his path I heard the frantic rattle and shove of bolts.

When Dysart was trying to explain various philosophies behind movements in twentieth-century European art, he talked a lot about existentialism. He recommended books by Sartre and Camus and people like that to read. He lectured me on the mental and spiritual crises of post First World War Europe. How terrifying it had been, he explained, for that generation of young writers and artists to perceive themselves as utterly alone in a godless and therefore meaningless universe.

Well, frankly I didn't need to read Sartre or Camus to know these things. I got there all by myself. By the time I left Quaffingham, I was – not that I could have put a name to it – a committed existentialist. I discovered this in the months after Jenny's death. I discovered it in Mr Jackson's long silences. And I didn't find the prospect of godlessness terrifying at all. I found it a relief. It was wonderfully liberating. For the first time since I killed my sister, I began to feel safe. Dust and ashes, a little water, a few chemicals, some warmth from the continuing aftermath of an explosion: that's all anything is. Things live, they pass briefly through the vast silence, and then they die. How comforting this was. How much kinder it made me feel.

At the end of the track that led to Mr Jackson's cottage I was blinded by sudden radiance, by a hard, white, violent light, a light that hurt, a light that violated the darkness.

Out of the light and the roaring chug of an idling engine, came a voice. 'Excuse me, love,' it said, 'is this the road to Kingsley Abbot?'

I said yes it was, although I'd never heard of Kingsley Abbot. I shaded my eyes against the fearful glare. The lorry driver shoved a map through his open window at me. 'Where am I exactly?' he said. 'I thought this was a short cut through to the motorway.'

'Where are you going?' I asked him.

'Nottingham,' he said.

Since the chance had so fortuitously offered itself, I thought: Why not? It made more sense to move on to Nottingham than to go back to a dreary dance and Shura's litany of betrayal at the hall. I was finished now with Quaffingham. So I climbed up into the cab beside this driver whose name I have forgotten. He wore a red baseball hat perched on his balding head. His shirt was stretched tightly across bulging rolls of fat. He was a kind man. He bought me a pot of tea and a doughnut at a service station, and required nothing in return. We drove through thick, looming, isolating darkness and listened to his tapes. He was an early sixties freak: Chuck Berry, Jerry Lee Lewis, the Everly Brothers – another of these people who are far too interested in their own obsessions to ask questions. He dropped me off somewhere near the centre of Nottingham. 'This'll do fine,' I said. 'I have friends near here.'

So there I was, alone in a wet, unknown city at half-past eleven at night. I had no coat, no money, no plans. Impulses, I remember thinking as I stared down at the lights reflected in an oily puddle, are always a mistake. In my case they are invariably destructive.

Further along the street, on a corner, was a pub which looked as if it was still open. It was called something like the Dog and Whistle. Lights glowed in the downstairs windows. I thought at least there would be a ladies' room where I could sit for a while and get warm. Flapping damply above the door of the pub was a strip of sheeting on which was written DOUG AND SHIRLEY – HAPPY ANNIVERSARY. Inside a private party was going on. The place was packed. I slid between hot bodies. Someone was passing back glasses of iron-rich Guinness from the gloom of the bar to the far side of the narrow lounge.

I took one.

No one seemed to think this odd. More glasses passed by overhead on this human chain. 'Excuse me,' I murmured, 'excuse me,' and I bumped my way, the Guinness slurping creamily over the rim of the glass, to a quieter corner of the lounge bar, away from the howls of laughter and the shrieking gossip, where the grannies and the ancient aunties sat in patient boredom, dragged out in their best Crimplene for the occasion, and longing for their beds, or for renewed youth. The air reeled with smoke. We sat in an ashy haze.

'You're looking well,' one of the grannies remarked as I sat down opposite her. She peered at me suspiciously. 'Is your Mabel better now?'

'Much better,' I said.

'That's good.' She nodded and relapsed into distant, dreaming silence.

I drank the Guinness and helped myself from the dish of peanuts on the table. I had, I decided, three options. I could hitch a lift back to the Astoria where my clothes were, I could hitch a lift home and stay there for a bit, or I could do something else altogether. By the time I'd finished the Guinness I'd made the decision.

'Just going to make a phone call,' I muttered to the grannies as I eased myself past their knees.

The phone was in a dimly lit lobby by the toilets. I was used now to the dread as I dialled my Mum's number, to the shifty unease as the phone rang at the other end. The noise from the bar and the constant clanging of the toilet doors would, I hoped, add an authentically foreign ambience.

My Mum cried when she heard my voice.

It occurred to me too late that I had probably woken them.

'Didn't you get my postcards?' I said. Oh, I could do the astonished regret so well now. I was an expert. How cleverly I implied that the postal service was entirely to blame for yet another of my long silences. Impossibly busy, I said. Life was frantic, I said.

'So it's going well, is it, the modelling?' she said.

'Who is it?' my Dad yelled down the stairs. I could hear the fear in his voice. No one rang at this hour unless it was a death in the family.

'It's going fine,' I said. 'But the season's finished now. We're having a big end of season party.'

'I can hear,' she said. She yelled up to my Dad: 'It's our Sand ringing from Rome.'

'At this hour?'

'It's a different time over there.'

'We fly home tomorrow,' I said. How easily, with what practised ease the lies came slithering out. So would it be all right, I asked, if I popped home to see them for a week or two?

Her joy was terrible. I closed my eyes and staggered back against the wall as if I'd been hit in the stomach, as if

I were winded. 'I'll see you sometime tomorrow then,' I said with a bright, fixed smile on my face and a loathsome weight under my ribs.

The wall I clumsily staggered back against was soft with layers of coats and jackets hanging four or five deep on a row of hooks. A coat, I thought, would be a useful thing to have. I sorted through them as if I were looking for my own, and chose from near the bottom a navy-blue one which looked as if it might be long enough for me. There was a fiver and some small change in the pocket. Kicked into the shadow under the coats was a squashy blue sports bag which I helped myself to because I would need some luggage and it was the nearest thing to luggage I was likely to find.

A small thin man with a moustache came out of the gents.

'Just looking for my scarf,' I said.

'Are you Lisa?' he asked.

'No,' I said.

'I thought you might be Lisa. In accounts. Shirl talks a lot about you. I'm Doug.'

'*The* Doug?' I asked.

He nodded. I congratulated him on his anniversary.

He slewed towards me. He was very drunk. 'Thirty years,' he said. 'A life sentence. You don't get that for murder. So you must be one of Shirl's other mates, then?'

'Yes,' I said.

'From work? From aerobics? Where from?'

'Aerobics,' I said.

'Beautiful earrings,' he remarked, and added lewdly, 'beautiful ears.'

'Thank you.'

He staggered slightly and fell against me. His breath was hot and beery under my chin. 'Beautiful fucking tits and all. Let's go upstairs, eh, come upstairs, there's a room up there . . .'

'You at it again?' A tiny woman with ginger hair and a

huge, white, powdery décolletage stood in the archway through to the saloon bar. She wore a very tight black dress. Her eyes glittered with hatred.

'He tripped,' I explained.

'Hello, Shirl, love,' Doug said blearily. 'Just telling this lovely young lady you don't even get thirty years for frigging murder.'

'You're getting embarrassing,' she spat. 'Find another joke. A funny one.' Tottering with boozy elegance on three-inch heels she fixed a black, demented eye on me. 'Who are you?'

'Lisa from aerobics,' said Doug.

'You shut up,' she told him.

'I'm Mabel's niece,' I said.

Shirl's face rearranged itself into an expression of respectful concern. 'Mabes's niece? Aah, poor Aunty Mabes, bless her. This is Mabel's niece, Doug. So how is the poor old duck? Any better?'

'Much better.' I had managed to get Douglas more or less perpendicular again. 'But I don't like to leave her on her own for too long, so I'd better get off now.'

'You do that, love,' said Shirl. She kissed me on both cheeks. 'And I hope that dirty bugger wasn't bothering you too much,' she whispered ginnily.

'Not at all,' I said. 'Thanks for a lovely party.'

'Thanks for coming, love. And give our best to Aunty Mabes.'

'I will.' With a small familial wave I disappeared into the crowd round the bar.

I used the five quid for a taxi to the station where I managed to spend the rest of the night in a waiting-room without being moved on. The coat I had helped myself to was in good nick and very warm. I wore it like a blanket. I lay along the torn plastic-covered bench underneath a poster of some castle or other. The sports bag I'd taken had some gym gear in it which I ditched, and also – which I didn't ditch – an envelope with a Marks and Spencer's token in it. Inside the card was written 'To Doug and Shirl. Here's to the next thirty years. Love, Eddie and Madge.' The token was worth fifty quid. In the morning I spent it all on clothes: some jeans and a couple of shirts which seemed more suitable to arrive home in than a Saint Laurent jacket. One lift up the motorway from Nottingham, one lift west, and I was back again where I started from – in Belmont Road.

My Mum and Dad welcomed me home in true prodigal-son style, except that we ate roast chicken and bread sauce instead of fatted calf. They hugged me, they wept, they laughed, they rang round the relations and invited the neighbours in to gawp at me. They accepted with bewildered pride that I had been working abroad for months. Their reproaches were delicate and subtle. My mother's chief complaint was that she hadn't known where to send my twenty-first birthday card, but never mind, I was here now, I'd just have to have it a bit late, that's all. She rooted through a pile of debris in a kitchen drawer and pulled out an envelope. The card was huge. It was padded scarlet satin. Inside were five ten-pound notes.

My sister Beverley took a less generous and more sceptical view. Her piggy snout was knocked thoroughly out of joint.

'So where were you staying then in Rome?' she asked. She stood stolidly at the end of my bed watching me unpack the meagre contents of the sports bag.

'In the suburbs.'

'What suburb? What was this suburb called?'

'You wouldn't know it,' I said.

'No, and neither do you, do you?' she sneered. 'You haven't been to Rome at all. You haven't been near it. All those mean, rotten lies about sending postcards. And what about those, then?' She prodded the bag. 'What's this supposed to be? I thought models earned big money. I thought at least they could afford proper luggage.'

'Well, you thought wrong,' I said.

'And where are all your designer clothes?' she jeered.

'I like to travel light.'

Her lip skewed upwards in disbelief. I could see her slimy gums. 'I don't think you're a model at all,' she said. 'I think you're just one great big lie. I've never seen you in any magazines.'

'No,' I said patiently. 'That's because I don't do anything for English magazines.'

'Prove it,' she challenged. 'Prove you've been working in Italy.'

'OK,' I said. 'What's this then?' I fished out the jacket Shura had given me, and pushed the label into her face. 'Yves Saint Laurent,' I said. I dipped into the pocket and pulled out two long, deep green icicles, like drops of frozen sea water. 'Emeralds,' I said.

That gave her self-righteous certainty a knock.

(Don't, by the way, imagine that I stole Shura's earrings. I didn't. I just never got round to sending them back.)

'I bet they're not real,' she said sulkily.

'They are,' I said. They were too. I had them valued when I got back to London.

'Try them on,' I said.

She held the emeralds up to her ears. Time had not been kind to her. She was nineteen but she'd pass anywhere for thirty-five. Her neck had grown fleshy. It was plumply ringed as if she wore rubber bands round it. Her skin was the colour of diesel oil. She suffered from pores the size of volcanic craters and a bottom so large it was practically deformed.

'Real emeralds?' she said wistfully, turning her head to get the effect in the dressing-table mirror. Her piggy eyes softened. The emeralds flashed against her dull-skinned neck. 'So what's it like living in Rome then?' she asked. 'Is it all that pasta and stuff?'

One day, while I was still at Belmont Road, I decided to surprise Duffy. I caught a bus into town.

The studio wasn't there.

At first I thought I'd made a mistake and forgotten which street his studio was on, but I hadn't. It was now a lingerie shop. The window was full of glass female torsos wearing black brassières and lacy knickers.

'What happened to the photographer down the road?' I asked the woman who ran the sandwich bar.

'Sold up and moved on, love,' she said. She couldn't remember where he'd gone. Abroad somewhere, she thought.

I was disproportionately upset. The idea of seeing Duffy again had really excited me. I'd even chosen a day when I was looking my best in case he remembered that I'd stolen twenty quid and a suitcase from him, neither of which I felt I was yet in a position to pay back. I stood outside the lingerie shop feeling cheated. All I'd wanted was a self-indulgent, self-confirming visit to the past – not a lot to ask – and now the past wasn't there any more.

I couldn't think what else to do instead.

I wandered back to the bus station. A driver was rolling the destination display on a waiting bus. It said 'Sprockley Station via Garsditch'. The frustrated urge to visit the past was now so strong I climbed on board and watched the familiar streets bump past me. I sat on the top deck so I could remember more viscerally that poor, shadowy, raging Sandra Fox who once travelled this route, so that I could check back on exactly where it was I'd come from before I went on any further.

At the stop beyond the Crown I got off and walked along the dual carriageway. This was the pavement I wheeled Keith's pram along. There was the short cut I took through the estate to the light-bulb factory. There was the scrubby grass where chocolate wrappers and crisp packets bloomed. I counted the houses. Numbers 101 and 103 whirly cream stucco, number 105 curiously clad in some kind of plastic-looking pink stone, number 107 (the Foxes') grey, blistered pebble-dash.

It hadn't changed at all. I stood on the opposite side of the road and stared at it. The window frames were painted a pale blue gloss. The garden was concrete. The front step was cracked. New flounced lace curtains hung at the windows.

It seemed a long way to have come just to stand outside a house and breathe in lungfuls of toxic air, so I crossed the road, walked up the concrete path and knocked.

No one came. After a while I rang the bell.

Lorries roared past. Through the bubbly glass of the front door a dark shape slowly trembled into focus.

'Nan'll bring you one in a minute, lovey,' Marilyn said as she swam up the hall. She opened the door. She turned white.

'You're not taking him,' she hissed, as if I were an avenging angel who had swooped down from heaven to snatch Keith's soul away. 'I don't care what you say. We'll fight you through every court in the land if we've got to, but you're not taking him off us.'

She slammed the door shut.

'I haven't come for Keith,' I shouted through the glass. 'I swear I haven't. I just came to say hello.'

After a second or so, she opened the door about six inches. 'I can't ask you in,' she said. 'I'm cleaning.'

I could tell that by the pink nylon overall she was wearing, and the bleak blast of disinfected air.

'New curtains,' I commented.

'Yes,' she said, warily. 'From a catalogue. "Viennese Boudoir blinds". We did the whole house out with Ted's Christmas bonus.'

She opened the door a little wider and leaned against the jamb.

'So how *is* Keith?' I asked.

'Fine.'

'And Billy?'

'He's doing OK. He's working at Ted's place now.'

'Still playing in the band?' I asked.

'Most weekends. He's courting again now. Her name's Brenda.'

'Is she a nice girl?'

'We like her,' said Marilyn pointedly. 'She's from Wigan.'

Over her shoulder I could see the narrow hall where I had once passed either on my way out to test light bulbs, or on my way in to eat liver and onions and watch telly.

A child's voice shouted, 'Nan?'

Marilyn tensed. 'You stay in the kitchen, love,' she called. 'Stay there, Keith. Do as Nan says.'

But either he was too curious or he was just plain disobedient. He came padding up the plastic runner. When he saw a stranger at the door he ran to Marilyn and buried his face in her thigh. She stroked his head, pushing it gently into her skirt.

'He's shy,' she said fondly. 'It's a phase he's going through.'

'Hello, Keith,' I said.

He pulled his head away and stared up at me. I waited for a pang, a wrench of the heart, but I felt nothing.

'He's turned three now,' Marilyn said. 'And he's talking brilliant. He knows the names of all Ted's carpentry tools.'

In a sticky whisper Keith asked, 'Who's that lady, Nan?'

His hair was darker than I remembered, a soft mouse brown with a kink in it, like my Dad's. His eyes were an odd mixture of yellow and grey.

Marilyn said nervously, 'This lady, pet . . .' She broke off. Over Keith's head she mouthed, 'We've never told him. He doesn't know he's got an M-U-M. Shall I say you're his aunty?'

'I'm Sandra,' I said to Keith.

'We *will* tell him, of course,' she mouthed. 'Before he goes to school. But not yet. He's too little.'

Keith had lost interest in these adult secrets. He buried his nose in Marilyn's skirts for a quick comforting draught of warm female leg, and then ran back down the hall into the kitchen.

'He sees your parents still,' she said, as if I had accused her of reneging on some agreement. 'He knows they're his Nan and Grandpa. It's just that we haven't explained about . . . about what happened yet.'

'Tell him whatever you want, Marilyn,' I told her. 'It's up to you.'

Marilyn and smoothed down her nylon overall. Neither of us could think of another topic of conversation. Eventually she said, 'Well, I'd like to invite you in for a cup of tea, Sandra, but I've got to finish the lounge and then get the dinner on.'

I left her standing on the doorstep. She watched me walk away, her arms clutched round her thin, tough body.

The bus stop back into town was next to a row of dying shops. Weeds grew up through the cracks in the pavement. The ground was littered with strange bits of rubble. An abandoned trainer had been kicked into the gutter. It looked as though I had wandered accidentally into a war zone. I stood in the bus shelter outside a launderette taking note of everything, marking the details, the grimy drab of poverty, storing it up, so that whatever happened next, however bad things got, I could remind myself how infinitely much worse they might have been.

When I got home there was a large youth sitting by the television. Bev was perched on the arm of his chair. They were watching the news.

I said hello.

The person leapt to his feet. My mother, alarmed by such exuberant politeness, spilt most of the cup of tea she was about to hand him.

'He does that all the time,' Bev said irritably. She slapped at him to make him sit down again. 'For goodness sake, you don't have to be polite to Sand,' she told him.

'This is Grahame. Bev's young man,' said my Mum, pouring tea from the saucer back into the cup. It was the first I'd heard of Bev having a young man. 'I hope you don't mind your tea a bit on the coolish side, Grahame.'

'Not at all, Mrs Bagnall,' he said.

'I'm Sandra.' I held out my hand. His palm against mine was awash with sweat.

'Bev, love,' said Mum, 'you're going to miss your film if you don't get a move on. Go and get changed.'

Bev was still in her Marks and Spencer's uniform. She was hoping to join their trainee management scheme soon.

'I'll be two minutes,' she said to Grahame. She gave him a look of heavy warning.

Mum went out into the kitchen to freshen up the teapot. I asked Grahame how long he and Bev had been going out together.

'About six months,' he said.

It was difficult to guess what he saw in her. He could have done ten times better. In an oafish way he was quite attractive. He had huge shoulders and a sweet, smooth, stupid face, like a horse.

'Grahame's studying at the tech,' Mum called from the kitchen.

'Building trades,' he explained. 'I'm doing an OND.' He looked at me with a shy smile and then blinked and gazed down at the cup in his hands. 'You're not a bit like I expected,' he mumbled.

'What did you expect?' I asked.

'Well, when Bev said her sister was visiting . . .' He swallowed the rest of the sentence in a frenzy of embarrassment.

'What did Bev tell you about me?' I persisted.

He was bright red. 'Nothing. Nothing at all. She's never said a word about you. She just . . .'

The door flew open. Beverley had taken precisely three minutes, forty seconds to change. She must have thrown her clothes on. It certainly looked like it.

'So shall we go then?' she said. She was itching to get him away from me. 'Come on, leave that.' She whipped his cup away from him. His brown, horsy eyes hung on to me as she pushed him out into the hall.

'He's a nice boy, Grahame,' my Mum said. 'They've been courting since the summer.'

What a strange old-fashioned word: courting. It sounds like the preliminary mating rituals of some sort of African water bird you see on television wildlife programmes.

'So it's serious then?' I said.

'Well, she's determined to have him,' said Mum, who was always far more realistic about Bev than she had ever learned to be about me. 'So I don't suppose the poor lad stands much chance.'

I stayed at number 22 for three weeks. Any longer, and Bev might have put rat poison in my Weetabix.

The night before I left, my Dad came into the kitchen where I was washing up a trayful of cups. He took a wad of tenners out of his pocket and peeled off ten of them. 'There you go, love,' he said. 'For a rainy day. I know it can be a bit of a dodgy business, this modelling lark.' He picked up the tea towel and started wiping a mug, something he never normally did, so I knew there was something else he wanted to say, something too difficult to approach directly without a legitimate job to occupy his hands and eyes. 'Listen, Sand, love,' he said, 'I know you're travelling about a lot, and I realize it can't be easy, but try and stay in touch a bit more regular this time, eh? For your Mum's sake. She breaks her heart over you. You're very special to her, you know. Right from a baby you were special.'

How painful these things are. These ties, these birth ties. I understood that now. I knew what he was saying.

On the train back to London I made a discovery. I was searching for my ticket because I could see the ticket collector lurching along the carriage towards me. In one of the more inaccessible pockets of my purse I found a scrap of folded paper. It had a telephone number on it, a London number. I puzzled over it for a moment and then remembered that it was the number Jordi's actor friend had given me. At Euston I went straight to the phones and dialled it.

A voice said, 'Premier Studios. Sammy Rubin speaking.'

I told this Sammy Rubin that I was a model. I asked if I could come and see him. He wanted to know what kind of experience I'd had, so I told him I'd done a lot of work in Liverpool for a photographer called Alisdair Duff. This was the right thing to say. He was impressed. Apparently he knew about Duffy. He said if I wanted to go round for a chat he'd be in the studio until about six.

I found a reasonably priced hotel near to the British Museum. It was nothing at all like the Astoria. It was discreet and hushed. The flowers on the reception desk were real. There were credit-card stickers on the glass-panelled front doors. My room had a mushroom-coloured carpet which was hardly stained at all, and a shower room en suite. There were white towels hanging on a heated rail and free bottles of shampoo in a little basket.

I took a shower and lay on the bed for a bit watching the television and weighing up whether or not I would go and see Sammy Rubin. It started to rain. I wasn't sure if I could be bothered to go out. The room was warm and I liked lying there watching other people's lives in a second-hand and painless sort of way.

On the other hand I needed a job.

Premier Studios was a terraced house in Battersea. The whole of the lower half of the house had been ripped out and boarded up to block out the light. On the door, which was painted black and looked like a cinema exit, someone had scrawled 'Premier' in yellow chalk. I looked for a bell or some conventional way of making my presence known but there was nothing like that, so I pushed on the door and walked in.

This was how I met Sammy Rubin.

His real name was Michael Hedges. He chose to call himself Sammy Rubin because he was obsessed with New York and wanted to sound like he came from Brooklyn. He could recite vast chunks of Woody Allen films off by heart. His ginger hair was wispy and uncombed. His face twitched with neuroses. He wore sleeveless Fair Isle jumpers and tiny wire-rimmed glasses. His studio was the whole of the bottom floor of the terraced house. He used the lean-to kitchen at the far end as a dressing-room. Upstairs were two bedrooms where he did soft porn work.

He'd already forgotten I was coming. We sat on a battered sofa with our feet up to avoid the fierce draught at floor level, and drank mugs of tea and gossiped. He knew everything about everyone who was famous. We were on our third mug of tea and were savaging a legendary film star when I thought maybe I ought to get to the point.

'OK,' he said. 'Strip off then. Let's see what you can do.'

He turned the electric fire on to full and found me a pair of white stockings with lacy tops and a suspender belt. I posed topless first on a bar stool that kept collapsing, and then in various ridiculous positions both on and over the battered settee. I had a whale of a time. Whale is a good word. It's what I felt like. I seemed to have an enormous surface area of glistening skin. I was monumentally large and damp, and smelled slightly fishy.

Sammy Rubin was very clever at what he did. I suppose his photographs of me were blatantly exploitative. People said they were. But he himself never was. His camera saw me as a provocative, erotic image, but his own eye, his homosexual eye, only ever saw me as Sandra. Most of the time he was making me laugh. The famous shots of me, the one of me in a man's ripped vest, the one – you must know it – the staggeringly vulnerable one where my lips are caught in a glistening pout and my eyes are misty as if about to fill with tears, were miracle pictures taken at the precise moment before I collapsed into gelatinous laughter.

He shot a whole roll of film very fast and then sent me off to the kitchen to put my clothes on. When I got back he had written me out a cheque for fifty pounds.

'What's this for?'

'Payment,' he said. 'To tide you over.' He tore off the corner of his cheque-book and wrote a number on it. 'Ring this guy. His name's Colin Cheeseman. He's straight, he knows the business, and you're going to need someone to handle you, because unless you fuck up badly, Sandra, you're going to make yourself one hell of a lot of money.'

I did too. Acres of money.

Money is like a comfort blanket. It wraps you up and keeps you warm. It insulates you. It gives you a deep, babyish pleasure. I made so much of it because I was the best. Absolutely the best. No one can ever deny that. I bounced pneumatically out of page three of the tabloids. My image filled the top shelves of newsagents. I sold men's jeans with that heart-jerking picture in the ripped vest. I sold cars and ketchup. I was more famous as Kathy Kuriakis than I could ever have been trotting up and down the catwalks of Paris like a pedigree heifer in the auction ring.

Kathy Kuriakis was the name I worked under. Those of you who've been asleep for the last eighteen months will at last be able to put a face to me now. Or at least a body.

Sammy Rubin invented the name. He was good at names. Kathy, he said, had a homely ring to it. Kuriakis added an exotic edge.

I was making so much money I could afford to rent a flat in Holland Park. It had two balconies overlooking some garages. I had it done out by an interior designer. I spent as fast as I earned. I bought clothes and perfume and make-up. The whole of London was getting rich then. No, not the whole of London. I don't suppose for a moment that Mr Haskin or any of the Sinful Children were getting rich. Most of London, most of the country, was getting significantly poorer, but a few lucky people had just discovered that you could make vast sums of money out of nothing at all, and that you could get away with it. I was one of them.

I loved money. I am not ashamed to say so.

'The love of money is the root of all evil.' I remember that from RE lessons at the Sacred Heart. Sister Carmel once spent a whole period on the morality of making money as opposed to the immorality of enjoying it. It was the *love* of money, she said, that was the dangerous and corrupting passion, not the creation of it. The love of money forced people into the paths of evil in order to feed their inflamed appetites.

I said I thought poverty was far more corrupting.

'You've misunderstood my point, Sandra,' Sister Carmel said. 'I am not talking about fifty pence for the gas meter. I am talking about large sums of money, the kind of money that equals power. Let us not forget that money is the fuel on which the whole world runs.'

I remember that I was shocked by this pragmatism. She was not supposed to say that. She was supposed to say that religion was the fuel which turned the engines.

Anyway, I don't think the love of money is necessarily evil. I think it's just good fun. Money poured into my account with the generosity of a summer garden. It grew like vines. I handed out ten-pound notes to people begging in the street. I bought extravagant presents for my friends. In Harrods I once bought a cashmere dressing-gown and a moss-coloured pure wool cardigan which I had wrapped and delivered to Mr Haskin at the Astoria. I wonder if he guessed who they came from. Or if he saw any of the Kathy Kuriakis pictures and recognized them as me? Or if he still keeps my clothes (which I never went back to collect) in case I should one day come for them?

I ordered a hamperful of exotic bulbs which I had dispatched, also anonymously, to Mr Jackson at Quaffingham. I loved doing things like that. I wrote on the note which accompanied the bulbs 'From a Student and an Admirer'.

My first real extravagance was a package holiday to Madeira for my Mum and Dad. I paid off their mortgage. I sent them on luxury cruises. I did what I could in compensation.

It was very hard for them. Changing my name and lightening my hair were no protection. It was hardest for my Dad. He had no idea how to handle it. He was the sort of man who occasionally bought himself a rude magazine, but he was always open about it. He said he liked looking at naked girls. What was wrong with that? Men will be men. Until the pouting, tousle-haired blonde opening up her lace corset to expose her vast, globular, gold-nippled breasts was his own daughter: then it was disgusting. Then it was obscene. It was impossible to make him see how illogical he was being.

He got over it quickly enough, though. Once he learned to take the jokes, once he learned to control his urge to punch every man who ever bought a girlie magazine or a copy of the *Sun*, or who gawped at my posters in the tube, then he grew increasingly proud of my burgeoning celebrity. He hated what I did, but he loved the fame that came with it.

What distressed my Mum was something different. I don't think she was bothered much about men fantasizing over me in toilets. Men will be men was her philosophy as well. I think – though I am not sure – that what distressed her was my huge, unequivocal, adult femaleness. It made her uncomfortable. 'I just don't think they're very nice,' she said, covering the pictures up or pushing them away. I could see they made her fingers shaky and her mouth dry. She didn't want to look at them, not even the most tasteful ones, the ones Sammy Rubin shot in Panama, for example, for a corporate calendar, or that series advertising jeans in which I starred, or the last calendar of all I did with Sammy in which there is really no nudity at all, the one we shot at Bayreuth during the festival.

I was Kathy Kuriakis for nine years. I opened supermarkets in the outer suburbs of London. I became a household name, the punch-line of affectionately smutty jokes, the answer to a Trivial Pursuit question. I was mentioned in sitcoms. I was photographed at premières. I gave my opinion on issues of the day (like what I ate for breakfast and whether I preferred blankets or duvets). I was denounced in the press by furious feminists. Journalists wrote serious columns in an attempt to analyse what the phenomenon of Kathy Kuriakis told us about the state of our society. I became a symbol, an icon, the property of the nation. Photos of me accompanied the lads across the Atlantic to the Falklands. When the whole fiasco was over and the first ships returned home, there was a television interview with some of the marines on the quayside. The reporter asked a bunch of them what it was they'd been fighting for, and one bright spark held up a two-page spread of me and yelled, 'That's what *I* was fucking fighting for, mate.' The reporter's follow-up question was drowned by lewd cheering from the massed troops. This incident made front-page news. The leader columns chewed over the meaning of patriotism. There was a cartoon of me as Britannia in *The Times*. 'Rule Britannia,' the caption said.

I had become a myth.

This morning Faith asks me a question about those days. Our friendship – if that's what you can call so delicate a thing – has progressed this far. We are making small probes to see how far we can go. 'So what does it actually feel like to pose naked?' she asks shyly.

Cold, is probably the answer. Cold and ridiculous.

I say that I have never posed completely naked, which, since I'm answering now on behalf of Kathy Kuriakis, is true. The only naked poses I ever did were for Duffy. Curiously, those are considered Art.

'Actually, it was always a bit of a joke,' I say. And this is true too, although I never thought of the work itself as a joke: I took that very seriously. I am not ashamed of what I did. You may think that because I have whizzed through nine years in a couple of pages that I am less than proud of my incarnation as Kathy Kuriakis. On the contrary, I considered the work to be a kind of sacred trust. I mention it so briefly not because I want to gloss over it, but because there is very little to say. There is never much to say about a time in which one has been happy. The work was enough. I treated it as a vocation. I drank moderately and slept eight hours a night. For the whole of those nine years I remained strictly celibate. It never occurred to me to do otherwise. I belonged to all men. It would have been a betrayal to involve myself exclusively with one. Besides, I had little time for that sort of luxury. My circle was small, and on the whole – Sammy Rubin, for example, and Colin, my manager, who was straight only in a business sense – largely gay. I attracted all kinds of things but seldom love. This may have been because I wasn't looking for it, or possibly because I frightened people off. The fantasy of Kathy Kuriakis was one thing: she had all the lovers she wanted in bathrooms throughout the land, and in the end she was only paper. But the real thing, the flesh and blood and bone, seemed to unnerve them.

'I'd be useless at anything like that,' Faith says philosophically. She pokes at her hips. 'I'm totally the wrong shape.'

Poor girl, I feel sorry for her – to be so aesthetically out of balance with herself, so firmly earthed by those massive thighs.

'But did you never feel exploited?' she asks.

I am tired of this question because I have never yet found a satisfactory answer to it. 'Not really,' I say. And to be honest those Kathy Kuriakis pictures were pretty harmless. Most of them were only ever used to wrap chips or to wipe up the cat sick from the floor.

Faith changes the subject. How am I getting on with *Jane Eyre*, she asks.

The experiment in random picking – which, of course, isn't random at all since the chosen book is supposed to be personally significant – has failed. When I left the library last week, the book I took with me, the one I thought was *Jane Eyre*, turned out to be *Great Expectations*.

'No, that's all right,' says Faith happily. 'That's good. Obviously you were meant to pick up the wrong book when you left. That's the one you're *supposed* to be reading.'

'"*Supposed*"?' I say. 'By whom? Who is this intelligence deciding what I need to read?'

'You,' says Faith. 'Obviously. It's your intelligence.'

I am afraid that not only does she have thick thighs, she is also more than a bit dotty. She probably believes in astrology and aromatherapy and diagnosing diseases from the soles of your feet. On the other hand today she has Mars Bars in her tin so I am prepared to overlook almost anything.

'All right, then, how are you getting on with *Great Expectations*?' she asks.

Mr Rick Thomas has started work again this morning after two weeks' leave, but his mind is somewhere else. He keeps looking round the office as if he can't remember what it is he does here. He shuffles through files pretending that they mean something to him. It must be alarming for him. If he can't rapidly rediscover the significance and the urgency of his work, then perhaps it isn't as significant and urgent as he thought it was. Perhaps it isn't significant or urgent at all.

He has also completely forgotten what we covered in our last session.

'So,' he says, 'where were we?'

Skilfully I manage to collide my two London arrivals.

'I was telling you about coming to London,' I say. 'This hotel.'

'That's right,' he agrees, although I can see that he's completely forgotten.

I pretend that the second arrival in London was the first. I left Duffy, I tell him, I arrived in London, I stayed at this hotel where the Sinful Children of God met. I tell him that an actor I met there gave me Sammy Rubin's telephone number and my career as Kathy Kuriakis was launched. In this way I deftly excise eighteen months out of my life and sew up the wound with invisible thread.

Mr Thomas has some photographs of the new baby. They are going to call it Bruno, poor little tyke. It looks like a newborn hippo wrapped in a shawl. Its face is greyish purple and squashed and whiskery. 'He's a tough little bugger,' Rick says. 'They had him in an incubator for the first three days.'

He tells me that Lesley had a rough time.

'The thing about childbirth,' I say, 'is that there's no language for it.'

'What do you mean?' he says. 'Yes, there is. Of course there is.'

'No, I mean no proper words, no special words, nothing big enough.'

'Like what?' he says. His voice is slightly huffy as if I've personally offended him. 'What kind of words do you want?'

'Well, I can't tell you what kind, can I?' I say logically. 'Because there aren't any. That's my whole point.'

He gives up on this conversation. It makes no sense to him. He passes me the next photo in the pile. 'That's Les with all three kids,' he explains.

'They look sweet,' I lie. I give up trying to discuss the shortcomings of language with him.

When they release me, I shall probably be in my fifties, so there is no chance that I shall ever have another child; but oddly enough these photos do not disturb me at all, I look at them with dispassionate interest.

Well, not all that much interest actually.

I was just thinking about my flat in Holland Park. I haven't thought about these things for so long. How rapidly I was catapulted into fame. One minute I was cleaning the Astoria, the next I was rich, the next I was the face – and body – of the eighties.

Settees. That's what I remember about that flat. I had two of them. They faced each other. Two white leather settees. Dysart blenched when he saw them. Between them was a low, rectangular glass table with chrome legs. I arranged various interesting jars and pots on it which I filled with bits and pieces – stones and feathers and marbles. I tried to make them look like Duffy's pots but they never quite worked.

In the bedroom – the only bedroom in my life that I have ever furnished myself – I had a massive divan with cream silk sheets and the whole of one wall was a wardrobe. And the kitchen. Oh, that kitchen. The fridge! It was almost tall enough to stand in. I filled it with things that were never heard of in Belmont Road. A ripe mango. Greek yoghurt. A bottle of champagne. A plastic tub of falafel. Fresh basil, ripe tomatoes, crunchy lettuce . . .

No, stop it. Don't start thinking about salads.

Why did I start this? How did I get into the kitchen?

I haven't had a proper salad for months. In here, salad is a couple of damp leaves of lettuce, a slice of pale, tasteless tomato and some cubes of beetroot killed by vinegar.

What else was in my fridge? Pesto sauce which Sammy Rubin got me hooked on: I liked eating it out of the jar with my fingers. Some dark chocolate. Butter. Eggs.

Eggs.

I would love an egg now. A boiled egg. A smooth-shelled egg to crack open. A clean, hard white and a golden yolk. A knob of butter inside. Crusty bread smelling of yeast. Black pepper. Salt. A cup of tea.

Anyway.

That was a mistake. I should know better. I do not have an egg. I do not have a fridge full of delicious things. I do not have cream silk sheets or a glass table. I must be very clear about all the things I do not have. And I must regret none of them. Regret is such an insidious enemy. It eats away at things. It is like death-watch beetle gnawing at a roof beam till the centre of it is dust.

Go on to something else.

It's getting hotter. The sun hits my wall all afternoon. Yesterday the temperature was in the high seventies. It is a damp, airless heat. Despite this, despite the fact that it's early June, they have still not turned off the central heating. We steam and bake and broil in here. Women are slowly braised in their own sweat.

\*

'So tell me,' says Rick. He is back on form today. The miracle of childbirth has shrunk back to a normal, everyday sort of size, hardly a miracle at all. This has allowed everything else to resume its proper proportions. He has remembered how vastly important he is and how vital is the work he does. 'Tell me about Kathy Kuriakis,' he says.

He's been wanting to ask me about this for weeks. He composes his face into a bland mask of professionalism, he pretends to be staring vaguely out of the window, but he can't hide the prurient glint in his eye.

'What would you like to know?' I ask.

He shrugs as if the subject is really of no interest to him at all.

'Well, for example,' he says, 'did you never feel exploited?'

That one again.

'Is that really the best you can do?' I ask.

He flinches. He covers his surprise with a series of intense facial twitches. His beard jerks up and down as if he's chewing on something. 'Interesting,' he mulls, 'that you leap straight to the attack when I ask you that.'

Oh, piss off, Mr Manly Macho Tedious Rick Thomas.

If I had any sense I would shut up now. I would let him witter on with all his nonsense and remain aloofly inscrutable. But I am too keen to set the record straight.

'I'm not leaping to the attack,' I say. 'I just happen to think that's a very boring question.'

He glances at me with those dreadful knowing eyes. He nods gravely. Now what have I done?

I should know better. What I've done is to confirm his assumptions. In his book, denial is proof he's on the right track: denial is confirmation. There's no way I can win. You never can with people like him.

'All right,' he says, 'let's put it another way. Did it never occur to you that you were perpetrating the image of woman as sex object?'

The man must go to bed with sociology magazines. 'Look,' I say, 'don't blame me for whatever perverted ideas your sex have got about women. That's their fault, not mine.'

I can think of plenty of things that exploit and demean women far more than anything I ever did. I could make a long list. Unequal pay for one. Man-made religions for another. I might even include psychiatrists.

'Don't talk to me about images,' I snap.

I have just read the beginning of that book I picked up by mistake – *Great Expectations*. It's quite interesting. I think I saw the film once but this is a lot better. I like Pip Pirrip. I recognize him. I also recognize his sister, the one who sweeps Joe Gargery out of her kitchen. She's got a lot in common with Marilyn Fox. It's amazingly true, that part. It made me laugh. I'm not so sure about Miss Havisham and Estella, though. I enjoy those bits, but they seem more like a dream than anything real.

I've just got to the bit where Pip learns about his expectations and has gone up to London.

So nine years passed. I turned thirty. Younger and more beautiful girls broke into the business every year. Their skin was fresher, their flesh was firmer, their expressions of sweet, salacious, schoolgirlish idiocy got them plenty of work. Few of them made any real mark, but they were there and they got bookings. I, on the other hand, was used a little less often every year. Colin, my manager, started looking for ways to cash in my celebrity while it was still marketable. One week he was considering a range of Kathy Kuriakis lingerie, the next he was negotiating for me to write a column in one of the tabloids. He took more and more of my money away from me and invested it in bits of paper like pension funds and unit trusts. He was always talking business. His voice grew more and more urgent. He wanted decisions from me all the time. When the bubble burst, he said, I would need a solid safety net of investments, I would need capital. He was in negotiations for me to front a fitness video, make a record, start my own agency, star in a series of tomato-sauce adverts.

I didn't much want to do any of these things. I was happy just being a symbol.

'Oh, stop panicking, Colin,' I told him. 'I'll be all right. Something'll turn up.'

Something did.

I can replay that moment, that entirely insignificant moment, as if it is still happening, as if it is a continuous loop in time. The details are still so clear to me. Colin is sitting on one of the white leather settees. He is wearing his grey suit, the one with the thin chalky stripe in it. I see his mouse-fine hair as he bends over a letter he is reading. He is going through my post for me. His wrists are disturbingly thin and delicate, like a young girl's wrists are supposed to be, although mine never were. His shirt cuffs gape. I can see him pick up another envelope, square and cream. He inserts a long, white finger under the flap and rips it open. Now he takes out a card. He looks up. He has one of those little boys' faces that are slowly drying up and going hard.

'Well, well, well,' he says. He is intrigued and impressed. 'So when did you meet Dysart Stevens?'

Such moments should come garlanded with banners, lights should flash, trumpets should sound. We should be warned that they are by no means as insignificant as they appear.

'Who?' I say. The name means nothing to me, although it clearly means something to Colin.

He waves the card at me. 'He's invited you to a party.' There is – or did I imagine it – a whiff of envy in the air. More – an implicit accusation. He suspects I have deceived him. I am suddenly not what he thinks.

'Never heard of him. Who is this Dysart Stevens?' I say.

'Well, he's obviously heard of you,' Colin says. 'So is this a pose, or are you telling me you genuinely don't know who Dysart Stevens is?'

I genuinely didn't.

I stuck the card on the mantelpiece along with the other invitations to open this supermarket or lend my presence to that charity bazaar.

And so the insignificant moment passed and we moved on to other things, and as usual I missed all the signs. Only in retrospect do I discover it preserved perfect and whole in my memory, and so heavy with import that I am amazed I failed at the time to recognize it for what it was.

I had to be careful of invitations from people I didn't know. Once I was invited to a party by someone called the Hon. Christopher Whittenshaw. I arrived to find that the only guests were a group of overfed young men, sleek as otters on a river bank. They flopped carelessly round the room with champagne cocktails in their hands, sniggering and making schoolboy jokes. I saw at once that I was to be the entertainment. These rich, stupid, over-stuffed young men were surprised when I walked straight out again. The Hon. Christopher himself could not understand it. 'Just a bit of fun,' he blustered.

So almost invariably I turned down invitations from men I didn't know. But this one – what strange bubblings from the bottomless well of my vanity prompted me to accept *this* invitation? I wore a black dress. Black is always safe.

The house was in one of those squares I looked for the first time I came to London. It was built from great white shiny slabs. There were steps up to the door and a portico. Through the engraved-glass upper panels of the double door I could see crystals dripping light.

The door was opened by a florid young man in a suit. He took my coat and led me into a room big enough to hold a dance in. The floor was polished wood like Duffy's but with a nacreous inlay round the edge. There were two marble fireplaces and four chandeliers. The walls were covered in paintings. Far too many. They looked cluttered to me.

The young man said, 'Mr Stevens will join you in a moment. Will you have a drink while you wait?'

This was distinctly fishy. 'Where are the other guests?' I asked.

'Arriving shortly,' he said.

I asked for a red wine. I always like to make the taxi fare worth while.

The young man brought me a glass of wine and then disappeared through a door in the panelling.

I sat there alone on a kind of settee. It was upholstered in watery blue silk. I sipped my drink and looked round at the pictures.

Dysart Stevens let himself into the room so quietly I had no idea he was there.

'Miss Kuriakis?' he said.

I jumped. The remains of the red wine leapt out of my glass and fell like a spray of fresh blood on to the pale silk.

'Oh, shit,' I said.

I started dabbing at the stains with a tissue which I fished out of my cleavage.

'Leave it,' he said. 'Bradley will deal with it.'

I assumed Bradley was the florid young man in a suit.

He took my glass and refilled it. He pulled up a velvet armchair for me. 'You'll find this more comfortable,' he said.

I apologized for ruining his settee. He winced slightly, but he hid it well. 'It's an ottoman,' he said. 'French. Second Empire.'

'Well, I'm sorry for ruining your ottoman, then,' I said. 'You must send me the bill. I'll pay to have it recovered.'

'It's French watered silk,' he said. 'Over a hundred years old and irreplaceable. No, don't worry. I'll get an expert in to deal with it in the morning.'

'Well, send me *his* bill,' I insisted.

He was drinking something colourless. It was probably water. He sat down opposite me.

'So tell me, Miss Kuriakis,' he said, 'where does the name come from? Is it Greek?'

'I don't know,' I said. 'It's not real. A friend of mine made it up.'

He focused the full force of his attention on me. It was like the switching on of the lamp in an interrogation room. It blocked out everything else.

'I really ought to be going now,' I said in a foolish panic, trapped there like a scorched moth.

'You can't leave yet,' he said. 'I invited you to a party.'

'Yes,' I said, 'but what as?'

'As what,' he murmured.

'And where is it, this party?'

'Upstairs.'

'So what am I doing down here then?'

'I asked Bradley to bring you in here. I wanted the chance to have a proper chat with you first.'

'Just tell me straight,' I said. 'Am I supposed to be the entertainment or what?'

'Do you often entertain at parties?' he asked politely.

'No, I don't. I don't strip. I don't jump out of cakes. And I'm not available for any kind of party games whatsoever.'

I watched his eyes widen with shock. 'You think I asked you here to provide my guests with that kind of entertainment?' he asked.

'Didn't you?'

'No, I did not. I would never dream of it. What an offensive idea.'

I stood up. I felt cheap and in bad taste. My skirt was too short. Dysart shook his head. He wiped a hand across his face in tired disbelief at yet further evidence of the bestial nature of human beings. 'I asked you to my house, Miss Kuriakis, because I wanted to meet you,' he said. 'Nothing more.'

The problem with writing about Dysart is that I can't see his face any more. It has gone. I try to reconstruct him feature by feature but he eludes me every time. This was true even when I lived with him. I could never get a clear or an accurate memory of his physical presence, so that every time I saw him again in the flesh the reality surprised me. I can list his features for you one by one, I can list all his qualities, but I doubt if I can make any of it add up.

His features first: the overall impression is elegantly distinguished, even a little frightening. He was both icily reserved and yet charmingly warm at the same time. And yet how can that possibly be? Sometimes I thought that the only explanation was that although the core of him was cold, the surface was warm. Sometimes I thought no, no, you have got him wrong, it was other way round: his coldness was a kind of protective reserve, a form of shyness.

What else? Details. His hair was silvery grey and thick. His skin was very pale, so pale it was almost green except where shadows of stubble darkened his cheeks and chin. Two sharp lines were etched into the left side of his face as if the memory of some great pain had lodged itself there. He was tall – an inch or so taller than I was, and thin. If you didn't know him, you would imagine that he was broad shouldered and wide chested, but that was an illusion created by expensive tailoring.

He was fifty-four when I met him. I had just turned thirty.

'Sit down, Miss Kuriakis,' he said. 'Please.'

His voice – I haven't mentioned his voice yet, have I? That too was contradictory: sometimes as warm and as smooth as well-cradled brandy, sometimes as authoritative as a knife blade. I loved his voice.

I sat.

I behaved as if I had been hypnotized.

'Actually,' I said – under such concentrated attention truths slipped out of me – 'my real name is Sandra. Sandra Bagnall.'

'Then we have something in common.' He leaned forward. 'My real name is Howard. Howard Stevens. Dysart is my mother's maiden name. So now you know something about me which I've successfully managed to keep hidden for the last forty years.'

'I could blackmail you,' I said stupidly. It was meant as a joke.

'Please do,' he said. 'It would be a pleasure to be blackmailed by someone as beautiful as you. Do you mind my saying that?'

I shook my head. I have never minded people saying I am beautiful. I expect it. I become anxious and confused if they don't.

'Your eyes are quite extraordinary,' he said. 'Even those appalling photographs can't cheapen those eyes. They look straight at the lens entirely without guilt. Guiltless and I think fearless. From which I conclude, Miss Kuriakis – I beg your pardon, Miss Bagnall – that either you've reached a philosophical position which allows you to live at peace with the world, or that you're so immensely stupid, you have no idea what either fear or guilt mean.'

'Well, in that case,' I said clumsily, 'I must be immensely stupid.'

He shook his head. 'Ah, but you see, I don't believe that. I was prepared to believe it was a possibility before I met you, but not now. Not now.'

He stood up. 'Shall we join the party?' he said.

One of the good things you can say about my present situation is that I won't have to go to another party for a good fifteen years. Parties have never amused me, not the sort where you stand around with a drink in your hand and talk to boring people about nothing of any interest to anyone except possibly another boring person. At this party they were all yattering on about something called 'the Biennale' and discussing people I had never heard of: conceptualists and post-modernists and various other kinds of '-ists'. I left after about half an hour. I gave my address to the florid young man called Bradley so that Mr Stevens could send me the bill for cleaning his ottoman. In the taxi on the way home it occurred to me that I needn't have bothered because he already knew my address, otherwise how could he have sent me an invitation?

He rang the next day. He made arrangements to take me out to dinner.

I shall regret this, but I can't help it.

I am now going to write down exactly what I ate the first time Dysart took me out.

Food is an obsession now. My day is measured out by meals. The whole of my session this morning with Mr Rick Thomas was spent talking about it.

Food is another of his specialities. It is like guilt. He claims they are closely related. Food, he says, is our first experience of the world. We learn to understand our environment initially through taste. As babies, he says, our mouths are our chief interpreters. (He's obviously been studying the habits of his youngest sprog.) We suck the nipple or the teat, we suck our own flesh, our mouth is the channel through which we receive all our initial sensory impressions. From day one, he says, food is the prime factor in our relationship with our mother. He goes on for ages about it: food and control, food and despair, food and punishment, food and sex.

Fuck all that. I just want the food.

The meal with Dysart, then. First of all we had fresh asparagus, lightly steamed, with a lemony hollandaise sauce.

Oh, the soft, buttery taste of asparagus. Already saliva is shooting into my mouth. It gathers on my tongue. How do you describe the texture of asparagus, the crumbling tips, the exquisite sliminess, the juicy fibrous bit at the end dragging through the teeth . . .?

What next?

Tiny pieces of plaice rolled round a soft centre of salmon mousse, so delicate, so delicious, it was as subtle as a poem. (Dysart said that, of course, not me. I hardly knew any poems, and the ones I did know weren't a patch on the rolled plaice.)

I think we had a Sancerre with the asparagus and the fish.

For the main course we had slices of pink lamb roasted with garlic and rosemary and served with a dish of *pommes dauphinoises* and sweet green peas. And a bottle of Médoc.

After that I was so full I couldn't eat a sweet.

'Dessert,' Dysart corrected. 'Or pudding.'

He ordered strawberries. They came served on a leaf. We shared them, eating them in our fingers and dipping them in the sugar bowl.

Then there was coffee and . . .

I shall have to stop now. I'm going to have to lie down, and go through the whole meal again slowly. I shall fall asleep with the smells of roasting lamb and rosemary in my nostrils. And the thought of a piece of thin dark chocolate yet to come.

We have a date for the appeal. My solicitor, the unhealthily clean Mr Roebuck, came to see me again today. The hearing is fixed for early in the new year. He is in a low-key mood. His eyes droop. He mumbles into his papers. He says I am not to get my hopes up.

I have no hopes, none at all, so that's all right.

'If there had only been just one or two mitigating circumstances,' he says wistfully, 'or some emotional angle we could have played on.'

The poor man is baffled by me. He would like it best if Dysart had beaten me or subjected me to hideous sexual perversions. Then at least he would have something to work on. Then at least he would have understood.

As he shuffles papers and drones on about witnesses, I find I am thinking about that first appearance at the magistrates' court. They drove me there in a car. I was handcuffed to a policewoman. The car turned the corner. A crowd forty or fifty deep had gathered outside the back entrance to the court. The air buzzed with a strange hissing sound, like the noise of escaping gas. It grew louder and stranger. I was baffled by it.

'Keep your head down,' the policewoman said suddenly.

I understood what it was then, this noise. I grasped it from the tone of her voice. It was the release of massed lungfuls of pent-up fury. The crowd sprang forward. They poured over the car. They banged on the roof, they thumped on the windows, their hands slid greasily across the glass. Their faces pressed into the side windows like hideous fish looming up against the glass of an aquarium. Their lips were squashed. They bared their teeth. They shouted things that made their faces distort with hatred.

The policewoman was sitting on a blanket. She dragged it out from under her and covered me with it. She held it down while the car rocked wildly and the driver panicked.

'When I say "Go" make a run for it,' she said. 'Keep the blanket over your face.'

Nothing happened for a moment, and then I felt movement, a brush of air, a soft intimate bump of bodies as she climbed across me. There was a click. 'Go,' she yelled above the roars. There was a sharp pain as the handcuff tugged viciously on my wrist. I fell blindly out of the car.

In the police cell where they took me to wait, I was brought a cup of hot sweet tea but I couldn't drink it. I couldn't keep the cup still against my lips. My teeth rattled as if the rocking of the car had knocked them loose. Tea splattered down my clean shirt in long brown streaks.

The same crowd was there for the first and every subsequent day of the trial. I had upset their vision of an ordered society. I had stirred up the murky sediment at the bottom of their mass consciousness.

'Pretend they don't exist,' the police advised.

But they do exist, these law-abiding citizens who come to savage those who remind them of their own darker natures, of the beast that lurks in the muddy depths of their own souls. They do exist. They come to rejoice in their own probity, to be purified, to spew out all their filth. They come to be collectively and individually purged. They will be there again for the appeal.

Mr Philip Roebuck drones on. I am bored with his legal subtleties.

I interrupt him. 'So what will you do tonight?' I ask. His skin is so smooth it can hardly be real.

'Tonight?' he asks.

I've embarrassed him now. He bares his perfect teeth in a nervous neigh. I am not supposed to trespass into his private life.

'Well, I've got quite a bit of work to do,' he says. 'And then I shall have dinner of course.'

Dinner.

'What will you have for your dinner?' I ask. My voice is thick with greed. I can feel my eyes narrowing, and my lips grow moist.

'I don't know,' he says. 'It depends what my wife has cooked.'

So he's married then. Interesting. I had not considered that.

He's rapidly gathering up his papers. His suit is perfectly pressed. He has presumably worn it all day, out there in this muggy heat, but there are no creases, no sweaty crumpling. Dysart was the same.

'So what's her speciality?' I ask. 'Fish? Chicken?'

Food has become my chief erotic pleasure. I am desperate for him to satisfy me, but he clicks the briefcase shut. He rings to be let out.

'Please,' I beg. 'Please. What does she do best?'

My urgency alarms him. He backs himself against the door. He clutches his briefcase to his chest like a shield.

'Tell me,' I demand. 'Give me the recipe. What do you *hope* she's cooked for you tonight?' I make a strange noise which sounds like a feral grunt. Saliva gushes into my mouth.

'Well,' he says, 'she does a very good thing with veal and Marsala.'

Oh, the words – veal, Marsala. The remembered tastes.

'Is it creamy?' I ask. 'The sauce . . . is it rich? Are there mushrooms in it? Does she fry the veal in butter?'

But I am left to invent the details for myself because the door opens. Someone has come to let him out. He escapes rapidly, looking for a moment almost dishevelled. But perhaps I imagined that bit.

Now he will drive home through the hot streets. The air will be hazy with traffic fumes. He will go back to his smart flat somewhere near Regent's Park perhaps, the sort that still has its Edwardian lift. He will let himself in and straight away, of course, he will take a shower to scrub away the smell of prison and of me. His wife, who is cooking veal escalopes in a Marsala sauce, will bring him a glass of wine. 'Poor darling,' she will say, 'was it dreadfully hot? And did you have to see that fearful woman again today? How was she?'

'She's going mad,' he says. 'She pinned me up against a wall and forced me to talk about food.'

I imagine his wife is Italian. I call her Graziella. She will sit on the settee all evening flipping through *Vogue*, while he works his way through his legal papers. Later they may watch a little television, and later still practise a spot of stylish and hygienic lovemaking.

I, on the other hand, will read some more *Great Expectations*, eat meat-paste sandwiches and drink a mug of tea.

In the late evening light the bricks in the wall opposite have gone mysterious shades of grey and purple. A last splash of setting sun has caught the extreme edges of the brick high up almost out of my sight. Here the colours are peach and rose and silver. The day's heat burns out of the brick. How beautiful it is. How rich. How complex. Nothing has any fixed colour. It is constantly changing. Colour becomes a function of light. Is that what I mean? It's the sort of thing Dysart said all the time, but then he knew what it meant.

\*

I finished *Great Expectations* last night. I read it through to the end as greedily as if it were a dish cooked up by the imaginary Graziella Roebuck. I gorged on it without pausing to chew. Now I'm trying to digest it. It's full of the sort of blinding coincidences that life is also full of.

Faith asked me on Friday how I was getting on with it. I said I thought Pip was brilliant but everyone else was just a caricature.

'That's the trouble with Dickens,' she said.

But I've been thinking about this since, and it seems to me that what Faith complains of as Dickens's trouble, is actually his greatest strength. I think everybody else is *always* a caricature. In real life, I mean. But perhaps that's the trouble with *me*.

I wish I had not finished it. Now I have nothing to read. I prowl around feeling uncomfortable and hungry and not knowing what kind of thing I am hungry for.

A few days after our first dinner, Howard Dysart Stevens rang again.

'Goodness,' said Colin. He rolled his eyes and sucked in his cheeks. 'No offence, Sand, but I would never have had you down as Dysart Stevens's type.'

A chauffeur-driven car was sent for me. This time we ate at Dysart's house, in a smallish high-ceilinged dining-room hung with weird pictures. They looked like the stuff the really depressed patients at Quaffingham did in art therapy: bright, mad daubs with things like goats and sewing-machines and young girls whirling round helplessly.

'Chagall,' he said. 'Do you know his work? And over here,' he took my arm and guided me away, 'this one's a Modigliani – his mistress Beatrice Hastings. The one above it is a Gaudier-Brzeska sketch.'

None of these names meant anything to me. 'Who *is* Chagall?' I asked.

'You don't know Marc Chagall?' He looked pained. He patted his mouth with his serviette. (Napkin. Sorry. He corrects me even from the grave.)

'Well, I meet quite a lot of photographers,' I explained, 'but no artists. Not as such.'

'No, no, no, he's dead,' Dysart said.

'Oh,' I said. 'Oh, I see.'

This Chagall guy was obviously barking mad anyway, so maybe it was a blessing he was dead.

'Well, that proves you guessed right first time,' I said. 'I *am* immensely stupid.'

'Uneducated, possibly,' Dysart said. 'Stupid, no.' He picked up my hand and examined it. 'They would have loved you, you know. Matisse. Seurat. Braque.' He spread my fingers and examined them. 'Big, strong, hands. The shoulders. The neck. They would have loved all that. Those eyes. That skin.'

He dropped my hand and stood up. 'Let me teach you about Chagall,' he said. We walked round the dining-room as if it were a gallery, looking at each of the paintings in turn. His pleasure in them fascinated me. We moved from Chagall to Modigliani.

'Am I boring you?' he asked.

'Not at all,' I said, and truly I was not bored. I liked listening to him. Not to what he said – I hardly grasped any of that, it didn't interest me, something about Post-Impressionism – but to the passion behind it. He spoke of paintings the way my Dad spoke of football, only more so.

I knew about the Post-Impressionists anyway. Well, I knew all about the Impressionists – they were people like Renoir and they painted in blobs with lots of light – so presumably the Post-Impressionists were the ones who came after them.

We stopped in front of a darkish painting. It was a picture of a pewter plate. It didn't look quite real. It wasn't sitting properly on the table. But it gleamed in the semi-dark, with only the light of a fire or perhaps the dying sun on it. Beside it were some brownish apples and a floury loaf of bread. 'Cézanne, of course,' he said. 'You know Cézanne?'

It seemed rude to know none of the painters who were so important to him, so I said yes, of course I knew Cézanne. He talked for a long time about someone called Roger Fry and some exhibition that had happened in 1910 – there was a link apparently between the pewter-plate guy and this Fry person, but I couldn't grasp what it was.

I ought to have asked him some intelligent questions, but I wasn't clever enough to know what an intelligent question sounded like. How dumb, how brutishly unimpressed I must have seemed by this blinding wealth of genius: the Chagalls, the Modiglianis, the Cézanne, the Seurat, the Braques. How disappointed he must have been in my response. I was being shown one of the most envied private collections of early-twentieth-century paintings in the country, arguably in the whole world, and all I could do was stand about, large and crude, like a big-boned, dimly dreaming cart-horse. I was thinking about dessert and whether or not there would be some, because I was still hungry.

We stopped to look at a small Matisse – one of his series of 'Odalisques'. Dysart stood in front of it the way old women kneel at the altar rail, caught in a moment of intense, rapt communion. 'I was recently offered fifty thousand for that,' he said. 'I refused, of course.'

'Fifty thousand?' I said, boorishly. 'Can a piece of canvas and a few daubs of paint be worth so much?'

Dysart took my hideously crass remark with complete seriousness. 'Oh yes,' he said. 'Yes. Because what the buyer is getting is the vision of a genius. A glimpse of another man's soul. A great artist, Miss Bagnall, can take a few very base materials, a few chemicals, and out of these he can produce a work of transcendental genius.'

He decided then that I had seen enough. It was not wise to overdose, he said. One must look only at a few paintings at a time. We moved to a small upstairs sitting-room (Picasso sketches) where coffee was served.

So obviously there was to be no dessert.

Dysart asked me about my childhood. His concentrated curiosity inspired me. I created for him a warm and funny picture of a working-class Catholic childhood in a northern city. It was not that far off the truth. In self-defence I wanted this man to understand that I was from a very different background from his. I wanted him to understand that I was an earth-bound creature, a philistine, a lump of clay, but even so the salt of the earth. I told him about Bev. I made him laugh. I drank two cups of coffee. After a while we ran out of conversation. Eventually he sent for the car to take me home.

'It's been a great pleasure, Miss Bagnall,' he said. He shook my hand. His goodbye was so formal that I assumed whatever curiosity he had felt about me had now been satisfied.

I did not expect to see him again.

Today I had a bath. The bathroom here is strictly functional, like a hospital bathroom. It is all white tiles with stained grouting, and rusty chrome. It's the sort of place where people dab carefully round bandaged wounds they cannot yet bring themselves to look at. There is no proper mirror, just a small sheet of rusty glass above the washbasin. I can't see myself full length.

In the books I used to read, the sort of books I bought at airports, the heroine always looks at herself naked in a full-length mirror at some point during the opening chapters. It's one of the rules of the genre. She notes with smug self-congratulation her firm, flat stomach, her tapering waist, her long legs, her round, high bosom, etc., etc. Her skin gleams with effulgent radiance. Complacently she worries that her neck is a fraction too long, her mouth a little too wide, her nose a little too retroussé.

Mirrors are dangerous things. I look through the trickling condensation into this one, and I do not like what I see. The older you grow the more the images in the mirror multiply. I am at a stage now where I can see too many versions of myself. It's like those transparencies police artists use to compile a likeness of a criminal. These days my eyes can too easily slide the transparencies about. There – still there, if I want to see her – is the young Sandra. But there too, with a slight adjustment of the eye, is the old woman, shadowy but unmistakable, implicit in the softening of the jawline, the downward pull. I have only to shift my focus a fraction and there she is, waiting. How sinister this is: the dead Sandras and the unborn Sandras all there one behind the other in a rusty mirror.

In the bath I notice that the skin above my knees is beginning to wrinkle. I read my own mortality in this. I will die. Here is another sign that I am already well advanced on the journey. The skin on my thighs is turning papery. My stomach is scarred with silvery lines and an incipient blubberiness. Every year – a disturbing thought – every year the day passes, my death day, the day on which I will die.

I soak in the bath and remember my obsession with Joanne's rotting body. At least I saved her this: the contemplation of her own living decay. I can claim that much in my own defence.

Perhaps I should have looked after myself better. I should have rubbed cream into my knees and joined a gym. This is what the new generation of young girls do, the ones who took my place. They pump iron and cycle and jog, they have personal trainers, they are all bone and muscle and sweat. The trouble is I believed for too long that I was immortal. I thought mortality was another of those things from which I was exempt. Really I should have known better.

Mr Rick Thomas is looking tired. He is tired of domesticity, of broken nights and the smell of stale breast milk in the bed. Possibly he is even a little tired of his sensible, Girl Guide wife. I shouldn't be surprised. I think he would like an adventure. I see it in his eyes when he looks at me.

In some lights and in some moods, I am still the stuff of which fantasies are made. Mr Randy Rick can see no signs of mortality in me. In himself perhaps, but not in me. He is too blinded by rogue testosterone to notice the bags under my eyes and the loose rough skin round my elbows.

This morning I come straight to the psychiatric unit from my bath, so I am still a little wet. My face is unusually pink. My hair hangs in damp corkscrews. 'I've just been having a bath,' I explain.

His eyes flicker. His mouth opens. It glistens, a moist red hole in the hairy abundance of his beard. His tongue slides slowly over his bottom lip and rests there, a slab of fat, purple-veined, obscenely noduled flesh. It's like something in a butcher's refuse bucket. He breathes unevenly. He says eventually, 'I thought today, Sandra, it might be useful if we talked a little about punishment.'

Punishment! Goodness me, Mr Thomas, what can you be thinking about? Shall I put on a gymslip for you and lean over your desk while you administer this punishment? Or do you want me in black leather and high heels brandishing my whip?

Punishment, he says earnestly, is part of the complex equation which starts with acknowledging guilt.

I wonder if the hearty Les dresses up for him. Probably not. A plastic cagoule is probably her limit and then only for hiking across the moors.

I ask Faith what I should read next. She says I should try *Jane Eyre* because that's the book I originally picked. I say why can't I read something more modern, but she says I need a firm foundation. It sounds like a corset advert. She says prison is a good place in which to read nineteenth-century novels. I forget now why she thinks this. Partly because the pace of one suits the pace of the other: partly – I think I've got this right – because prison is a useful metaphor for the nineteenth century. Or was it the other way round?

Sometimes I wonder if Faith is quite as clever as I think. Or even as *she* thinks.

Today for lunch I had shepherd's pie. There was a shard of bone in the mince. I thought I had found a bit of decayed tooth. I panicked. More evidence of physical decomposition. I felt round my mouth with my tongue. I stuck a small handbag mirror into my mouth. But everything seems to be all right. Odd the way teeth decay so rapidly in the living mouth and yet remain intact for centuries after death, long after everything else has putrefied. If I have to live on this diet for another fifteen years my teeth will almost certainly rot.

I eat mounds of potato, and gingery steamed puddings, and thick pastry with gluey treacle on it, and wedges of dried up macaroni cheese. My skirts are tight and my face is acquiring that odd, bloated look that so many women here have. When I first came I thought it was brutish stupidity. Now I know it's the food. But I'm growing very fond of this cuisine. I crave it. I have rediscovered a passion for sausages and baked beans. I adore sliced white toast, cold, slightly leathery, spread with margarine. I dream of chips gone soggy with vinegar. How comforting it is, how solid, this reversion to the dishes of my childhood. How securely a stomachful of toad-in-the-hole and mash anchors you to earth. In the afternoons, after these sturdy dinners, I lie on my bed exhausted by my own weight, and doze and dream and chew silently on the cud.

Dysart ate very little. He was an obsessively abstemious man: he believed that overeating wore out the system. The less the body consumed, he said, the less matter there was to fester in the gut, the less weight the skeleton had to carry and consequently the greater the chance of longevity. My greed fascinated him.

After the dinner at his house there was a complete silence. I was surprised to find how disappointed I was.

And yet, of course, not surprised at all by the silence itself. Weeks passed. I got a cameo part in a film, a dismally unfunny comedy in which I had to play a Roman page-three girl. Colin was excited about this: he thought it might be the beginning of a new career, but the film was dreadful and I was stiff and dull in it. All I got out of it was a generous fee and confirmation of what I already knew: that I had no talent at all for acting.

One day a huge bunch of white and yellow roses arrived for me. They were from Dysart Stevens. The note said that he had been in America for the last month or so but was now back in London and would very much like to see me again if I were free. Shortly after this Bradley phoned me and arranged a date.

This time we ate again in the small dining-room, observed by the dizzying Chagalls. Dysart talked about America. He had been on some kind of lecture tour. He spoke of a young painter – a genius, he said – whose work was causing huge interest on both sides of the Atlantic and whom he hoped to commission. He spoke of some marvellous private collection in Philadelphia which he had seen.

I cut myself a small slice of runny cheese and wondered what I was doing there. Such a man, a man of such knowledge and intellect, must surely by now have grasped that most of what he said was lost on me. He certainly hadn't invited me for the brilliance of my mind or the wit of my conversation. But then maybe that was the attraction: maybe he had a secret fetish for women who did not belong in his rarefied and cerebral world. In that case, I assumed that he must have designs on my body, although I had seen no evidence of it. He was, if that was his game, an unusually slow mover. Strangely, the idea of being seduced by Dysart Stevens excited me. I liked the slow pace. I liked the dinners and the flowers and being the focus of his powerful attention. I loved his passion and his knowledge.

That most of all.

I wasn't looking for a man. That was the last thing I wanted. I was perfectly happy with celibacy. But when

Dysart suggested after weeks, after months, of occasional outings and chaste dinners that perhaps we should go upstairs, I never even paused to think. I stood up and followed him blindly, like a curious cow stumbling after a farmer. We climbed the main stairs. At the end of a passage, Dysart opened a door. The room he led me into was the size of a bedroom, but there was no bed in there. It was empty of furniture. Dying summer light from two tall, curtainless sash windows slanted across bare floorboards. Three of its four walls were stark white and blank: on the fourth hung a framed photograph.

There was something strangely smooth and expectant about the room as if we had walked into a Magritte. In fact – I'd forgotten this – there was a cast-iron bedroom fireplace on one wall. Had I known about Magritte at the time I should not have been at all surprised to see a small train emerge from it.

'You recognize it?' Dysart asked. He was talking about the photograph.

I did recognize it. It was 'Woman in the Bath'. There I stand, nineteen years old, in Duffy's claw-footed tub. My stomach is ridged with jagged leaf-shaped shadows. My face is heavy and dull.

Dysart said, 'I found it years ago. In Leeds. The only thing worth looking at in an otherwise uninspired provincial exhibition.' He glanced at me. 'It is you, isn't it?' he said.

It wasn't a question. He knew it was me. The first time we met, the time I threw wine over his ottoman, *then* he had not been a hundred per cent sure. I understood now why he had been so curious about me.

'It was Bradley who tracked you down,' Dysart said. 'He was convinced Kathy Kuriakis and the girl in that photograph were one and the same, but I had my doubts. My problem was that I found it hard to see past those offensive poses in the tabloids.'

'You find them offensive?' I said. I was myself offended by his judgement. He didn't answer. He was absorbed in line and texture.

'Deeply offensive,' he said after a long silence. 'And in comparison with this . . .'

'Oh that,' I said. 'I hate that photo. I look so heavy. And that awful hairy armpit.'

'I had to have it,' Dysart murmured.

Well, naturally I was flattered. Who wouldn't be? I found the whole incident really quite romantic. How gratifying that this clever and distinguished man should have become obsessed with a photograph of me. I glowed, I felt enormously pleased with myself. And also with him. If he had made the expected pass that night, then I would have almost certainly succumbed. But he didn't, and this confused me. He kissed my hand briefly when I left. His lips were hot and dry. And on subsequent occasions he was equally reserved.

Once or twice a week the phone rang and it was Bradley. 'I have Mr Stevens on the line for you,' he would say as if Mr Stevens were my solicitor or my bank manager. Then there would be a long pause, and then I would hear Dysart's voice inviting me to dinner, or to the theatre, or to a private viewing, or to meet a couple of his friends. It was amusing to watch the faces of these friends as they struggled to remember where they'd seen me before. I always accepted these invitations. I never thought of refusing. I could not keep away.

Sometimes I caught Dysart looking at me and I thought now, now he will say something, now he will touch my hand or my thigh, now I will understand what this is about. But I was always wrong.

I have got athlete's foot.

What an inappropriate name. I have done nothing remotely athletic so why am I cursed with this eponymous affliction? Is that the right word, eponymous? I don't know if you can use it for diseases of the feet. Perhaps it's exclusively reserved for literary things.

What an ignorant person I am. For so long I have lived

in my warm bubble of self-satisfaction with no grasp at all of the vastness of my ignorance. Now it becomes clearer to me every day. Recently I've been having particular trouble with words. For example, I have all these words in my head (like eponymous) which ought to belong to me but don't because I have no real idea how you use them. On the other hand there are things like childbirth and whatever it was that happened between me and Dysart for which no useful words exist. It is a kind of dispossession. I am a dispossessed person.

My ignorance depresses me.

Apparently this athlete's foot is a fungal infection. I have got it, they tell me, by not drying my feet properly. My personal opinion is that the climate in here is to blame. They still haven't turned off the heating. My cell is so hot I wake up at night drenched in sweat. Such a warm, damp, airless environment is perfect for fungal growths. It's like dry rot. The spores multiply. They dig deep. The skin between my toes turns white and cheesy and peels away in thick strips. Sometimes a whole piece comes away shaped like a small goblet or an inverted mushroom, the exact shape of the space between one toe and the next. Every night I peel away gobbets of dead, dense, fungal-infested skin, and the next night another layer has formed.

My hair is also falling out. I am not alarmed by this because it's thick enough to take it. Anyway, I always lose hair at this time of year. But I find this shedding of self very interesting. I have started a collection. Yesterday I combed the thick weave of fallen hair out of my hairbrush and wrapped it in a little envelope which I made out of a sheet of file paper. In another envelope I have put the peelings from my feet. I am going to make two more envelopes, one for my fingernail clippings and one for my toenails. I find this very satisfying. It pleases me to think that there are insensible bits of me stored away neatly in paper packages. I am going to label them: 'Sandra Bagnall – skin', 'Sandra Bagnall – hair'. I shall also date them. I shall keep them on the shelf, tucked in between my books.

Dysart would understand this. He had a small bowl of bones – human bones – on the table beside his bed.

I have been thinking about God again lately. God and athlete's foot. On the whole, athlete's foot is easier to think about than God. I find wrestling with something that doesn't exist a tiresomely complex process, although I'm sometimes sorry now that he doesn't exist because I would like to have a worthy enemy again, a powerful adversary to grapple with as my skin withers and bits of me fall off. I think I could accept this process of destruction more easily if I'd been a more creative person. It would make more sense then. But I have destroyed indiscriminately and created nothing. Dysart felt much the same. He would have given all his money and his knowledge to have painted one great picture. Unfortunately he had no talent.

Anyway, let me skip on now. Let me get on with it. I am wasting too much time. These days I am far too absorbed with food and decay.

In short: Reader, I married him. (You can tell I've been reading *Jane Eyre*, can't you?)

He proposed formally one night after the ballet. I was not expecting it. I had come to the conclusion that whatever else it was, his interest in me was not sexual, and beyond that my imagination failed. Marriage had never seriously occurred to me. I simply did not consider myself in his league. Oh, I could put on a limited act: I had brightened up my northern vowels, I knew how to dress. I did not go round in diamanté-studded, bulging bodices and stiletto heels. But underneath the acceptable surface what was there that a man like Dysart Stevens might value? That such a man could be interested in me made me almost drunk with self-love. I started to delude myself that maybe he had seen more than I knew was there. Or rather – no, this is better – that he had instinctively recognized what I had always known was there. I am, I thought, even more extraordinary than I thought I was.

Anyway, he proposed, and I said yes. It was a formal proposal, formally accepted.

We did not kiss. We did not hug. We did not dance up and down on the pavement. We did not rush to a bar and drink champagne or leap into bed together. We did not, as far as I remember it, declare our love for one another. He simply squeezed my hand and then let it go. He seemed profoundly moved, so moved that he couldn't for a time speak. He took out a handkerchief and blew his nose, something I had not seen him do before. It seemed an intimate and thrilling thing. Eventually, in a choked voice, he said, 'I shall talk to Bradley about the arrangements.'

Thinking about it now, I am surprised how few questions I asked. And yet I must have known even at the time – I did know – that it was a strangely incongruous match. Perhaps he regretted asking me the moment I accepted. He must have realized what an outlandish thing he was doing. He must have woken at night sweating, and baffled by his own rashness. The truth is I have no idea what was going through his head: I can't even guess what prompted this proposal. It was as strange to me as Duffy's proposal after he'd tied my head up in a scarf.

When the papers got wind of the engagement they jumped gleefully on the parallel between us and the Arthur Miller/Marilyn Monroe liaison – the Culture Guru and the Bimbo, the Art Collector and the Centrefold Nude, the Intellect and the Body. They made it sound as if Dysart, struck by some middle-aged crisis exacerbated by years of dry intellectualism, had finally fallen prey to his hormones; and that I, the juicy, air-head porno queen was making a laughing-stock of him.

He took it very well. He was even amused by it.

But the reasons Dysart married me were far more complex than the tabloids' analyses. They were so complex that I am still puzzling over them.

The reasons I married him, on the other hand, were

blindingly simple. I was dazzled by him. I was dazzled by his wealth, his house, his reputation – the extent of which I was only just beginning to grasp – his intellect, his influence. Marrying him seemed to be a kind of validation. It told the whole world that I was more than just a mass fantasy: that I was a woman of substance.

At the trial, the prosecution claimed I had married Dysart for his money. It wasn't a new idea. From the beginning the tabloids had implied with a nudge and a wink that the only reason a young woman like me would marry a desiccated aesthete like Dysart was for his loot. They were right. I can't deny it. I don't see anything particularly reprehensible in it either. Is it morally pure, then, for a woman to choose the poorest man she can find for a husband, or is it just plain stupid? The point is that I didn't marry him *only* for his money, or even *primarily* for his money, although I am not ashamed to admit that his wealth was a large part of his potent mystique. How hypocritical to pretend it wasn't. There were also practical considerations. I had grown used to money, and none of the alternative futures Colin suggested held any appeal for me. On the other hand, marriage to Dysart seemed like a glittering triumph, like a crowning reward. It had the shattering ring of destiny.

Dysart perfectly understood the importance of practicalities. One afternoon, for example, we went to see his lawyers. He suggested I took Colin with me. I was given a contract to read. It was largely designed to stop me from cleaning Dysart out in the event of the marriage failing. It was a very fair and perfectly reasonable contract. When Colin was satisfied that I was sufficiently protected, I signed it. I had no difficulty with this because I could see how easily an unscrupulous woman could take Dysart to the cleaners.

He was much richer than I'd realized, unimaginably rich. He was the last surviving member of a dynasty of Victorian entrepreneurs, brothers and cousins, who had all made fortunes: cutlery in Sheffield, diamonds in South

Africa, precision instruments in Scotland, oil in Venezuela, port in Portugal. Dysart himself was one of the South African Stevens. He spent the first twenty-odd years of his life in Johannesburg. You could hear it sometimes in his accent. When he disapproved of something, when he withdrew into reserved politeness, his vowel sounds tightened. His life now was largely devoted to art. He bought paintings both for private collections and for himself, he lectured, he wrote books and articles, he formed critical opinion, he commissioned artists and advised galleries throughout the world. He was vastly famous. No, 'famous' is the wrong word. My Mum and Dad, for example, had never heard of him: but in his own circle, among the international intelligentsia, he was more powerful than God.

The wedding...

It was in all the papers. You probably saw it: 'Kathy Kuriakis Marries Millionaire Art Dealer', 'Our Kath Weds Billionaire Art Boffin'.

It was all very different from the sad affair at St Joseph's thirteen years before. No Billy Fox in his sharp blue suit and his kipper tie, no cosmic laughter to whip off my veil, no ham sandwiches and pints of Guinness and bottles of pomagne at the Three Feathers.

We were married in a register office. Everyone was there: my family, Dysart's friends and colleagues, my colleagues, Sammy Rubin, Colin Cheeseman, and, of course, the press. It was a fresh, cleanly washed day in June, a day of puffed clouds and fragile china-blue skies. If I had still believed in God I would have taken the weather as a sign that this time he had looked down and was pleased with what he saw.

It is all there in the photographs. There I am, newly incarnated as Mrs Sandra Stevens. Kathy Kuriakis is dead and finished with. Her flat is empty and on the agents' books, her furniture is sold, her white settees have gone for ever. The newly minted Mrs Sandra Stevens smiles with quiet restraint at the camera. She wears a cream lace dress. Her hair blazes. Her face is more finely drawn than the face of that raging child with the muddy veil: it is thinner, more honed. It suits her. She looks touchingly happy. She looks, Dysart said, when he saw the photos, like Lizzie Siddall.

And there is Dysart standing beside me with a stoical expression of bewildered endurance. It is not, I think, the marriage itself which has brought this on, but his shock at the massed barrage of cameras waiting for us on the pavement. The road was blocked by them.

There is my Mum in violet chiffon with a henna rinse in her hair. She is an animated Lautrec poster. She's worried sick about making a show of me. And beside her there is my Dad looking in one photo like a demented crane-fly, and in another like a 1920s matinée idol. How nervous they both are. You can see it. They're floundering way out of their depth, but they're pretending to have both feet firmly on the bottom.

And there is our Bev, Mrs Beverley Birtles, in a floating yellow two-piece. Clustered in front of her are the three little Birtles, all uniformly hideous, all uniformly overweight. Bev is scowling, although whether this is because the sun is in her eyes, or whether it's because she's consumed with jealousy it's hard to tell. Jealousy, I hope.

Behind her stands Grahame Birtles, who has filled out nicely. Shortly after this he will make a fool of himself by drinking too much champagne and whispering in my ear that he has always loved me, from the first moment he saw me, or words to that effect.

People did a lot of whispering in my ear at the reception.

'Jesus wept, love,' my Dad whispered when he walked through the double front doors and into the hall, 'you've fallen on your feet this time, girl.'

The house in Essex Square stunned them. They wandered round dazed and humbled.

Beverley hissed, 'He's a bit old for you, isn't he? I'd have thought you could have found someone younger.' She refused to be impressed by anything. 'Oh, look,' she said to Mum, 'see those curtains? Me and Grahame have got those curtains. Only ours are newer.'

'Be happy, love,' whispered Mum as she hugged me to the tightly packed violet chiffon. 'Be very happy. You deserve it.'

*FOUR*

Beverley was here again today. She is looking thinner. The onset of early middle age – she must have turned thirty-seven now – suits her. She was always destined to be middle-aged. She is coming, as they say, into her own. Her hair is stiffly set. She wears a lot of gold. Beneath the delicate trace of Anaïs Anaïs is a tougher, more powerful whiff of matriarchy.

We kiss.

We try to spar, we try hard to establish our normal relationship, but it seems we both lack the energy for it. Our hearts are not in it this afternoon. In the absence of insults and resentments we are a little lost. We struggle for conversation.

After a while she gives up on small talk and gets to the point. She tells me that Mum and Dad would like to come and see me. I see at once that this is the real purpose of her visit: they have sent her to intercede for them.

No, I say.

I am adamant about this. I haven't seen them since the trial. That was bad enough. I do not want them to see me here. Better if they quietly bury me. Let them think of me as an experiment that failed. But then, in the middle of this conversation, I am pierced by one of those helpless sadnesses that seem to come more frequently these days. How sad it is, I think, that neither of them will live to see the inevitable re-evaluation of my image, how tragic that they will never know the unique place I shall one day hold in the history of art. When eventually things come round full circle, and I become respectable again, they won't be there to see it. I may not even be there myself.

'No, really, I do think you ought to see them,' Bev says. 'It would be kinder.'

*Kinder?*

No, it would not. Kinder to whom?

I cannot bear my Mum to see me in this place. It's not the place itself, although that will distress them enough. It's me. I will not have her see my mashed-potato skin and my exhausted docility.

'Think about it,' says Bev.

What makes it worse is that my Mum was so fond of Dysart. It will be hard for her to avoid his name. At first she was afraid to be left in a room alone with him in case she said something stupid, or bored him with her chatter. But he was always at his most charming with her, at his most human and accessible. She warmed to him. In the end I think she grew to love him. She once knitted him some gloves for Christmas and he wore them. He envied me my mother. Both his parents had died when he was quite young. My Dad liked him too. They talked sport together, which was kind of Dysart because he was not a sportsman. He said he found my Dad very perceptive. I explained this was because my Dad was a steel erector and saw things from a distance. Dysart and my Dad were the same age almost to the day.

At least twice a year we invited my parents to stay with us in London, and Dysart lent them the villa near Fiesole whenever they wanted it. He never, as far as I remember, went to Belmont Road, but that was entirely out of consideration for my Mum. He knew she would have felt it necessary to paint and redecorate the house from top to bottom and would have been ragged with anxiety had he ever accepted an invitation to stay there.

'You know how Mum feels about you,' Bev says. 'Let her come.'

I say clumsily, 'I can't. I can't bear it.'

Bev reaches a hand across the table and clasps it over

mine. It is smaller and smoother than mine and heavy with rings: wedding ring, engagement ring, eternity ring, all those binding symbols of respectability. 'It's all right,' she says. Her voice is warm and soft. Did she always have such a kind voice? 'It's all right,' she says. 'Don't worry, you're still faultless in her eyes.'

I am comforted by this. I do not take my hand away. I clasp hers tightly.

'Does that make you jealous?' I ask her. I cannot meet her eye. We have never spoken of these things. Jealousy seems such a contemptible emotion. It is not really what I mean.

She shakes her head. 'I got over all that long ago,' she says. After a pause, she adds, 'And I've nothing to be jealous of now, have I?'

I look up. Is this a dig? Are we, thank goodness, back to our old familiar ways? But no, she is just telling the truth. She says it almost sadly as if she too is sorry that the old state of affairs between us has changed.

Now – God, how tiring – we shall have to go through all the trouble of inventing a new relationship.

We sit holding hands tightly until the bell goes for end of visiting.

Dysart's villa – the Villa Berlinghieri – was in the hills north of Florence. It was a square building on three floors, covered in dark apricot stucco. The shutters were green. In the front was a walled courtyard with an arched gateway, and at the back, overlooking the valley, a balustraded terrace ran the full length of the house. Below this the garden fell away, level after level, each level connected by stone steps.

This is where we honeymooned.

The couple who looked after the house had opened all the windows and aired it through. After the long darkness of being shuttered off from the sun, the rooms were cool and smelled of orange blossom. Jars of dried flowers were set in exactly the right places on the rough tiled floors. The fabrics were simple, the furniture solid and provincial. Even the lemons in the deep blue bowl on the kitchen table looked as if they had been chosen on the criterion of style. It had that glossy-magazine look of highly designed, self-conscious rusticity.

We climbed the wide stairs.

'I thought this would be your room,' Dysart said. The walls were whitewashed. On the bed was a simple white quilt. The wooden floors were painted a powdery greyish blue and covered with cotton mats. There was a dressing-table, a cheval mirror, a chest of drawers, a magnificent wardrobe and two blue armchairs. On the walls were small wooden panels painted in brilliant colours with a lot of gold. They seemed to be mostly religious pictures. Three tall windows opened out on to a long balcony. My suitcases were already standing on the floor.

It must have been mid-evening by then. We'd flown straight from the reception to Pisa. In the plane I had suddenly grown frightened and cold. Planes are always cold. They drone from one reality to another. You hang suspended there in this cold tube, out of time, out of place, out of self. I held my coffee-cup out to the stewardess, and took the opportunity to look straight at Dysart's profile, the thin nose, those two deep lines. I thought: what shall I say to this man? How will I entertain him? What will we talk about alone together day after day? For although our courtship – I don't know what else to call it – had been very brief and curiously impersonal, a matter of a dozen dinners and a handful of visits to theatres and galleries, I'd already told him what little there was to tell. I had nothing left to say. I had exhausted my conversational resources.

'Are you all right?' Dysart asked as we hummed over central France.

'Fine,' I said.

He was reading a magazine, some art review.

'Is it interesting?' I asked.

'Very,' he said.

'Good,' I said.

'Have *you* something to read?' he asked.

'Yes, thank you,' I said.

I pulled the magazine out of the pocket in the seat in front of me and flipped through it. Perhaps, I thought, you could get through thirty years or so with courteous inquiries and polite responses. There was nothing in the magazine that interested me. What *did* interest me? I couldn't think. Nothing. I went on flipping pages back and forth, reading nothing, tracing imaginary journeys along red lines that spurted out from Rome and Pisa and Venice like arrows of blood. But as soon as we touched down, as soon as we were back on earth and the early evening sun hit us as we crossed the tarmac at Pisa airport, the cold panic calmed. I reconnected. And here, now, in this villa, in this white room with the long balcony I was again awash with warm draughts of optimism.

Dysart could see I liked my room. He was pleased. 'Mine is just along the passage,' he said.

This arrangement suited me fine. It was what I would have chosen for myself. Except for that brief spell with Billy Fox, I have always had my own room. I was used to sleeping alone, so I perfectly understood Dysart's need for privacy. It was one I shared.

A door from my room led into a bathroom. It was like a vast marble hall, like a ballroom. The bath-tub was in the middle of the room, attached to the floor by ancient decorated pipe work. It was one of those old tubs with clawed feet like the one in Duffy's flat.

Beyond the bathroom was Dysart's room. It was similar to mine but less pastel, more definite. Odd how indeterminate pastel colours are traditionally associated with female things. Below us, from the terrace, came the ring of plates and the clatter of cutlery. 'I think it's warm enough to eat outside tonight, don't you?' Dysart said. 'I've asked them to lay dinner on the terrace.'

There was a table in his room with books on, and a magnifying glass, and also a bowl of strange white objects like chicken bones. I picked the bowl up to look at these more closely. 'What are these bone things?' I asked.

'That's exactly what they are,' he said. 'Bones. Tarsals. Metatarsals.'

'*Human* bones?' I said. I put the bowl down.

'Oh, certainly human, yes,' he said. 'From the old cemetery above the village. Half of it was washed away a couple of winters ago.'

'You keep them in a *bowl*?' I said. 'In your bedroom?'

He laughed, a soft, self-deprecating laugh as if he suspected that what he was going to say might sound ridiculous. 'I keep them to remind me of my own mortality,' he said.

I stared at him. My mouth fell open.

He tried to explain. 'Of the nature of death. Of the terror and yet the inevitability of nothingness. Those hands . . .' he sifted among the bones and picked up a small handful, he held them in his palm, '. . . have peeled vegetables, picked grapes, played the piano, stroked a lover's skin.' His voice trailed away. He let the bones roll back into the bowl. He spread out his own fingers in front of his face and looked at them against the light. 'When you're my age,' he said, 'you'll understand.'

I nodded. And, of course, I did understand. More or less. On the other hand I was slightly shocked. What seems like a natural and understandable obsession of one's own, looks very like perversion in someone else.

It was almost dark by the time we ate. Bats wheeled through the soft dusk. The air was sweet with the smells of cooling earth. We ate milky cheeses and raspberries from the garden. Dysart opened a bottle of the local wine. After all, it turned out that we still had something left to talk about. He told me about his childhood in South Africa, and the difference between the star canopy there and here. The sky above us had turned creamy with the density of stars. The moon drifted from one side of the terrace to the other. We discussed the moon. We talked about his first marriage and a disastrous honeymoon in Scotland. I knew already about this marriage.

Her name was Anne. It had lasted nearly twenty years, although it had never been a happy one. She was now a Professor of Fine Art at a Canadian university. She wrote books and learned papers about eighteenth-century pastoral painting. I imagined her as a tallish, slightly overweight woman with heavy pale swatches of hair that she piled up in a bun. I imagined she wore big glasses with transparent frames and that her lips were thin and dry. In fact, I'd seen a photo of her and she wasn't like that at all, but that's how she was in my head.

We discussed my disastrous first marriage. This made him laugh in a way that the failure of his own did not. But then, of course, I always tell it as if it is a joke. I drank three quarters of the bottle of wine. I remember thinking hazily that it would be wiser not to tell him all the details of the Fox fiasco so that I had something left over for another night, for the next $x$ number of years.

I remember, too, while we were on the subject of marriage, saying to him with a kind of scientific curiosity: 'How do you feel now?'

He paused in his peeling of a peach. 'In what context precisely?'

'Today. Being married,' I said. 'How do you feel about it?'

He thought for a moment. 'Enormously privileged,' he said. He repeated it. 'Enormously privileged.'

I was touched by this.

A silence fell. It felt edgy with embarrassment as if neither of us was quite comfortable with such simple sincerity.

Eventually Dysart caught sight of something. 'Those earrings . . .?' he said.

'Emeralds,' I told him.

'You were wearing them the first time I met you,' he said. 'And I remember thinking that a woman who chose to spend her money on such exquisite jewellery must have intrinsically good taste.'

'Actually,' I said, for I felt his earlier admission deserved an offering of equal honesty on my part, 'I didn't buy them. I stole them.'

'*Stole* them?'

I wish I could remember his face. I loved those moments when I surprised him, when he was still delighted by the novelty of me, when the shock of me still gave him pleasure.

'Yes,' I said gaily. 'I stole them from a girl I knew. She was very rich. I don't think she missed them.'

'You *stole* them,' he repeated. His eyes widened.

'Well, they were so beautiful,' I explained. 'I just wanted them. I had to have them.'

He was caught in suspended motion, the peach in his hand, the knife pulling away a strip of skin, the juice dripping on to his plate. Suddenly he laughed, a bark of excited laughter.

'You had to have them,' he chuckled. 'Well, of course. Of course. You had to have them and there they are.' He stabbed his knife in my direction to make the point.

Annunciata brought some coffee. We talked on about this and that. I was very comfortable. I thought – and was surprised by the thought – this will work. It will be all right.

Quietly, the exhaustion of the day caught up with us. We left the table and went upstairs. Outside my room Dysart took my hand and kissed it. Then, for the first time, he kissed me on the lips. It was not unpleasant. 'We're both tired,' he said. 'I'll see you in the morning.'

I was not sorry. It had been a long and difficult day. I was ready to sleep.

In the morning, the room was full of moths. I had gone to bed without closing the windows or pulling the tissue-thin curtains. Small, deltoid corpses lay on the floor. The ceiling round the light was crawling with powdery, concussed insects in a state of shock. This explained why, in the night, I had dreamed of things brushing my face, of lips on my neck.

I stepped over the bodies and went out on to the balcony. All this, I thought, leaning over the ironwork, all this is mine.

When I got tired of exulting and congratulating myself, I took a bath. I lay in the tub, as if I was drifting in it across a vast marmoreal sea. No one else seemed to be up. I sang. I blew soap bubbles. I admired the length and the shape and the colour of my legs. The house was silent. I dried myself on the balcony. On the terrace below the table was set for breakfast. I went down. No one seemed to be about. I wandered off into the garden to survey the extent of my empire.

Below the terrace was a strip of grass. On the far side crumbling stone steps overgrown with pads of thyme and wild strawberries led down to a lower patio where, among torrents of ivy, were cracked terracotta pots like old wine jars full of brilliant flowers, and mounds of lavender humming with drugged bees. Further down I found a sunken Roman pool. Sharp-leafed shrubs sprouted like mythical swords out of the rock. On a lower level still was an olive grove. Down and down it went, level after level, mystery after mystery. Oh, Mr Jackson, you would have loved all this.

A bird whistled a fierce bubbling exultant song of joy, and this is what I felt too: a deep sweet joy, an eruption of exultance. Is there such a word as exultance? There is now, because that is what I felt. (No, sod it, the word is exultation, isn't it, which is not right at all. Too many syllables. Exultation is a pompous word, a religious word, a military word: something to do with angels and trumpets.)

How I preened myself in that garden on the first morning of my honeymoon, how I purred, how I gloated. I breathed in lungfuls of perfumed air. I laughed out loud and the laugh became a kind of shout. I was puffed up like a toad with self-satisfaction. I thought: There you are, God. Note how well I've done without you.

\*

That was the day we drove into Florence. Dysart had business at the Uffizi. The sun was beginning to burn through the early freshness as we drove down from the hills. Below us the city of Florence shimmered through a mist. It was stacked with tourists. The car crawled through the streets. Dysart grew irritated. He spoke of rationing the place to those few who could truly appreciate it. But I was glad we went so slowly. I gobbled up the crowds. I gorged on the smells of exhaust fumes and dark chocolate and warm floury dough.

At the Uffizi serious people in suits came to shake Dysart's hand and to be introduced to me. 'Signora Stevens,' they murmured reverently and dissolved back again into shadowy offices. If they were surprised by me, they were too discreet to show it.

'Will you be all right?' Dysart asked me.

I said of course I would be all right. His business, he said, would take perhaps a couple of hours. He would come and find me when he was finished.

I drifted through the Early Italian rooms. I was eager to learn. I had a book Dysart had given me. Start with Giotto and the thirteenth-century Italian School. In room 7, he said, study the huge Uccello. I knew better now than to assume he was talking about some kind of medieval musical instrument.

I looked at everything he suggested. After about twenty minutes, I had done the Early Italian rooms and was on to Botticelli and Leonardo da Vinci. I started again from the beginning. I sat on a bench and tried to read the book but it was the sort of book you can read whole paragraphs of without anything going in.

The rooms began to annoy me. They were too full of space. Everything was at the edges and nothing, except the odd wormeaten chest, in the centre. People shuffled in circles round the walls whispering to one another, consulting guidebooks, murmuring piously as if this were a cathedral. The still air and the artificial light drained away their human colour. They were like ghosts, pale and illusory in comparison with the blazing jewels on the walls. Guides droned cultural information in foreign languages. A Japanese group was being instructed on the fourteenth-century Sienese School. They looked bored. Outside, the traffic hummed and hooted; outside, people ate pasta and drank wine and sat on walls quarrelling with one another and examining their sore feet. I thought maybe I could slip out and walk in the city for a little, have a drink perhaps at one of the cafés I'd seen, but I was afraid that I'd miss Dysart and then he would know I'd got bored and be disappointed in me. I was somehow disappointed in myself.

'Did you enjoy it?' Dysart asked when he came and collected me.

I said that I'd enjoyed it very much. My eyes were still watering after a spasm of involuntary yawning.

He asked me questions about what I'd seen. I found it hard to answer them. I mumbled incoherently. He seemed pleased that I liked the Early Italians, and it was true. I did. Very much. I liked the bright, clean colours, the exuberant flatness of people, the cheerful disregard for human perspective in contrast to the loving respect for the details of daily life. I also liked the portraits of richly dressed Florentine girls haughtily challenging anyone to come near them, and the sly, thin, dark, crafty young men, their hands resting lightly on their daggers, and the serious Botticelli angels who made me think of Jenny. But I didn't know how to look at any of these paintings for more than a minute or two. What was I supposed to see there that would involve me longer than two minutes? What experience exactly was I supposed to be having?

'Is it time for lunch yet?' I asked.

My rapacious appetite was still a sort of joke to Dysart, a source of amused wonder.

He took me to a restaurant near the river. I caused a small stir as we walked between the pink-clothed tables. Heads turned. Conversations dangled from open mouths, heads swivelled, forks hovered, the chatter was punctuated by sudden silences and indrawn breaths. I saw Dysart's face as he sat down. His thin cheeks flushed. He muffled a smile which seemed to be at once both smug and strangely excited.

I leaned back and breathed in the noisy, lusty, air and the glorious smells of food cooking, while Dysart translated the menu for me. The waiter caught my eye. He wore a white shirt, tight trousers and a slip of white cloth tied round his hips. He weaved between the tables, showing himself off. He knew exactly which women in the restaurant – and perhaps which men – were watching him.

'What would you like to do after lunch?' Dysart asked. 'We could go back to the Uffizi, I could show you the Duomo, or perhaps . . .'

'Let's go home,' I said.

I had in mind a spot of seduction for the afternoon. I thought it best to get this side of things over with as soon as possible.

In all honesty I can't say that it was an entirely successful enterprise, but then I hadn't expected it to be. Dysart's passions had never, I suspect, been centred in his loins. This suited me fine. In this, as in most things, we were surprisingly compatible. I am not, I think, a passionate woman. I do not have the capacity. On the other hand, I have never been much interested in my own body whereas Dysart was obsessed and terrified by his. He was repulsed by the physicality of it – the tubes, the mucus, the fibres, the fluids. In his day-to-day affairs he could rise above his physicality: he could deal with his brief bodily necessities in private and the rest of the time revert to pure intellect. But the sexual act was *not* private, and it involved all those things he most feared: bodily intimacy, hair, juices, smells, sweat, stickiness. It involved a surrender of logical thought. It culminated in a kind of death. Sex was an occasional, a very occasional, necessity to him, like blowing his nose: it was never a fundamental drive. It simply did not suit him. Naked, he was seriously diminished. He was the sort of man who should never take off his clothes. Clothed, he was a kind of god; unclothed he was like a plucked bird, like a skinned rabbit. How cruel it is that alone among animals human beings have no covering, no sleek pelt of glossy fur, no brilliant feathers, no shiny scales, nothing to hide the hideous vulnerability of our ageing skin.

Curiously, Dysart did not seem to be at all afraid of my nakedness, as long as I kept it at a viewing distance. He liked to observe it, but not to tangle with it. He liked sitting in the room when I bathed. It gave him pleasure to watch me undress and walk about the villa with nothing on. The contemplation of my body excited him. What he did in private after these lubricious viewings was entirely his own affair.

But here, you see, was yet another thing about Dysart that suited me. I loved to be watched. I lapped up admiration as greedily as a starving cat laps milk. It was the thing I did best. I have made a career out of it. I am a professional object of unconsummated desire.

Nevertheless, this first brief, limp, uninspired coupling was a necessary hurdle. We could not avoid it, we could not pretend it did not exist. But how relieved we were when it was cleared. Neither of us, I think it fair to say, felt any pressing need to repeat the experience at least in the foreseeable future; but as a consequence of it we came to understand each other perfectly. In this area at least, we were so entirely complementary that we were able to give each other unparalleled satisfaction.

I have just finished *Jane Eyre*. What a book. I have stuffed it down in undigested chapterfuls. I could not get enough of it. It interests me that Jane Eyre should be so small and plain and yet inspire such a great passion. How did she do it? How does a woman get through this life without the smile, the hair, the body? Well, I shall have to learn soon enough. I must try and look on it as a challenge. What frightens me, though, is that when I am fat and dry, and my skin drags, I shall still instinctively fall back on all my old tricks – the moistened lips, the widening eyes, the walk. I am afraid of becoming grotesque, a joke, an embarrassment to the young and powerful.

Mr Rick Thomas is now inquiring into the reasons why I seem to have such a weakness for men old enough to be my father. (Or even grandfather in Mr Haskin's case.) He wonders whether I am looking for some father substitute.

Rubbish, I say. I have a perfectly good dad of my own, on whose behalf I find this suggestion most offensive. I don't need substitutes.

This one he has got completely wrong.

But he is not always as stupid as I pretend he is. This morning I say to him that I am beginning to think I am essentially a shallow person. I say it a little sadly in the hope that he will contradict me. I want proof that I am still able to fool other people if, perhaps, no longer myself. And he does contradict me.

'On the contrary,' he says, 'I think you've buried yourself so deep no one can ever find you.'

The bastard is right. How does he know this? But is burying yourself deep the same thing as being a deep person? I don't think it is.

'I suspect,' he says, 'that you buried yourself along with your sister.'

This sounds like the usual ridiculously neat psycho-speak. I open my mouth, but nothing comes out. I have nothing to say.

Could he be right?

My new library book is *Middlemarch*. I chose it on the same principle as I chose *Jane Eyre*, only this time Faith arranged a circle of thick nineteenth-century novels on the floor – Tolstoy, Thackeray, Balzac, Trollope, Henry James, Mrs Gaskell – and then spun me round again. What a stupid game for two grown-up women to play. I cheated. I noted where *Middlemarch* was and then stumbled upon it with convincing helplessness. I wanted it more than any of the others because it was a paperback and there was a nice picture on the front and it looked somehow less daunting than the alternatives. Actually, it turns out to be extremely daunting and very hard work, but I am persevering because I'm hungry now for a solid book. I like the weight of it in my hands. It's like holding a whole alternative world. That's what I want – something with deep roots. I want depth.

So the days passed and the honeymoon continued. We breakfasted and dined alfresco. I sunbathed. Dysart had occasional business in Florence. He spent a lot of time working on a series of articles he was writing. Sometimes we drove into the countryside.

One day an extraordinary thing happened: one of those coincidences that are so far-fetched they can only happen in books. Dickens would have loved it. I was in Florence. I was by myself because Dysart was in Rome for the day on business. Bernardo – the male half of the couple who ran the villa – had driven me in. He drove with one hand on the wheel, his left arm hanging out of the window and a fag between his badly stained teeth. He could flip the cigarette from his teeth to his lips in a deft, showy routine that included taking it right into his mouth and keeping it there for minutes at a time. He angled the rear mirror so that he could see me on the back seat. His eyes, lazy as a snake's, flickered from the road ahead to his mirror view of me.

Oh, what a morning that was – I am just remembering it – a morning smelling of hot oil and flowers. I got rid of Bernardo; I sent him off to find somewhere to park and told him to meet me at four. I ate a huge ice cream. I bought clothes. I walked up and down alleyways, holding my head high, smiling enigmatically at the tongue-licking, lip-kissing Florentines who hung about in open doorways: thin-faced, crafty young men whose hands rested dangerously on the belts of their jeans like the portraits in the Uffizi. I bought ridiculous touristy things, plates emblazoned with 'Benvenuto a Firenze', a doll dressed in Tuscan peasant dress, a fistful of postcards for everyone I knew.

At lunch I stopped at the restaurant by the river, the one with the pink tablecloths and the sexy waiter. I ordered a cocktail with an exotic name. Under the midday sun colours had gone manic, like a Matisse canvas. The Arno had turned a dull burning copper. Above it, the sky was navy blue. The buildings were baked clay. Already, you see, I was beginning to think in terms of paintings. I was filtering things through some dead painter's eye. I was learning to define my vision of the world in terms of Art. A stretch of water in the shimmering light of late afternoon, and I thought Monet. Hot, mad colours fractured by the heat, and I thought Matisse.

Across the road a plump man with sparse, greying hair was sitting on the wall looking out over the river towards the far bank. He was taking photographs. I glanced at him briefly and dismissed him. When I looked back again, he was still there, perched on the wall, but now he was facing the restaurant. He was putting his camera reverently to rest in a case. It was Alisdair Duff.

I stood up so suddenly that I knocked over a glass of bread sticks.

'Duffy!' I shouted.

He stared up at the sky in confusion as if God had spoken to him.

'Duffy,' I yelled. 'Over here.' I waved wildly.

He spotted me. For a moment he didn't recognize me. I pushed my sunglasses back on top of my head. 'It's me,' I shouted.

His mouth fell open. He stepped into the road. A delivery van screamed to a halt. There was a soft thump, and Duffy whirled away into the gutter like a small, fat ballerina pirouetting across the stage. Women on the pavement shrieked and cried out to God and their mothers, and crossed themselves. Duffy was doubled up clutching his stomach and gasping for breath. The crowd that had gathered from nowhere insisted that both parties should be taken to hospital at once, but the driver, who was relieving himself of a stream of hysterical swear-words, was too busy examining the front of his van for dents. By this time Duffy was under the van looking for his camera case. He looked ridiculous wiggling himself out backwards. He emerged yellow with dust. Frowzy scraps of detritus clung to his wisps of hair. I helped him across the road and sat him down at my table. The state of his camera was his only concern. He checked and double-checked it with anxious little grunts. He took a photograph of me to check that everything was working.

I ordered him a brandy.

'It's an Ikon Praktika,' said Duffy, patting at it lovingly with the pink napkin. The brandy arrived. He gulped it down like a glass of water.

'Good God,' he said, looking at me properly for the first time. 'Sandra. Sandra Fox.'

'Sandra Bagnall.'

'Yes, of course. Sandra Bagnall.'

'Except it's Stevens now. I married again. I'm on my honeymoon.'

He shook his head and rubbed his eyes as if he thought I might be an optical illusion. 'Good God,' he said, 'you look wonderful.' He was wearing a short-sleeved shirt and creased tartan trousers. He'd aged. The skin hung in a loose tired bag under his jaw. He kept shaking his head in bewilderment. 'This is incredible,' he said. 'In the middle of Florence. After . . . how long is it?'

'Years,' I said.

He nodded. 'Years,' he said.

He took a whole reel of me, burbling all the time about how extraordinary it was that after all this time, etc., etc.

'Shall we have lunch?' I said. There were so many questions to ask we would need time. I signalled for the waiter. Duffy laughed softly, watching me through the eye of his camera all the time.

'Sandra Bagnall,' he murmured. 'Sandra Fox.' He was full of questions too. 'Where are you staying?' he asked.

'Near Fiesole. My husband has a villa in the hills.'

'Good Lord,' he said. He was impressed. 'A villa?'

'What about you?' I asked.

'I'm here with my wife.'

'You're married then?'

He smiled foolishly. 'Nearly ten years now, would you believe,' he said. 'She's from Vermont. I moved to the States, you know. Actually,' he smirked, 'I've done rather well over there. Made a bit of a name for myself.'

'I know,' I said. 'And do you have children?'

'Just the two stepsons,' he said. 'Grown up and flown the nest now. What about you?'

I thought about Jenny. I considered telling him that once he had had a daughter who would now be eleven years old. He had the right to know. And such a wild coincidence had put me in the mood for dramatic confessions. But looking at him across the table, I found it hard to believe that this ageing dwarf with his wispy baldness and his toad-like skin could conceivably have been Jenny's co-creator.

The waiter brought two menus. He gave Duffy a curious glance.

'He thinks I'm your father,' Duffy murmured.

We browsed through the menus.

'So what about you?' Duffy asked. 'What have you been doing?'

I laughed. 'You honestly don't know?' I said. 'You don't see the English papers?'

'Well, not often, no. England's a long way away, you know. It seems very small and a bit marginal when you've been in America for ten years.'

'So you've never heard of Kathy Kuriakis?'

'Well, yes, I know the name,' he said. He frowned and clicked his fingers. Suddenly light dawned. 'Kathy Kuriakis?' he said. 'Yes, of course. Girly pics for the tabloids? Am I right?'

He struggled to hide his shock. 'Not quite the kind of modelling you wanted to do, then?'

'Not exactly,' I said.

'Isn't it strange how things turn out?' he said. I watched a sentimental nostalgia creep over him. Slowly his eyes filmed over, his smile grew sillier. 'Sandra Bagnall,' he murmured. 'Do you know,' he said, 'I still think about you. The fact is, I owe you everything. No, really. If it hadn't been for you – if you hadn't walked out on me – I'd never have gone to America. And when I got there, it was those photographs of you – the one in the bath, the "Surfaces" sequence – those were the ones that got me started. They made my name. Plus I made a lot of money out of a couple I sold for album covers. I'm not joking. I owe you everything.'

'And I owe you twenty pounds and the price of a suitcase,' I said.

He laughed. 'Shall we call it quits then?' he said.

I should really have added to the list of things I owed him (a) a rich and distinguished husband and (b) a daughter. But I kept quiet about the seminal part he had played in both these major events in my life.

The waiter came and took the order. He had seen me there before with Dysart. He oozed a thick layer of respect over the perpetual undercurrent of raw sex. He called me Signora Stevens.

Duffy murmured, 'You seem to be very well in here.'

'They know my husband,' I said. 'Dysart spends a lot of time in Florence.'

Duffy nodded. There was a moment of thought. Then he choked on the bread stick he was nibbling. He coughed violently. He had to be thumped on the back and given water. Tears dribbled from his bloodshot eyes. 'You mean Dysart Stevens?' he croaked. '*The* Dysart Stevens?'

'Do you know him?' I asked casually, but oh, inside – inside how smug I was, how triumphant.

'Of course I bloody know him,' Duffy said. 'Everybody knows him. What do you think?' He poured himself more water and gulped it down. 'You're married to Dysart *Stevens*?'

'Yes,' I said, as if it were the most natural thing in the world. 'Shall we have a bottle of something? A local red?' and I leafed knowledgeably through the wine list. Me, Sandra Bagnall, 22 Belmont Road, Andwall. I'd come a long way since the morning I walked out of Duffy's flat.

So we ate lunch together. Every so often conversation died. After we'd got over the surprise and exchanged brief updates there was, in fact, very little to say to each other. In the silences we stole surreptitious, wondering glances at each other over our forks. I thought, how weird life is, how random it seems, how random it *is*, and yet, viewed from a distance, how clearly plotted. While Duffy talked about his wife – who had studied in Pisa and who was off for the day visiting old friends – I half listened to him, and half marvelled that a decade or so ago this warty dwarf and I should have met briefly in a cold, black northern town, and should subsequently have had such a profound and continuing effect on each other's lives. And how curious that we should meet again now, as if the meeting were predestined, as if there were some deeper significance to it than just bizarre coincidence.

We ate, we drank, I paid the bill – which, incidentally, came to considerably more than the twenty quid and the price of a suitcase – we hugged goodbye, we parted. We neither of us felt the need to suggest another meeting.

Dysart came back from Rome.

'I met an old friend while you were away,' I told him. 'We had lunch. Alisdair Duff. The photographer.'

'Really?' said Dysart. 'Where's he staying? We should have dinner.'

I lied. I said he had already flown back to the States.

I was happy in Italy.

I've just been reading the chapter in *Middlemarch* where Dorothea Casaubon is sitting sobbing bitterly in the apartment in the Via Sistina in Rome. My honeymoon in

Florence was a hundred per cent more successful than hers.

I remarked on this to Faith. I said wasn't it odd – something I seem to be saying a lot at the moment – that Dorothea and I should have both spent our honeymoons in Italy. Faith looked at me as if I were speaking in an obscure foreign dialect. I suppose it was a rather foolish thing to say. It's just that I am so absorbed in Dorothea, it seemed significant that we had so much in common, although Dysart was nothing like Casaubon, nothing at all, and Dorothea and I are more than a century and a half apart. Also, of course, she is a fictional character, which I suppose makes a difference. Does it? Maybe not. I keep forgetting these people are not real.

After Florence we flew briefly to Rome and then on to Paris for a week. It satisfied me to think that finally I was staying in all those places I had once lied about. It somehow justified the lies: it made them not lies at all, just slightly premature claims.

Dysart was happy too, I'm sure of it. I worked hard to make him happy. I looked on this marriage as my job, so I took it as seriously as I took my work as Kathy Kuriakis. Since this was how I intended to support myself for the rest of my life, I naturally devoted all my attention to it.

It wasn't an easy job. Despite our compatibilities, the vast differences between Dysart and me could not be ignored. Frequently in conversation he dropped names or made references which meant nothing to me. In Paris he spoke of someone called Danton and quoted a poem about some fierce girls in the Sacré Coeur café. He mentioned Balzac and Hugo and Verlaine, none of whom I had ever heard of, and Joyce, who at first I thought was an old flame of his, and Gertrude Stein and Diaghilev. Names and knowledge, knowledge and names, a whole language from which I was excluded. I didn't know what was history, what was fiction, what was art. But I discovered that my ignorance, which I assumed would be a problem, touched him. It made him smile tenderly. Also it excited him. It was as if I were some noble savage – Rousseau was another name he dropped – that he had netted, a modern Pocahontas, or even some rare and exotic animal still smelling of hot dung and the jungle. He loved my ignorance because it allowed him not only to teach me, but to rediscover his own pleasure in things that had begun to tire him a little. No, not tire him. I am wrong. He was never tired of these things. But perhaps the sharp edge of his passion for them was slightly blunted, and this frightened him.

And yet, of course, my ignorance was a diminishing asset. The more I learned, the more my value to him decreased. On the other hand, if I learned nothing, then there was no point in his teaching me. I could see the problem. I was not stupid. And that was what he loved, my raw, brutish, uncultivated intelligence which was now entirely at his disposal to shape as he chose. I was his blank canvas.

In Paris there was one small crack in our mutual satisfaction.

I bought a statuette of the Eiffel Tower. I saw it and I wanted it. I wanted to buy it for for my Mum. It was proof that this time and for ever more when I said I was in Paris, then I *was* in Paris, so it became a symbol of my success.

Dysart was offended by it. It was about a foot high and set in a heavy marble base.

'What on earth do you want that rubbish for?' he said.

'Because I want it,' I told him.

I was about to explain that it was a present for my Mum, when Dysart said, 'Put your money away. I absolutely forbid you to spend it on offensive tack like that.' I'd never heard this firm, paternal voice before, this voice of ultimate authority, except when he spoke on television. Never to me.

'It's my money,' I pointed out huffily, and so it was. I had savings and investments of my own, I didn't need to touch the quarterly allowance he had contracted to pay into my account. 'So I shall buy what I want with it.'

He shrugged. He tried to pretend it was some amusing little whim of mine, he made a joke of it. But the fact that I bought it disturbed him. He was embarrassed and a little repulsed by this evidence of my innate vulgarity. And yet – another contradiction – he also liked it. I quickly learned to recognize and to exploit this odd ambivalence in him, his attitude to my proletarian tastes. He loathed it when I ate vinegar-sodden chips in the street, or wore a dress that was fractionally too tight. On the other hand, these things gave him a secret, almost erotic pleasure: they were proof that his wild beast still stank of the jungle.

It was during that brief stay in Paris that the collection was born. I mention this in case students of art history are interested in knowing the definitive moment of conception.

We dined one night in a restaurant with friends of Dysart, three young men, all artists, two French, one Polish. They stood up as we approached their table. Their eyes flickered over me with surprise. They shook Dysart's hand. I saw how they looked at him with renewed respect. They deferred to him as if they were young bulls and he was the dominant male. None of this was lost on Dysart.

'Let me introduce you,' he said, his hand in the small of my back. I could feel his satisfaction, his pleasure, vibrate like an electric shock down his arm. 'This is my wife. Sandra.'

And how it gratified him to note that all through the meal, the young men, the young painters, gazed at me greedily.

Dysart was particularly affectionate in the taxi back to the hotel. He took my hand. He said my sort of beauty was wasted on the lens. The lens vulgarized and cheapened it. What it needed was something subtler. It needed, he said, the eye of an artist to see through to the core of it, to illuminate the soul. He was, I think, a little drunk. 'That Polish chap,' he said, 'what did you think of him?'

I said I thought he was very nice.

Dysart laughed.

'Nice?' he said. 'He is very possibly a genius.' For a moment he stared out of the cab window. Then he said, 'I think if you have no objection, Sandra, I might just possibly commission him to paint you.'

That was it: the moment of conception. Rather dull really, but then I suspect most conceptions are pretty dull.

I took the Eiffel Tower statuette back to London with me and stood it brazenly in one of the arched recesses in my bathroom. I did not give it to my mother. I kept it to remind me of something: possibly of what my value was to Dysart and also of how far I could go.

Have I described the Essex Square house yet? The glittering white slabs, the portico, the chandeliers, the reception rooms? Yes, I have. Of course I have.

My room there was a self-contained suite consisting of a bathroom, a private sitting-room, and the bedroom itself. In the sitting-room – dove grey and ivory – the major exhibits were two Dufys, an early Rouault sketch of a naked woman and a Vlaminck. Sometimes I lay in bed – a Whistler, a John Piper in view – and thought triumphantly of my other bedrooms: of the boxroom overlooking the cemetery in Belmont Road, of the disinfected peach soufflé at the Foxes', of room 11 at the Astoria, of the basement room where Jenny was born and where Mr Haskin slipped in and out under cover of darkness.

Now I had all this. This, a villa near Fiesole and a flat on the Upper East Side. Now I had truly come into my own. Except to start with it was not my own. It took time to impose myself on Essex Square. The rooms were tall and silent; the air was oppressively still. The walls, stiff and pale, stared in hostile mistrust at each other like four enemies met to parley. I entered a room and felt immediately that I had disturbed something serious and profound, something stern and momentous which could only resume when I had gone again. I was too trivial for these rooms. They were full of echoes and the low hum of traffic in the square, like a municipal art gallery on a wet afternoon. But slowly I learned how to subdue these arrogant spaces, how to sit unflinching in a room until I had won the battle of wills. I learned not to take these rooms at their own value. I turned up the music and hung my feet over the backs of sofas. I defied them by leaving magazines and discarded shoes about, by lying on the floor, by spilling coffee and bringing mud and bags of shopping in. You could hear them sighing, you could hear them whimper a little and give up. Something was released. The walls relaxed. The rooms resigned themselves to a new regime. The house softened and grew warmer.

The Polish painter came to stay with us. He painted me in almost the same pose as Duffy had photographed me. I stand in a tub, one of those galvanized iron things that people kept in the backyard and brought in once a week for the ritual bath in front of the fire. He has used a strange technique of swirling brush strokes and inhumanly pale flesh tones so that I have an ectoplasmic look as if I am rising out of the tub like a voluptuous ghost, like a haunting cloud of steam. The background is a heavy grey. I did not like the painting. 'I'm a hundred times more solid than that,' I complained to Dysart.

I have no colour in that painting, no life. I hardly belong in the canvas at all. The main character in it is the viewer, the voyeur, the painter himself. It seems to be some guilty childhood imagining of his, some brief, dreamy, half-remembered glimpse in a steam-drenched kitchen of a naked woman, his mother perhaps, or his sister, some enduring personal image.

The Polish painter fell in love with me.

This amused Dysart. It gratified and excited him. He enjoyed the idea. It added a temporary pinch of spice to our brief, occasional and unnecessary couplings. He rather liked the painting. He said it captured a certain ethereal quality in me, and also, he said, both a timelessness and a grasp of roots. He hung it in the empty room where Duffy's photo hung.

I feel unaccountably depressed these days. I think it must be the food.

The other day I met another prisoner from this wing in the showers. I'm allowed to mix a little more now. I'm getting to know people's names. This woman is called Iris. She has bluish lips which are badly swollen and covered in bites and sores. She pulls at them with her teeth all the time. She gnaws away the skin inside her cheeks. This, she says, is a side-effect of the drugs they put in our food to keep us quiet. Her eyes dart about like angry wasps.

I assumed at the time that she was mad, because everybody in this wing is considered to be off her head in one way or another. But perhaps she's right. They certainly pile enough processed white bread into us. Dysart was always convinced white bread was poisonous. He would never touch it. He said it was full of bleaches and dangerous brain-damaging chemicals.

There's another girl I have met here called Julie. She's as thin as wire and vibrates like a tuning-fork as if there is not enough fat on her to hide the twitching messages between brain and muscle. She seems to be listening to something no one else can hear, so I'm always afraid to talk to her in case I'm interrupting something more important. She moves, trembling, in a thick invisible wrapping of silence. Actually, I'm quite scared of her. I meet her sometimes in the corridor outside Mr Thomas's office. Her stick-thin arms are wrapped in bandages. She cuts herself. I find myself thinking about this: is she punishing herself, or is she proving to herself that she's really there, that she's human enough to feel pain and to bleed? I am afraid of such extremes.

Why did I mention her? I forget. My brain is going.

Mr Rick Thomas has given up talking to me about punishment. The subject of the week is death. I can hardly keep awake through his sessions. I am heavy with porridge and rubbery white toast and gloom. I flop about over his desk, my head on my arms, and push his pencil-sharpener round a miniature Grand Prix track I have devised. It consists of a pile of papers, a jar of pens, a bottle of Tipp-Ex and a framed photo of his tail-wagging family. Brmmm, brmmm I mumble softly to myself as I rev up to take a particularly sharp corner. I am dreadfully bored. I want to sleep. I want to be lighter. I want to be so light that they have to tie ropes round me to keep me from floating away into space. I want to be light with goodness.

Goodness.

What an odd ambition.

No, I want to be deep.

'Are you concentrating?' asks Mr Rick Thomas. He raps on the desk and clicks his fingers at me. 'Concentrate. Tell me what you're feeling.'

Heavy. Tired. Stuffed full of food, all bulk and no substance.

'Let's consider what it is you've done,' says Rick Thomas. 'Let's address it face on. Pulling no punches. The fact is you've killed. You've taken another human life.'

And not just one.

'So tell me,' he asks, 'what you feel about that?'

I shrug. This annoys him. It is too casual, too dismissive. He wants a proper answer, but what does he expect me to say? It's a ridiculous question. I don't know why he asks it. Perhaps he's checking whether or not I have a proper respect for human life. But that depends what you mean by 'proper', doesn't it? It also depends how you interpret 'respect'. It also, now I come to think of it, depends what you mean by 'life'.

For the last two days I have done nothing but read *Middlemarch*. There are chunks I skip. I try not to but I can't help it. Some characters interest me more than others. I'm glued to the page when I'm reading about Lydgate and Rosamund Vincy, but I tend to lose interest when I get to bits about Fred Vincy and Mary.

Dorothea interests me most. What I admire about her is her depth. I told her not to marry Casaubon, I begged her to marry Sir James instead because he was kind and a bit dim and would do whatever she wanted. But of course her story is already written so she didn't pay any attention.

How stupid I am getting. Listen to me!

The thing about Dorothea is that she is shot through with goodness and a genuine love of learning. In comparison with her I am as shallow as a puddle.

How do you get to be deep?

I was thinking today during Mr Thomas's session that if I had been born fifty years earlier they would certainly have hanged me months ago. A life for a life. By which, of course, they mean a death for a death. I don't know what 'a life for a life' means. It's the ultimate euphemism, I suppose.

I am still collecting things in my envelopes; bits of fungal-infested skin, nail clippings, threads of hair. I now have one labelled 'Scabs'. I could collect congealed nose pickings and ear wax. I think I will. I shall make two more envelopes this afternoon. The ones I have are still wafer thin, but as the years go by I expect they will get thicker. What interests me about them is that these small bits of me are already dead.

How many years will it take for the dead parts of me to equal in bulk the living part? I could create a whole new body out of these insensate sheddings.

Have you ever seen that painting, by the way, the ectoplasmic vision of the Polish genius? What do you think of it?

I am beginning to irritate myself now. Who is this 'you' I keep addressing? I chatter away mindlessly on paper, I ask direct questions, as if I am presupposing that in some distant future these jottings will be read. I am also presupposing that one day the ectoplasmic painting will be on general view. Neither of these things are guaranteed to happen. But I go on storing words on paper like I store my discarded skin in paper envelopes.

\*

Anyway, after the painting was finished and the Polish genius had gone back to Paris, there was nothing specific for me to do. Dysart was busy. He was frequently away. At that particular time he was doing something in Glasgow. I forget what.

If I'd been a wifely person I think I'd have been at a complete loss. There was no role at all for me. I did not, for example, sew on Dysart's buttons or take his jackets to the cleaners. There were people to do that. There were people to do everything. Bradley, Dysart's porcine secretary and amanuensis, ran the whole Essex Square operation with a small, efficient and largely invisible staff. I didn't much like Bradley. He looked like a young Conservative politician, fleshy and sleek. His colourless eyes were steely with ambition.

So for a week or two after the Polish painter left, I drifted about like a jellyfish washing back and forth on the shore line. I visited my friends, but they had other things to do. I no longer fitted naturally into their world. I made them uncomfortable. The gossip at Sammy Rubin's place was about girls whose names I hardly knew, and people whose secrets I was no longer entitled to pick over; and the business lunches I used to have with Colin in warm, poky Italian restaurants – too much wine and spicy gossip – fizzled out for lack of legitimate business to discuss.

Dysart saw that I was floundering. He invited selected friends round to entertain me (and probably to entertain himself as well, because although my conversation amused him, he must have longed occasionally for something more challenging). His friends accepted me generously, which was kind of them because privately they must have thought Dysart was suffering from a menopausal madness. To my face they were charming, but behind my back how they sneered. I'm sure they did. How they speculated with sighs of false concern and barely camouflaged fears for Dysart's sanity.

Once I found myself sharing a wash-basin in the ladies'

room at the Opera House with one of Dysart's closest friends, a woman called Francesca Harding. She was probably a little older than I was. She wore her dark hair pulled tightly back from her face like a dancer. Her clothes were discreet and expensive and always, like her hair, in subtle shades of brown. She was one of those alarmingly intelligent girls who manage to get degrees from almost every university you've heard of and several you haven't. I always thought she would have been the perfect wife for Dysart, and I suspect this is what she thought as well.

'How are you settling in?' she asked as we rinsed our hands under the taps.

'Fine,' I said. I compared us in the mirror. She was a study in understatement. She made the other women in the room look like shrieking parrots. She wore one splash of white, an almost hidden blouse, and a thin gold chain on her narrow wrist. It was enough.

'None of us thought Dysart would ever marry again,' she said. 'I can't tell you what a surprise it was. We none of us thought he was the marrying kind.'

'Really?' I said vaguely. This ladies' was one of those rooms in which I am always too big. I blaze in them. I get in everyone's way. People stare.

'Well, he seems to be very happy,' she said with a dry, patronizing smile. I was not offended by it. I saw that it hurt her to say this, so I was impressed by her generosity.

It was a pity that we had nothing much in common beyond our species, our gender and Dysart, because it would have suited us to be friends. We hovered on the edges of some kind of friendship for several weeks. A couple of times we met for lunch like two typists in their dinner hour. We pretended valiantly to an intimacy we couldn't crank into life. She was too contained, too subtle for me. We greeted each other with kisses and expressions of pleasure, but the gulf was too great for there to be anything real underneath. I think we kept up the charade largely for Dysart's benefit.

Was I jealous of her?

Yes, I was.

I was jealous of all Dysart's friends. They made me feel hopeless. Hopeless and then angry. They laughed at jokes I didn't understand. They had heated arguments I couldn't join. They smiled knowingly at quotations I didn't even know were quotations. All this excluded me. It cut me off from Dysart. When I was alone with him my ignorance seemed fresh and charming and sometimes funny. The presence of his friends exposed it for what it was: uneducated ignorance. And yet what could I do about it? They were born knowing things: they had a whole lifetime's start on me. There was no way I could catch up, even if I had the will, even if I had the ability, even if I had that much stamina. Where would I begin?

I tried pretending that it didn't matter, but it did. I disliked making myself look ridiculous. I hated the way I was either forgotten about, or deliberately drawn into a politely modified conversation scaled down for my benefit. In the end I fell silent.

Dysart watched me. He saw that I needed something to fill my time, something of my own. So he commissioned a second painting.

This time he chose the Grand Old Man of Modern British Art whose name is legendary, and whose studies of the naked human form revived representational painting in the last quarter of the twentieth century. You'll know him, of course, you'll know his mercilessly honest eye, his fascination with human bulk and skin textures.

He was in his seventies then. The idea of being commissioned seemed to have bemused him. He sat opposite me in my sitting-room fiddling with a Tesco plastic bag he was carrying. When he spoke it was very warily, as if he thought I had bewitched his level-headed friend Dysart into some act of uxorious madness. (Uxorious! I am showing off now. By the way, they did let me have a dictionary. You can probably tell.) A faint grey fuzz covered the GOM's scalp. He told me that he'd shaved his head to stop himself sticking brushes and pencils into his hair.

Then – I can't remember the connection, but there must have been one – he started talking about Stanley Spencer and his wife. This was exactly the kind of thing I liked to know – gossip. While he talked, he produced various things from his carrier bag like a magician drawing things out of a hat. Triumphantly he whipped out a huge maroon handkerchief on which he blew his nose. Next he extracted some throat sweets and offered me one. Finally he took out a small pad and a child's fluffy pencil-case, and started to make rapid sketches of me.

'Dysart,' he said, 'has given me a very open brief. Do you object to nakedness?'

'Whose nakedness?' I said.

The GOM laughed. 'It might be fun to paint you in the bath,' he said. 'A proper bath.'

It seemed that he knew about the ectoplasmic painting. He was not impressed by the Polish genius. He sneered a little at modern French painting in the way people who are a bit jealous always sneer. Then he got sidetracked into chatting about Bonnard. All the time he was sketching, a frenzy of swift lines before flipping over to the next page and starting again. Bonnard, he said, was fond of painting women in the bath. The trouble, though, he said, with all Bonnard's women was their sexless vapidity. No real flesh to get hold of, he said. All shimmering mirages of women. He talked a lot about flesh: flesh in water, flesh squashed into the confines of a bath.

But in the end he painted me lying across the end of an unmade bed. I am wearing my kimono but it's undone and gapes open. I am curled on to my left side like an overgrown foetus, resting my head on my hands. My breasts are squashed under my bent arms. My stomach swags a little, dragged down by gravity, a soft little bulge which I quite like. It would be all right if he hadn't been so enthusiastic with a mad scribbling of silver stretch marks. Most of them are imaginary, as is the anxious strained expression on my face.

\*

I was sorry when the painting was finished. I enjoyed the occasional sittings. The GOM made me laugh. I grew fond of him. But to tell you the truth I wasn't as impressed by the finished painting as Dysart was. That face, that strained, sad expression – I am not a sad person. I don't have the stamina to be sad for long. Trivial people can't manage anything more than a fleeting sadness. It bores them.

Dysart hung the painting in the empty room. Except that now it was no longer empty. There were two paintings in it, a photograph and a chair which he sometimes sat on to consider them.

He started to call that room 'The Gallery'.

I'm very tired today.

I flop about, shapeless and greasy like an old toy. My hair is the texture of matted wool. I can't even sit up properly. I slump in the chair. There are dark hairs on my legs. I noticed them a week or so ago. They are growing thicker.

Actually, I've developed this ridiculous fear. I know it's ridiculous, but I can't control it. I think I am turning into something else. If I rest my chin on Mr Rick Thomas's desk my arms sweep the floor.

Did they always hang so low? I can't remember. I think I am reverting to some kind of subhuman ancestor.

There are other signs as well. Yesterday, in the shower, I found a burst of black hairs on the knuckle of my big toe. Was that there before? Surely not. Soon my whole body will be covered with hair, and my arms will swing beside my calves. Soon I will lose the power of speech. I will gibber and shriek. I will rattle the bars of my cage and beat my breast. I will be condemned to do tea-bag commercials for a living.

No wonder I'm so tired. No wonder I write stupid things. I realize now I have been going backwards for weeks.

'Are you all right?' asks Mr Rick Thomas. 'Is something wrong with your arms?'

'With my arms?' I say. 'No, nothing.' I try to wrap them away naturally on my lap but they don't seem to fit anywhere.

'What about a game?' he suggests. 'A word game. I say a word, and you have to say the first thing that comes into your head.'

Oh, *that* one.

'Mother,' he says.

You'd think he'd try and disguise his tracks a little more subtly than that.

'Short,' I say.

'Father.'

'Tall.'

'No, you've got to do it properly,' he says.

'I am doing it properly.'

'All right. Sky.'

'Blue.'

'Sea.'

I think for a minute. 'Turner,' I say.

'Quicker,' he says.

'Thicker.'

'No, no, no!' He runs his hand through his hair. 'No, I was telling you to be ... oh never mind. Start again. Green.'

'Emeralds,' I say.

'Light.'

'Night.'

'Rain.'

'Pain.'

He tuts irritably. 'It doesn't have to rhyme.'

'I know it doesn't,' I say.

'Just say whatever comes into your head.'

'I can't help it. Rhymes are what come into my head.'

I can't even do a stupid game like this properly.

We play another game, which is designed to show whether I am an emotional extrovert or a rational introvert, or any combination of these possibilities on some kind of sliding scale. I am at the absolute extreme of rationality and more than averagely introverted according to Mr Rick Thomas and his little chart.

I laugh.

'What's so funny?' he asks with a quizzical, slightly nervous look on his face.

I am laughing because I don't think there's anything remotely rational about believing one is turning into an ape.

My arms are definitely growing. I know they are. The tips of my fingers are almost at my knees. I measure them obsessively, every ten minutes or so. It's the first thing I do when I wake up. I have to check. I want to be wrong, I try to convince myself that I am wrong, but I can't. I've made a series of biro marks on my thighs and there's no doubt about it. My arms are growing.

I show Faith my legs. 'Look at all this hair,' I say. 'Look how long my arms are. Something terrible is happening to me.'

She laughs. 'What, you mean like Gregor Samsa?'

*Who?*

'In "Metamorphosis",' she explains. 'He turned into a beetle.'

That's the thing that really annoys me about literature and art and stuff. It denies you any experience or vision that is uniquely yours. Some bloody writer has always gone and done it already. Whatever new and remarkable thing happens to you, it can always be back-referenced to some book: whatever vision you see, some painter has always got there first.

Faith finds a ruler and uses it to measure my arms. She says they are thirty-three inches long from the shoulder to the tip of the longest finger. I measure hers. They are inches shorter. She says obviously hers will be shorter because she's nowhere near as tall as I am. I make her mark the exact place on my shoulder from which she measured so that we can make an accurate comparison next week.

Or maybe in ten minutes.

\*

I have finished *Middlemarch*. Dorothea's life, Lydgate's life, both have become almost more real to me now than my own. They *are* more real. Their fictional world grows huge in my head, while around me my own world shrinks and fragments.

I can't stop thinking about the end of that book. 'Her full nature ... spent itself in channels which had no great name on earth ... but that things are not so ill with you and me as they might have been, is half owing to the number who lived faithfully a hidden life, and rest in unvisited tombs.'

This has upset me. It has made me angry and uncomfortable. I pace about my cell. Such pious littleness is simply not enough. It's not enough for anyone, and certainly not for Dorothea. She is far too good for that. She deserves great triumphs.

But perhaps this is where I have gone wrong. Perhaps goodness is essentially unremarkable. That is to say it needs no remarking. It requires no drum rolls nor sanctification.

Anyway, I have thought of an extremely good but 'unremarkable' thing to do. It will not be easy for me either, so it's doubly good. I am going to send a visiting order to my Mum and Dad. I want them to come before I turn irreversibly into an ape. Also, I should like to speak to them one final coherent time before my mind goes. My head buzzes these days like a wasps' nest: things fly about, nothing settles. I can't hold on to a thought for more than a moment. Unless, of course, it's a thought about food, in which case I can concentrate with loving and intense clarity for minutes at a time. Today for breakfast I had porridge, thick, slightly grey, and covered with delicious gritty white sugar, followed by two slices of white toast with margarine and marmalade, solid marmalade that tastes of nothing but an indeterminate sweetness. All the same it was very good. I think I like it better than real marmalade now. I think the taste of real orange might be too much for me.

\*

I have seen the authorities about sending off the visitor's order. Bev will be pleased. I might write her a letter. Except then I will be publicizing my act of goodness.

Faith has just measured my arms again. She says they are exactly the same length as they were last week. I find this hard to believe. I know they're still growing. They bang into my thighs, they flap about and trip me up when I walk. At night I don't know where to put them. They ache. I come across them in the bed and think for a moment in terror that they are someone else's arms.

She must be mistaken. I think she is measuring from the wrong place. If my arms are growing from the shoulder then obviously the mark she made will have moved further down. Obviously it will always be the same distance from the biro mark to the tip of my longest finger. She must start from higher up.

She asks if I have come for another book, but I am not ready to read anything yet. I am still thinking about *Middlemarch*, and wondering about that last statement, and about the nature of goodness. It's odd that I know so little about it. I've met enough of it in my life.

It's difficult to discuss my metamorphosis with Faith because she won't take it seriously. She laughs at me. I show her how the hairs on my legs have thickened and darkened since last week. She says that means nothing: her legs have also got much hairier since she's been inside. She thinks it's something to do with lack of fresh air. If this is supposed to reassure me it won't work. There is simply no comparison between her hairiness and mine. She has quite a thick growth it's true, particularly under her plump, dimply knees, but her hairs are so fair and insipid you can hardly see them. Mine are long and black and getting coarser.

She laughs so much her glasses steam up. 'So have you told this psychiatrist man of yours yet that you're turning into an ape?' she asks. She can never remember Mr Thomas's name. She's never met him. She isn't on my wing. Fraud is considered a natural female crime. Unlike the murder of a husband, it does not denote some serious psychological maladjustment.

The idea of telling Mr Rick Thomas anything real is almost enough to make *me* laugh. It's certainly enough to make the hairs on my legs stand on end.

They are almost an inch long now. The hairs, not my legs.

Today for lunch we had chicken with a dried-up lump of packet stuffing, greasy roast potatoes and Brussels sprouts. The sprouts were yellowish brown with crispy bits where they had dried out in the ovens. The gravy had gelatinous lumps in it. But every mouthful was a treat. I eat too fast now as if there is a rat in the pit of my stomach gnawing a hole which has to be filled.

This is the day my Mum and Dad come.

They stand by the door a moment looking for me. They're looking old. They're shrinking. My Mum's astonishing orange hair is streaked through now with coarse threads of white which shoot out at odd angles from her head as if charged with electricity. Her upper arms are flabby. She has a pale, bristly moustache. The skin pulls in a tired drag from shoulder to elbow. She pats at her pallid face with a tissue. The heat, she says. Such a hot, muggy day. The train was a nightmare. I am politely surprised. I have lost touch now with such raw sensations. These breaths of reality no longer touch me. In here, the seasons are perfectly regulated. I have grown used to being permanently too hot and to breathing stale air. I can't remember anything different.

My Dad's skin has a strange, white, dusty patina to it now, like the powder that clings to stale chocolate. He grows thinner. He stoops a little. His high-stepping prance has slowed almost to a shuffle as if his long bones are too fragile these days, too skeletal to carry the weight of all that natural nobility.

Have I done this to them?

Yes.

No. Time has done this.

No, time and I together have done this.

And yet they hold no grudges. They are as loving as ever. Unquestioningly they are on my side. They hold out great and unrealistic hopes for the appeal. My Mum clutches my hands tight in hers. My Dad has read up about appeal procedures. Their faith in the judicial system and in my innocence is absolute.

My Dad says I look well. He is obviously lying to keep my spirits up. I know exactly what I look like. My lardy face is pimpled with spots. My hair hangs in lank ropes. I am growing fungus in the damp folds of my body.

'No, honest,' he says. 'A bit of weight on your bones – it suits you.'

How good they are, my Mum and Dad, how neat, how sweetly smelling. Possibly even a little stupid. No. What a disloyal thought. (But I think it all the same.) I think that they *must* be stupid not to have rumbled me by now. But then perhaps I am the stupid one: perhaps they rumbled me from the beginning, but it never mattered to them. They forgave me anyway and will go on forgiving. They humbly forgive the fact that I am slowly killing them because this is the natural fate of all parents.

I wish they would go. I have caused them too much joy and too much grief. I am responsible for too many deaths in this world.

When they leave I am so heavy with self-disgust I can't move. It's like cold cement poured into my legs. My heart is a dead weight. I think maybe it has atrophied. I think it has dried up and become a rattling leathery husk.

Dysart commissioned a third artist, one who was nearly as old as the GOM and equally venerated, but nowhere near so much fun. He painted me walking up a passage. I am wearing a loose, unbelted dress with an uneven hem. My hair blazes like a fire round my head. Literally like fire: the strands of hair are painted as tongues of flame. The skin of my face is translucent. My eyes stare ahead as if I am sleepwalking. I am barefoot. The walls of the passage are geometric panels cut from the sky. They have clouds on them. I look like a figure in someone else's dream. It's a horribly smooth painting. There are strange things on the floor of the passage – a tuft of grass growing out of a crack, a broken birdcage, symbolic-looking things which presumably are supposed to carry some meaning.

So now there were three paintings in the empty room. In the gallery.

I have been thinking about rooms.

I was remembering Sister Ambrose's custard-yellow cell at the Sacred Heart Convent which is almost identical to this one. There must be a reason for this beyond the obvious one that they are both institutional rooms. It's not just the shape and the sparse furniture. It's the quality of the silence in them. They are both rooms where people are in the process of casting things off.

Dysart's room, on the other hand, which I have also been remembering, belonged to someone still in the process of acquiring things. The walls were thickly encrusted, like a jewelled cave, with hundreds of paintings which glowed through the opulent gloom. Heavy gilt frames crowded up against medieval panels. The fabrics were ponderous dark browns and crimsons. Above the bed hung a fearful picture – perhaps a Munch, I don't know – a painting of a pale girl, her face dissolving and falling away as if the flesh is already rotting on the bone. She's very pale. She stands, ashamed of her putrefying decay, covering her nakedness with large, raw, knuckly hands. And there is another figure in the picture, a man, whey-faced and hollow-eyed, a dark shadow, unearthed, floating behind her. A lover perhaps, or maybe something more sinister. On the same wall were two paintings by Otto Dix, two scratchy cartoons in shades of red of an ageing harpy with orange hair and monstrous genitals.

On the opposite wall was a dark mirror, the sort of

mirror that has seen centuries of betrayal and has learned now only to reflect shadows. There was also a most beautiful Whistler, a waterscape across the Thames at dusk.

Sometimes we sat together in there late at night and drank whisky and water and talked about which dead painter could best capture me on canvas.

Sometimes I took my clothes off for him – slowly – and stood in front of the mirror brushing my hair. Nothing more. That was sufficient. That satisfied us both.

Something very strange happened today – two strange things – one after another.

I was summoned to the governor's office. One of the screws, Mrs Hutchman, a plump woman with tightly curled black hair, came to fetch me. I trot obediently behind her along corridors and down stone stairs. My arms hang disturbingly low. I try standing up straighter to see if that makes any difference. It does, of course, but I am only fooling myself.

The governor's name, by the way, is John Witherspoon. His office is beige and smells of dinners cooking. He still treats me with nervous deference.

'Please,' he says. 'Sit down.'

With a boyishly clumsy gesture he indicates a chair, and as a consequence knocks over a vase of flowers.

'Oh dear,' he says, disappearing on to the floor to pick up the mess.

It must be strange for him to work in such an intensely female place. The smells must be so alien to him. How kind we are, I think, to be so passive, to let him herd us into stalls and keep us penned here. Strange how quietly we collude in this bizarre arrangement.

He stuffs the flowers back in the vase and sits down. 'A rather odd letter came the other day,' he says.

I assume it is something to do with the appeal.

He passes two sheets of lined notepaper across the desk. The address at the top is not one I recognize. The letter is written largely in capital letters. It reads:

Dear Miss Stevens,
   I have been reading the papers and following your case with great intrest you look very like a girl who used to work at the Astoria Hotel for Mr Leonard Haskin about twenty years ago and I am wondering if you are one and the same Person. She was also called Sandra, if so then we would like you to know that our Prayers are with you.
   Kind regards
   *Janice Broomfield nee Hobbs.*

PS. The Sinful Children are still going strong and send their regards and wish to be remembered to you. Mr Haskin died in 1988 of a Heart Attack. Phyllis had to be put to sleep on account of kidney failure soon after you left. No one knew were you had gone.

PPS. If it is not you please ignore this letter, although our Prayers are with you anyway.

PPPS. I am married now to a gentleman I met in Bournemouth and we have two girls.


'Do you know this woman?' the governor asks.
'Yes,' I say. 'I did once.'
'I thought it might have been from a crank. I'm afraid you receive a lot of that kind of stuff.'
'Do I?'
'We tend to chuck it in the bin. It's not very pleasant.'
'Hate mail, you mean?'
'Some of it.' He bows his head and looks down at his crotch for a moment, tactfully allowing me to absorb this information unobserved.
'I hadn't realized,' I say.
'So although this seemed a perfectly harmless letter,' he says, 'I wasn't quite sure.'
'Well,' I say briskly, 'if that's it . . .'

But clearly it isn't. There is more. He has taken a bottle of sherry out of his filing cabinet. Will I join him in one, he asks.

Sherry is not my favourite drink, but after three months' abstinence I am happy to drink anything. It's a new bottle. He has to break the seal. He half fills two styrofoam beakers.

'Cheers,' he says. 'Don't mention this to anyone else, will you? Strictly against the rules. If this gets out it will be like the fly in the soup.'

I suspect that what seems like a friendly if rather reckless gesture on his part is actually a carefully planned strategy. He probably nipped into the off-licence on his way in to work, and discarded his first choice, whisky, on the grounds that it was (a) too expensive and (b) too obviously medicinal.

So I am sipping this rather sweet cream sherry when Mr John Witherspoon says casually, 'One other thing before you go, Sandra. I've had a letter from someone called Keith.'

I can't think who he means. 'Keith?' I say stupidly.

'Keith Fox. He claims he's your son.'

I need something stronger than sherry. I drain the beaker. It burns the back of my throat. 'Keith Fox?' I say. 'He *is* my son.'

'He's written to ask if he can see you.'

This is so strange, so unexpected, I think I must have misunderstood him.

'Can I see the letter?' I ask.

He passes it to me. The address is somewhere in Durham. I do rapid and muddled sums in my head. I have no idea how old Keith is. I never think about him. I work out that he must be twenty-one. His letter is perfectly spelled. It's very brief. It says that he is my son from my first marriage and that he would like to see me. Nothing more.

I don't know what to think.

Mr Witherspoon pours me another sherry.

\*

The fourth artist Dysart commissioned was a Brazilian. He painted old men, grey and twisted like roots, as if they had grown in great but solid agony out of the earth. He painted women standing at windows, their solid bodies as fierce as tigers tensing for the kill, their faces lost in a dream of elsewhere. This was how he painted me – against a long upstairs window. I wear a dark dress. Diaphanous white curtains blow inwards against my face. He wanted, he said, a sense of air, of imminent flight. The curtains billow out beyond my shoulders in a suggestion of wings. The light in the painting is very strange. A flat, lifeless sun hovers in the window but all the light is coming from me, from my skin.

The Brazilian liked working from sittings. He came two or three times a week. He was one of those painters who suffered from a temporary lust for me. This gave Dysart a peculiar kind of satisfaction. He liked to drop in on the sittings. He said that the paintings which emerged from a thwarted passion were the ones that had real power.

The Brazilian told me stories while he worked. One was about a girl in his parents' village, a contemporary, he said, of his grandmother. This girl had miraculously started to grow wings.

'Really?' I said.

'No, not really,' he said. 'It was some kind of deformity. Some growth on the shoulder-blades. But the people in the village longed to see physical signs of holiness. They wanted it so badly they wouldn't entertain any other explanation. She was very famous, this girl. People travelled miles just to be touched by her.'

'What happened to her?' I asked.

'She died,' he said. 'Of tuberculosis.'

'How big did these wings grow?' I asked.

'Oh, not big. Just little stumps. She died before they had a chance to develop properly. My grandmother went to school with her. She said that for weeks, when the phenomenon began, the little girl complained that her back was itching.'

I was very interested in this story. I thought about it a lot: about how special this girl must have felt herself to be, how she must have thought herself marked by destiny. And yet all the time – how cruel, how terrible – this manifestation of holiness was nothing more than the ravages of a fatal disease.

Funnily enough I have had some itching just under my shoulder-blades recently. There are certainly lumps there. I can feel them. Although in my case I think they are mosquito bites.

This is the day my son, Keith Eric Fox, comes to see me.

All morning I am sick with nerves. I can settle to nothing. I have washed my hair and put on lipstick. This is a ridiculous vanity, I know it is. It makes me look worse, so I smear it all off again with the back of my hand. Now my mouth looks bruised and shapeless, as if I have been crying. The colour does not match my spots. My face looks like a stale raspberry soufflé which has catastrophically collapsed.

My heart flutters and thumps in my throat. I choose a table and sit down. The visitors are let in. They smell of outside. Their coats smell of fresh rain, their skin carries the greasy odour of chips. Their eyes sweep the room, looking for their wife, their daughter, their girlfriend. You can tell the ones who are visiting for the first time. They hang back: they make themselves narrow. There are several of these today. They bunch together by the door, two or three young men, any one of which could be Keith.

I sit at the table facing two empty chairs. I try to breathe slowly, to swallow my heart back down into my chest.

In the end it's obvious which is Keith. He is the only one left. He is tall, well over six feet. His hair is ruddy brown and has a slight kink in it. It is cut in a thick wedge. His skin is paler than mine. His hands are very big, and dangle against his thighs.

I am the only one now without a visitor. I watch him realize who I am. He smiles tentatively. I don't recognize the smile. I recognize nothing about him. He comes over. 'Hi,' he says.

I cannot speak at all. My throat has gone into paralysis.

'All right to sit down?' he asks.

He sits. His legs spread out in all directions. His feet appear to be enormous.

'Thanks for letting me come.' He has a Lancashire accent. His voice is as awkwardly deep as his limbs are uncontrollably long. He hasn't yet grown into himself. 'I was a bit scared I wouldn't recognize you,' he says. 'I've got loads of photos but they're all from about ten years ago.'

'Photos?' I croak.

His skin flushes slightly. 'I used to go to the newsagent every day on the way back from junior school and buy anything that had a picture of you in it.' He laughs as if this is a joke.

'Where did you get the money from?' I ask stupidly.

'Dinner money,' he says, 'pocket money, whatever.'

He leans back in his chair and stares round. 'It's not as bad as I thought it would be, this place,' he says. 'I was a bit nervous, actually.' He spots the WRVS canteen in the corner. 'Shall I get us a drink?' he asks. 'What would you like?'

'Coffee,' I say.

He gets up and lopes off to join the queue. He is wearing jeans. This great, self-possessed creature with a Lancashire accent, this adult person, is my son. I watch him. He turns and grimaces at me: the queue is hardly moving. We smile at one other. When he gets to the head of it, he gives me the thumbs-up sign and winks.

How weird this is. I made this person. I made him with my iron-thick blood.

He lollops back with two coffees and two buns. I can't think of anything important to say to him. I would really like to say something important because I assume this is what he has come for: some word of wisdom from me.

Either that or money. But all I can do is stare at him.

'I hope you like those currant things,' he says. He means the buns.

'Are you still living with Marilyn and Ted?' I ask him.

'No,' he says, 'not for ages. We moved to Wigan when my Dad married again. Gran Bagnall's got my address. Didn't she tell you?'

Perhaps she did. I don't remember.

His mouth full of bun he says, 'They keep in touch, Gran and Grandpa Bagnall. They always remember my birthday.'

This sounds like a reproach. I say so.

He looks straight at me. His eyes are greyish brown with flecks of yellow and frighteningly honest. 'Is that what you think I've come for?' he asks.

'Haven't you?'

He shrugs. 'I never expected presents from you,' he says. 'Never.'

'What did you expect?' I ask. This is a pointless question. I regret it immediately. Whatever it is he expected of me I have failed him.

'That's a tough one, actually,' he says. 'I don't really know.'

A strange and unidentifiable feeling swells under my ribs. What is it? A sadness? An emptiness? A regret?

'I haven't come looking for a mum if that's what you're thinking,' he says. 'I've had Bren since I was four. And then there's Nan Fox. I've got too many mums already. I don't need another.'

I am gripped by a sudden attack of subcutaneous trembling, so deep under the surface it doesn't show at all. My hands lie still and calm on the table. They look older than I remember.

My son thinks he has hurt me. His baby face puckers. And maybe he has hurt me. I am too confused to know. 'No,' he says, 'don't get me wrong. What I mean is I don't need another mumsy kind of mum. Bren's enough for anyone.'

Now something odd is happening in my head as well. The sounds of the room drain out of my ears like a receding tide. I have to concentrate hard to hear what Keith is saying. I think I may faint.

'They've got three girls,' he says.

Who have? I struggle to make sense of this, to stay conscious. 'Your dad and Brenda?' I ask.

He nods. 'Three girls. The eldest is ten.'

Billy and Brenda. Billy and Bren. 'And how is he, your dad?' I ask. I think of Billy Fox in the back of Dead Meat's Transit van and am sad to think that he must have turned forty.

'Fine,' he says. 'He's got a good job with the gas board.'

'And what about you?'

'Last year at uni,' he says with his mouth full of bun. 'Just finished finals.'

At *university*? The child that Billy Fox and I made casually in the back of the Transit van is now at *university*? How can this be? Where did he get enough brains from?

'Durham,' he says. 'I'm hoping to get a research scholarship. Archaeology.'

'Archaeology?' I repeat.

'Yeah, well I like old things,' he says. He grins sheepishly. I can see this reply is a defence he uses. He probably has to use it a lot back home in Wigan. I think how gently he must patronize Billy Fox and Bren with these joky self-deprecations. He must have learned to keep the larger part of himself hidden from them.

'So what did you do with all those pictures you bought from the newsagent?' I ask him.

An embarrassed pinkness rises from his neck. 'I kept them in a box,' he says, 'under the floorboards in my room. It was because . . . well, I really wanted to meet you, just to meet you, that's all, just once, but Dad wouldn't let me. They didn't even want to talk about you. So I collected pictures instead. I had this special box I kept them in. With a padlock I bought in Woolie's. I hid it under the floorboards like in the films.'

Can this huge, blushing young man with his outsize feet really be that iron reptile I grew inside me, that ancient tortoise I gave birth to? How quickly the focus moves on. How fast you slide from centre stage into the past. 'Keith,' I say. I want to apologize to him. There is so much I have to apologize for. Beginning with his awful name.

His eyes widen in surprise. 'What's the matter with it? It's OK. Keith Fox. I quite like it.' He finishes his bun. 'Sir Keith Fox. Sounds good to me. Sounds spot on for an eminent archaeologist.' He laughs and wipes his hands on his jeans.

I have no idea why he's here. What does he want?

'Do you realize,' he says, 'I'm older now than you were when you left Dad.' He offers this fact triumphantly as if it is some kind of gift to me. 'No, the thing is,' he says, 'I just wanted to tell you that I don't blame you for getting out. I never have. Honestly. I mean, if you ever felt bad about it, then don't. I'm OK.'

'Don't forgive me too easily,' I hear myself say.

'Nothing to forgive,' he says. He sounds as if he means it. I don't matter enough for him to resent my loss. 'Actually,' he says, suddenly shy, 'I used to boast about you at school. Nobody else had anything half as glamorous to boast about. Well, there was someone in our year whose uncle was a racing driver, but some third-rate Formula One guy was never a patch on you.'

The bell for end of visiting goes.

'Is that it then?' he says. Around us people start to shuffle with coats and bags. Lovers kiss. 'Can I come again?'

'Do you want to?' I ask.

He stands up. 'Next month OK?'

'How tall are you?' I ask, awestruck.

'Six foot two and a half,' he says.

I see him wonder whether or not he should kiss me. He leans awkwardly across the table and wraps his elongated arms around me. Perhaps he has inherited these simian arms from me. The kiss he means to land on my cheek crashes into my hair.

'I don't know what to call you,' he says. 'Do I call you Sandra?'

'Whatever,' I say. 'Sandra's fine.'

I wonder whether or not I would like it if he called me 'Mum'. The idea gives me an odd feeling, like a pain, like the first stirrings of queasy bowel.

'Did you really kill your husband?' he asks ingenuously. I think I catch a touch of awed admiration in his eyes.

'Yes,' I say.

'Jesus,' he says. 'Bloody hell.'

I watch him lollop out. He turns and waves at the door.

All evening in my cell I interrupt myself with bouts of soft, helpless laughter.

The more I think about it the less I understand what has happened. Is this, finally, a gift of reconciliation? Or is it yet another cosmic trick?

I can't sleep. Thoughts flap around my brain like trapped moths. It's dawn now. A milky light slides across the brick wall. It will be a dry, clear day out there. The sun will shine. My son will wake up soon and stretch his long body. My son.

Well, I can mend nothing and I can change nothing. So there is no point in worrying about it.

And yet I do. I do worry. Now that my head is suddenly so full of this large, lolloping creature, now that I have something real to think about, the other fear has completely disappeared. How absurd it seems, how embarrassing. Of course I am not turning into something else. I never was. The truth is I have always had long arms and a tendency to hairiness. I'm ashamed now to think I got so hysterical about something that was patently ridiculous. No wonder Faith laughed. I must watch my mind carefully. I must remember how slyly it betrays me.

They will come with breakfast soon. Good. I'm ravenous.

I tell Faith about my son. She says, on cue, 'Twenty-one!

You don't look old enough to have a kid of twenty-one.'

What a bright girl she is.

She gives me a bar of chocolate and a book called *The Mayor of Casterbridge* to read. She says I might find it relevant under the circumstances.

An odd thought: not one of the artists Dysart commissioned painted me as a mother. None of them saw me as a Madonna, although now I come to think of it the Grand Old Man painted me with heavy, drooping breasts and a forest of stretch marks, all of which imply motherhood. But then maybe in the initial stages, Dysart discouraged the artist from any kind of sentimental approach to the commission. I don't know what instructions he gave them.

One of the artists, the fifth, painted me as a wolf. It is quite a small painting, very detailed. A mass of thick, perpendicular tree trunks like pillars in a cathedral fill the canvas. Slipping through the narrow darkness between them is the figure of a naked woman with thick, ruddy hair and dangerous yellow eyes. Her mouth is slightly open, her teeth glisten, and there is a trickle of blood on her chin. It's a remarkably good likeness.

The sixth painting was an exuberantly childish explosion of colour, a spillage joyously uncontained by the bold outline of a female form, which was sketched in one continuous thick blue line. Dysart was very interested in these markedly different responses, particularly since both painters suffered a passing but intense infatuation for me. The 'wolf' painter begged me to run away and live with him in Stockton-on-Tees.

Dysart was fascinated by this attempt to steal his property. We sat at night in his encrusted room, drinking whisky, while I replayed for him the hopeless passions of the young artists respectively from Stockton and Glasgow. Sometimes I had to repeat the latest instalment several times. Sometimes I had to make up embellishments because he wanted more than the reality.

The seventh painter was German and unequivocally gay so he didn't fall for me. He was a cold man. He painted me as if I were a biological specimen laid out for dissection. He skinned me, and painted a sort of emblematic cardiovascular system, a complex twisting of red and blue tubes, like some modernistic waste-disposal system. On top of this, where the skin divides and is pinned back, he has painted an unblemished and photographically perfect face.

For the eighth painting Dysart commissioned a woman. On the whole he felt 'woman' and 'artist' were contradictory terms, but this particular woman's work had impressed him. She was Portuguese. She painted me as flat and one-dimensional as anything in the thirteenth-century room at the Uffizi. It is a child's painting. I float stiffly and horizontally across the canvas in a triangular skirt like a ballistic missile. On my face is a beatific smile. Below me is a field full of delicately detailed but wildly improbable flowers. There is something very scary about this painting, something distinctly dangerous.

The ninth painting ... but for goodness' sake I can't describe every single one in detail. It would take pages.

One day, though, when I am old, when all the paintings are gathered together again and on public exhibition, I will write my definitive memories of each artist. And people will come from all over the world to see me, to touch the hem of my robe, to gaze on the woman who inspired such a unique, such a glorious collection.

I go over and over the conversation with my son, Keith Eric Fox, who is six foot two and a half and an archaeologist.

'Did you really kill your husband?' he asks me again and again my head.

Yes, I did. I did kill him. Although now I find it almost impossible to believe. I'm not sure if I've ever really believed it. From the beginning it has always seemed to me as if the arrest, the trial, the sentence were connected not with Dysart but with Joanne, as if I were arrested, sentenced and tried not for his, but, finally and belatedly, for her death.

It's true. I still expect Dysart to come and see me. I miss him.

Mr Rick Thomas is talking about dreams today. I have no interesting dreams to offer him. Perhaps I will make one up.

Now we are on the subject of dreams I would like to state that I have never had a single dream that was connected with the killing of Dysart. I have never been plagued with them like I was plagued with dreams of tunnels and headless angels and beating wings. I never dream of a floating flannel in the bath, or a statuette of the Eiffel Tower, or chips of bone in a towel. What does this mean?

Mr Rick Thomas is so anxious for a significant dream that I feel obliged to invent one for him, but he rumbles me immediately. Clearly my heart is not in it.

So instead we do the *Guardian* crossword puzzle. He is teaching me the tricks. Believe it or not I am rather good at them.

One day soon my son will come to see me again. One day it will occur to him to ask the next logical question. After 'Did you really kill your husband?' comes inevitably, 'But *why* did you kill him?'

I must have an answer ready for him.

I suppose the paintings were at the root of it.

You will note that 'root' is an anagram of rot and o – rot and love. The clue is: 'Love rots and gets to the crux of it.' Love and rot. This is the kind of thing I think about nowadays.

On our fifth anniversary there were twelve paintings hanging in the room Dysart called the gallery. Individually each was important enough in its own right, together they formed a significant collection. Dysart started inviting people in to see them. Occasionally he lent one out for a particular exhibition. He insured them heavily. They were known about and discussed. They represented the work of twelve of what Dysart considered to be the most interesting painters of the late twentieth century.

They also began to represent something a great deal more personal. Not only was the collection potentially priceless, but he came to understand that it was going to secure his immortality. He saw it as his one act of almost pure creation. If his other work – his criticism, his committees, his influence – was forgotten (and these things generally are) then what did it matter, because some part of his self, his soul, the collection would survive, and with it his name.

Also, of course, my name. There I was, Sandra Stevens, hanging, no, hung, no, hanged – which way round is it? – twelve times over. For as long as art is valued and written about I shall be famous. The Virgin Mary, La Gioconda, the Venus de Milo, Rembrandt's Saskia, Lizzie Siddall and now Sandra Stevens. So this, this finally was how I would make my mark on history; not as a saint, not as a tabloid phenomenon, but as a Muse, one of the great Muses of the Western World. I would blaze down the centuries into eternity. This was the absolute achievement of my boundless egotism.

We became utterly obsessive about those paintings, Dysart and I. Obsessive. Sometimes, if I woke in the early hours, I slipped along the passage for a quick fix, for the comfort of seeing myself immortalized, for the reassurance of guaranteed fame, only to find that Dysart had beaten me to it. He sat there in his dressing-gown, lost in a private ritual of communion. Sometimes he turned and caught my eye, sometimes not.

How I loved those paintings. There were some that individually I liked less than others, but as a body, God, how I loved them. How they fed that fat greedy worm which lay curled in my gut, which grew fatter and greedier with every passing year.

But the curious thing was, the sad thing – how did this

happen? – the thing that started slowly and reeled out of control, was that as the number of paintings in the collection increased, so proportionately Dysart's interest in me seemed to decrease. Gradually the paintings became the real focus of his interest, the reality. They were the true gold. In comparison I was slowly turning back into dross.

There must have been some point in our marriage, some fulcrum – a word I have learned from crossword puzzles – when the balance subtly changed, but I never noticed it. Perhaps I was not clever enough in my juggling act: maybe I learned too much or not enough. In my warm, self-satisfied delusion I thought that we had a reached a plateau of perfection. I thought we had the ideal marriage, Dysart and I – not a conventional marriage but a marriage that was sublimely complementary. And the magnificent monument we had built to celebrate our union was a collection that would illuminate the world for centuries after we had gone.

Perhaps I gloated too much and grew too pleased with myself. I think I became careless. I failed to notice things were shifting until already they had slipped too far away for me to haul them back. Too late I realized that Dysart had come to prefer the paintings to the real thing.

I panicked.

The fact is that I had lost my freshness for him. I had lost the dangerous stench of the jungle.

Let me give you an illustration. Once, when we were in New York – where one of the greats of the American establishment was painting me, and a young tiro was discussing the possibility of a commission – I escaped for a whole day and caught the train to Coney Island. I drank beer and ate popcorn and hot dogs and went on rides. I watched families of fat Americans waddle down to the beach. But something had gone wrong with me. Here, where I should have been in my element, I no longer fitted comfortably. I brought with me the stink of civilization, the reek of class. It wasn't just the shoes I wore and the haircut; it was on my skin, it had invaded my blood. People stood aside to let me pass. The hucksters, who once upon a time would have whistled, whose eyes would have glinted with cheerful lust, spoke to me in muted, respectful tones. They almost tugged their forelocks. They waited until I had passed. I brought a silence and a stillness with me, a deathliness. People waited politely for me to go. Only when I had gone did life start up again. And this is what Dysart sensed, that I had lost something vital.

All this, of course, was inevitable: I'd been aware of the danger from the beginning, and yet when it started to happen I was baffled by it. I grew more and more distressed. I snarled and twisted and bit in my distress like a caged fox.

And yet the paintings were still working. The old American painted me as a series of interlinking, overlapping red and black circles. The young American did something very similar to Duffy's 'Surfaces', a smooth wash of undulating pale gold sand-hills blown smooth by the wind: a desert.

Now fourteen women hung from the walls like the lifeless bodies of Bluebeard's wives. It was not enough. Despite the bewildering distance that was growing between us, we were still held together by this one consuming lust, we were both obsessed by the possibilities of the fifteenth painting.

I dreamed last night of that room in the Essex Square house.

I dreamed that I was walking down the passage. A light under the door dribbled on to the landing carpet. I went in. Hanging round the walls, from great butchers' hooks screwed into the ceiling, were naked and half-naked women all in states of dreadful decay. Their mouths were stretched in skeletal smiles. Some twirled idly on their hooks. Blood had dried in black pools under their dangling feet. Flies swarmed round the viscous intermittent drips from open wounds. And in the middle of the room, in the middle of this ghastly abattoir, sat Dysart, exactly as

I had so frequently found him on those morning visits when I was driven to check on my immortality.

I knew it was Dysart, although his face was blank like a white balloon.

There's a dream to keep Mr Rick Thomas fed for weeks.

The fifteenth artist failed to fall in love with me. He suffered neither an old man's sentimental fondness for me, nor a young man's sexual infatuation. There was no excuse for this: he wasn't gay, he wasn't blind, he wasn't senile. He didn't even particularly dislike me. He was just indifferent.

This sent a fear like a cold, cold wind through my bones.

Dysart was dissatisfied with the fifteenth painting. He debated whether or not it should join the others. It stayed stacked against the wall, unhung.

There was no talk of a sixteenth painting.

After that, we had a series of functions which interrupted our usual habit of drinking whisky in his room late at night and gossiping before bed. When the run of late nights ended, the habit was not resumed. Dysart always had some excuse. He stopped visiting my room on occasional mornings to watch me bath. Both rituals were quietly dropped and I could find no way to resuscitate them. There were other signs. Too many. I could chart a million such small instances of a healthy marriage taking a sudden, unexplained chill and dying slowly of it.

One such instance – a dreadful and humiliating memory – happened at a dinner party.

I am trying to remember who was there. Let me think. The usual crowd: Gerald Mockridge, who is the editor of *The Reddington*, which, if you don't know about these things, is a magazine devoted to contemporary art. Archie Powell, who is a critic, a misogynistic gay who adores dogs. You know the type. He looks like a vicious cherub. His face is pink and dimpled under a tonsure of thinning copper curls. His thick lips are sweetly malicious. Francesca Harding – she was definitely there. She was always everywhere Dysart was. Also a woman called Zoë Patanian, who claimed to be a performance artist.

We ate chicken, I remember. Way above my head a conversation on some obscure '-ism' rumbled to a close. I had learned to stay quiet during these discussions. I preferred to look as if I were thinking about something more profound, more real, more in touch than any of them, crippled by their dry intellectualism, could ever aspire to.

'Don't you think so, Sandra?' Archie Powell said suddenly.

If I was asked a direct question it was my habit to smile vaguely and murmur an amusing *non sequitur*. They seemed to be discussing what was currently happening in Japan. Personally, I thought that what was currently happening in Japan was pretty much what was happening anywhere else in the world: people were being born, people were dying, people were desperate, or euphoric, or in love, or out to grab all they could get. Politicians were as devious and corrupt as they always are. All the usual stuff. But of course Dysart's friends weren't talking about life. They were talking about Art. They couldn't even talk about the weather (as I no longer can) without relating it to a Turner sky. I looked round the table and felt a sudden recklessness, a desire to say precisely what I thought, to recapture that fresh philistinism that had once simultaneously appalled and fascinated Dysart. I said, 'Do you really want to know what I think, Archie?'

He didn't, of course. His occasional attempts to draw me into this kind of conversation were entirely motivated by malice.

'I think we'd all like to know that, wouldn't we?' he said with a gallant little sneer at his fellow guests.

'All right then,' I said recklessly. 'Well, I think there's probably a hundred times more interesting things going on in Japan than whatever a couple of conceptual artists are doing with a pile of fish bones and a dead rabbit.'

There was a burst of laughter.

'But seriously,' said Francesca, 'doesn't one measure the

health of a society by its art?' She leaned across the table in an earnest effort to rescue me – and therefore Dysart – from any possibility of looking stupid.

'So Sandra thinks there are more important things to discuss than art?' said Gerald Mockridge, his voice thickened by a glass or three of Traminer and the pleasurable possibility of an equally good row. 'Well, frankly, I think she may well be right.'

'What, for example?' said Archie with a thin snigger.

'Well,' I shrugged. 'I don't know. The political situation . . . ?'

Dysart said gently in an attempt to close the subject, 'A fairly dull and labyrinthine subject, I'd have thought.'

But Archie was in his stride now. 'Good,' he said. 'Politics. So give us your views on the current Japanese government, Sandra.'

'I would,' I said, 'if I had any. But I haven't.'

'Sandra passes on politics,' Archie announced to the table at large. 'How wise. What about philosophy?' What a poisonous little toad he was. His cheeks bulged with gleeful venom. 'Modern Japanese philosophy. Is that a more interesting subject to you than conceptual art?'

'Almost anything is,' I said.

Zoë Patanian laughed nervously. 'Well, I'm afraid you'd have to count me out on Japanese philosophy.'

'Me too,' I said. 'Don't look at me' – although no one except Dysart was. The skin over the bridge of his nose was turning livid yellow, like the colour of the dead strips I peel off between my toes. 'I've never pretended to know anything about philosophy,' I said, 'Japanese or otherwise.'

'Then tell me, Sandra,' said Archie. 'What exactly are these important things about Japan you wish us to discuss?' He bounced about in his chair waving his fork at me. His eyes glittered with spite. It was the kind of performance he sometimes gave on television. It was his favourite sport: demolishing in public people he personally considered of no worth. He could disembowel a writer, a poet, a painter in less than five minutes. 'Theatre?' he suggested. 'Do you consider theatre important?'

'Not particularly.'

'Or film. Would you prefer us to discuss the work of Oshima?'

'I've never heard of Oshima,' I said.

Dysart closed his eyes briefly as if he were dreadfully tired. He tried rescuing me. He tried to change the subject but Francesca and Zoë insisted on pursuing it.

'Oh, yes, I'm sure you have,' said Francesca nervously. 'You must have done.'

'*Ai No Corrida*,' said Zoë. 'You can't have missed that. Although, actually, I have to say, I do take Sandra's overall point.'

'Really?' said Archie. 'You *have* to say that, do you? You "take her point"? Despite the fact that she has no idea what she's talking about?'

'Ignorance,' Dysart remarked drily, 'has never prevented most of our revered colleagues from offering their opinions on a whole gamut of subjects.'

'And that includes you, Archie, my dear,' said Gerald Mockridge.

'Quite,' said Dysart. 'If you insist that people should know what they're talking about, Archie, before they venture an opinion, then our media would be bankrupt.'

Zoë Patanian leaned across to me. 'Darling,' she said, 'if you really haven't seen *Ai No Corrida* then you absolutely must. The whole thing is texturally so profound.'

She probably didn't say 'texturally profound' but it was something equally meaningless.

'No, no . . .' Archie insisted. 'We can't let Sandra off the hook as easily as that. She has thrown down the gauntlet. She has accused us of triviality. She says there are more important things about Japan to discuss than its art. So let's hear these interesting things. Come on, Sandra.'

'I wasn't suggesting,' I said, 'that you should discuss anything in particular. I was simply wondering aloud whether sometimes you talk about art as if it were more real than life.'

Archie sniggered.

Dysart said sharply – it was a warning not to get in any deeper – 'It's our capacity to create art, and to be moved by it, which raises us from the level of animals.'

I watched Dysart cut a small piece of chicken breast and lift it to his mouth.

'And what about that chicken you're eating?' I said.

He paused in mid mouthful. 'I beg your pardon?'

'How do you know,' I said, 'that a chicken isn't moved by art?'

Gerald Mockridge spluttered.

'I don't think that's a question that deserves a serious answer, do you?' Dysart said. He turned his attention pointedly away from me. 'Zoë, have some more salad.'

But I was not to be put off. 'Yes, it is,' I insisted, somehow adrift now on some line that was off the point, and yet seemed to be central to some other mysterious argument I was engaged in with Dysart alone. 'You know nothing about it. How do you know what a chicken thinks? It may find wonderfully beautiful patterns in the mud. Or in the sky. Or maybe . . .' I was floundering a bit, '. . . you know how chickens suddenly stand absolutely still with their heads on one side? Well, how do you know that isn't because they've just been struck by some deeply profound thought?'

'Tautology,' said Dysart. 'You don't need both deeply and profound.' He smiled at his guests – an invitation to join him in indulging me. 'I'm not quite sure why I'm discussing this absurd proposition of yours, Sandra,' he said lightly, 'but since I am, let me just remind you that chickens do not paint, they do not sculpt, they do not write poetry, they do not compose music, they have no language.'

'Sorry, Sandra,' said Gerald Mockridge. 'Won't do. Doesn't hold water, this argument of yours.'

'It isn't an argument at all,' said Dysart. 'It completely ignores several million years of human evolution. But then, of course, you could argue that Sandra herself is still fairly low on the evolutionary scale.'

Why did he say that? Did he mean it as a joke? He pretended it was a joke. He wrapped it up with an air of amused, indulgent kindness, but it was not funny. It was not kind. Had I lost so much value in his eyes that he no longer cared how much he hurt me?

The rest of the table chose to take it as it was presented to them. There was a ripple of laughter. Archie sat back in his chair smiling beatifically.

I pushed the rest of my chicken to the side of my plate. It was too late for this particular bird to have even the smallest of profound thoughts, but now I had made such inflated claims for her, it seemed wrong to eat the poor creature.

'You're like one of those pompous old Victorian missionaries,' I said to Dysart. 'You think you're the ultimate. You think civilization and culture have finally reached their peak in you.'

'Not at all,' he said coldly. 'I should be very foolish to think that. The trouble with Sandra,' he said, smiling round the table, 'is that she's still insufficiently equipped to offer a properly reasoned argument.'

'The trouble with Dysart,' I said, lashing back like a wounded cat, 'is that he's insufficiently equipped to offer a good fuck.'

There was a dreadful silence. A long and dreadful silence. Distantly I heard Archie's high-pitched snicker. Francesca and Zoë studied their plates. Gerald coughed several times, then he chuckled nervously. 'Well, well,' he said. 'There you go. I feel I ought to say "a bit below the belt, Sandra", but perhaps that's less than appropriate under the circumstances.'

For dessert we had poached Italian pears with a dark chocolate sauce. I choked on every mouthful.

Much later, when the guests had left, Dysart and I passed each other icily on the stairs. 'Never,' he said, 'never do that to me again.' His voice was glacial. 'Never humiliate me like that in front of my friends.'

We did not discuss the incident again.

We discussed less and less. We were afraid of what new symptom of this disease, this rot, we might inadvertently reveal to each other. We spoke only of necessary things. But, oh, how polite we were with one another, how nice, how delicately we skimmed over the surfaces like two water-boatmen prancing on the oily tension of a lake.

I watched the marriage dying and grew desperate. I grasped at solutions. I took a lover.

What a perverse and irrational response this seems to me now. I did not want a lover, I wanted Dysart. I did not want afternoons of tediously repetitive sex in bland hotel rooms. I wanted reassurance. I wanted confirmation that I, Sandra Stevens, was as luminous as any of the paintings. I wanted Dysart, who had chosen me, still to find me worthy, to find me still full of substance.

The man I chose was my sister Bev's husband, who had lusted after me devotedly, and more or less silently, like a large, dim dog, for the last fifteen years. I conceived the idea in the silence of an Essex Square afternoon. I told Dysart that I was going north for a few days to visit my Mum and Dad. In the muddled pit of my mind, I thought that if I could recover that old power that had once come to me with such baffling effortlessness, then as a side-effect I might also revive whatever equally baffling enchantment I had once exercised over Dysart.

I chose Grahame Birtles because he was the easiest pickings I could think of. I knew that his hopeless dreams of me had compensated him for a life of nagging and social climbing with Bev. These days he was buying up land and building on it. Strings of small exclusive estates on the outskirts of the city displayed his maroon and gold logo: 'Birtles Executive Homes'. He'd just built a house for Bev and their noxious children on a prime site at the end of Bexton Lane, a detached, five-bedroomed mansion with

Elizabethan leaded windows, a Georgian portico and a Victorian conservatory. If I had never married Dysart I would have envied Bev this house, but I had learned now to sneer.

'Of course it's not as grand as your place in London,' Bev said. She was giving me a guided tour. She patted her hair complacently. It was very clear from her tight, smug smiles which of the two houses she preferred.

Grahame dragged round after us, pointing out details of plumbing fixtures and forcing himself not to look at me too much. His eyes were dazed with longing.

Finally and triumphantly Bev brought us back to the lounge and left us there alone while she went to the kitchen – a miracle of technology, white surfaces and chrome dials like the nerve-centre of a nuclear power station softened by flowery prints and frills. While she was brewing tea, I made a direct approach. I told Grahame that I was booking a room in a hotel. I suggested he might like to meet me there.

He reared back in his chair. His face turned pale as dough, a yeasty mixture of fear, wonder and disbelief. He mumbled something. It turned into a cough. Choking, he hurled himself to his feet and stumbled out of the room, colliding with Bev and her gold tea trolley in the doorway. 'What's the matter with you?' she snapped. 'He's always doing that. It drives me mad. The moment I've got a meal ready, he disappears. He could win prizes for it. "The Most Irritating Man in the World Award".' She laughed. 'He'd win that one hands down.'

I waited for him downstairs in the hotel bar. I was doubtful whether in the end he'd have the courage to face his dream head on, but he did. He walked across the reception area with 'deceit' written all over him. We sat side by side on a squashy maroon sofa drinking vodka and tonic. 'Shall we go up now?' I said.

He swallowed. He wiped his damp hands on his trousers. 'I'm afraid I'm a bit sweaty,' he said.

I walked across the thick pink carpet towards the lifts. He followed me. Together we travelled in dizzy silence to the fourth floor. 'Are you sure you know what you're doing?' I asked as I opened the door to my room. I thought in all fairness I ought to give him one last chance to change his mind, but he didn't take it.

Despite his nervousness and his constant apologies about the state of his sweat glands, we spent really quite a satisfactory couple of hours in room 403. Surprisingly satisfactory.

After that we met once a month or so, somewhere anonymous off the M1. Goodness knows why I went on seeing him. He was a terminally dull man, nice but dull. Fifteen years with Bev had smashed to a pulp any delicate conversational buds that in other circumstances might have successfully sprouted. I lay in his thick, muscly arms – he had a good body – and longed for something else, for Dysart's easy knowledge and his quiet wit, for his murmuring elegant phrases to wind themselves in and out of my ears, for a less messy, less physical, more subtle communion.

So we conducted ourselves, Grahame Birtles and I, almost entirely in silence. His breath was always mildly fishy, as if he'd just eaten a sardine sandwich. He splashed himself with body sprays and deodorants to mask any rank smells from which he was convinced he suffered. He was afraid the musky oozings from his glands, his rough, tradesman's stink, would offend my delicate sensibilities. Sometimes he tried to speak as we heaved and rolled on the bed together, but his words broke up into choking helpless gasps. How anxious he was to please. Sometimes, he tried to tell me how much he loved me, but the strength of his emotion always defeated him. It was better when he said nothing. Then these mute couplings had an illusion of significance. Afterwards we lay side by side, and exchanged the odd word about the weather or the traffic on the motorway. We looked at our watches, we dressed, we had a quick drink together in the bar. By this time gratitude and a giddy sense of his own manliness had gone to his head: he experienced a brief flush of volubility. Football was his chief subject. He'd just been made something or other on the board of the city's football club. His only other subject was his chairmanship of the local Rotarians. I was always anxious by that point to get away. In the car park we shook hands in case anyone who knew him was looking. We climbed into our separate cars and drove off in opposite directions.

The subject for this week is significant men.

'Who,' Mr Rick Thomas asks, 'just as a matter of interest, who would you say have been the most significant men in your life? Apart obviously from Dysart and your father?'

He has to repeat the question. I am not really listening. I am thinking about croissants. I have forgotten what they taste like. It's hard to drag my mind round to men.

'I once knew a gardener,' I say.

'A gardener?' says Rick. 'And in what way was he significant?'

'I don't know.' (The problem is I can still visualize a croissant, I can see the flaky yellow texture, but I can't recapture the feeling of it in my mouth.)

'Then why did you mention him?' says Rick, for whom everything must have a reason.

'I just think about him sometimes,' I say. A memory drops into my head. I am standing on a doorstep. I am wearing a thin jacket, damp with November drizzle. 'I once asked this gardener,' I volunteer, 'whether or not he believed in God.'

'And what did he say?'

'I can't remember. Nothing, really. He said: I just get on with my work.'

'Voltaire,' Rick murmurs with a mocking smile. I assume it's a mocking smile. It's difficult to tell, with so much growth about his lips.

'No,' I say, to be annoying. 'Mr Jackson.'

I can't think of any other significant men, except Duffy, of course, and Mr Haskin and Mr Webster and Mr Noble and Sammy Rubin and Colin and all the others.

And my son.

That dinner party, the awful one, the one that marked the beginning of the end ... I have replayed it again and again in my head recently. I have been trying to work out what it was that Dysart and I were really arguing about under the convenient cover of chickens and the absolute superiority of the human race. I think it was something to do with the way he looked at things, the way he assumed that things must inevitably be the way he saw them: that in the end his vision must irrefutably be the only vision because it was his.

My son (what a curious, shy pleasure it gives me to write that), my son Keith, came to visit me again today. He brought with him a photograph of his girlfriend, who is also an archaeologist. She is pale and freckly with a small tough face. She's the sort of girl who looks nothing much, until one day it occurs to you that she is beautiful. She reminds me of a young Katharine Hepburn. Her name is Lizzie. It suits her. She comes from Sheffield. She is not a bit like me.

As well as the photo, he also brings me some biscuits and a box of chocolates.

I still can't get over this son of mine, with his wedge of hair and his leather jacket and his limbs which are not made on a human scale. His face is unmarked, except by stubble. It glows. He seems to me so gloriously simple, so wonderfully undaunted by the world. I stare at him all the time, greedily, stupidly. He is ten times more beautiful than any of Bev's children.

I pray to something or the other, to the world perhaps, or to life itself, not to hurt him too much, not to crush him too hard. I think of him in a few years' time, ten perhaps, when he is established in his profession, when he is working somewhere in the Middle East. I see him in khaki shorts and sun-glasses supervising a dig. His hair will be bleached by the sun. He and Lizzie will live out in the desert in a tent and ride camels and discover fragments of long-lost lives. And then I think of those people whose lives burned brightly thousands of years ago, and who, in their time, have no idea that one day, unimaginably far into the future, my son, Keith Eric Fox, will retrieve their shattered dinner plates from the sands of time (and also, of course, from the sands of the desert). I wish I could tell them. It seems to me his work has vital importance, not from a historical/sociological point of view, although that's quite interesting if you like that sort of thing, but from the point of view of continuity, of distance, of insignificance, of understanding one's place.

He hugs me when he leaves. He has eaten half the packet of biscuits. A son after my own heart.

'Bye, Mum,' he says, casually, without thinking about what he has said, without even realizing that he has said it.

It's odd the way people reappear in your life, as if everything moves in smaller or larger circles, like planets, like the seasons, and will ineluctably come back again.

Late one night, I returned from one of those silent pointless encounters off the M1 with my sister's husband, to find the chandeliers blazing in the hall and Dysart alone in the downstairs drawing-room waiting for me. He was pacing up and down.

I thought, this is it, he knows about Grahame. Now it would all come out. Now we would fight, I thought, faint with exhilaration and fear, now we would cry, now we would prod and poke this dead thing back to life. And I was so excited, because I was sure that now I could hook him again, now I could reel him in. I would shock and enchant him by a new level of vulgarity.

'You're very late,' he said.

'I told you I would be late,' I said. I took off my gloves,

peeling them away from my fingers slowly like women do in old films. On the surface I was quite calm. I sat down very carefully on the ottoman, arranging myself, taking my time, gathering my wits.

Dysart could hardly contain himself. I saw the dreadful question bubble up and explode into his mouth. I was ready for it. I had my strategy planned. And here it was ... here it was ...

'Who is she?' he demanded.

I remember blinking several times and wondering if time had slipped and I had missed half a conversation. The question made no sense to me.

'Who is who?' I said. My mouth must have been slack with amazement.

Dysart made a sharp grunt of exasperation. 'This woman. This Rezvani woman. She's upstairs. I told Bradley to put her in your sitting-room.'

Now I was utterly confused. Now I was no longer in control.

'She's drunk,' he said. 'She refuses to go away. She says she's an old friend of yours.'

In my sitting-room – ivory and dove grey, two Dufys, a Rouault and a Vlaminck – a middle-aged woman was examining the Bohemian Millefiore perfume bottle that Dysart had bought me for our fourth wedding anniversary. She was vastly fat, a mass of hanging things, of dripping things, of wispy scarves and lengths of fur and trailing hems. I had no idea who she was.

'Good evening,' I said.

She turned. Still I didn't recognize her. Her hair was dustily grey as if a mass of ancient cobwebs were caught in it.

'Sandra,' she shrieked.

She flung open her arms. There was a gaping split between the sleeve and the body of her dress. 'How wonderful to see you after all this time.' Her face floated offensively close to mine in a reeking haze of spirits. She pecked my cheek. 'I meant to get in contact ages ago, but you know how it is.' She waved an arm vaguely.

*Still* I was at sea. 'I'm so sorry . . .' I murmured.

She laughed, the sudden, high-pitched bark of an hysterical dog. 'You don't recognize me, do you?'

'I'm afraid I don't.'

'Shura,' she said triumphantly as if she had just successfully executed some wonderful sleight of hand. 'It's me, darling. It's Shura.'

And then, of course, vaguely, I did remember her.

She sat herself heavily down on the sofa. 'You will forgive me,' she said, 'for disturbing you so late. I'm afraid your husband . . . such a charming man . . . is not too pleased about it, but I knew you would understand because it is such an emergency.'

Suddenly she burst into noisy tears. 'He has thrown me out,' she wailed.

'Who has?'

'The landlord of my flat. He is a rat. A grasping rat. I am penniless, Sandra. Penniless and friendless. I have no roof over my head. I shall sleep on the streets, I shall die of cold.'

It looked to me as if she was already sleeping on the streets.

'What about your father?' I asked, remembering dimly that her father was some kind of oil tycoon.

'My father?' She gave another of those strange hysterical laughs. 'Don't speak to me about my father. My God, if you only knew.'

She then proceeded to make sure that I did know. It was a long, confused and bitter diatribe interspersed sometimes with sobs, sometimes with harsh barks like the cries of a distressed sea lion. Her father, it seemed, had married yet again, this time a grasping schemer, a failed starlet, who had borne him a son, and then persuaded him to change his will. A month or two later he died of a heart attack, leaving his multitudinous ex-wives and his daughter each with such a pathetic pay-off she could hardly expect to keep a cat alive on hers. Obviously, she said, they'd contested this will, but the new wife had locked herself in with such a clever bunch of lawyers there was nothing they could do. So, obviously, Shura was left with no choice but to marry for money. She found herself a suitable rich Iranian, an older man, but he had turned out to be a swine and nowhere near as rich as she had imagined. The marriage had been miserably unhappy, and in the end he had tricked her out of what little money she had left and deserted her. Now she was in the most pitiful state. Her landlord had changed the lock on her flat for non-payment of rent. He had taken her few meagre possessions as part payment. From riches to rags, she said. Literally, she now had nothing.

'But then,' she sniffed, 'then I remember that in the whole wide world I still have one friend left, my old friend Sandra from so long ago when we were girls.' She dabbed at her eyes with the end of one of the bits of material slung round her neck. Her skin still looked as if she had rubbed ashes into it. 'I have followed your career, you know, with such interest. And I have often thought how nice it would be to get in contact again. But the weeks pass, the years pass, I am abroad so often. Then I see the photographs in the paper. The wedding.' She laid a plump hand on my knee. 'And when this disaster strikes me I think immediately of my dear old friend. Please . . .' she clutched at me with repulsive, clawing fingers, 'please help me.'

I put an arm gingerly round her shoulders. In a soft, horrible response, her body slumped against mine. Her hair smelled powerfully of rancid cooking oil.

This is how Dysart found us when he came to find out what was happening.

'My husband,' I said, 'Dysart Stevens.'

'We've met,' she said, extending her hand as if she expected him to kiss it. 'I feel I know you intimately. I watch you so often on television. I read all your articles.'

Dysart nodded. 'Well,' he said, 'if you'll forgive me. It's getting very late . . .'

Shura took the hint. She struggled to her feet. There was a dreadful, pale, bloated look about her as if she had just been fished out of the river.

'If you could just lend me a couple of hundred,' she murmured.

Suddenly her milky eyes rolled upwards. Her colour changed from ashen to corpse white. She collapsed like an empty bag on to the floor.

'She's fainted,' Dysart observed unnecessarily.

'She's very drunk,' I said. 'We'd better get her to bed.'

Dysart blenched. 'You want her to stay?'

'Well, what else can we do? We can't throw her out on to the street.'

Together, we heaved her up on to her feet. We bumped and hauled her along the landing and rolled her on to a spare bed.

'She smells,' said Dysart, his face a mask of fastidious horror.

Her skirt was rucked up round her waist. Her legs were like two fat, pale rolls of sausage meat stuffed into bulging skins. I pulled the covers over her. She stirred and then burped, a loose, loud belch. After a moment she started to snore.

'Who is she?' Dysart said. He was rolling his shoulder as if he'd strained it.

'No one,' I said. 'A vague acquaintance. I met her very briefly years ago.'

I could see that he did not believe me.

He looked dreadfully tired, tired and sad. It hurt me to see how tired he looked. 'You go to bed,' I said. 'I'll bring you a whisky along in a moment.'

I thought perhaps now, perhaps in this moment of weakness, I might manage to revive our lapsed habit. I might soothe him with whisky and stories to make him laugh of Shura and Quaffingham. And then I might take off my clothes in front of the tall mirror on the far wall, and things would slide back to how they once were and we would be happy again.

He smiled, a smile as thin as damp, wintry sunshine. 'A little too late for that now, don't you think?' he said.

I must just pause here a moment to note that *The Mayor of Casterbridge* is a superb book. It interests me deeply. Too deeply, really, for me to be able to grasp it properly. I can't think about it as profoundly as I want to. I start to think, and then my brain flaps and flutters away and lands briefly on something else. That's one of the really sad things about being stupid and having an uneducated mind.

All the same, I've got this far: Michael Henchard is not a good man, not by conventional standards of right and wrong, not in the way, for example, that Dorothea Casaubon is good. But actually I think he is transcendentally good. (This is Dysart's word, 'transcendental'. He used it often to describe me. The verb 'to transcend'. It makes me think of soaring up above the clouds where the sun blinds you, and thick dazzling puffs of solid glittering white float below, that moment of rising above, of starting a journey.)

Shura was awake when I knocked at her door in the morning. The room smelled of cheese, of unwashed flesh, of grease. I ran a bath for her and poured half a bottle of perfumed oil into the water. While she bathed I found her some old clothes of mine.

'How beautiful,' she murmured, stroking the white shirt I found for her, 'it's such a long time since I saw such exquisite clothes.'

I also found her some leggings. On her massive limbs the fabric was stretched to the limit. 'Oh, my God,' she breathed, waddling from room to room in these leggings of mine. 'How elegant it is. What a house. What exquisite furniture. And the paintings. Sandra, my God, did you know you have a Cézanne on the landing? And these, did you know these are Picassos?' She touched one reverently. 'He must be so wonderfully rich, this charming husband of yours.' She linked arms playfully with me. 'Do you remember, Sandra, those happy days we had at Quaffingham together, you and me? I've never forgotten our talks. But we were so young then, you know. So young. And now look at us.'

The ravages of time had actually been immeasurably kinder to me than they had to her, but she seemed blithely and insultingly unaware of this.

'Oh, Sandra,' she said, 'believe me, if I had married a man like your husband, such a cultured, such a generous man . . . is that a Klee? My God, a Paul Klee on your wall. And a Derain. And this . . . look at this superb ottoman. Second Empire, is that right? What perfect taste. Do you know, I feel so comfortable here, so much at home.' She bounced fleshily away to examine something else. 'Oh my dear, this table, I love it. French. Eighteenth century. I adore it. So tell me, Sandra, how did you meet your husband?'

I started to tell her but she was already off to examine another find.

'I tell you what we should do today,' she said suddenly. 'We should go shopping.'

'You've got no money,' I reminded her.

She frowned in a distracted way as if some trivial thought had eluded her, then she clapped her hands. Her wild grey hair writhed round her face. Her chalky face was radiant with pleasure. 'Never mind,' she said. 'This is no problem at all. You will lend me some.'

I had other plans altogether. I took her straight to my bank. She stood beside me in the queue for the cashier, smiling and nodding like a madwoman, and staring up at the marble pilasters.

'So where exactly is this flat of yours?' I asked her.

'I'm not going back there, not to that flat,' she muttered. 'You can kill me first, but I will not go back.'

The people queuing behind us pretended not to notice her. They shrank discreetly away. I scooped up the five hundred in cash I'd taken out of my account, tucked my hand under the flaccid flesh of her arm and marched her out across the hushed floor.

'Tell me the address of this flat,' I insisted.

'No, I will not,' she said mutinously. 'He is a bad man.'

'But your clothes are there.'

She snorted. 'You think I am so shallow a person I care only about clothes?'

'We'll go there now,' I said. 'I'll pay off all your arrears, and we'll find somewhere better. How much do you owe?'

She cringed back against the front window of a sandwich bar. 'No, please, Sandra,' she whimpered. 'If I go back he'll call the police.'

I was exasperated by all this. It was none of my business. If she wouldn't go back to her flat then she wouldn't. I couldn't force her. But for goodness' sake, she wasn't my responsibility. She had no claim at all on me. Except possibly the price of a pair of emerald earrings.

Her face brightened suddenly. She seemed able to switch her mood in seconds. Her moment of terror was utterly forgotten. 'All that money,' she crooned. 'Let's go and buy something nice with it.'

I lost my patience with her. I told her that if she would not go back to her flat then I would find her a hotel. That was the limit, I said, of what I was prepared to do. We were not friends, I said, and never had been.

I waved at a taxi. It pulled in to the kerb. I grabbed her by the arm and dug my fingers hard into her flesh in a sudden exquisite desire to hurt her badly. She gave an indignant shriek. I shoved her into the taxi. 'Shut up and get in,' I said.

She fell like a bulging refuse bag on to the back seat and burst into tears. The taxi swerved into the traffic. Her lax body tumbled against mine. I tried to nudge her back into an upright position. 'You are the only one left, Sandra,' she mumbled. 'I have no one in the world now but you.'

The hotel I found for her was pleasant and relatively inexpensive. I paid for a week. Her room had a small en suite bathroom, a television and a mini bar. I left her sitting on the floor examining its contents. She looked like a large angry child playing with a dolls' house.

'I'm going now,' I said. 'I'll come and see you tomorrow.'

'Go then,' she said mutinously. 'Go.'

'Is there anything else you need?' I asked, trapped in the doorway by a sudden need to expiate some guilt.

'There's a draught,' she said. 'Shut the door and go.'

So I shut the door and went.

I've just been remembering the pleasure of coming home to the house in Essex Square on those grey January afternoons when the wind, swollen with sleet, blew cold from Russia across the marshes. I am thinking of the fire in the upstairs drawing-room, or in my private sitting-room. I'm remembering the shaded lights, the musky Earl Grey tea and dark chocolate Liebnitz biscuits, the brightness and the opulence of the Kandinskys and the Dufys. I am remembering how warm, how safe, how rich I felt then.

The lawyers will have put that house, my house, on the market now. So who will inherit all of Dysart's money?

Not me. They will surely not let his murderer inherit his fortune.

After I left Shura, I stopped at a café and had a cappuccino and two sweet, sticky Danish pastries covered in almonds. Then I went home. I lay on the sofa watching a little television. I was drifting into a quiet doze when Bradley woke me.

'She's here again,' he said. 'That woman. She came back. What shall I tell her?'

An unease, a fear, slithered like an anxious worm through my veins. I could see this moment repeat and repeat itself into eternity. Now she had found me she would never let me go, she would move in, she would take me over, there was no escaping her. She was like some dreadful reflection of myself in a mirror.

She was standing in the hall. She carried a brown paper bag from which the neck of a bottle protruded. 'I have come back, Sandra,' she announced, reeling slightly. 'I cannot stay in that place. Such a nasty hotel, such cheap furnishings. The chair came apart in my hand.'

I found myself defending the hotel to Bradley who was listening to this. It was actually, I said, a very nice hotel. It had, I said, at least two stars.

'No, no, no, you were deceived,' Shura said. 'It was a flea-pit. There were things in the bed.'

'What kind of things?'

'And the manager was rude to me.' She swayed dangerously, like a comedian whose shoes are anchored to the floor. 'I will not stay in a place where people are rude.' She stumbled up the stairs towards me in a shimmering fug of alcohol. 'You will hardly notice, my darling,' she announced, 'that I am here. I am the perfect guest.'

There was no point in forcing her into another taxi and finding another hotel, not until I'd sobered her up. No one would have her like this. And anyway, a couple of hours and the entire contents of a mini bar later and she'd be back again.

I steered her into the bedroom. She collapsed on to my bed like a waterlogged and disintegrating corpse. She held out a fat white hand to me. I was afraid to touch it. It looked as if it might crumble away into hunks of flesh. Under the sweetness of the perfumes I had doused her with, I could smell the sickly stench of rot. She grasped my hand and pulled me down beside her. 'Oh such fun we had at Quaffingham,' she said. 'Do you remember? The dances. The tennis.' She made it sound like a country house in the nineteen thirties, the sort of place I used to read about in Mr Haskin's mildewed novels. She made it sound as if we had shared some long idyllic girlhood together. Her eyes were dark with sadness. 'Do you remember the day we first met?' she lisped in a dreadful, wheedling, little girl's voice. 'On the stairs? And you mistook me for your sister. Do you remember that? I wish I *was* your sister.' She snuggled up to me, wrapping her fat body round me. 'I would like that so much,' she said, peering up flirtatiously from under her purple eyelids. Suddenly an idea occurred to her. She clutched my arm. 'Let's pretend I *am* your sister. Let's pretend she didn't die.'

Her softness, her flesh, revolted me. I stood up.

'Don't go, Sandra,' she said. Her hand was tight as a claw, her nails dug into my skin. 'Don't leave me.' Her eyes reddened and filmed over. Tears trickled down her floury cheeks.

Down the front of the white shirt I had lent her was a long brown stain pitted with dry tomato seeds. The last dregs in the whisky bottle dribbled on to the bedspread. 'So good to be back again,' she muttered. A gobbet of spittle gathered at the side of her mouth and slithered like a slug trail down her chin. I left her to sleep it off.

I had a very interesting letter from Beverley this morning, a friendly letter. She says how pleased she is I took her advice and let Mum and Dad come and visit me. It's put their minds at rest, she says. It's actually quite a funny letter, quite witty. I enjoyed it.

According to Bev, Grahame is working himself into the ground. 'I never see him these days,' she writes. 'If I didn't know him better I'd think he was having an affair!!'

There are two exclamation marks to emphasize (a) that this is a joke and (b) that it's a perfectly safe one to make because the idea of Grahame having an affair is so absurd. She's right: it is absurd. He was never cut out for adultery. How relieved he must have been when it ended. How desperately he must have prayed that no hint of it came out during the trial. The Rotarians would have drummed him out of their lodge. Poor, silent, dim, muscle-bound Grahame. And yet for a few blazing moments in those hotel rooms I illuminated his life: I gave it meaning. At least, on his deathbed, he'll have the consolation of knowing that once upon a time, if briefly, he lived. And really, you know, thinking about it, I took nothing from Beverley that was hers: certainly nothing that she wanted. As far as Grahame Birtles is concerned, I don't think I have much to reproach myself for.

Last night I finished *The Mayor of Casterbridge*. I cried through most of the last third of the book. Mrs Hutchman, who popped in with a message from my solicitor, was quite upset to see the state I was in, and was relieved when she realized it was nothing serious, only a book. She says she cries non-stop through *Brief Encounter* every time she sees it. Strange to think that a woman with so powerful a moustache can be so easily moved.

She is equally surprised by me. She says, 'I never thought you'd be the crying type.'

Actually, I suspect that I am quintessentially the crying type. Only shallow people cry as easily as I do, only trivial people manage to exorcize their pain so cheerfully, so quickly, with such a warm, delightful rush of tears.

It's just occurred to me that if I had an airtight bottle I could catch all my tears in it and keep those as part of my growing collection of physical trimmings – skin and hair and horny claws, stuff that will not decay. My envelopes sit in a neat row on my bookshelf. Unfortunately, they are still very thin.

'She's still here then?' Dysart said. He had met her on the landing early in the morning. She was dressed, he said, in my dressing-gown.

'Yes,' I said. 'I lent it to her.' I told him about the hotel fiasco. 'Don't worry,' I said. 'I'll sort it out today.'

'Please do.'

He was drinking tea. How immaculate he looked: his dark jacket, his silk shirt.

'I still haven't grasped who she is. Is she some kind of schoolfriend?' he asked.

'She isn't any kind of friend,' I said. 'I met her years ago. At a kind of psychiatric nursing home.'

'Really?' I heard the flicker of interest in his voice. 'What on earth were you doing at a psychiatric nursing home?'

'Convalescing,' I said.

He laughed softly. 'After all this time you can still manage to surprise me,' he said. 'But of course I don't believe it. No one could be saner than you.' He drained his cup. 'Well,' he said, 'she's your responsibility. Make sure she's gone by tonight.'

'I will,' I said. 'I'll get rid of her.'

But I couldn't. I tried. Daily I tried, but she would not be budged. She was like a limpet. She was like an incubus, sucking us dry. Days passed. All my strategies failed. She would not be parted from me because I had become the central figure in this mythology she had invented for herself, her one true friend. I belonged to some lost golden time that she had convinced herself we had shared together, a time of magical innocence.

Every evening we sat, the three of us, round the dinner table, while she remembered events that had never happened, and drew on a debt that had never been incurred. Dysart was unfailingly polite to her, but he sat in cool silence through these meals, his face drawn, the lines in his cheek unnaturally deep. He ate less and less.

'How long?' he asked me. 'How long is this going to go on?'

'I don't understand,' he said. 'What hold has this woman got on you?'

Oh, the schemes I devised to get rid of her, this ghastly *doppelgänger*, this fat, raddled, shrieking, cringing lump of despair who slept on my sheets and contaminated my rooms, and touched my exquisite possessions. They grew wilder and wilder, these schemes, as one by one the rational ones failed. I planned to give her all my money, all the investments that Colin had salted away for me during the nine years I was Kathy Kuriakis. I planned to buy her a house at Land's End, no, further – on an island. A house on the Isle of Man. On Corsica. On some uninhabited lump of rock a hundred miles off the coast of Australia. I contrived ways to get her arrested for some crime. I planned in precise detail how I could poison her.

But I did none of these things. A kind of lethargy paralysed me. I became passive and hopeless. There was such an inevitability about Shura. I saw her as a kind of nemesis. I began to believe that she was my punishment.

On the night which at the trial they constantly referred to as 'the night in question', Dysart brought a crowd of people back with him for drinks. It was the usual bunch: Gerald Mockridge, Zoë Patanian, a titled person on the board of the Royal Opera House, the TV arts guru who was fronting the series of programmes Dysart was presently working on, plus his producer, an amazingly pale woman, pale hair, pale face, colourless watery eyes... all in all, I think, nine or ten people of this sort gathered together in a softly lit room, each holding a glass and chattering like agitated monkeys about the one subject to which all other subjects in their minds were viscerally connected. Francesca Harding was there, of course. We kissed. We held hands and said sweet things about each other. I circled the room, smiling, playing the hostess, offering drinks and flattery, canapés and small jokes.

Fortunately, Shura had been suffering from a headache all afternoon and was lying down. I left the party from time to time to check on her. She was flat out, which was fortuitous but hardly surprising since earlier on I had given her a glass of hot milk laced with two heavy-duty sleeping pills.

Plans were eventually made to move on to a restaurant for dinner. People were putting their glasses down, stubbing out their cigarettes, discussing whether the general mood was in favour of Thai cuisine or something more European. Suddenly the double doors burst open. There, framed in the doorway, stood Shura, trailing new expensive scarves, her grey hair as tousled as a well-used Brillo pad. She flung open her arms. Tears trembled in her vast, liquid-brown eyes. 'Such a wonderful thing,' she trumpeted. 'I have seen it. This magnificent temple to Love.'

The room fell silent. Dysart's friends froze with looks of polite astonishment on their faces. Shura wrapped her arms round me. Her salty tears rolled down her cheeks and splashed on to my chest. 'How he must love you,' she wept. 'All those superb paintings. My God,' she said, releasing me and flinging her arms round Dysart, 'it's like Dante and Beatrice, like Antony and Cleopatra, like Heloïse and Abelard, like . . .' but she had run out of comparisons.

Dysart released himself. His face was livid. A tic pulsed in his cheek. I said hurriedly, 'This is a friend of mine, Shura Rezvani, who is staying with us.'

'God knows what was in that milk, darling,' Shura said. 'I am stumbling about like an old drunk. And for heaven's sake, I go barging into completely the wrong room. But thank God, because there they were . . . these extraordinary paintings.' She gazed up at Dysart, shaking her head in drugged wonder. 'Such a man,' she said. 'So romantic. Such a beautiful gesture. This man, Sandra, he must love you more than anyone else on earth.'

There was another of those embarrassed silences at which Dysart's friends excel. They know exactly at what pitch to clear their throats, at what angle to raise their eyebrows, at what pitch of amazement to set their smiles.

'Oh, what fun,' Shura said. 'A party. The parties we used to have when my father was living in New York . . .' she stepped backwards into a table. The impact of her weight sent it rocking wildly. A Meissen figurine slid elegantly down its tilted surface and smashed on to the floor.

'It's all right, it's all right,' said Dysart in a tight voice, his South African voice, his voice like a steel blade. The room was breathy with gasps. 'It's perfectly all right,' Dysart said. 'Leave it alone. Bradley will deal with it.'

Shura stood with her hand clasped over mouth in horror.

'So – dinner,' Dysart reminded everyone. 'Have we decided yet?'

Conversation bubbled nervously up again. Zoë Patanian bent to pick up the pieces of smashed porcelain. The guests started to wander out on to the landing. They drifted, chattering, down the stairs.

Shura clasped her hands together like a child. 'Where are we going?' she asked.

Francesca Harding called up from the landing, 'Are you coming, Dysart?' She was looking, I remember, particularly sleek, like a Burmese cat.

'You go on,' I whispered in Dysart's ear. 'I'll get Shura back to bed.'

From the top of the stairs I watched them gathering. I watched Dysart hold Francesca Harding's coat for her.

'Where are they going?' Shura asked.

'Nowhere interesting,' I said.

I sat with her, holding her fat white hand, until she fell asleep again.

When Dysart eventually came home from the restaurant, I was running a bath. He wandered into my bathroom carrying two glasses of whisky and water with jangling ice cubes in them. I looked up at him. For a second I felt the familiar ballooning of joy: I thought whatever has been wrong for this last year has somehow during the evening magically put itself right. I thought he had come to gossip about friends, to tell me what had happened in the restaurant, what everyone had eaten, who had said what, what scurrilous stories had circulated. I thought perhaps he had realized that the problem of Shura, this shared, external problem, had somehow united us against a common enemy.

I wish I could remember his face. It is like a Cubist painting to me now ... an eye here, a nose there, details which float about accurately and independently in my head but which I can't put together. Mr Rick Thomas says I don't want to; he says I have deliberately blotted it out. This is not true. I long to be able to have Dysart's face clear in my mind again.

'Is she asleep?' he asked.

How grave his face suddenly was, how pale. I saw that he had not come to gossip. He had come, on the contrary, to say something very serious, something I did not want to hear. I grew afraid. I looked away. I watched the flannel undulating like a strange flat fish swimming along the bottom of the bath.

'I gave her some more sleeping tablets,' I said.

He sat down beside me. I remember he was wearing a cream-coloured jacket. A white silk scarf hung round his neck. Even perched on the edge of a bath he was uniquely elegant.

'Poor Sandra,' he said. How kind his voice was. He took my hand and kissed it. There was something horribly formal and final about that kiss. 'Poor Sandra,' he murmured.

I stood up. I undid my skirt. I thought that perhaps the sight of my body might stop him from saying whatever dreadful thing it was that made his face so grave and pale and his kiss so valedictory.

The skirt dropped to the floor. I stepped out of it. 'Did you enjoy dinner?' I asked. 'Tell me what happened.'

'Sandra,' he said. 'Let me just say this straight out. And let me make it quite clear, absolutely clear – none of this is your fault.'

The word 'fault' frightened me. I felt my knees loosen. I sat down again, skirtless, on the cold edge of the bath.

'It's me,' he said. 'I am entirely to blame. But you must know as well as I do that in the last year or so things have gone very wrong between us.'

'No,' I said in a blind panic of denial. This was not what I was expecting. This was not something we could talk about. I was expecting dramatic accusations of infidelity, something powerful and dangerous, something to reignite his obsession.

He said quietly, 'I've been trying to understand. But how does anyone ever understand these things? Something died. The mistake was mine.'

'There was no mistake,' I croaked. In my throat was a

monstrous painful swelling like an abscess. I found it hard to get the words out. 'It isn't a mistake.'

He shrugged. We sat in miserable silence. A tap dripped. I looked at my knees. I smoothed them.

'I know you have a lover,' he said eventually. 'At least, I assume that's why you book rooms in Trusthouse Forte hotels. I can think of no other reason.'

In the long silence that followed I wondered if I should deny it.

Dysart murmured, 'I'm sorry you found it necessary.'

I saw that my adultery neither hurt him nor excited him. He felt neither passion nor curiosity about it.

'It doesn't matter,' I said. Such a sad, such a hopeless ache had settled in my chest, like a great fat bird that could not be shifted.

'No,' he said, bleakly.

'Dysart,' I said, making conventional responses, pleading with him as if I thought he cared, 'please don't misunderstand this. It was just a trivial thing. It means nothing. I won't see him again.' But I could see that what I did or didn't do was of no real consequence to Dysart any more. The silence grew thicker and more intolerable. The ice in my whisky had melted. Through the glass I could see the skin on my forefinger slightly magnified so that the perfect lines became very clear, like ridges on a hillside.

'So what do you want, then?' I said eventually. 'Do you want a divorce?'

This surprised him. He looked up. 'I thought maybe a trial separation,' he said, 'just to see. Just to find out whether we're any happier apart.'

How could he *say* these things? Was he not happy then? Did I make him so miserable? The idea that he was not happy with me was so distressing I was struck dumb.

'A separation,' he repeated.

*I* was happy. I was very happy.

He looked vaguely around him as if there might be some way out of this conversation. His eye fell on the statuette of the Eiffel Tower I had bought on our honeymoon. He picked it up and examined it. 'This is very difficult for me,' he said. 'After the first disaster with Anne, I swore I would never marry again. And I meant it. What happened when I first saw that photograph of you ... when I first met you ... it was a kind of madness. I thought with you ... someone so open, so fearless, so unspoiled by all the usual things ...' He gave up and shrugged. 'I thought it might work, that's all.'

'It *has* worked,' I insisted.

He shook his head sadly. 'No,' he said. 'No, it hasn't. Be honest. I was wrong to insist on marrying you.' He held the statuette out in front of him as if he was looking at it for the first time. 'What a dreadful thing this is,' he remarked. 'Why on earth do you keep it?'

'You want a separation?' I said, trying to get this clear. I was gripped by panic. He was going to move me out of this house; he was going to banish me. I would land up like Shura, fat and rootless, a mad, destructive woman wandering from place to place, embarrassing my friends – who had never really been my friends – pretending pathetically to be what I no longer was.

'So what about the collection?' I said.

Dysart stared at me in confusion. 'The collection?' he said as if I'd introduced some absurdly irrelevant subject.

'Has that obsession worked itself out as well?' My voice was very tight. Some thick stuff, like escaped blood, or like pus, was bubbling in my throat. 'There'll be no more paintings, then? Is that what you're saying?'

His eyes froze over. 'Is that all you care about?' he said.

'That and the house,' I said coldly. Although it was not true, that was by no means all I cared about.

Dysart looked at me, a long, strange, blank look as if he was waking out of a dream. 'What a monster you are, Sandra,' he observed. 'I hadn't quite realized just how monstrous.' He handed the statuette of the Eiffel Tower to me. 'There you are,' he said. 'That's yours.'

And then in a quiet voice he started to talk about arrangements, things he had already discussed with his lawyer, where he would live, where I would live, my allowance, the weeks he would be using the villa, the weeks I could have it. On and on he droned, a distant, slightly sad smile on his face, on and on, as if he were discussing the details of a funeral. And that's exactly how it was. I could see that. I was dead to him. In my place he had gathered a whole bevy of new wives, a troop of them hanging neatly and silently on the walls. He had captured everything he wanted, every last drop he craved from me had been extracted and was locked away in his special chamber. This was the essence of possession. In the gallery was housed his harem of silent women who would secure for him his immortality. Now he was discarding the husk. And he was being very fair about it. Such a long list of arrangements. On and on. How sweet his voice was, how rational. Have I ever mentioned how much I loved his voice? The cool charm of it, the accent with just a hint of South Africa in the vowels, the kindness?

'And who will have the paintings? How will we divide those?' I said. I was shaking. I knew the answer.

'What a monster you are, Sandra.'

I can still hear him say it. I remember that dazed, bewildered look on his face as if a spell were slowly breaking. I loved his face.

Where did this terrible and unstoppable rage come from? God knows. I didn't even realize I was angry. I thought I was afraid. I thought what I felt was the horror of things slipping uncontrollably away from me. I had no idea that it was rage. Without any warning – except perhaps for that soft viscous bubbling in my throat – it tore out of me like the bursting of a monstrous abscess, or the sudden ejection of fiery streams of glittering lava. Oh, the force of it. It left me breathless. It knocked me half-unconscious. The blood swept into my eyes and blinded me. Its roar was like a great train exploding from a tunnel.

They asked me time and again what happened next, the

police, the endless queue of lawyers. How did the statuette of the Eiffel Tower get into your hand, they asked. Did you pick it up deliberately? With what intention? Was it your intention to hit your husband with the statuette?

'I don't know,' I said.

I *don't* know.

They thought I was lying, of course.

Had you hit your husband in anger before, they asked. Had he hit you?

'Never,' I said.

What do you remember, they asked.

'Nothing.'

I didn't then. That was the truth. Almost the truth. But now I do. I remember selective things. The roaring in my ears, the smell of something vile, something sulphurous or maybe metallic, the look of sudden appalled disbelief in Dysart's eyes. I saw him lift his arm as if I were so luminous that he was blinded by me. There was a thud, a crack. Blood sprayed in the air. I heard Dysart sigh as the air rushed from his mouth. He tumbled tidily forward on to the bathroom floor.

I stared at him in amazement. I thought briefly – did I think this or is it later invention? – that he must have fainted. Until I saw the dark gash in his hair.

Blood smells. It has the smell of butchers' shops, the hot iron stink of secret fears. It was on my hands. It was smeared across the base of the statuette. Dysart lay at my feet. He was moaning. As instantly as it had ignited, the rage drained out of me. I was limp with horror. I am limp with horror now at the memory of it. That dreadful noise. What had I done? I had killed him. He was dying at my feet. And yet – the most fearful thing of all – he was not yet dead. He was still whimpering, still making these thin, terrible noises. He was trying to drag himself across the tiles. He reached out for my ankle. I skipped back in terror. The muscles of his face contorted. Already his eyes were filming over like the eyes of a dead fish. In a burble of blood he whispered something. 'Please . . .' he breathed.

'Please...' So I lifted the statuette in both hands, and this time, with absolute deliberation, I smashed it hard into his skull. It was an act of love, I swear it was. Because I did love him. I have never loved any man so much. I never will. Pinpricks of blood spattered the floor. Dark gobbets of it, like scraps of best ox liver, gleamed on the bath mat. Splinters of bone had caught in his hair. From the hole I had made in his head something bulged slowly out, something grey and spongy like old porridge. I dropped the Eiffel Tower. It cracked an Italian ceramic tile. I shut my eyes tight, I gritted my teeth, I slammed the heels of my palms into my ears until my head hurt. I blocked it all out, all of it.

When I opened my eyes again he was lying quite still with his mouth slightly open. The viscous bubbling noises had stopped. He was as peaceful as if he were asleep.

I slid down on to the floor beside him and lifted his poor, damaged head into my lap. For hours we sat together like that, Dysart and I, his head cradled in my thighs. I wept a little for what I had done: I am not so irredeemable a monster that I didn't weep for him, but shock had paralysed my normal functions. I couldn't move. I think I hardly swallowed or blinked. The tears failed to flow properly. The water in the bath grew cold. I heard Bradley go past on his way to his room. And together we sat on through the night, Dysart and I.

In the early hours I grew tired. My knees locked. I found it hard to shift them without disturbing Dysart. The silence echoed like a horrified gasp through the house, silence upon silence upon silence. I was sick with horror to realize that it had happened again, I had done it again, I was back in this place. The American who had painted me in a series of red and black circles knew exactly what he was doing. What will happen now, I thought. It would be very different this time. This time no kind person would come and find me. No one would comfort me or absolve me, no one would spoil me with Mars Bars.

Somewhere I heard a soft whirring like the sound of

wings. I froze. But then distantly in the dark vacuum of the house a clock struck. The resonance hummed quietly through the stillness. Four o'clock. A second clock followed, a higher pinging chime – the clock in the room next to mine. I tried moving my leg. It was numb. With immense care I wrapped Dysart's poor bloodied head in a towel and laid it gently on the floor. I would have liked to kiss him goodbye but it seemed indecent. I had to hold on to the edge of the bath to pull myself up. I rinsed my hands in the cold bath water and then dipped the Eiffel Tower into it. Tiny scarlet worms curled away from it and turned the water pink.

This is what I did next. This next part is very clear to me. I put on a bathrobe and hobbled down the landing. My legs were on fire with pins and needles. I opened the door of the room where Shura was sleeping. She was rolled up in a fat mess of bedclothes, whistling damply as she snored. I shook her.

'Shura,' I said. I put my fingers on her lips. 'Listen. I have just killed Dysart.'

The good thing about mad people – or at any rate about the kind of mad that Shura was – is that nothing surprises them. They have lost the distinction between mundane and bizarre. Shura accepted everything with the same kind of blithe enthusiasm. 'Do you know,' she whispered back, her eyes sticky with sleep, 'I envy you. I wish I'd killed mine. I wanted to. Goodness, how much I wanted to. Only he was such a violent man and so big. I could never find the right moment.'

I pulled back the bedclothes.

'Quick,' I said. 'Put some clothes on.'

She swung her lumpen rolls of legs out on to the floor. I forced a blouse on to her. Passively she held up her arms like a small girl and allowed herself to be dressed. She let me button her up, staring down at my shaking fingers with frowzy interest.

'What are we going to do?' she asked. 'Are we going to bury him?'

I had no idea what we were going to do. I suppose I was thinking in terms of getting her to help me carry the body down to the garage, and then driving it to some deserted spot where we could roll it off a cliff into the sea, but the moment Shura asked what we were going to do I knew these were ridiculous options, out of the question, the sort of stupid thing people did in films.

She stood looking down at Dysart's body curled on the bathroom floor. It shocked her into a moment of temporary lucidity. 'Oh, Sandra,' she said. 'Oh, how dreadful. They'll put you in prison now. You'll lose everything.' She became agitated. 'We must hide the body,' she said. 'You could say he's gone abroad.' She prodded him lightly and fastidiously with her toe as if he were the corpse of a dead animal lying across her pathway. 'It's such a strange thing, death, isn't it?' she observed. 'One minute here, the next minute whoof! Such a shame. He was a nice man. And so rich. And he loved you so much.'

I put my finger to my lips to remind her to be quiet. 'I'm going to ring the police,' I said.

She nodded vaguely.

'You must leave before they come,' I said. 'Don't get involved.'

'Where will I go?' she asked, her eyes wide with sudden excitement as if we were having an adventure. 'I've got no money.'

I gave her my jewellery. I pressed Christmas and birthday presents from Dysart into her hands, rings, bracelets, necklaces, some diamonds that had belonged to his mother. I also gave her back her emerald earrings. She didn't even recognize them. She licked her lips. Jewellery dribbled between her fingers and spilled on to the floor.

'Sell the lot,' I said.

I gave her my purse as well. She counted the notes, her eyes moist with greed.

Oh, the panic, the confusion, the muddle in my brain. I had no idea what I was doing. All I could think about was money, enough money to get Shura safely away. This was not altruism: I was terrified of her being there when the police came. Irrationally I was afraid that if she was in possession of the place when the police came, then she would never go, she would take it over. I had a vision of her standing in the doorway waving as the police car drove me away, as if the house and everything in it belonged to her.

'Stay there,' I said to her.

I ran down the landing in bare feet. There would be more money in Dysart's room. It was so hushed, so still in there the noise of my own thundering heart filled it. I was afraid to turn the main light on. I felt my way across to the bed. The noise of something slithering to the floor as I bumped into a chair made me rear back as if I'd been electrocuted. My blind hands patted the air until I found the bedside lamp and traced my way down to the switch. How cold the room looked in the small pool of light, how the walls shrank away from me. The Munch girl stared manically from the hollow circles of her eyes. The Otto Dix women sniggered through their scribbled red lips. I could smell him in there, the delicate resinous perfume he wore, like boxwood, like the breath of cypress trees in the afternoon heat. I opened the drawer of his desk and found roughly three hundred pounds in an envelope. There was another five hundred in the safe. I took it all, and ran from the room in a helpless sweat of terror, streaking silently along the landing. But then I stopped. I turned back. I could not leave this house without one last look at the monument to egotism, the magnificent thing we had made together, our joint act of creation. There they hung, silently on the walls, the fifteen paintings. I pulled the chair into the centre of the room and sat there humbly, where I had so often found Dysart contemplating his work of genius. And it seemed to me then that I could not leave them there, not all of them, I must have one. At least one. Even if I had forfeited the right to anything else, I was surely entitled to one of these paintings. Oh, the lustrousness of them, the light that shone out of them. I agonized,

I hovered, I could not decide which one to take. In the end it was a choice between the GOM's 'Nude in a Bed', or the Brazilian's 'Woman in Black Dress at a Window Contemplating Flight'.

I chose 'Woman in a Black Dress' because it was less earthbound (and also smaller so a lot easier to carry).

'This,' I told Shura, 'is something very important I want you to keep for me.' We were still whispering, not just because I was afraid of waking Bradley on the floor above, but also because of a natural reticence, a fear of disturbing the dead. 'Look after it for me,' I told her. 'Don't lose it, don't sell it, keep it till I come for it.'

She nodded gravely, but she was so busy counting the money I'd found in Dysart's room I don't know if she grasped what I was telling her. I still don't.

I rang for a taxi and we waited for it silently in the unlit hall. The clocks in the house struck five. 'Isn't this weird?' Shura whispered. Her disembodied voice hung for minutes suspended in the darkness. The silence was like an indrawn breath. We waited.

Lights slewed across the double front door. An engine stopped. I slipped Shura quietly out of the house and into the taxi. The painting, wrapped in a blood-flecked towel, was perched beside her on the back seat.

'Where am I going?' she asked in a sudden panic.

I told the driver to take her to a hotel I knew somewhere off the M1.

She wound down the window and blew me a kiss. I heard her say, 'Drive on, cabbie,' as if she were starring in some Hollywood film set in foggy Victorian London.

And that was the last I saw of her.

While I waited for the police to come I took a bath. I was still damp and slightly steaming when I opened the door to them. This did not go well with me in the press.

They took me away in a car. There were five or six police cars parked carelessly across the square. Goodness knows why they needed so many for just one woman. Dawn was breaking. The sky was streaked with patches of shell-grey light. A harsh wind blew the ribbon they used to cordon off part of the street and made it twirl and flap. I heard myself think, 'It's an ill wind that blows no one any good', which seems a pretty obvious conclusion to me and hardly one worth bothering to turn into an adage. I was glad I had put on several layers of clothing. The policemen's faces were pinched and yellow. We drove through empty streets where the wind blew a loose dustbin lid along the pavement. An abandoned supermarket trolley lay on its side in a shop doorway. I thought, if this were a film I would have a street-cleaning lorry round the next corner, and there it was, on cue, rolling its brushes noisily along the gutter. I laughed. This too was somehow picked up by the press and did me no good.

It was an old police station. The walls of the interview room were unplastered brick painted a thick yellowish cream like the top of milk that has gone off. It smelled of Dettol. How strange, I thought, that this is finally where I should land up. Strange, but fitting. It was like the loop of another circle. It had a comforting inevitability. It was right. I was very glad, very relieved, finally to be there.

At night I have started to hear my heart. It gallops along with odd squelching noises. It sounds like an engine, which, of course, is exactly what it is. This is all I am really: an engine-room. What I still can't grasp is the precise function of this engine. What am I for?
  Am I a monster?
  Am I?
  If I am, then the God of my childhood is also a monster, for there is little to choose between us except a gender. I am indeed made in his image.
  'Do you believe in God?' I ask Mr Rick Thomas.
  'It rather depends what you mean by God,' he says.
  *I* don't. I daren't.

My friend Rick has given up on me. He claims I am one of his few failures. He says I have shut the door on myself and thrown away the key. I am as sane as he is, he says, and he can do nothing more for me. This implies (a) that he is sane, and (b) that he has done something for me already. I would question both those assumptions. No one who studies psychiatry and marries a physics teacher can be entirely sane. Also, what exactly does he imagine he has done for me? Nothing that I've noticed. He's taught me how to unravel cryptic clues, that's all. Anything important that I've learned since I came here, I've got from books.

Anyway, despite the fact that he's given up on me, the weekly sessions continue. We do crosswords instead. Together we try to finish the *Guardian* puzzle and *The Times* within the hour. It's good fun. Better fun than when he was trying to peer into my soul. Anyway, I am convinced now that I don't have one.

It may, of course, be possible to grow one. In time. I don't know. I'm still not sure what they are. Or if I really want one. Is the word soul a synonym for depth?

I am sitting at the table now in my cell. The sun is setting. It has coloured the wall a fierce wintry gold. There will be a frost tonight but we won't feel it, not in here. We are warm. My stomach swills with cocoa. I listen to the processes of my body: the thumping, the squelching, the gurgling, the swilling, the slapping. I think – a sudden thought as crystal clear and as potent as a drop of distilled liquor – that I am ready now. And then I get confused because I don't know where that thought came from or even what it means. Ready for what?

The police station.

I was there for hours. Days. The same questions, the endless cups of milky tea.

'So tell us in your own words, Mrs Stevens, exactly what happened as you remember it,' the policemen asked.

The trouble was I remembered nothing clearly.

They leaned across the table in the custard-coloured room. Their voices were kind and quiet. Officers came and went. I lost track. Some were in shirtsleeves. They had pitted, damp complexions like crumbling cheese. Some had moustaches. One of them smoked. Occasionally they brought me a mug of tea. 'Tell us what happened,' they said. They recorded everything on tape. 'Yes,' I said, 'I did. I did kill my husband,' because I know that I did. I remember doing it – a mercy killing. That's why I was sitting there in that room talking to them.

But then I lost faith in this statement. I didn't believe it any more. It was impossible. The idea was inconceivable. 'I'm sorry,' I said. 'I don't know what happened.' And I don't. That eviscerating rage – where did it come from? Whatever it was, it was surely never directed at Dysart. Why would I want to hurt him? I wanted to keep him. I loved him. So then – in that mood – 'No,' I said. 'No, of course I didn't kill my husband.'

At first they suspected Shura. By this time, Bradley had been interviewed. He told them that a friend of mine, a strange woman, had been staying in the house. The police thought that her sudden disappearance in the middle of the night was highly suspicious. Bradley also told them that he'd found the safe open and money gone. My jewellery and a valuable painting were also missing. The police worked for a while on the theory that Dysart had disturbed Shura while she was thieving from my bedroom, but the theory didn't hold up for long and they soon abandoned it.

So then the interviews started all over again.

The good thing is that Shura was never found. She disappeared from my life again as completely as she vanished from it in the seventeen years between the dance at Quaffingham and the night she turned up in Essex Square.

I like to think she is living somewhere exotic, a small pink hotel on a Caribbean island. I imagine her sitting on her balcony among the palms and the bougainvillaea like an overblown retired whore. She is drinking rum punches and watching the sun set over the sea. I imagine that on the whitewashed wall of her room my painting still hangs in luminous state.

The appeal starts today. I am going to it. There are questions they want to ask me. Mrs Hutchman came to wake me at a quarter to six but I am already up. I am wearing a suit I bought once in New York, the one I wore for the trial last year. I have to borrow a safety pin because the skirt won't meet across my bulging hips. We are on first-name terms now, Mrs Hutchman and I. Hers is Doreen. I brush my hair and tie it back. I do not bother with make-up. I wish I'd thought to have all my hair cut off. It wastes so much time and energy.

My friend Rick Thomas has come in early in his pale blue 2CV to wish me luck. The governor gives me a rose. I don't know where he found a rose from in the middle of January, nor what I am supposed to do with it. I borrow another pin from Mrs Hutchman and stick it to my lapel. I look as if I am going to a wedding. They see me off, a small group of well-wishers on the steps, waving to me, as the officer on court duty escorts me to the waiting van, but I am handcuffed so it is hard to wave back.

'Good luck,' they shout. 'Good luck.'

Am I *really* a monster?

I think so, yes. Don't you?

What do you think?

*FIVE*

The appeal failed.

I knew it would. Although there was always the fear that Mr Roebuck and my clever barristers would pull some legal rabbit out of the hat at the last moment. What a relief they didn't.

'Home again, miss,' says the officer who brings me back. He's a cheerful little man with a pock-marked face and greasy black hair. We drive in and the gates roll closed behind us. He asks me for an autograph. He wants me to sign it 'To Lenny, with best wishes from Kathy Kuriakis.'

'Do I look like Kathy Kuriakis?' I ask him. I'm curious to know because all that seems such a long time ago. I am overweight now and suet-skinned.

'What do you mean, do you *look* like Kathy Kuriakis?' he says blinking at such a stupid question. 'You *are* Kathy Kuriakis.'

Inside, the home team are all waiting for me: the governor, Rick Thomas, Doreen Hutchman. They pat my back as if I have just lost the match, and mumble their distress. What they don't know is that inside I am ablaze with joy. The decision of the Appeal Court is not a disappointment to me but a glorious release. I scuttle joyfully back to my cell like a small animal burrowing back into its nest. This is where I can breathe. I have things to do here, important things, things that will take time. I have a sentence to serve, an old and unpunished crime to expiate, a long journey to go on.

I think of woolly, sheep-like Sister Ambrose, who must have scurried gratefully back to just such a cell after the horrors of teaching ink-stained little girls about the God of their Fathers. I am almost a nun myself, a nun in nearly every particular, except that I am without God.

Without her God anyway.

I know about God now. Where I have gone wrong all these years is thinking of God in terms of a person, a male person with axes to grind and scores to settle and small-minded prejudices. God is not a person at all, of course not. God is a process: the inexorable process of destruction. I can't think why it has taken me so long to realize this. Or why I have only just grasped how gloriously creative, how divine this process is.

In this small space, three by four, with its blue-striped narrow bed and single window I plan to get to grips with these things. As I quietly and slowly decay, I plan to make myself. But into what? What shall I make myself into?

I shall make myself human. That's what I'll do. It ought to be possible. Other people must have done it. I have several excellent patterns to work from.

Well, I honestly thought that was the end. I did. I thought there was nothing more to write and that I was about to embark on a life of contemplation and self-improvement. But something new has happened.

They told me yesterday that I am to be moved to another prison. Home Office orders. The prison I am going to is somewhere in Leicestershire. I suppose it will be all right. To be honest, I feel rather apprehensive about it. I hope the cocoa is as good there as it is here.

Rick Thomas and I have our last session together today. We manage to do *The Times* crossword but the *Guardian* defeats us. Our hearts are not in it. He has brought in a cake which the lovely Les has baked specially for the occasion. It has a single candle on it, one candle to mark our year together.

'Blow it out,' he says. 'Go on. Make a wish.'

The flame gutters and snuffs out.

What do I wish for? Suddenly there is a great silence in my head. I can think of nothing. There is nothing I want.

'Have you wished?' he asks.

'Yes,' I lie.

When the hour is over, we hug as if we are intimate and loving friends who fear they will never see each other again. Which we won't. Then he kisses me. On the lips.

Faith is devastated. This always happens, she says. The moment you make friends with someone they get transferred. She promises to write to me.

She gives me a goodbye present: a large KitKat and a paperback copy of *Tess of the d'Urbervilles*. This is the book I gave up on when I arrived here. I remind her of this.

'No, you'll like it now,' she says. 'It'll mean a lot to you. I think it's absolutely the book you ought to read next.'

I flip through it. The subtitle is, 'A Pure Woman'. I'm afraid Faith has a rather romanticized view of me. Never mind. Despite her massive thighs and her rampant cellulite, I must not judge her. She has been a good friend to me. More than a good friend. And I will miss her.

I leave early tomorrow. This is my last night in this room. I am all ready. My things are packed. I have said my goodbyes. Earlier today, while the window was open, I slid my hands between the bars and emptied the contents of my home-made envelopes into space. It seemed inappropriate and a little tasteless to take them with me. Also, I felt it was unnecessary. I had forgotten why I was keeping them. Soft, frouzled mats of faded hair drifted away like dandelion seeds into the air. Nail clippings and shreds of skin tumbled into the frosty sky. It was like scattering my own ashes.

What a strange life I have had so far. And it gets stranger.

Now I am sitting on my bed gazing at the wall beyond the window, learning it, before it gets too dark to see. I watch the sharp January light falter and fade.

I am to be a proper prisoner now. I shall have to

integrate and work in the laundry or something. I might even have to share a cell.

Life. This is what I am sentenced to: Life. How encouraging. How wonderful. What a splendid phrase. I take it literally.

In legal terms, Mr Roebuck tells me, this translates as maybe fifteen years. The thought of fifteen years does not dismay me, not at all. I shall need every minute of it if I am going to make myself. I am tired of being one-dimensional, of being so many false, flat images, reels of celluloid, washes of paint, surfaces and circles, lines, shadows, skin and flesh, the stuff of countless fantasies. I am sick of being processed through other people's imaginations. I have been far too pleased with all that. The trouble is that one life is nowhere near enough compensation for two deaths, so I shall have to make myself twice as deep, twice as wise, twice as everything. But believe me, if I can do this well – which I will, I will – then after all, when the fifteen years are over, I may turn out to be twice as special, twice as extraordinary, as I once thought I was.

But then I would think that, wouldn't I?